To Helen

Enjoy the read!

love Donna

THE SUITCASE MAN

by

Michael K Foster

Michael K Foster

Typeset in Bembo Std

Editing, design, typesetting and publishing by UK Book Publishing

UK Book Publishing is a trading name of Consilience Media

www.ukbookpublishing.com

ISBN: 978-1-912183-47-0

Cover images:

Eye © Thomas Tolkien – flickr.com – CC BY 2.0

For Marilyn

By **MICHAEL K FOSTER**

DCI Jack Mason Crime Thriller series:

THE WHARF BUTCHER
SATAN'S BECKONING
THE SUITCASE MAN

Acknowledgements

As all my DCI Mason and David Carlisle novels are works of fiction based in the North East of England, there are so many people without whose help and support it would have been difficult, if not impossible, to write with any sense of authenticity. Suffering from dyslexia as I do, my grateful thanks go out to the late Rita Day and my dear wife Pauline, whose belief and inspiration has never waned.

I am indebted to Detective Constable Maurice Waugh, a former member of the Yorkshire Ripper Squad, and Ken Stewart, a former member of South Shields CID, whose technical assistance in the aspects of how the police tackle crime has allowed me a better understanding of what takes place. Their efforts have helped me enormously.

To single out a few other names who helped make the difference to this book, I would like to thank Paul Foster and Lynn Oakes for their encouragement and unqualified support in developing the initial cover graphics. Finally, I would express my heartfelt appreciation to the Beta reader team: Jan Duffy, Dan Line, Mark Duffy, Daniel Inman, and Brenda Forster, without whose help this book would never have made the bookshelf.

Michael K Foster
Co Durham England
michaelkfoster.com

Chapter One

Gateshead 2014

Jack Mason's iPhone rang the minute he stepped out of the Area Commander's office. The details were sketchy, but the truth when it came shocked even the most hardened police officers on the team. Now kitted out in white protective coveralls, shoes cover and face mask, the Detective Chief Inspector took another deep breath and poked his head in through the open doorway. The flies were the giveaway. Thousands of them, along with an overpowering stench of rotten flesh. No matter how many precautions he undertook, it always had the same effect on him. Mason had read somewhere that blow flies weren't the only organisms scavenging on the human corpse. Bacteria, fungi and vertebrates were also in competition. The thing was, blow flies used an antenna to sniff out dead meat and usually got there first. Not that he was an expert or anything. He wasn't.

Maggots troubled him most; the damn things got everywhere. No longer than a grain of rice, once a larva had metamorphosed it would mature into a fully-grown blow fly and join the rest of the goddamn swarm. If they did have a useful purpose in life, it was to tell him how long a person had been dead. Shit happened, but this was ridiculous.

'It's not a pretty sight,' the Crime Scene Manager said by way of introduction.

Early fifties, with an unruly shock of jet black hair, Stan Johnson had a touch of the eccentric about him. Not one for mincing his words, Johnson was more than capable.

With sunlight bleaching through a chink in the curtains, Mason's eyes toured the room. Johnson was right. It wasn't a pretty sight. Now taking centre stage, the dead woman's bloated body looked surreal. From what he could see, the corpse was showing early signs of blistering. Blood everywhere, the head had fallen back slightly, and the tongue forced out of the mouth. He could see the wrists had been bound to the chair armrests with heavy duty duct tape, and her ankles strapped to the base. He'd seen evil before, but nothing compared to this.

From the outside, the house had looked ordinary. Inside was a different matter, of course. What had begun as a routine enquiry was now a full-on murder investigation.

The small knot of forensic officers had grown.

'Do we know who she is?' Mason asked.

Dr Colin Brown, a lean, long-backed, balding man, with a stern flushed face and thick bushy sideburns peered back at him from the corner of the room. 'Her name's Jennifer Oakwell.'

'What do we know about her?'

'Neighbours say her ex-husband is doing time in Durham prison.'

'That complicates things.'

The doctor shook his head resignedly. 'It gets worse.'

'Worse?'

'There's been another incident.'

'What do you mean. . . incident?'

'Upstairs,' the doctor said, pointing a finger at the ceiling. 'There's blood everywhere, but we've yet to find a body.'

Mason peered at the woman's corpse and stiffened. He wasn't a tall man, five-nine, Mediterranean looking with a moon-like face that had seen more than its fair share of trouble.

'What about forensics?'

'No. Nothing yet,' the doctor replied.

'Another grudge attack by the looks?'

'I've counted at least thirty stab wounds to her head, neck, and body. The chest wall has been punctured, penetrating the lungs and heart chamber.' The doctor ran his spatula over the dead woman's upper body and shifted his stance. 'He used a long-bladed knife by the look of things, but don't quote me on that. Not until Home Office Pathologists have completed their findings.'

The doctor's voice sounded lame, as if his cage had been rattled.

'The suspect may have been disturbed at some point,' Johnson added. 'After he'd finished his business down here, he then set about the upstairs victim.'

Mason bristled, pen poised. 'Any sign of a struggle?'

'By the amount of force used, I'd say it was over in seconds.'

Mason checked his notes. 'It's a bit over the top don't you think?'

'Whoever he is, he intended to leave his trade mark behind.'

Mason swung sharply to face the Crime Scene Manager. 'Trade mark, what mark is this?'

'He's drawn smiley faces on the upstairs bedroom walls, using the victim's blood.'

'That's all we need.'

Johnson shook his head. 'It takes all sorts I suppose.'

'What about neighbours?'

'University students mainly. It's half-term and many have gone back to their parents' homes.'

'Who found her, Stan?' Mason asked.

'A close friend; she was on her way to work apparently. When Oakwell's mobile phone kept ringing out, that's when she decided to call in.'

Still grappling with his emotions, Mason brushed another annoying blow fly from his face and stepped back a pace. 'What time was this, Stan?'

'Half seven this morning.'

'Has she given us a witness statement?'

'I wouldn't go there if I were you. She's in a bad state of shock by all accounts.'

Mason tilted his head back in thought. 'She obviously had a key to the place.'

'Yes, she did.'

From what Mason could see, the dead woman looked mid-fifties. Not tall, plump, with a rounded face and square jawline. The front of her dress had been torn away, and dried blood covered her breasts and lower limbs. These weren't random killings; these murders had been planned, he reasoned. Once they knew more about the victims' backgrounds, it would be a simple matter of legwork.

Mason ran his hand over his short-cropped hair and felt a knot in his stomach tighten. It wasn't a particularly large room, drab, with plain painted walls and cheap second-hand furniture. The living room carpets were worn, shabby in places and badly stained. Truth be told, the victim and assailant were probably known to each other. There were no signs of forced entry, and all the ground floor windows were shut.

His next question, when it came, was more direct.

'How long has she been dead?'

'I can't swear to it – not longer than a week.' The doctor glanced back at him, then down at the dead woman's hands again. 'No doubt Dr Gillian King will fill you in with the rest of the details during the post-mortem examination.'

'Jennifer Oakwell, you say?' Mason said, looking over the top of his notebook.

'We've run a database check over her ex-husband,' said Johnson, 'he's currently serving a twenty year stretch for armed robbery. His name's Frank Wiseman, and he's a nasty piece of work by all accounts. Six months ago, he was involved in a minor dispute over prison visitors' privileges. A few days later a scuffle broke out in the prison canteen, and he beat the living daylight out of one of the prison officers.'

'CV's don't come much better than that.' Mason grimaced. 'Is there anything else I should know?'

'Like I say, it's still early days.'

The real horror lay in the upstairs front bedroom. Blood everywhere, graffiti-filled walls; it was like stepping into a slaughter house at the end of a long day's shift. The room smelt of fear, reminiscent of another case he'd recently worked on. Whoever had died here had certainly met a horrific ending.

Mason stood in silence for a moment, thinking.

The report would come later, after he'd cleared his head of unpleasant thoughts. The problem was, Mad Frankie Wiseman didn't exude charm at the best of times. The man was a moron, and not to be taken lightly. But there was more to it than that. There had to be.

As he made his way back downstairs, he tried to get his head around it all. Without a second body to work on, it was difficult to get a real feel for what might have happened here. Judging by the amount of blood spatter, it looked a prolonged attack. There was no sign of a scuffle, and no quarter given. And yes, Mason thought, whoever had killed these people had a definite point to prove.

Before leaving, he checked in with the Crime Scene Manager, and made a few observations. More importantly to Jack Mason was the pub on Bensham Road. It was Friday, and the start of his weekend was fast slipping away from him. He needed some thinking time, and right now he could murder a drink.

Chapter Two

It was chucking it down, and the air felt oppressive as if a thunderstorm was brewing. Three floors up at Gateshead Police station, overlooking Matalan car park and the Magistrates' Court, Jack Mason glanced at a new set of crime-scene photographs he'd pinned to his corkboard. Not good, he thought. Two murders, one body, and a shit load of unanswered questions to resolve. Some crimes left a nasty taste in his mouth, and this was one of them.

Now forty-six, Mason had risen to Detective Chief Inspector at an early age. Not all had been plain sailing, though. When he was six his father had walked out on his mother. The marriage over, Mason was brought up on a rough council estate in the East End of London and quickly learned to adapt. A rebellious child, had it not been for a caring uncle, God knows where he would have ended up. Having messed up badly at school, his sole ambition was to be a policeman. The competition to join was tough at the time, and Mason didn't have a single qualification to his name. It was a hard slog, but after knuckling down and studying hard he somehow muddled his way through the entry exams. Known as a risk taker, he soon caught the attention of his superiors. It was this, and a natural talent for detective work, that had earned him the pips on his shoulders.

Now onto his second cup of coffee, Mason glanced at the small assembled team of police officers now sitting in front of him. They were a mixed lot. He liked to think he'd created a common bond between them but was having second thoughts. Not all were perfect, and a few carried baggage. At least he could depend on them to give one hundred percent, and that's all that mattered to him.

Mason pointed to the corkboard. 'This isn't the most difficult of crimes to solve, and there's a stack of evidence to work on.'

'What do we know about the dead woman?' asked DS Rob Savage.

'Her name's Jennifer Oakwell, and she worked as a receptionist in the Bensham area. After failing to turn up for work last week, at around eight-fifteen on Friday morning, she was discovered by a friend at her home on Rectory Road. Bound to a living room chair with heavy duty duct tape, she'd been stabbed to death and her decomposing body had lain there undetected for a week.'

'How did her friend gain entry?' someone asked.

'She had a key to the property.'

'Anyone reported hearing or seeing anything?'

'No,' Mason confirmed. 'Uniforms are carrying out door-to-door enquiries.'

Mason explained in a little more detail before delivering the punchline. 'For those not aware, her ex-husband is a notorious gangster called Frank Wiseman. He's currently serving time in Durham prison for armed robbery—' Mason paused as the noise levels heightened.

'What about the post-mortem results?' DS Savage asked.

'According to Dr Gillian King, the senior anatomical pathology technologist, Oakwell had suffered multiple stab wounds to the neck, back, and chest. The main cluster of wounds was to the left chest region, penetrating the right ventricle and aorta. There were four stab wounds to the left side of her neck – two severing the carotid artery. This was a violent knife attack, no one should be in any doubt. There were ten stab wounds to the back, five of them penetrating the lungs, and one penetrating the abdominal viscera.' Mason made a little stabbing motion. 'These were classic downward arc stab wounds, and of some considerable force I might add. We know her attacker is right handed, and approximately five-ten in height.'

'What do we know about the murder weapon?' asked DS Holt, in a broad Geordie accent.

Tom Hedley, the senior forensic scientist, raised a hand to speak. 'The wounds to the back and chest are elliptic in shape and indicate the knife was double edged. Small contusions found above and below each of the stab wounds suggest it had some sort of finger guard attached to it.'

'Sounds like he'd lost control,' said Detective Constable Harry Manley, trying to make his presence felt.

Mason nodded. 'It would appear so. Unable to defend herself, any one of twelve wounds could have been fatal.'

The silence that followed was short lived.

'We believe the weapon used was a double-edged combat knife,' Hedley added.

Mason nodded. 'Yes, that would fit perfectly.'

'Any further developments on the second victim?' asked DS Holt.

'No, we still haven't found a body.'

Hedley pointed to the corkboard. 'Looking at the SOC photographs, you'll notice there's a lot of arterial blood spread over a wide area. Stabbed numerous times in the chest and back, the victim now fought their way to the landing where another vicious attack took place. Judging by the blood trail, the victim's body was dragged to a position at the top of the landing stairs before it was removed from the premises.'

'Blimey,' DC Manley sighed. 'This bastard doesn't hang about.'

'Apparently not,' Mason bluntly replied.

Hedley referred to his forensic report again. 'We uncovered a footprint trail leading from the upstairs landing and down into the street. In other words, this was a pre-meditated attack, suggesting the killer intended to remove the victim's body all along.'

'So why leave Jennifer Oakwell's body behind?' Savage shrugged.

'He could have been disturbed at some point.'

'He may well have been,' Mason agreed, 'but he still had plenty of time to return and finish the job off.'

Hedley shuffled awkwardly. 'Which suggests our second victim may well have been a case of witness elimination.'

Harry Manley shook his head dejectedly. A muscular man, early forties, with a thick bushy mop of black hair, the detective constable was undoubtedly the joker in the pack. 'Not necessarily,' Manley announced. 'He could be sending out a warning message.'

Mason gave a thin, wintry smile. 'You're right, Harry. That would account for the smiley faces he's drawn on the victim's bedroom walls.'

'What do we know about her ex-husband?' Holt asked next.

Mason explained. 'Shortly after Frank Wiseman was sent down for a string of armed robberies across Tyneside ten years ago, Jennifer Oakwell divorced him. Codenamed operation *Black Rock*, the officers involved in the case described the gang as well organised and violent.' Mason took a sip of his coffee. 'After targeting a string of local betting shops, supermarkets, and outlying sub-post offices, the gang's overall haul was more than ten million quid.'

Unease all round.

'What's your take on it, boss?' asked Savage. 'Do you think there could be a connection here?'

The smell of death still clinging to him, Mason tried to steady himself. The mechanics of murder could be quite overwhelming at times, but the visual memories of a crime-scene even more difficult to eradicate. 'The thing to bear in mind here is that none of the gang had shown the slightest remorse. As a result, they were each given a sentence ranging from ten to twelve years. It was a long drawn out trial, lasting well over ten weeks.'

'I can't speculate on that,' said DS Holt, 'but what I can say is, because of Wiseman's previous convictions and the fact he'd masterminded the whole operation, the judge sentenced him to a minimum of twenty years.'

Mason nodded. 'Thank you, George.'

Manley blew through his teeth. 'The word on the street is the money the gang made off with has since gone missing. Well over ten million quid. Some say it was squirrelled away into Swiss bank accounts, others say their accountants made a killing from it, laundering it into offshore bank accounts. The thing is, anyone caught with their fingers in the till usually faces the consequences with these people.'

'You're clutching at straws, Harry,' said DS Rob Savage, shaking his head. 'We're talking ten years ago here.'

'That's my point,' Manley replied. 'Apart from Mad Frankie the rest of the gang are now out on parole.'

Mason dutifully stroked his chin in thought. Manley had a point, and a good one at that. Even though Frank Wiseman was behind bars, it didn't mean he wasn't active. He made a mental note of it and pushed on.

'Looking at the SOC photographs, apart from heavy bruising to the victim's ankles and wrists, there don't appear to be any other surface injuries to her body.' Mason opened his hands expansively, the ripples of a grin racing across his face. 'If there are no signs of a struggle, perhaps she knew her killer?'

'Even so, why kill her?' asked Holt.

'Therein lies the motive, George.'

'It could have been a mistake.' Manley shrugged.

The room fell silent again.

'This second victim,' said Holt pointing to the corkboard. 'What about personal effects – a wallet, driving licence, a mobile phone, or something with an address on it?'

'We found nothing,' Mason confirmed.

Manley's face lit up. 'He could have been giving her one. . .'

'If he was, then during the post-mortem Dr King would have found semen traces in Jennifer Oakwell's body. She didn't.'

'Bugger,' Manley huffed.

'All is not what it appears to be. Find the second victim's body and we're halfway to solving the case.'

Mason thought a moment. Manley had unwittingly raised another valid point. Why kill Wiseman's ex-wife in the first place? There again, he thought, what if she'd been acting as a go-between? Relaying her ex-husband's instructions to the rest of the gang? This case wasn't as simple as he first thought, far from it. And, if he was completely honest, he still wasn't ruling out a revenge attack. At least she was local, which made his investigations a lot easier.

'What are we doing about the gang members who are now out on parole?' asked Manley.

'We need to speak to these people, Harry. Find out where they were on Friday 21st February.' Mason consulted his notes. 'While you're at it, let's check out the local area CCTV and see if anything unusual crops up.'

As the team left the room, Mason put his head in his hands and muttered under his breath, *God! What a mess.*

Chapter Three

David Carlisle checked his scorecard and did a quick mental calculation. Hole eighteen, where to start? Two hundred and twenty yards, a long par 3, with out of bounds left, right and long. In anyone's books, this was the kind of hole that could ruin a good scorecard. There were trees down either side of the fairway, and four large bunkers protecting the green. Minutes earlier Harry Manley had sliced his tee shot, sending his ball into the long rough. It was a lousy shot, and an impossible position to recover from.

Sucking in air, Carlisle took out his trusty 3–iron and stepped up to the tee box. Aligning himself with the flag, he pushed his tee into the soft ground and stepped back a pace. Jack Mason had struck a perfect tee shot from this very position – *straight down the middle of the fairway*. After landing heavily, it had carried a further thirty yards before pulling up just short of the eighteenth green. The tension was mounting and there was no getting away from it, this was now a pressure shot.

Addressing the ball, Carlisle took a practice swing. The wind was starting to pick up, making conditions even trickier. After watching the trajectory of Mason's ball, he'd decided to aim left. If the wind carried his ball towards the right-hand side of the fairway, he was in with a chance. Then, as the head of his club connected with his ball, it soared into the air like a rocket. Seconds later it hit the fairway, bobbed a few times, and pulled up just short of the right-hand bunker. Perfect, he thought.

'What a cracking shot!' Manley called out.

'Thanks mate.'

As the next player stepped up to the front of the tee box, you could have heard a pin drop. Wearing a bright orange sweater, matching trousers, and black brogue golfing shoes, George Holt was out to impress. Or that was his intention.

'Easy, George,' Mason chuckled, 'there's sixty quid resting on this shot.'

'No pressure then,' Holt replied.

After taking a massive divot out of the front of the tee box on his practice swing, the detective sergeant addressed his drive with a little more caution. As the head of the club struck his golf ball with a resounding thwack, it shot up into the air and disappeared into the distant treeline. Seconds later it came to rest in a bunker.

'Bollocks!' Holt cursed.

Now out of the running, Manley dropped his Ping 5–iron back into his caddy bag and turned to face them. 'It looks like we have another bucket and spade job, lads.'

'Sod off,' Holt replied.

'Given the choice, I fancy my shot rather than yours, George,' Manley said smugly.

'It isn't over yet.'

The tension was mounting, along with the snide remarks.

Carlisle hadn't got off to a particularly good start that morning. Had it not been for a fluke shot on the fourteenth green, he would have been well out of the running. When he was younger he could hit a 250-yard drive to within three feet of the hole. Not anymore. Fast approaching forty-four, his reactions were slowing as was his concentration. He'd never intended to be a private investigator; it had happened quite by chance. After accepting voluntary redundancy from the Northumbria police force, that's when he'd decided to set up his own business. It was nothing ambitious, enough to earn a few quid and see him through to retirement. Well that was the theory, and he was sticking to it.

Having given up all hope of ever finding Harry Manley's ball, Mason declared a penalty stroke. Then, just when they were least expecting it, the detective constable pointed to a small patch in the long grass.

'Here, lads—'

Holt looked on in bewilderment. 'Are you sure that's your ball, Harry?'

'Well, this is where it landed.'

'But yours was a white ball, and this one's pink!'

'What the hell,' Mason cursed. 'He's not going to win bugger all from here.'

Fast losing patience, Manley slammed his golf club into the ground and turned to face them. 'Oh. Watch this!'

Three shots later, Mason was proved right.

Now down to three possible contenders, the Detective Chief Inspector was in a rich vein of form. Taking out his trusty 9—iron, he addressed his ball with an air of confidence. It was another crap shot, and Carlisle had fared little better. The moment his ball hit the back of the green, it scooted off and disappeared into the trees.

All eyes now turned to George Holt.

With little room to manoeuvre, the Sergeant shuffled his feet in the bunker sand and addressed his ball with a lofty wedge. Then, as a huge cloud of sand flew into the stratosphere his ball dropped to within an inch of the hole. It was a magnificent recovery shot, leaving Holt with a simple tap in.

Mason checked his scorecard.

'Bugger me, that shot makes you sixty quid better off.'

'The winner was never in doubt,' said Holt.

They all fell about laughing.

'Well done, gentlemen,' Mason acknowledged. 'This calls for a small celebration.'

Manley was quick off the mark. 'Does that mean the drinks are on you, boss?'

'Sod off, Harry. Tradition has it the winner gets the first-round in.'

Things were livening up, and after they'd changed into more suitable clothes, they made for the bar. Still unsure as to why Jack Mason had invited him here today, Carlisle trod with caution. Behind the narrow-lipped smile was an unbending ruthless streak. Mason was thick skinned, arrogant, and difficult to work with. Everything had to be done his way, which left you little room for manoeuvre. The minute the DCI rounded on him, Carlisle realised he'd been conned.

'What do you know about Mad Frankie Wiseman?' Mason asked.

'Not a lot. Why?'

Mason cocked his head to one side. 'I'm told you did some work for his son recently.'

'Yes, I did. His lawyers asked me to resolve a problem for them.'

'What kind of problem?'

Carlisle felt the cutting edge of Mason's tongue. 'Why? Is there an issue?'

'There could be.'

'If you must know, his son Robert was getting a lot of grief from a group of local thugs who lived on a nearby council estate in Wallsend. They were threatening to burn his pub down if he didn't pay the protection money they were asking for.'

'And what was your part in all of this?'

'Low key stuff mainly, surveillance work, talking to local people, that sort of thing.'

'So, it was the family lawyers who hired you, and not Frank Wiseman's son?'

'That's right. They were keen to get to the bottom of it.'

'You certainly pick your clients,' Mason grunted. 'What's wrong with going to the police nowadays?'

'Knowing Frank Wiseman, the police would be the last people he'd want to deal with.'

Mason thought a moment. 'Yeah, I suppose you're right.'

'Besides, his son was trying to make a clean break of it and didn't want his old man getting involved.'

Mason grinned. 'So, they hired you to sort things out for them?'

'You could say that, yes.'

'Some things never cease to amaze me, my friend.' Mason wiped the beer froth from his lips and turned to face him. 'What about the son's mother? Did you ever bump into her at all?'

'No, I never met her. Why?'

Mason cradled his glass. 'Knowing Frank Wiseman, it was lucky you didn't.'

'Oh, and why do you say that?'

Mason took another swig from his glass. 'It's not general knowledge, but a few days ago his ex-wife was brutally murdered in a vicious knife attack. Her name is Jennifer Oakwell.'

'So, that's what all the fuss was about?'

'Uh-huh. Oakwell was her maiden name.'

Carlisle reflected on Mason's statement. 'How the hell did you manage to keep that one from the media?'

'It goes with the territory.' Mason tapped his nose. 'If you want my advice, you stay well clear of Frank Wiseman's lawyers in future.'

'Thanks for the advice.'

'Good, at least we've sorted something out.'

Now deep in thought, Mason fiddled with his watch strap. However much he could annoy you at times, he still had his positive sides. Not many, though. Still pondering over the DCI's hidden agenda, Carlisle decided to throw him a hook line. 'If I can help in any way, you know where to find me.'

'I'll bear that in mind.'

'So, where do you go from here?' Carlisle asked.

'It's strictly a police matter at this stage, but that could all change in due course.'

Mason didn't elaborate.

Chapter Four

Jack Mason stood in the shade of the arcaded cloister and checked his mobile phone was switched off. It was 8.50 am, and West Road crematorium was now bathed in glorious sunshine. He could hear the distant hum of the rush hour traffic but could not see it. Soon it would ease off, and things would get back to normal again. Whatever normal meant.

His brain stuck in overdrive, Mason had barely paid attention to the Garden of Remembrance that morning. His mind was on other things. Security was tight. It had to be. Frank Wiseman was a high security risk, a category 'A' prisoner who wouldn't think twice about beating your brains out just for the fun of it. Not that there was any chance of that happening. Everything was under control – *or so Mason believed*.

Among those paying their respects that morning were some of Newcastle's most notorious villains. It was a large turnout, a solid show of support for a fellow gangster whose ex-wife had been brutally murdered under very suspicious circumstances. If this was an inside job, whoever the killer was he'd be nervously looking over his shoulder right now. The big guns were out for him, and it wouldn't be long before the streets of Newcastle threw up another dead body.

The killer's, hopefully!

This gathering was different, though, the likes of which Mason had not witnessed before. Not in his lifetime, nor in anyone else's come to think of it. It was surreal. Dressed in a smart black mohair suit, white button-down shirt and black silk tie, Frank Wiseman descended the Group 4 prison van steps flanked by four burly prison guards. Eyes hidden behind wrap-around Ray-Ban sunglasses, his face bore a look of indifference. What was going on inside the prisoner's head was anyone's guess. Now under a heavy security screen, he watched as the prisoner was whisked through one of the west wing side doors and into the chapel beyond. It was a tense stand-off. No one spoke. They were dealing with professional criminals here, people at the top of their game who wouldn't think twice about breaking your arm.

As the two police motorbike outriders sped off towards the rear of the cemetery, the Group 4 prison van followed in their wake. Nothing was left to chance. Everything that needed to be done was being done. Now stationed at intervals around the perimeter wall, a strong presence of armed police officers could be seen. Wearing their familiar black combat overalls and black Kevlar body armour vests, the police were taking no chances. If there was trouble to be had, it would start after the service and not before it, Mason thought. He knew how easy it was to fall flat at the first hurdle. It only took a second, but in that moment in time everything could turn on its head.

Having prepared for every eventuality, nothing could move in or out of the place. Not without his permission, that is. Then glancing up, Mason caught his first glimpse of the beautiful horse drawn hearse. Pulled by a pair of handsome black Belgian horses, they carried black drapes on their backs and wore tall black ostrich feather plumes on their heads. High up on the open top seat, he noted the driver and groom were immaculately turned out in traditional Victorian livery. No expense spared, he smiled. Mad Frankie's ex-wife was getting the best that money could buy.

Mason knew from experience that events such as these always carried a high element of risk. It was the budding reckless young wannabes who scared the living daylights out of him. The mindless thugs who turned up in outlandish twenties pin-striped suits and posed like henchmen in an Al Capone movie. And another thing, why were funerals always such morbid affairs? Having spent the past twenty minutes listening to the sounds of religious piped music invading his privacy, it was doing his head in. He'd often wondered what kind of music they'd play at *his* final send-off. Something livelier, he hoped – Iron Maiden or Guns N' Roses, something with a little more humph.

The DCI had barely reached the chapel door when he felt his coat sleeve being tugged. Turning sharply, his heart sank. Tony Fox was the Godfather of all Godfathers – a notorious Newcastle gangster who controlled the north side of the city.

Mason gathered his composure.

'Nice of you to turn up, Jack. A friend of the family, was she?' said Fox.

'No, just keeping a watchful eye on proceedings.'

'It's always nice to know when the police are looking after my interests, Jack.'

'Yeah, that's what we're paid to do.'

'It's a sad affair,' said Fox, feigning empathy.

'Someone out there had it in for her, and whoever he is, I want the bastard taken down.'

Fox looked down at him and smiled. Six feet six, and built like a brick shithouse, he stood head and shoulders above everyone present that morning. It wasn't common knowledge – or maybe it was – Fox had homosexual tendencies and was attracted to young boys who frequented his night clubs. Not that anyone complained. They didn't. And those who had were now pushing the daisies up.

'Now here's the thing,' said Fox, chewing on an ivory toothpick between gleaming whitened teeth. 'Why would someone go to all the trouble to murder such a sweet, innocent young lady like Jennifer Oakwell?'

'I've no idea, Tony. You tell me.'

The gangster's eyelids flickered, enough to display his contempt. 'It's not the same old city anymore. Not since these Eastern Europeans moved in.'

'Pissing in your pot, are they?'

'Who knows?' Fox shrugged. 'Like I say, it's not the same city. These recent killings have sparked off a whole load of unnecessary trouble, and I do not like what I'm hearing. The sooner this bastard is taken off the streets, the better I'll sleep at night.'

Mason stroked his chin, pondering the gangster's statement. Walls had ears, and if a useful piece of street gossip was about to come his way, then he'd be eternally grateful. Not that that was ever going to happen; it wasn't.

'It's strange you should say that,' Mason replied, 'cos it's been awfully quiet over at the station lately. These foreigners you talk of, do you think they could be involved?'

Eyes like daggers, Fox glared down at him. 'Don't put words into my mouth, Jack. It doesn't suit you.'

'You know me, Tony. It goes no further.' Mason's eyes scanned the perimeter wall looking for any signs of trouble. 'More to the point, how's the second-hand car business doing nowadays?'

'Why do you ask?' said Fox, arms folded across his chest in a defensive stance.

'There have been an awful lot of high-end rollers going missing lately, and we're keeping a watchful eye on all the ferry terminals. Someone out there is stealing them to order. Mind, I can't say as I blame them, not at some of the amazing prices they're fetching. There's a big demand out in the Middle East, I'm told, and a waiting list as long as your arm. How times have changed.' Mason kicked the gravel under his feet as if to make his point. 'Someone's making money out of it. Maybe it's these foreigners you talk about. Who knows?'

'Well it ain't me. I can assure you of that.'

'Your name never crossed my mind, Tony.'

Fox made a little stabbing gesture with his finger. 'Who told you I was dealing in second-hand cars again?'

'Nobody did, I just thought I'd mention it, that's all.'

The gangster tapped the side of his forehead with a finger. 'I'll bear that in mind,' he replied sarcastically.

Mason stared at him for some moments in silence. 'You scratch my back and I'll scratch yours. If you do happen to hear anything, you know where to find me.'

'Quid pro quo.'

'You could say that, yes.'

'I'll look out for—' the gangster's voice tailed off at the last syllable.

Joined by a pug-faced associate with short cropped hair, and a mouth full of gold teeth, there followed a long awkward silence between them.

'It's been nice talking, Tony,' said Mason, extending out a hand. 'Enjoy the service.'

The lump in his throat now the size of a tennis ball, Mason turned on his heel. There was nothing more to be done here. Not now there wasn't. Minutes later and sat inside the undercover pool car, he suddenly realised who he had been mixing with.

Chapter Five

Tommy Harris wasn't a particularly talkative man, not by any means. He preferred his own company if the truth was known. Close to retirement, Tommy had salted enough money away to live out the rest of his days in relative comfort. Never one for taking holidays abroad, he thought them too expensive. The last time he'd done that was a bus trip to Paris with his wife Peggy. Blimey, that was almost ten years ago, Tommy chuckled. Local B&B's were as far as they ever got nowadays. Preferably the coast. Somewhere where they served up generous portions of fish and chips and the beer was cheap.

Having arrived early for work that morning, Monday had started bright and cheerful enough for him. Now onto his second pot of tea, he finished his drink and realised he'd better check the weekly complaints log. It wasn't a taxing job, and the hours suited Tommy down to the ground. Halfway along Forth Street and within easy walking distance of Newcastle Central Station, the Storage Company was ideally located as far as he was concerned. What a lot of people didn't know – or perhaps they did and weren't letting on about it – was that Tommy was born in Quetta, India and educated at Seahouses Middle School. Aged eighteen, he'd followed in his father's footsteps and joined the British Army. Apart from a short stint in Northern Ireland, he'd never fired a gun in anger. Even so, he'd won a silver medal to prove it and kept it hidden in a bottom drawer. Nothing exciting ever happened to Tommy these days.

He lifted his arm and checked his watch. Nine fifteen, and the start of a brand-new week. There were rumours doing the rounds that the company was about to change hands. How much was true, Tommy dreaded to think. It was a great company to work for and judging by the five-star reviews the company was getting nowadays there wasn't a bad word to be said about it.

The thing was, Tommy was an expert at choosing the right locker size and giving the customers what they wanted. Described in the brochure as the size of a hatchback car boot, the small storage lockers were the most popular. Not so with the larger storage rooms. At two-hundred and fifty square feet, these were similar in size to a thirty-foot articulated lorry. And, according to Tommy's calculations, they were the most profitable units to fill. They seldom came up for hire, though, as the customers who rented them had mostly upped sticks and gone abroad to live. And that was another thing he liked about his job. If a client didn't continue with their quarterly payments, the contract was closed, and the locker contents auctioned off. It was a nice little earner.

The early morning sunshine was flooding in through the office window when Tommy logged on to his computer. He scrolled down the list of complaints and made a mental note of them. The hand dryer in the ladies' toilets was still broken, and there was a problem with the main entrance CCTV camera. Then, moving down, he spotted the kitchen boiler was out of action again. Not a good sign, he thought. This was the third time in as many weeks it had failed him. He'd been onto the suppliers at least a dozen times and was sick to death of the excuses they were giving him. Why couldn't they repair it, or send him a replacement? At least the lights in the corridor had been fixed, and that was a major plus.

Then he spotted what the electrician had been whingeing on about – *a nauseating smell coming from Locker Room 2.* Never a dull moment, he thought. You fix one problem then another crops up in its place. It was probably the street drains. The last time this had happened, one of the local kebab shops on Grainger Street had been caught tipping hot boiling fat into them. Damn foreigners, he cursed. Why couldn't they conform like the rest of us? Still, Monday wasn't the busiest day of the week to get things fixed. That was on Friday. It was all linked to the trains – people storing their hand luggage whilst touring the streets of Newcastle. At least it made sense, if nothing else seemed to that morning.

The electrician was right. There was a nasty smell coming from Locker Room 2. A pungent smell that made him retch the moment he stepped into the room. Just out of curiosity he checked the toilets, but everything was in order. Then he poked his nose down the kitchen drains, but nothing from there either. Returning to his desk, he quickly ran his cursor over the long overdues. There were five in total, and all posted in Locker Room 2. The thing was, some people never returned to collect their belongings as the overdue rental costs far outweighed the value of their possessions. It was a regular occurrence, and it was time the company put a stop to it.

Numbered one to eighty-two, the first storage locker Tommy opened in Locker Room 2 was number 21. Crammed full of rucksacks and personal effects, there wasn't much in the way of value in it either. Pushing his head in through the open locker door, he caught a strong whiff of sweaty feet. Clearly these people weren't coming back, which wasn't good.

The moment he opened locker 56, his stomach lurched. In all the years that Tommy had worked for the company, he'd never experienced anything like this before. The smell was so overpowering he could barely breathe let alone think straight. Pinching his nose between finger and thumb, he slid the large blue suitcase towards the front of the locker. It felt heavy. He prodded it with his finger, and watched it move. Taking a closer look, he noticed it was pad-locked and secured with two thick luggage straps. He tried to open it and wished he hadn't.

Panic gripped him, and before he'd even reached the end of the corridor he'd thrown up at least a dozen times. Shaking violently, he clawed his way back to the main entrance. He was sweating profusely, and the thought of what might be hidden inside the blue suitcase simply terrified him. His world falling apart, his whole body felt as though a thousand insects were crawling over him. Fast sinking into a bottomless pit full of writhing snakes, he gulped at the air in snatches and tried to steady himself. No matter how hard he tried to rid himself of bad thoughts, the sweet sickly smell of death clung to him like a thick blanket of fog.

Who had brought it here that night?

Was he alone?

The only thing that made any sense to Tommy was the customer had had one hell of a struggle in lifting it into the locker that night. Then he remembered, he'd worn a black hoodie pulled down low over his head and mirror lens sunglasses guarding his eyes. The rest was lost in a sea of confusion, and he was too scared even to go there.

What to do next?

Alone with his thoughts, Tommy was fast drowning in a sea of uncertainty. The more he thought about it, the more it sent his blood pressure soaring. The thing was, he knew exactly what was inside the blue suitcase and there wasn't a damn thing he could do about it.

It was still there, waiting for him in locker 56!

Chapter Six

Within hours of the Storage Company owners contacting Northumbria Police, Warwick Street was awash with newspaper reporters. News travelled fast, and the number of outside broadcast vans had grown considerably these past few hours. There again, the discovery of a headless torso wasn't an everyday occurrence. The city was in shock, with some people even too scared to venture out at night.

David Carlisle had watched the press conference unfold from his iPhone that morning. All the major networks were there. It was a big turnout. As well-known news presenters jostled for prime positions, the proceedings were beamed live across the nation. In front of a packed media gathering, DCI Mason gave a brief statement appealing for witnesses to come forward. The details were sketchy, inconsistent, but the mere mention of a headless torso had fuelled the public's imagination. Dubbed *the Suitcase Man*, the media's insatiable demand for answers was unnerving. It's what sold newspapers, what pushed editors to write great headlines.

Dressed in full police uniform, the Superintendent appealed to the public for calm. Even a heavy police presence had brought little comfort to the student community. People feared for their lives, and anyone seen dragging a suitcase around the streets of Newcastle was immediately stopped and questioned.

It was ten o'clock when David Carlisle entered Gateshead police station. Harassed by overzealous reporters, the desk Sergeant wasn't his usual happy-go-lucky self that morning. According to Police Central Control, the station was awash with hundreds of hoaxers claiming to be the killer. If there were any positives to be had, it was that blood samples recovered from Jennifer Oakwell's property matched that of the torso. All that remained now was to find the second victim's missing body parts, and the rest of the pieces would fall into place.

Taking the stairs two at a time, Carlisle reached the third floor amidst a hub of activity. These latest developments had certainly caused a major stir amongst the senior backroom staff, and many were demanding answers. The problem was, no one had any to give.

The moment Carlisle entered Jack Mason's office, he knew things were serious. The DCI's look was stern, and his approach direct. 'No doubt you'll have heard about these latest developments.'

'Yes. I saw you on the telly this morning.'

'Hmmm. What did you think?' Mason asked.

'To tell you the truth, I thought you looked a right shifty bastard.'

'Let's not even go there.'

Mason shuffled a few papers around an untidy desk and made a big show of adjusting his computer screen. Not the best of starts, thought Carlisle. Making you feel uncomfortable the moment you stepped into his office was one of Mason's favourite little tricks.

'This latest discovery has sparked off all kinds of unimaginable panic,' Mason began, 'and Forth Street will never be the same again.'

'No, I guess not.'

Mason took a sip of water from a glass. 'Remind me of your involvement with Frank Wiseman's son. What exactly did you do for them?'

'I thought we'd already discussed that issue,' Carlisle retorted.

Pen poised, the DCI glanced up at him. 'We have. But this is for the record.'

'If you must know, I did some work for his son's solicitors. Low key stuff, undercover surveillance, that sort of thing.'

'And what else did you do?'

'What do you mean?'

Mason looked down at his notes. 'What was the nature of your investigations?'

'Wiseman's son was having a spot of bother with a group of local thugs. They were threatening him with violence if he didn't pay up.'

'Drugs related, was it?'

'No, these people were trying to extort money from him in return for a protection racket they were supposedly running.'

'Did they know who his father was?'

'Yes, apparently.'

'And yet they still went ahead with it.' Mason shook his head in disbelief. 'So, how did you finally resolve the problem?'

'I was owed a few favours.'

Mason's eyebrows raised a fraction, the serious side surfacing. 'This wouldn't involve one of Frank Wiseman's associates, would it? The reason I ask is there could be a connection here.'

'That's interesting,' Carlisle replied thoughtfully. 'So, you think these murders could be linked to his son's recent threats?'

'No, I didn't say that.'

'Linked to whom then?'

'I'm not at liberty to say, as it's strictly a police matter at this stage.'

Mason was bluffing, and Carlisle had picked up on it. Two could play at this game, he thought. It was time to dig his heels in. 'Without seeing the case files, then how do you expect me to comment?'

Mason put his pen down and poured some more water from a jug. He admired his colleague's approach but thought it a waste of time. He knew how the system worked, how Jack Mason operated. First, he'd prime you full of bullshit, then try to pick your brains in the process. And yes, these recent murders had all the hallmarks of a gangland killing, but it was far from the truth. Whoever *the Suitcase Man* was, he'd certainly stirred up a hornet's nest.

'This latest victim has yet to be identified,' Mason confirmed. 'Find the answer to that, and we're half way to solving our problem.'

'You think it's that simple?'

'Probably not.' Mason raised a finger, then tapped his computer screen. 'We know Jennifer Oakwell was his intended target, as it was her he killed first. After attempting to dispose of the second victim's body, he must have got side-tracked at some point.'

Carlisle swallowed hard. 'Surely, you're not suggesting the killer intended to return to Forth Street to pick up the suitcase, are you?'

'That's how we see it.'

'He left it a bit late, don't you think?'

'What do you mean. . . late?'

'According to the press, the body stank the place out.'

Mason glared at him. 'This was a gangland execution, and that's why they removed the victim's head and hands. It's a classic method these people use. Eliminate the witness. . . get rid of the evidence.'

'It would have been far easier to bury or burn the body, don't you think?'

'Well, that's how we see it.'

'So, what is it you want from me?'

Mason shrugged. Having got off on a bad footing, things weren't going to plan. 'I'm still intrigued by this work you did for Frank Wiseman's solicitors. The guy you dealt with wouldn't be Tony Fox, would it?'

'No. I can't say as I've ever heard that name before.'

Mason explained. 'Fox runs a second-hand car dealership in Bridge Street. It's high end stuff, big turnover, and all of it stolen to order. We've been watching him for several months now, and a lot of money is changing hands.'

'No. That name's not familiar, so what's the connection here?'

'Just curious, that's all.'

'Wait a minute—'

Mason interrupted him by raising his hand. 'We also have it on good authority there's a power struggle taking place, and someone is trying to muscle in on Frank Wiseman's patch. If the rumour holds true, then it could have links to these killings.'

'So how can I possibly help?'

'You can't.' Mason shrugged.

'So why invite me here?'

Mason shook his head despondently. 'To be frank with you, it was your involvement with Wiseman's solicitors that got me thinking. I was rather hoping you'd shed some new light on the subject.'

Carlisle was curious as to where Mason's interests lay, then he understood what was happening. He was using him as a go-between, a means of gathering information. No way, he thought. It was totally out of the question.

Chapter
Seven

A pall of fear hung over the city that morning, and parts of Forth Street were still cordoned off. It was headline breaking news, and tales of headless torsos being dragged around the streets of Newcastle were running rife. Sometimes Mason wondered why he even bothered to attend press conferences in the first place. No matter how hard he tried to dress things down, reporters overhyped it. News travelled fast, and the crowd of curious onlookers now gathered outside the Storage Company was growing by the minute. What were they expecting to find for God's sake?

Despite his early start, Mason's investigations had unearthed very little in the way of fresh leads. A few people had been interviewed, but nothing of any significance had turned up. Throughout that morning, a team of specialist undercover officers had examined every access route in and out of Forth Street. It was painstaking work, and with hundreds of hours of CCTV footage to sift through, he was confident of making an arrest. Anyone caught on camera within a mile of the Storage Company the evening the case was dropped off, was now under suspicion. Not everyone was willing to come forward, though. Those that hadn't were now under scrutiny.

Thanks to some good PR, the number of possible sightings had grown considerably over the past forty-eight hours. So much so, that a team of officers had been tasked to deal with them. Uniforms had worked tirelessly too, distributing thousands of leaflets to jog people's memories. Someone out there must have seen or heard something, surely, he thought. It was a matter of weeding them out.

Mason stared at empty locker 56, as if mesmerised. The trouble was, CCTV covering the storage company's main entrance wasn't working that evening, nor were the lights in Locker Room 2. The only thing in his favour, if there was such a thing, was the manager hadn't opened the suitcase. Once forensics had arrived on the scene, it meant they had a clean sweep.

As his gaze drifted along the lengthy line of storage lockers, Savage poked his head into the room. 'I've just come from the manager's office, boss,' the sergeant said. 'The guy who brought the suitcase in here that evening didn't have a strong local accent.'

'He's not a Geordie then?'

'No, according to the manager, he's not.'

'What else did he tell you?'

'The guy had one hell of a struggle lifting the suitcase into the locker apparently.'

Mason's eyes narrowed. 'I thought the lights weren't working?'

'They weren't; the manager carried a torch with him.'

'What time was this?'

'Around seven o'clock.'

'Did he say what this guy looked like?'

'He's still in a state of shock and can't seem to remember much.'

Mason checked his watch. Even with a good smothering of Vicks VapoRub under his nose, Locker Room 2 still stank to the high heavens. There was no smell like the smell of decomposing flesh; even the most hardened investigators retched at the first sniff of it when entering a crime scene. As a body decomposed, it released gases and the two primary chemicals involved were cadaverine and putrescine. Real crime scenes were nothing like the glamorous dramas played out on TV, he thought. Working at street level was a whole different ball game. The problem was, it usually took days before the nauseating smell that clung to your clothes disappeared. Even then, it hung in the memory.

Mason slipped out of his white coveralls and brushed the flecks of forensic powder from his trouser legs. Not the best of starts, he muttered. At least they'd made some progress, but it wasn't much. Outside, his lungs full of clean air, the young constable stood guarding the entrance tipped his peaked cap in salute. Normally he would have stopped to chat; not today though. What little daylight there was left, he would need to use sparingly. Despite all his efforts that day, there was still no simple explanation as to how the suspect had arrived here that evening. Sifting through hundreds of hours of CCTV footage took time, and he was having to rely on eye witness accounts. He knew from experience that the whole grizzly affair had been planned. But by whom?

Turning his collar against a stiff northerly breeze Mason walked towards the Central Station and tried to clear his head of unpleasant thoughts. Soon it would be dark, and the city would take on a different form. Strangely enough, it was something that DS Savage had said that stopped him dead in his tracks. Still full of indecision, he retraced his footsteps back towards Forth Banks police station. He wasn't a gambling man, but at seven o'clock that evening he was confident the killer would have arrived here by car. It made sense, if little else did. There again, he argued, what if an unsuspecting taxi driver had dropped him off? The only thing wrong with that line of thinking was the suitcase would have been extremely heavy to lift. Not the best of options, he thought. It would have raised too much suspicion.

★★★

Entering Forth Banks Police Station, a familiar face stared up at him from behind the desk screen. Sergeant Bronson was a distinguished-looking man, mid-forties, balding, with a sharp, public school accent. Mason disliked him intensely and considered him a knobhead.

'Name?' the sergeant announced.

'Mickey Mouse!'

Fingers poised over the computer keyboard, the sergeant lifted his head a fraction. 'I need a name, sir.'

'Is DS Wallace on duty?'

'First things first,' the sergeant replied stoically.

Mason held his warrant card up in front of the sergeant's face, and grimaced. 'DCI Mason, Northumbria police. Is DS Wallace about?'

'Thank you, sir. I'll check if he's in.'

The sergeant smiled meekly as he picked up the telephone receiver and punched a three-digit code into the keypad. Seconds later he turned to face him again. 'You'll find Detective Sergeant Wallace on the second floor, sir. It's the first door on your right.'

The operations room was open-plan and narrow. Five desks overlooking the East Coast main railway line, and all decked out with flat screen computer monitors. It wasn't a large room, but as police offices' go, it had a cosy atmosphere. He found Wallace staring up at a large wall map pinned to the back wall. From what he could see, his old workmate had piled on the weight since they'd last worked together. Unlike some of the hangers on he'd dealt with over the years, Wallace was a grafter and easy to get on with.

'Hello, Jack. What brings you to this neck of the woods?'

'Business, George.'

Wallace managed a wry smile as they shook hands. 'It wouldn't be about the *Suitcase Man*, would it?'

'How did you guess?'

Wallace gestured towards an empty seat opposite. 'How can we help?'

A phone rang, and the officer at the end desk picked up the receiver and began taking down notes. Mason cleared his throat. 'This one's a bit of a puzzler, George. We know the victim had links to Jennifer Oakwell, as we now have a positive DNA match. What we don't know, not even forensics, is who the hell he is.'

Wallace shook his head. 'I take it you still haven't found the rest of the body parts?'

'Not yet we haven't, but I'm not pinning any hopes on ever finding them.'

'Whoever killed him is obviously intent on making identification difficult for you.'

Mason shuffled awkwardly. 'He's a cunning bastard all right.'

Wallace glanced up at him. 'He could be sending out a warning, of course.'

'That had crossed my mind.' Mason sighed. 'As have a lot of other things lately.'

'Hindsight's a funny thing, but your killer sounds a bit of a loose cannon in the grand scheme of things.'

The two men looked at one another and smiled.

'It doesn't add up. It's as if —' Mason stopped himself mid-sentence, his mind switching to other things. 'This has all the hallmarks of another gangland execution in my opinion. The only problem I have with that, is who in their rightful mind would want Mad Frankie Wiseman's ex-wife murdered?'

'It could have been arranged.'

'He's not that daft, George. Besides, it would have been far too obvious.'

Wallace thought a moment. 'Why did Jennifer Oakwell split from her husband in the first place? As I remember she sat in the courtroom during the eight-week trial and supported him throughout.'

'The day Mad Frankie went down she was left facing a twenty-year separation. It's not something to look forward to in any marriage.'

'No, I suppose not.' Wallace frowned. 'And she never re-married?'

'No. Oakwell was her maiden name?'

There was a long drawn out silence.

'What about casual lovers?' Wallace asked. 'Did she ever team up with anyone?'

'What, you think Wiseman may have turned jealous at some stage?'

'Twenty years is a long time to be cooped up inside a prison cell, Jack. God knows what goes on in some people's minds.'

Mason thought for a moment but said nothing.

'It's not just her sex life,' Wallace went on. 'It's Wiseman's reputation that could have been at stake here.'

'That's a good point.'

'What about the rest of the gang members – I hear some of them are now out on parole?'

'We've already considered that aspect. The day Wiseman's ex-wife was murdered, they all had watertight alibis. I'm thinking more along the lines of this take-over bid that everyone's talking about who's trying to step into Frank's shoes?'

Wallace stroked his long-pointed chin, his eyes searching for answers. 'It's been exceptionally quiet around these parts lately, it's as if the criminal fraternity has gone into hibernation. I could put my feelers out for you. . . ask around. I know a few desperate lowlifes who could do with a few extra quid in their pockets.'

'Good man. That would be useful.'

'Tell me,' said Wallace, the look of concern still showing. 'Have you given any thoughts to contacting David Carlisle?'

'Yes and no,' Mason muttered. 'The Acting Superintendent's the stumbling block. She's not at all keen on the idea of bringing specialists in on the case, especially at this early stage in our investigations.'

'Police budgets, no doubt.'

'There is an element of that.'

Wallace nodded. 'She's probably right.'

'Even so, I'm still not convinced it's the right decision.'

'So where do you go from here?'

'You know me, George. I'm not one to shy away from a problem.'

Wallace stuck a yellow post-it onto the side of his computer screen and swivelled in his seat. 'The last I heard, Frank Wiseman was serving out his time in Durham prison.'

'He still is.'

'It might be worth paying him a visit.'

Mason sighed. 'Criminals aren't usually that obliging, George.'

'No, I guess not, but at least you'll know which side of the fence he's sitting on and whether he knows anything about his ex-wife's murder.'

Wallace was the third person to suggest a prison visit in as many days, and he wasn't overly impressed with the idea. He would need to sleep on it, think things through carefully before making any snap decisions.

Mason held Wallace's glances. 'If you were involved, how would you have transported a body to the Storage Company that evening?'

Wallace tapped his pen on the desktop in thought. 'I'd have driven it there by car. Think about it, who in their right mind would want to drag a heavy suitcase round the streets of Newcastle, especially with a headless torso stuck inside of it.'

'Unless you're the executioner!' Mason shrugged.

'True—'

'Do you think others could be involved?'

'It's possible, especially if this was an organised crime.'

'Who are the most likely candidates, do you think?'

The detective took a deep breath before answering. 'If there's a power struggle going on, it could only involve a few people. My money would be on Tony Fox, or one of Wiseman's counterparts from the east end of Newcastle.'

'Anyone else spring to mind?'

'There's a guy who operates out of Westgate Road, called Carlo Stefano. It may be worth checking him out. The trouble is, he has his fingers in an awful lot of pies these days and is a difficult person to pin down.'

'He sounds Mafia to me.'

'He probably is.'

Mason shook his head. 'So why bother with the Storage Company?'

Wallace shrugged. 'That's a good point.'

Chapter Eight

Whilst the rest of Newcastle slept uneasy in their beds that night, dozens of armed police officers had moved into Forth Street under the cover of darkness. Nothing was left to chance, and by first light that morning, the whole area was swarming with police. Not all had been plain sailing, but Jack Mason was pleased with the way things had gone. Barely a ten-minute walk from Newcastle Central Station, every inch of the ground had to be covered. It was a huge operation, involving hundreds of police officers. If the killer had arrived at the Storage Company on foot that evening, then someone must have seen him. It was this aspect that Mason was working on, and he was convinced he was finally onto something.

All along Forth Street and buried deep beneath the bowels of the East Coast mainline railway line, lay a network of tunnels. It was the perfect hiding place. Built of solid sandstone, not all archways had been turned into going concerns. Some were empty, and it was these the police were concentrating on.

Plagued by uncertainty, yesterday's press conference had come and gone. Mason hated media gatherings at the best of times, claiming they were minefields of unscrupulous reporters. The problem was, the Detective Chief Inspector had a nasty habit of putting his foot in it at all the wrong moments, and it wasn't good for morale.

It was now 4:30 am.

'We need to fan out, work in pairs,' Mason shouted. 'If this bastard is hiding in one of the side tunnels, we'll need to flush him out.'

'I'll get one of the dog teams involved,' Savage replied.

Twenty minutes later, Mason watched as a dozen police officers began their search of adjoining properties. Dressed in full combat gear, they'd prepared for every eventuality. Thirty feet down, beneath Newcastle's mainline railway station, passenger trains could be heard. It was a weird environment, and the people who worked here lived the existence of moles.

'I never knew this place existed,' Mason said turning to face Savage.

'I knew they were here, but thought they'd been blocked up years ago.'

'It's perfect.'

As Savage shone his torch into one of the ventilation shafts, Mason checked his surroundings. The deeper into the network system they ventured, the creepier it got. It reminded him of London underground, high arched ceilings, red brick walls, and a maze of secret passageways.

'What's it like back there?' Mason asked.

'There's a few offshoot passages, but nothing in comparison to some of the tunnels that run under the city.'

'So, there's more?'

'There's a few still in existence that I know of.'

'You've obviously been down here before?'

Savage bent and scraped something from the floor. 'When I was a young lad, my old man used to bring me down here. It was one of the many weird interests he had. There's one tunnel that runs from Spital Tongues colliery down to the River Tyne, and is over two miles long. It was used to transport coal down to the waiting collier boats back in the old days but was mothballed after the pits were closed.' Savage scratched the cleft of his chin as if living a bygone memory. 'They used them as air shelters during the Second World War, but many have since been bricked up.'

'You live and learn,' Mason said, shaking his head. 'Walk the streets of Newcastle, and you never know what lies beneath your feet.'

'It's another world down here,' Savage replied.

As footsteps broke the silence, a small group of police officers emerged.

'We found these two scoundrels holed up in one of the side tunnels,' Manley announced.

Mason took a closer look. 'What are they doing down here?'

'They're part of the city's homeless community by the looks.'

Mason gave them a once over, and quickly eliminated them from his enquiries. Too many people had fallen through the cracks of society for his likes. Securing a safe place to live was always difficult when you were down on your luck. He felt sorry for them, as many were vulnerable. People living rough on the streets of Newcastle were seventeen times more likely to have been the victims of violence – a statistic he wasn't proud of. Having grown up knowing hardship himself, Mason knew how easy it was to fall into the homeless poverty trap. Life was a vicious circle, and there was no easy solution to the problem.

Having caught a whiff of the suspects' stale breath, Mason took a step back. Cheap supermarket wine – another debilitating disease associated with the homeless community.

'Do you guys sleep down here?' Mason asked, inclining his head slightly.

The shorter of the two grinned through blackened teeth. 'Yeah, this is our home. Why?'

'How long have you lived here?'

'Six months. . . since the start of last winter.'

'Anyone else call this place home?'

'Not to my knowledge.'

'How can you be sure?'

'Cos we'd know about it.'

Sleeping rough in the middle of Newcastle could be harsh, but what if they'd witnessed something? Like startled sewer rats, the strangers stared at him as though he'd arrived from another planet. The smaller of the two, stocky, with short cropped hair, looked ex-military, Mason thought. He had an anxious look, emotionally detached, as though suffering from some form of post-traumatic stress disorder. Probably involved in some sort of military combat at some stage in his past. Avoidance of places, people, and reminders of traumatic events were the most common symptoms he looked for.

What to do next?

'Who else hangs around here at night?' Mason asked.

Neither spoke, which was kind of understandable under the circumstances.

Mason turned to Manley. 'What did your sweep of the other tunnels throw up?'

'Apart from these two scoundrels, nothing.'

'We need to question them. Find out what they know. While you're at it, see if the duty sergeant can't rustle up some bacon and eggs. . . they certainly look as if they could do with a hot meal.'

The moment Mason stepped back out into Forth Street, one of the locals confronted him. A stout man, with an overhanging belly and black shiny leather shoes.

'Are you one of the tenants?' Mason queried.

'Yes, what are you people looking for?'

Mason showed him his warrant card, as a team of police officers poured out of one of the adjoining archways. In what was now a well-oiled operation, they were soon about their business again. If the killer was using this place as a bolt-hole, they might even catch him red-handed. He smiled inwardly, knowing his imagination was running amok again.

'Are these units locked at night?'

'Why, is there a problem?'

Mason was thinking on his feet. 'What about CCTV?'

'There isn't any.'

'Any reason why not?'

The tenant shrugged but said nothing.

'What about these two reprobates. How do you explain their presence on your property?'

'With all due respects, Inspector—'

Annoyed with the tenant's attitude, Mason thrust his warrant card under his nose and said. 'Take another look. . . it's Detective Chief Inspector.'

He'd lost the plot again, and the man standing in front of him was probably squeaky clean. Not good, he reasoned. Why did he always fly off the handle at the slightest provocation? Was it his marriage breakup? He would need to calm down, think things through logically instead of recklessly jumping to conclusions. And that was another thing that worried him lately, he was back to his old drinking habits again. He would need to cut back – stop the late-night lock-in's – but how was the problem.

Mason noticed his hands were shaking and took another deep breath. 'Have you been watching the news lately?' he asked.

'What if I have?'

'So, you'll have heard all about the body we found at the Storage Company.'

The tenant shrugged. 'I may have done.'

Mason glared at him. 'No doubt you've made a statement to that effect?'

'No, I haven't.'

'Why not?'

'Cos, I didn't think it was necessary. Besides, it's been weeks since I was last down here.'

Mason took another deep breath and felt his fists clench. 'In which case, you'll need to accompany me back to Gateshead police station.'

The tenant was about to speak, but quickly thought the better of it.

'It's the law,' Mason said brashly. 'It's what I'm paid to do.'

The tenant glared at him.

'And this is a murder enquiry!'

Chapter Nine

Acting Superintendent Sutherland stared down at the coroner's report and raised her eyebrows a fraction. Not an unattractive woman, mid-forties, with a slim waistline and fair complexion, her hair had been cropped short at the sides and changed colour every fortnight according to Tom Hedley, the senior forensic scientist. At least she was approachable, which was more than Jack Mason could say about most senior officers in the division. A former pupil of Queen Elizabeth High School in Hexham, her father was an ex-Coldstream Guards officer. A strict disciplinarian, with contacts in high places, rumour had it that at some stage in his career he'd served as equerry to the Queen. If true, there was little wonder his daughter had made such rapid progress as she had.

Mason sat quietly waiting for the punchline.

'This male torso we found in Forth Street,' Sutherland began. 'Can we put a name to him?'

'Not yet we can't, ma'am.'

Sutherland was punctilious about the use of professional titles, and Mason hated it. It wasn't his style, and the word Ma'am always sounded empty and insincere to him. He watched as she annoyingly tapped the end of her pen on one of the case files, before turning to face him.

'Are you sure this is a case of witness elimination?'

Mason grinned inanely. 'If not, then someone's in an awful hurry to step into Frank Wiseman's shoes.'

'Talking of criminals,' said Sutherland staring at her notes, 'where are we with Mr Wiseman's associates? I hear that four of them have recently been released on parole.'

'Yes, that's correct, ma'am.'

She was quiet for a moment. 'There's rumours that some of the money the gang stole during their post office raids has since gone missing.'

'I believe so.'

'Could Wiseman's ex-wife have been involved?'

'It's feasible, but highly unlikely.'

'We need to keep a watchful eye on these people, Jack.'

'We already have, ma'am.'

'And?'

'They all have watertight alibis and have nothing to do with these recent murders.'

'Keep trying,' Sutherland insisted. 'These people cannot be trusted.'

Mason looked at her and shrugged.

'Perhaps you should arrange a visit to Durham prison. Let's hear what Mr Wiseman has to say for himself. He's bound to know something about his ex-wife's murder.'

'I doubt he'll talk.'

'I agree, but at least we'll know which side of the fence he's sitting on.'

Following on from Sergeant Wallace, the Acting Superintendent was now the fourth person in as many days to mention a prison visit to him. He wasn't impressed. Experience had taught him that interviewing inmates was never a clever idea, let alone Category B prisoners. No, he thought. He would refuse to go down that avenue again.

'I'm not convinced it will work, ma'am.'

'It must be worth pursuing. . . surely?'

Notebook open, pen poised, the Detective Chief Inspector's look was unyielding. 'And how would you propose we go about that?'

Sutherland's jaw dropped. 'I would have thought you talk to the prison governor.'

Mason cringed but said nothing.

'Tell me,' she said, the look of despair still showing. 'What was the outcome of yesterday's Forth Street operation?'

'There's been plenty of feedback, but nothing of any significance has shown up.'

'What about ANPR or the storage company's CCTV?'

'The main entrance cameras haven't worked in weeks, and the manager hasn't a clue what our suspect even looks like.'

'He must have filled in some sort of documentation, Jack.'

'He did, but the name and address don't add up.'

'Well there's a thing,' Sutherland shrugged. 'And what else did he tell you?'

'He mentioned a lot of things, but none of it is of any use to us.'

'And yet he still remembers a *blue* suitcase being deposited there that evening, so it can't all be worthless information.'

Mason thought about it before answering. 'Yes, but we still don't know how the suitcase initially arrived at the storage company that night.'

'Being so close to the railway station I would have thought it was dragged there.'

'I'm not so sure about that either. According to the manager the suspect had great difficulty man-handling it into the storage locker.'

Sutherland looked at him with frank surprise. 'So how do we know he's the killer?'

'We don't. That's my problem.'

The Acting Superintendent glanced up at a series of SOC photographs pinned to her corkboard. 'It's rather a large suitcase, and definitely looks awkward to lift.'

'And our suspect's not a tall man,' Mason added.

Sutherland hesitated, as she stared at the corkboard and wrinkled her nose. 'It does have sturdy runner wheels, nevertheless, which suggests it could have easily been dragged there.'

'It may well have been,' Mason replied.

'We need to revisit the CCTV footage again, let's see if we haven't missed something.'

Mason made a note of it, annoyed at having to go back over old ground. He lifted his head as if resigned to the fact. 'I'll get someone over there right away, ma'am.'

Sutherland pushed back in her seat, walked over to her filing cabinet and pulled out the top-drawer. She was making him feel uncomfortable, and he was finding it difficult to relax. It was then he noticed she was wearing flat shoes, more for comfort than fashion, he thought. Then, lifting one of the case files out from its folder, she returned to her seat.

'Shortly after Frank Wiseman was sent down, his wife filed for divorce. It wasn't a good relationship by all accounts, and he never put up much of a fight during the divorce proceedings. Not that Wiseman had any choice in the matter.' She smiled, as she flicked through the pages of the report. 'They had a son. Robert. He was twelve at the time. What with a father in prison and a mother keen to celebrate her newly found freedom, it wasn't the best environment to be brought up in.'

'Those were my sentiments, ma'am.'

Sutherland's shoulders sagged. 'She didn't hang about by the look of things. It says here in the report, that shortly after the divorce settlement she reverted back to her maiden name.'

'Most women usually do,' Mason said, speaking from experience having just gone through a very nasty divorce settlement with his own wife.

'Yes, but having gained resident parent over Robert, according to Social Services it wasn't a very good mother and son relationship either.'

'No. I guess not.'

Sutherland's eyes narrowed a fraction. 'It also mentions that Robert spent most of his childhood living with an aunt in Whitley Bay.'

'We've already covered that ground, ma'am. Robert went to the High School there but didn't do well in his final exams. After leaving school, he was in and out of jobs before finally ending up running a pub in Walker.'

'Ah, yes.' Sutherland nodded. 'And as I remember he got into a spot of bother over it.'

'He did indeed. Local impressionable thugs trying to squeeze protection money out of him.'

'Do we know who they were?'

'Yes, we do.'

Sutherland flicked through the pages of the report, and then turned to face him. 'And are things back to normal?'

'Yes, for the moment they are.'

'We need to dig deeper, Jack. Find out what Jennifer Oakwell got up to after the divorce settlement. As to why she was murdered, it may be hidden in the detail.'

'We've already done some digging around, but nothing much has come of it.'

'I understand she drank an awful lot. . .'

'She did.'

'And you're still adamant this is a case of witness elimination?'

'Unless we've missed something obvious, ma'am.'

Sutherland shook her head. 'This isn't as easy as I first thought.'

'No, ma'am. I agree.' Mason trod cautiously. 'The question remains, why did the killer choose to leave the victim's body in a storage locker in the first place?'

'Convenience, I would think. Proximity to the city centre. . . easy access to the Metro system?'

'If I may say so, it's a bit risky dragging a suitcase around the streets of Newcastle with a body stuck inside of it, don't you think?'

'What if he dropped it off for someone else to pick up?'

'It's possible, ma'am.'

Sutherland closed the case files and pushed them to one side. 'If anything, you need to concentrate your efforts on establishing who this second victim is. Once we know the answer to that, we'll be well on our way to solving the case.'

Mason experienced that sinking feeling again. Pity, he thought. He could have done with a few imaginative thinkers on the team. People like David Carlisle, quick thinkers who could move with fast changing situations. As usual, Sutherland's head was still stuck inside the rule book and seemed reluctant to venture away from it.

At least he was on his own turf.

'I forgot to mention it earlier, but David Carlisle was initially involved with Wiseman's lawyers over this protection racket that Robert was caught up in.'

'I thought it was his father's pub?'

'No, ma'am. Robert owns it outright. Besides, he's the innocent party in all of this.'

'You never mentioned any of that in your report.'

'With all due respects, I didn't think it had any bearing on the case.'

Sutherland kept silent for a few moments. 'If there *is* a power struggle taking place, then Frank Wiseman is bound to feature heavily in it. These people have a knack of keeping control over their empires, even when they're serving time in prison.'

'It's not just a simple case of protecting your assets, ma'am.'

'I know, but what if someone killed his ex-wife because of it?'

Mason shrugged but said nothing.

Sutherland gave him a stern look. 'Let's see what your visit to Durham prison throws up. Who knows, it may open up a whole new line of enquiries.'

Fat chance of that happening; Mason groaned. Answers were few and far between, and he was fast running out of ideas. Lateral thinking was the way forward, it had to be. If not, then it was back to the drawing board again.

As the meeting ended, the Detective Chief Inspector felt utterly dejected by it all. It didn't look good suddenly, and any hopes of an early breakthrough now seemed a million light years away.

Chapter
Ten

Over the centuries, HM Durham Prison had contained some of the country's most notorious criminals. Many, such as the Kray twins, Ronnie and Reggie, were household names. What many people didn't know, or perhaps they did, was that over one-hundred men and women had been hanged there. Ninety-one of these had taken place at the prison or nearby courthouse, and eighteen in public. Not that statistics concerned Jack Mason as he strolled into Old Elvet that morning, but at least he was well-informed.

It had started to rain when Mason entered the prison's main entrance hall. Far removed from the everyday hustle and bustle of normality, this was another world. On being stopped at reception, he showed his warrant card and was asked a series of questions as part of the standard security procedure. Next, he was given the once over by an inquisitive drugs dog who stared at him as if he were a dealer. Not finished yet, his personal effects, including wallet, car keys and mobile phone, were placed in a long plastic tray and stored in a security locker for safe keeping. After a walk-through body scan and pat-down search by an overzealous female security officer, Mason felt awkward and conspicuous.

'Follow me, sir,' the waiting prison officer announced.

He was led through a series of high security doors, then they entered a windowless room normally set aside for interviews. 'Make yourself comfortable,' the prison officer said; 'they shouldn't be long.'

Mason nodded and took up a seat.

The room was imposing and had an overpowering feeling of mistrust. Prisoners who came here were obviously in some sort of trouble with the law, that much was evident. Staring up at a 42-inch plasma screen normally used as a video link to connect to outlying courts, he felt he was being watched. Although much of the building had maintained its original character, several new features had been added. Security was tight – it had to be, as Durham prison harboured some of the hardest criminals in the land.

Several minutes passed, then Mason heard keys jangling. Flanked by two prison officers, Frank Wiseman entered the room handcuffed. Dressed in a standard blue prison shirt, black trousers, and wearing a pair of comfy deck shoes on his feet, his left hand was heavily bandaged protecting a broken finger.

Mason stared at him for a second. 'Mr Wiseman,' he began. 'I'm DCI Jack Mason, Northumbria police. I'm here to ask you a few questions if I may.'

The prisoner muttered something inaudible and slumped down in a chair opposite.

'This shouldn't take long.'

The voice was worn out, gruff like a smoker's. 'Are you for real, or what?'

'I'm sorry——'

Wiseman gave him a look. 'It's me who asks the questions around here.'

Mason's instincts told him not to rush into it, but he still couldn't get his head round the fact he was dealing with one of Newcastle's most notorious gangsters. God loves a trier, he groaned, but this was ridiculous.

'So, what is it you're wanting to ask me?'

'Don't fuck with me, Inspector,' Wiseman growled. 'You know what I want.'

Mason thought a moment, trying not to make eye contact. Any kind of contact! Wiseman had obviously kept himself in decent shape over the years, as most long-term prisoners usually do. It's what kept them apart from the rest of the inmates, what segregated the wheat from the chaff. Flexing your muscles was a big part of the prison mind-set, as it not only demonstrated your ability to smash someone's brains in, it established your prison credibility. No, Mason thought, he would need to keep a cool head on this one, even though it rubbed against the grain.

'I'm sorry to hear about your recent loss, Mr Wiseman.'

'Are you?'

'If that had been my ex-wife who'd just been murdered, I'd be hopping mad.' Mason let it sink in. 'Rest assured, we're doing everything in our power to catch the sick bastard who did this to her.'

'I'm listening, but I'm not liking what I'm hearing.'

'If there's anything——'

Wiseman interrupted him by raising a hand. 'Let's cut the crap. What is it you're after?'

'I'd appreciate some honest answers.'

Wiseman cocked his head to one side. 'It doesn't work like that, not around here it doesn't.'

'Really?'

'You heard me.'

As his grip on the tubular chair legs tightened, Mason gritted his teeth. If the prisoner was to kick off at any point, he would need to be quick on his feet. He stared at the heavily bandaged finger again, his mind all over the place. One false move and he would reach over and grab tight hold of it and watch the bastard scream.

'When did you last contact your ex-wife?'

'Not since the divorce.' Wiseman laughed. 'And I was glad to see the back of her.'

'What about relatives?'

'No. They don't bother me either.'

'Did any of Jennifer's family ever keep in touch? A prison visit. . . the odd Christmas card perhaps?'

'Why would they?'

'Just curious.'

'Let's get one thing straight here,' Wiseman said, as he leaned across the table and exhaled heavily. 'I've never talked to my ex-wife, not since the divorce settlement. What she got up to, and who she went out with, was none of my concern.'

'What about the sub-post office raid money that's gone missing. . . was she involved in that?'

Wiseman stared at him hard. 'What money is this?'

The tension was building, and Mason needed to cool things down. 'I was talking to Tony Fox the other day, about the Eastern European gangs who are moving into the north side of the city. The word on the street is they're muscling in on your old stamping grounds.'

'So what?' Wiseman shrugged.

'I just thought I'd mention it. That's all.'

Wiseman flexed his huge biceps in another show of resentment.

'What else did Tony have to say?'

'Not much. Although he did mention there was a lot of money changing hands.'

'What's that supposed to mean?'

'I have no idea, you tell me.'

Wiseman said nothing, but his face said it all.

'What do you know about the young guy who was murdered in your ex-wife's house?' Mason asked coldly. 'Would you know who he was?'

Wiseman's eyes narrowed a fraction. 'Without a name, how the fuck would I know?'

'He must have been there for some reason or other.'

'Is that not what you people are paid to do. . . find these things out?'

Mason shook his head. 'Right place wrong time, eh?'

The prisoner smiled at him, knowing full well he didn't have a name to give. The gangster was sizing him up, acting dumb and trying to establish what the police knew about his ex-wife's murder.

'Let's hope he was a friend of the family, and not one of your local thugs.'

'So why ask?'

'I'm just making general conversation, that's all,' Mason shrugged.

'You don't come across as a very intelligent copper. What the fuck do you think he was doing there?'

'I've no idea, Frank. You tell me.'

'Whoever killed this young lad, obviously knew where to find him.'

Plausible, Mason thought, but highly unlikely as everyone on the force knew Jennifer Oakwell was the killer's intended target. Even so, he still hadn't the heart to tell him as much. Not yet, he hadn't. That would come later, when he was treading on safer ground.

'Someone's obviously got it in for you, Frank. Whoever killed your ex-wife was extremely angry about someone or something. Blood everywhere, carpets and walls, it wasn't a pretty sight I can assure you. What puzzles me about it all is that nothing was taken from the property.'

Wiseman's look was stern. 'You're the copper around here, you're supposed to know how these things work.'

'True.' Mason nodded.

'Tell me,' said Wiseman, their faces almost touching, 'why do you think he killed the fat slag?'

'An old score to settle, or maybe—' Mason paused mid-sentence.

Eyes like daggers, Wiseman suddenly shot to his feet. 'Rest assured, Inspector. Whoever's responsible for murdering Jennifer will end up being fed to the pigs.'

'And who will do that for you, Frank?'

'You'd be surprised.'

'Nothing surprises me anymore,' Mason said calmly.

Face to face with a notorious gangster wasn't the most exciting experience in his life, but it came mightily close. This was another world, a world where every little victory was hard fought. It was all about posturing, flexing your muscles and trying to gauge what the other person was thinking.

'You ever been badly beaten up just for doing your job, Jack?'

'Several times. Why?'

'Do you know what it feels like to be beaten up by a real professional?'

'I know what happens to them.' Mason smiled.

Wiseman glared at him. Eyes glazed over, pupils dilated, his voice ice cold. 'I'm not talking about a bar brawl here. I'm talking about the real thing.'

'So am I.'

'What then?'

'The last guy who gave me a good hiding, we got thrown down a dark alley together one night.' Mason glared at him. 'Just the two of us. No witnesses. That's how I like to deal with your so-called professionals. He's in a wheelchair now. Drinks through a straw and has to be spoon fed three times a day, so I'm told.'

Wiseman said nothing, but Mason knew what he was thinking.

'Is there anything else you wish to talk to me about?'

The prisoner nodded weakly. 'No. I've heard enough bullshit for one day.'

'Any messages for the outside world?'

Wiseman flashed him an angry look. 'Why don't you piss off back to your cosy little warm office, and leave me to get on with it?'

As the door closed firmly behind him, Mason could hear the other inmates kicking off. It was show time, and Mad Frankie Wiseman was putting on a five-star performance. It was all about timing and striking the right balance. Not the greatest of interviews but getting the prisoner to talk was often enough. No, Mason thought, with any luck the feelers would soon be out, and the streets of Newcastle would cough up the answers. If not another dead body.

Chapter Eleven

I'll never touch another drop, Mason was thinking as he dragged his sore head from the pillow and gazed at his watch through one eye. Monday morning, and the start of a brand-new week. His tongue felt like coarse sandpaper, and the back of his throat dry. No more overindulgence, he groaned. Honest to God. It was 10:00 am, and he'd missed the morning team briefing, a meeting of his own instigation. Cursing incompetence, he'd considered calling the office, but quickly thought better of it. The world's worst liar, he was useless at making excuses up and his stories never sounded convincing anyway.

Unsteady on his feet, he staggered into the kitchen and made towards the fridge. Grabbing the remains of yesterday's milk, he gulped it down in the belief that it would pull him around. He was wrong, of course. Seconds later he was straddling the toilet full of remorse and self-pity, as the recycling process contacted the porcelain pan. Suffering the mother of all hangovers, the previous night's events were awash in a drunken stupor. All he could remember was boarding a taxi outside some sleazy back-street Chinese restaurant in Wallsend. The rest was a series of vague recollections, obscure incidents lost in a sea of alcohol confusion.

His phone rang.

'Is that you, boss?'

'Uh-huh.'

'It's DS Savage. You okay?'

Mason's tone sounded pitifully woeful. 'What time did we finish last night, Rob?'

'Two-thirty in the morning, boss.'

He swayed and grabbed the bathroom towel rail to steady himself. 'What's happening?'

'Where are you now?' Savage asked inquisitively.

'Why, what's up?'

'Don't tell me you've just crawled out of bed?'

'No, what gave you that impression?' Mason lied.

'You sound just like I feel. . . shit!'

Thinking on his feet, Mason feigned a more convenient approach. 'I'm checking out witness statements; what are you up to today?'

'I'm over at the Waste and Recycling Centre.'

'Oh. What's going on over there?'

There was another long pause on the other end of the phone. 'Haven't you heard? We've found another body. A young man, late teens. His hands and feet have been bound together with heavy duty duct tape, and it's a bit of a mess, I'm afraid. And, before you ask, we've been trying to contact you ever since the call first came in.'

'What time was this?' Mason croaked.

'Eight o'clock this morning.'

'Blaydon, you say?'

'Yes. I'm here with forensics.'

Mason felt as though his head was about to lift from his shoulders. He could barely think straight, let alone make conscious decisions. Having slept curled up on the sofa bed all night, his movements were sluggish, and he was struggling to stay upright.

What to do next?

'Who's with you now?'

'Harry Manley, Peter Davenport the SOC photographer, and a few other members of the team.'

'Who's the duty SOC manager?'

'Stan Johnson is, why?'

'Good man. What about the duty police doctor?'

There was another long pause, a moment of hesitation. 'It's Doctor Hindson. . .'

'Oh, shit. That's all I need,' Mason cursed.

'I couldn't agree more. He's not the best person to have around on a crime scene.'

'The old sod exudes arrogance from every pore in his body and isn't liked either.' Mason thought a minute. 'Hold the fort, Rob. I'll be over there as quick as I can.'

The moment he hung up, Mason grabbed the bottle of aspirins from the bathroom cabinet and dashed his face with icy water. Maybe it was denial, or perhaps avoidance, but this couldn't have happened at a more inconvenient time. Throwing his jacket onto the backseat of the undercover Ford Focus, he reluctantly slid into the driver's seat. He was probably over the drink driving limit anyway. Any hopes of a quick recovery clearly dashed, he gazed through the mud-spattered windscreen. Not having the best of mornings, he suddenly felt worse. Another body on his hands, and a shit load of explaining to do too.

Well, he thought, might as well get on with it.

★★★

Surrounded on four sides by a perimeter fence, the immediate crime scene had been cordoned off and a constable posted on guard. By the look of things, forensics had arrived in a Mercedes-Benz Sprinter Van – their attentions already drawn towards a large yellow skip full of household rubbish. It had spilled onto the road and was now being gone over with a fine-tooth comb.

His head full of self-pity, Mason signed the crime scene log sheet and made his way towards the knot of police officers now gathered in front of a large blue skip.

'What have we got?' he asked.

The constable dutifully tipped his peak cap in salute and rolled his eyes. 'Young man in his early twenties, sir.'

'Do we have an ID?'

'Not yet, we don't.'

'Who found him?'

'One of the site lorry drivers. . . around seven-thirty this morning. He was about to hook up his vehicle when he noticed body parts sticking out of the skip. At first, he thought it was a tailor's dummy, but on taking a closer look, that's when he raised the alarm.'

Pen poised, Mason lifted his eyes from his little black notebook and levelled them at the constable. In no mood for conversation, he was trying his best not to throw up.

'Anyone with him at the time?'

There was hesitation in the constable's voice. 'Nobody that I'm aware of, sir. These guys work pretty much on their own. It's a large site, and according to the site manager the place was shut down over the weekend for routine health and safety checks.'

Mason pointed to a large gathering of scavenging seagulls hovering over the back of one of the stationary skip lorries. 'Who's working the outlying area?'

'Uniforms are,' DS Rob Savage said, fast homing in on him.

Mason felt another bout of nausea wash over him, but somehow managed to contain it. Moving towards the front of a stationary dumper truck, he gulped at the air in snatches and tried to force some oxygen into his brain. They couldn't move or touch anything yet, not until Home Office pathologists had completed their findings. Even so, there were still plenty of things to be getting on with.

'How long has he been dead?'

'Hard to say. Not more than a couple of days.'

'What sort of state is the body in?' Mason asked.

'You best look for yourself, boss.'

Mason pointed to a huge mountain of garden rubbish in his attempt to stave off the inevitable. 'How's this stuff brought in here, Rob?'

'Vans, tow trailers, the back of people's cars, you name it. . .'

The moment he stared up at the body, Mason's mouth filled with bile. Not the prettiest of sights either, he cursed. The stench was unbearable and carried an odour of sour dreams. From what he could see, the head had been stuffed inside a bright orange carrier bag and pushed into a pile of household rubbish. On closer inspection, the face had a wax like appearance reminiscent of something out of Madame Tussauds. Eyes wide open, mouth frozen open in a cry of revulsion, the skin was drawn tight around the cheekbones. He'd seen human mutilation before, many times, but nothing compared to this. Then, looking up, he was met with an even more disturbing sight – *the contents of an opened suitcase.*

Moving closer, he could see the upper torso was covered in numerous puncture marks, the sure signs of a frenzied knife attack. The arms had been sliced away at the shoulders, and the hands bound together with heavy duty duct tape: not as he was expecting to find, so he pocketed his notebook and moved towards a small group of police officers barely twenty feet away. With so many environmental controls in place, the site would surely keep records.

His mind made up, he suddenly sprang into action. 'Okay. I want a list of everyone employed at the site, particularly those who worked here over the weekend. And, when you've done all of that, I need statements from everyone and anyone who dropped rubbish off here on Friday. Do I make myself clear on that?'

Nods of approval gathered pace.

'Who's in charge of site security?' he asked.

'The site manager's the best person to talk to about that,' DC Manley replied.

'Have a word with him, Harry. Check out what arrangements are in place. CCTV cameras, log sheets, etcetera, etcetera. . .'

'Will do, boss.'

'While you're at it, see what you can find out about the drivers who work the skip lorries, and don't take *no* for an answer.'

Mason mulled over the facts. Just when he thought he was getting to grips with things, the killer had struck again. There were too many unanswered questions, too many possibilities. Maybe this wasn't a gangland killing after all, maybe the profiler was right. One thing for sure, he would need to get the bottom of it and fast.

DS Savage turned to face him. 'You look like I feel, boss.'

'No thanks to you.' Mason groaned.

'You shouldn't drink so much. It's bad for your health.'

Mason brushed Savage's sarcastic comment to one side. 'If this murder is linked to those in Bensham, then we've got some serious thinking to do.'

'I hate to mention it, boss,' Savage said coyly. 'But Dr Hindson believes the head and hands belong to another victim.'

'*What!*'

'Something's not right. He's convinced that some of the body parts have been kept in a freezer.' Savage held Mason's glances as he habitually dug his hands deep inside his trouser pockets. 'No doubt the post-mortem will tell us more, but I have a real nasty feeling about this one.'

His biggest nightmares realised, Mason swung to face Savage. 'What's going on, Rob?'

'At least with the head and hands in our possession, we're able to identify who it is.'

'That's a point.'

'There again, what if the body parts don't match?'

Mason looked at him for a moment. 'Try explaining that to the powers to be.'

'I'm sure you'll cope.' Savage smiled.

Mason gazed up at the torso again and wasn't impressed. The sick bastard who'd done this wasn't right in the head. Perhaps it was time to bring some lateral thinking to the case, involve David Carlisle – that's if his boss would agree to it.

Mason shook his head. 'This certainly screws a lot of our theories up, Rob.'

'At least the driver had the sense to check his load before hitching his lorry up. Had he not done, then this would have been history.'

'You're right,' Mason agreed, with an element of irritation in his voice. 'We need to look at the positives.'

Savage blew hard. 'If you ask me, there seems to be a general pattern taking place here.'

'Yeah, this one likes to deliver his victims to us in suitcases.'

'Do you think these foreigners are involved?'

'Anything's possible. Whoever killed these people was determined to get rid of the evidence.'

'But why mix the body parts up?'

'God knows.' Mason furrowed his brow. 'If this latest discovery *is* linked to Jennifer Oakwell's murder, then we may find the answers we're looking for.'

'Do you think they're connected?'

'A good cop always follows his nose. Instinct is eighty per cent truth, the rest is bullshit and falls into insignificance.'

The approaching blue flashing spinner-lights told them more officers were arriving.

'Sounds like the experts are on their way.' Savage shrugged.

Mason stared into the distance. 'Yeah. Soon the whole area will be crawling with keen want-to-be police officers excited in the belief they're about to solve their first real murder case. In an hour from now, after sifting through millions of tons of unwanted household shite, they'll probably think differently.'

'I can't wait.' Savage chuckled.

The workings of the police force never ceased to amaze Jack Mason, especially moments such as these. A copper's luck was hard earned, and you could spend days working your bollocks off without a sniff of a lead, then all hell would be let loose.

Having pulled round a tad, Mason was beginning to feel his real self again. In a few hours from now, forensics would have a clear picture of what was going on. Only then would he be able to formulate new plans – whatever they might be.

Then, just when he was about to climb back into his unmarked pool car his iPhone buzzed in his pocket. He checked the display, and Sutherland's name popped up on the screen. Right now, he knew the square root of bugger-all, and guessed then why she was calling.

Never a dull moment, he groaned.

'Good morning, ma'am. How can I help you?'

Chapter Twelve

It felt good to be back, thought David Carlisle as he entered Gateshead police station leaving behind clear blue skies. He still hadn't a clue what the meeting was about, but guessed it was important from the sombre tone of Acting Superintendent Sutherland's voice, asking him to attend.

With only one prisoner in the holding cells to worry about that morning, the desk sergeant seemed his usual jovial self. Caught red-handed trying to steal a tray of pork sausages from one of the local supermarket stores, the culprit was still pleading his innocence when they slammed the cell door behind him. Some things never change, Carlisle thought and smiled.

Three floors up, after taking the stairs two at a time, he entered Sutherland's office with an air of trepidation. The moment he took up a seat next to Jack Mason, he guessed that something was up.

'I'll be frank with you,' the Acting Superintendent said by way of introduction. 'There's been a new development.'

'Nothing serious, I hope,' Carlisle replied.

Sutherland spread her hands out on the desk in front of her and sighed. 'I'm not sure how much you know about this case, but we've found another body.'

'Is that what this meeting is about?'

She paused, and then said softly, 'Yes, it is.'

'Where was this, ma'am?'

'Over at the Waste and Recycling Centre in Blaydon.' She turned to Jack Mason before continuing. 'It's not general knowledge at this stage, as we're trying to keep it from the press.'

'It sounds pretty ominous.'

'It is,' Sutherland confirmed, 'and I'm not going to tell you otherwise.'

The criminal profiler remained silent.

Sutherland sighed heavily, then took a sip of water from a glass and wiped the corner of her mouth. 'After conducting a thorough search of the rest of the recycling centre, we've recovered several body parts belonging to another victim. It's not what we were expecting to find, but it does strongly suggest the killer is trying to dispose of the evidence.'

'Do we know who the victims are?'

'One of them we do,' she answered directly. 'Blood sample previously taken from Jennifer Oakwell's property matches body parts recovered from the killer's second victim – the one found in the Forth Street Storage Company. His name is Colin Henderson, and he's a nineteen-year-old undergraduate who was studying computer graphics at Newcastle University.'

'What about the other victim. How was he found?'

Sutherland's bottom lip quivered slightly. A keenly intelligent woman, she was usually bursting with enthusiasm; today she wasn't. Having spent much of the morning studying SOC photographs and listening to police officers' first-hand grizzly accounts of dismembered body parts, she was obviously overwhelmed by it all.

'The head and hands were missing, but the legs had been severed mid-thigh and placed inside a large black suitcase along with the victim's torso. Looking at the SOC photographs, he seems to be adopting the same method of disposal for each of his victims.'

'I take it the heads and hands are still missing from the latest murder victim?'

'Yes, they are.' Sutherland nodded.

The profiler wanted to tell her they were dealing with a psychopath but refrained from doing so. That would come later, when he had a few more facts at his disposal. 'It seems your killer is deliberately mixing the body parts up for some reason or other, which suggests these murders are carefully orchestrated.'

'It would appear so,' Sutherland sighed, 'but I'm beginning to have reservations as to what his intentions are.' Sutherland raised her eyebrows a fraction and took another sip of water. 'After we carried out an extensive fingertip search of the rest of the recycling centre, we found nothing. Without the victim's head and hands at our disposal, identification is obviously proving more difficult.'

'He's organised, and deliberately keeping you guessing, ma'am.'

Sutherland peered at her notes, as if searching for divine intervention. 'According to Tom Hedley's forensic report, after this monster had dismembered Colin Henderson's body he'd kept some of the body parts in a freezer.'

'That *is* an interesting new twist,' Carlisle said, shaking his head.

'Yes, but what does it tell us?'

'It sounds like someone is on a murder rampage of some sorts. Whatever his reasons to kill, he's obviously gained a passion for the taste of blood. That's how some killers react. To them it's a game. By mixing the body parts up, he's not only keeping you guessing, he's spreading fear whilst deliberately maintaining control.'

'That's all very well, but I'm more interested in his motives. Why does he do it?'

Carlisle sat shocked at Sutherland's sudden outburst. This latest development had obviously rattled her. No, he thought. Unless he could give the problem his full attention, he knew it would be a waste of time.

'What makes him tick?' Carlisle replied.

'Yes, that would be very useful.'

'May I ask how the limbs were removed from the victim's body?'

Sutherland glanced at Mason, who nodded for her to continue. 'According to the PM report, the killer used a powered surgical saw.'

'The same one he used on Colin Henderson?'

'Yes, we believe so.'

'That is interesting.' Suddenly he remembered something. 'And what initially drew your attention towards Colin Henderson being a university student?'

'It was quite by chance actually,' Mason interrupted. 'When Newcastle University broke for half-term recess, everyone thought Henderson had returned to his parents' home in Nottingham. He hadn't, of course.'

'So, when did people first begin to realise he'd gone missing?'

'When Henderson didn't show at his parents' house they naturally became anxious. They'd tried calling him, but his phone kept ringing out. After talking to other family members who hadn't heard from him in weeks, that's when they contacted the police. The rest was a matter of leg-work. . . and elimination.'

'Do we know what Colin Henderson was doing in Jennifer Oakwell's property?'

'She's a family friend apparently, which would account for him visiting there before returning to his parents' house.' Sutherland paused to check her files. 'The course of our investigations has since led us to a student bedsit in Bensham, but after a thorough search of the property we found nothing much of interest. A statement from Henderson's university mentor released to us a few days ago confirms he was a hard-working young man who was well liked by everyone who knew him.'

Carlisle cocked his head to one side. 'Right place, wrong time?'

'It would appear so.' The Acting Superintendent leaned forward, both elbows on the desk. 'It seems we have another vicious predator on our hands.'

'Indeed, ma'am. But how can I possibly help?'

'What makes you say that?'

'Well,' Carlisle began, trying his utmost not to sound overly enthusiastic. 'You seem to have everything under control here.'

Sutherland blushed. 'It might appear that way on the surface, but beneath it I can assure you we're fumbling around in the dark.'

One thing for sure, looking around, these weren't gangland killings as the police firmly believed they were. Gangland executions were usually no-nonsense affairs. Swift. A bullet to the head, or a knife to the throat. These murders felt sinister, more controlled. Whoever was responsible for these crimes was suffering delusional paranoia. They had to be. If not, then who in their rightful mind would pick up a powered surgical saw and dissect their victims' bodies as if they'd worked in a slaughter house all day? No, Carlisle thought. This wasn't an everyday occurrence, and the person responsible for these monstrous wrongdoings was a sensation seeker. A cold calculated killer – *someone who enjoyed his trade.*

'What about Jennifer Oakwell's close-knit family and friends?' Carlisle asked.

Mason rounded on him. 'Why would you want to know that at this early stage?'

'Well,' he said, pointing to the SOC photographs pinned to Sutherland's corkboard, 'whoever killed these people certainly knew where to find them.'

Sutherland managed a thin smile. 'That's why we believe Jennifer Oakwell was his initial target.'

'I'm not so sure about that either, ma'am.'

'How can you possibly say that without even seeing the case files?' Sutherland asked.

Carlisle faltered and unfolded his arms. 'Call it intuition, ma'am.'

'Is that a criminal profiler thing?'

'Undoubtedly.'

Sutherland looked down at her notes, as if convinced. 'Is this the sort of case that would appeal to you?'

'It certainly has potential, ma'am.'

'You don't sound overly enthusiastic. Any reason why not?'

He sensed a contract was about to be tabled and tried to contain his excitement. 'This latest victim found at the Blaydon Waste and Recycling Centre, what do we know about him?'

'Not a lot,' Mason interrupted, 'but we do have a person in mind.'

'Does this person have a name?'

Mason looked at him like a dog with a bone. 'He's a local low-life called Thomas Wilkinson who has a long association with shop lifting and handling stolen goods. He's not a prolific offender as such, more a nuisance than anything.'

'Any involvement in drugs?'

Mason's faced drained. 'Let's not go there—'

'Any reason why not?'

Mason shook his head despondently but said nothing.

'We received a tip-off only yesterday,' Sutherland confirmed. 'Wilkinson was last seen drinking in the Eagle public house late on Thursday night. It's a gay bar on Scotswood Road.'

'I've heard of it, ma'am. Is that where Wilkinson hangs out. . . Scotswood?'

'No, Bensham mainly,' Mason cut in. 'And as far as we know he has no fixed abode.'

Carlisle removed his spectacles and breathed heavily on the lenses before giving them a quick wipe. The likelihood the killer still had unfinished business to fulfil, worried him. Serial killers started slowly and built up confidence until reaching a point where the killings became more frequent. He stared at the SOC photographs again. Three unsolved murders. One concerning a bright university student, another the ex-wife of a notorious gangster, and a third involving a homeless male who was yet to be identified. Crude as it was, why the killer had gone to great lengths to dismember only his male victims puzzled him. Were they known to him, or did he have a personal grudge against young males? Whatever his motives were, Carlisle felt a conflicting surge of emotions as if something wasn't right.

On the face of it, these crimes bore all the characteristics of a serial killer at work. Loath to admit it, he'd already made his decision. Business was business in his books, and if a contract was to be tabled, he could certainly do with some extra cash. What Mason didn't know, or perhaps he did, was that his private investigation business was in free-fall again. Things were relatively quiet these days, and the competition was tough.

'Well,' Sutherland said, shaking her head thoughtfully. 'Is this something you might consider taking on?'

'It certainly presents an interesting challenge, ma'am.'

'I take it that's a yes?' Mason said forcefully.

Carlisle trod cautiously. 'Before I do commit to something I may later regret, would it be possible to take a quick peep at the case files?'

Mason rounded on him again. 'I'll talk to you in the morning.'

'Thank you.' Carlisle nodded. He stood to leave. 'One further question if I may. This gangland unrest we talked about earlier, have you made any more progress in that direction?'

Mason stared at him. 'We'll talk about that too.'

Sometimes it was better to take it on the chin, act dumb and say nothing. If he did have an answer, right now he couldn't think of one. The only real positive, if he could call it that, was the press still hadn't picked up on the story. Some serial killers were notorious for keeping newspaper clippings and viewed them as a record of their achievements. Many took trophies and souvenirs from their victims, and he was hoping that this wasn't the case.

He should have come better prepared. He hadn't, and now he was out on a limb again.

Chapter Thirteen

Jane Collins simply adored cats, and the moment a stray kitten walked in through the open office door, it was only natural she would pick it up. Grave mistake. Carlisle hadn't lifted a finger since nine o'clock and could sorely have done without this. Not a cat lover himself, there was always the problem of what to do next. Switching to profiler mode, he guessed the young kitten's survival rate was based on a combination of mathematics and probabilities. And if his calculations proved correct, there was only a slim chance the kitten would find its mother again. Perhaps she was lying low somewhere, or out hunting for food. And yes, there were plenty of stray dogs in Laygate to scare the living hell out of her.

'I take it you still haven't found anything?'

'Not yet I haven't.'

'Did you check the waste ground at the end of the street?'

'Yes, of course,' Carlisle replied stoically. 'It was the first place I looked.'

'You poor unfortunate thing,' said Jane; 'what are we going to do with you now?'

Carlisle shuffled awkwardly. 'Well he can't stay here if that's what you're thinking.'

'So, what do you suggest we do?'

'Simple. We stick him outside with a bowl of milk and wait for his mother to appear.'

'That's utter nonsense, and you know it,' Jane retorted. 'The poor little thing wouldn't last two minutes on his own.'

'Who knows,' Carlisle shrugged. 'It's not my problem.'

Jane leaned back against the metal filing cabinets and regarded him through narrow eyes. There was no simple answer to this, but he wasn't giving in that easily.

'I'd take you home with me if I could,' his business partner said, talking to the kitten, 'but I doubt my two Siamese cats will take kindly to you moving in with them.'

Having grown tired of it all, Carlisle returned to his computer. Having received a bundle of case files from one of Jack Mason's young detectives, he cleared his head of feline thoughts and got down to the business in hand. These latest murders certainly had all the hallmarks of a gangland killing, but there were too many flaws in that theory for his liking. Besides, gangsters rarely used knives as it wasn't effective enough. Their methods of killing people were usually swift. A bullet to the head, or a shallow grave out in the countryside somewhere. And that was another thing that had crossed his mind that morning. Why leave Jennifer Oakwell's body behind?

He was still searching for answers when the young kitten suddenly appeared on his desk. At first, he couldn't believe his eyes. Without giving it another thought, he picked it up and dropped it back down on the floor again. The next thing he saw, when he turned his head, was his iPhone crashing to the floor.

'You little bugger,' he shouted.

★★★

It was late afternoon when Carlisle finally walked in through the main entrance of the Northeast Press offices in Sunderland. Now running late, he was met at the reception desk by an obnoxious middle-aged blonde, with heavy mascara and thick ruby red lipstick. Having been offered drinks from a nineties dispensing machine, he was then left to his own devices.

He didn't wait long.

Mark Patterson was a tall man, elegant, with wispy chestnut-brown hair swept back at the sides. A retired police officer now turned senior newspaper editor, Mark had an extraordinary talent for sifting out scandal. Determined to learn more about the west end gangland takeover bid, it was this aspect that had brought Carlisle here today.

'What can I do for you?' Patterson asked, taking up a corner seat overlooking the busy main road.

'I'm after some information.'

'This wouldn't be about Frank Wiseman, would it?'

'How did you guess?'

'I'd heard rumours that you'd been approached by the Northumbria

Police.' Patterson tapped the side of his head. 'The mere mention of that sad bastard's name was enough to send shivers down my spine.'

His phone kept ringing in his pocket, and Carlisle switched it to silent. 'There's talk of a power struggle going on in the West End of Newcastle. . . what do you know about it?'

'I've heard a lot of Eastern European gangs have been moving into the area lately, and it's causing friction between the ruling gang masters. People are jockeying for position, and nobody knows how to put a stop to it.'

Coffee and biscuits arrived, as Patterson filled him in with the details.

'So, what are these foreigners actually up to?' Carlisle asked.

Patterson moved his hand dismissively. 'There are agents and runners all over the place. Fake passports and visas are changing hands before the ink is even dry on the paper.' Patterson blew through his cheeks. 'An awful lot of money is changing hands, and people are getting twitchy. The Home Office is loath to get involved owing to the number of people caught up in it, and the local politicians aren't interested either.'

'Human trafficking?'

'Cheap labour and prostitution more like.'

'What about Border Patrol?'

'They're stretched to the limit nowadays, and it's mainly due to cutbacks.'

'That doesn't surprise me, but it doesn't bode well for the security of our borders.'

Patterson habitually whistled through his teeth. 'Nobody in authority is willing to grasp the nettle, it seems. Freedom of movement isn't all it's made out to be, and we're no longer in control of our own borders anymore. It's not the genuine people coming here to work that's the problem, it's the undesirables who follow in their wake.'

Carlisle thought a moment, not wishing to get drawn into a political debate. 'Is Frank Wiseman's old territory still under threat?'

'Anything's possible, especially with people like Tony Fox waiting in the wings.' Patterson brushed the biscuit crumbs from his trousers and leaned forward. 'Fox is ambitious, and not to be trusted. If he can't buy his way out of trouble, he'll revert to using force.'

'Capable of murder, do you think?'

Patterson roared with laughter. 'He's more than capable of that.'

'What about this recent Forth Street incident? Do you think Fox is involved?'

'Are you referring to *the Suitcase Man?*'

Carlisle nodded.

'I doubt it.'

'What makes you say that?'

'It's not his style. Fox is a sly bastard and knows how to play the judicial system to his advantage.'

'You mean bent lawyers, that sort of thing?'

Patterson lowered his voice. 'Nothing surprises me about Tony Fox anymore. When Frank Wiseman's gang did a hit on several sub-post offices more than ten years ago, they'd made off with over two and half million quid in used banknotes. Given the ease in which Wiseman masterminded the whole operation, they thought they'd got away with it. They hadn't, of course, and that was the gang's biggest mistake.'

Carlisle shrugged. 'What went wrong?'

'The police had a snitch in their midst. A guy called Sam Monday. It wasn't common knowledge at the time, but it was Monday who gave the police the breakthrough they'd been looking for. Not only did he spill the beans on who was involved in the raids, Monday told them everything they wanted to know.' Patterson laughed. 'And I mean everything. Who was working on the outside, who the contacts were, and who had masterminded the whole operation. A few days later, after they'd rounded up all the gang members involved, that was the end of Frank Wiseman's empire.'

'I bet he wasn't chuffed.'

Patterson thought about it. 'When word got out they'd been stitched up, that's when Fox got involved.'

'That would be almost ten years ago—'

'I know, and the mad thing is, Fox has hung around in the side-lines ever since. He's not daft. Like I say, he knows how to play the system.' Patterson stared at him. 'The only way to eat an elephant, is a piece at a time.'

'So, you think Fox was brought in specifically to do a job for Wiseman?'

'At the time, he was one of Wiseman's trusted lieutenants, and always featured heavily in his plans. It was the golden opportunity that Fox had been waiting for. . . a chance to make a name for himself.'

'Hmmm. So that's how Fox rose through the ranks as he did.'

'To cut a long story short, a week after the trial the nameless whistle-blower disappeared without trace.'

Carlisle felt a ripple of excitement running through his veins. 'What happened to him?'

'Rumour has it Monday was buried in the outside lane of the A1(M) during the motorway improvements.'

'What about the police, surely they must have known he'd gone missing?'

'At the time, they didn't. It was pure speculation. Besides, the police weren't going to dig up a brand new hundred-million-pound motorway in the hope of proving a point.'

'No, I suppose not.'

'Fox had it all worked out.'

Carlisle thought a minute. 'I'd heard Monday was under some sort of police protection scheme and whisked off to another country with a new passport and identity? Wouldn't that account for his sudden disappearance?'

'He may well have been, that's the thing. There were so many rumours doing the rounds at the time that nobody knew what to believe.' Patterson laughed. 'It made a great headline story, though, and you can't begin to imagine the number of newspapers we sold.'

'No, I guess not.'

Patterson wrinkled his nose. 'You asked if Fox was capable of murder. Well here's the rub. It was Fox and his crew who buried Monday in the motorway.'

'Well I'll be damned.'

Patterson tapped the side of his nose. 'Think about it, they don't call it Monday's Highway for nothing.'

'These people certainly don't mess about.'

'I wouldn't like to be on the wrong side of them, if that's what you mean.'

'Do you think Fox is running the show whilst Wiseman's inside?'

'The thing to bear in mind is that most of Wiseman's gang members are now out on parole.' Patterson snapped another biscuit in half. 'There's rumours doing the rounds that the money they stole from their bank raids has since gone missing.'

'So I've heard.'

'There were dozens of people involved in the handling of it, but no one knows where it is. Some say it was salted away into Swiss bank accounts, others say not. Whoever's story you believe, there's no simple explanation to it all.'

Carlisle thought a moment. 'What about Tony Fox?'

'Hard to say. But if you're looking to find out where the money's gone,

I'd stay well clear of Fox if I were you. Walls have ears, and you never know who's listening in on the other side.'

'You're the second person who's told me that recently.' Carlisle smiled.

Patterson pushed his empty coffee cup to one side. He'd been well advised. There was more to this than had first met the eye, and Carlisle was glad of some sound advice. Gang wars were one thing but cheating on fellow criminals was a lethal cocktail that no gang member would tolerate.

'I've often wondered how Fox paid for his nightclubs.' Carlisle smiled.

'I wouldn't delve too much into that either. Fox made his money through dealing in second-hand cars. Most of them stolen to order, and all of them shipped overseas.'

'You're right, these people do seem to have their fingers in an awful lot of pies.'

Paterson drew back in his seat. 'If anyone in the criminal world is tied up in these murders, you can forget Frank Wiseman. Fox is your man.'

'Thanks, Mark. I'll bear that in mind.'

Patterson stood to leave. 'Time's precious, I hope I've been of some help to you. If there is anything else I can assist you with, you always know where to find me.'

'There is one other thing,' Carlisle confessed.

'Oh! And what's that?'

'What do you know about stray kittens?'

Patterson's eyebrows shot up. 'I'm a newspaper editor not a bloody veterinary surgeon!'

'Just looking for some sound advice, that's all.'

'Sounds like it's been a long day.' Patterson smiled.

Chapter Fourteen

Having spent the best part of the evening reading through the Jennifer Oakwell files, Carlisle was done in. It was seven-thirty, and the TV news presenters were still deliberating over the state of the nation's economy. If it wasn't one thing it was another these days. Sometimes he wondered if the stock markets were rigged – people making vast fortunes out of shifting their money around. Not that he could do anything about it; he couldn't. But it still annoyed him nevertheless.

The moment the toaster popped on the kitchen unit, Benjamin was on to it like a flash. Paws outstretched, the young kitten had caught the slice of toast mid-air. He had certainly been in a mischievous mood that morning, and the distractions were driving Carlisle mad. Having already watched the kitten climb up the living room curtains in a show of contempt, he'd tried pinning tin-foil to them to prevent him. When that didn't work he decided to put his foot down. Not that Benjamin was concerned – he thought it was a game.

It had started to rain when David Carlisle pulled up outside Jennifer Oakwell's terraced property in Bensham. Not the best arrangements at nine o'clock that morning; he could sorely have done without this. Now holding open the driver's door to his Rover P4 100, Mason burst out laughing.

'What the hell are all those scratch marks doing on your face?'

'Don't even go there.'

'It looks like you've been in a fight, my friend?'

'Yes, with a twelve-week old kitten.'

'You're joking.'

Carlisle nodded, but refused to be drawn in.

Still off-limits to the public, the blue and white police cordon tape still attached to the front door was fluttering in the breeze. All the locks to the property had been changed, but Mason had a key. He would have preferred to visit there alone, but the Detective Chief Inspector had insisted on quickly bringing him up to speed.

Darkness embraced him the moment he stepped into the narrow hallway, never-ending and sameness. The air felt oppressive, tinged with a musty smell that clung to the back of his throat like a thousand forgotten nightmares. This was one of those moments he disliked most about the job: stepping into a murder victim's shoes.

The living room was small. It had plain emulsion walls, a high ceiling, and a north facing bay window overlooking the main road. At the far end of the room, next to a small bookcase, stood a large flat plasma TV screen. It seemed at odds with the rest of the furnishings, which were inexpensive and outdated. Taking centre stage, directly below a central hanging pink lampshade, stood a straight back wooden chair.

Mason pointed to it. 'This is where Jennifer Oakwell finally met her end. Ankles strapped to the chair legs, arms bound to the armrests with heavy duty duct-tape; the medical cause of death was given as sharp force wounds to the back, neck, and chest.'

'Nasty!' Carlisle cringed.

Mason pointed down to the heavily blood-stained carpets and stepped back a pace. 'To say this was a frenzied attack would be an understatement. According to the PM report the killer inflicted no less than thirty-two stab wounds to the victim's upper body. We know he's right handed and is approximately five-ten in height.'

Carlisle nodded. 'What do we know about the murder weapon?'

'He used a double-edged combat knife made from high carbon stainless steel. It had a spear point four-inch fixed blade and some sort of protection guard to it.'

'Any fingerprints?'

Mason turned to face him. 'Not according to forensics, the killer wore surgical gloves. They are a common brand and can be picked up in most pharmaceutical stores. There's plenty of footprints scattered around the place. . . size eight to ten Nike trainers. These are a popular brand but have no distinguishing wear to the soles.' Mason's eyes toured the room. 'It's pretty cramped in here, so there's not much room for manoeuvre.'

'Any sign of sexual motive?'

'No, nothing of that nature.'

'What about self-masturbation?'

'Funny you should say that,' said Mason. 'This one is more intent on dismembering his victims for some reason or other.'

Carlisle tried to put himself inside the killer's shoes. Unable to protect herself, the woman's ending must have been horrific. But why bother to restrain her, and how did she get into that position in the first place? The only thing that struck a chord with him was that it was a kitchen chair he'd restrained her in. Strange, he thought. There were no signs of a struggle, no forced entry, and nothing of value had been stolen from the property. Having killed her, and now in a heightened state of frenzy, had events overtaken him? At least it made sense, if nothing else seemed to at this point. The more he thought about it, the more convinced he was that the answer lay in the upstairs bedroom.

'Initial impressions?' Mason asked.

'What about neighbours?'

'Nobody reported hearing or seeing anything suspicious, if that's what you're thinking.'

'That's odd. You would have thought someone would have seen something.'

'The fact she'd lain here for the best part of a week, sort of backs that theory up.' Mason gazed at him with narrow eyes. 'It wasn't a pretty sight I can assure you of that. Flies everywhere, the early signs of bloating, and a smell that beggared belief.'

'What about the curtains. . . house lights?'

'The curtains were drawn, as I remember. As for the lights, the house was in total darkness when Oakwell's friend discovered her.' Mason smiled. 'Her fingerprints were all over the hall light switch.'

Still early days, Carlisle was still waiting for his brain's synapses to kick in and provide him with inspiration. Then he remembered. 'According to the PM report no alcohol or drugs were found in her body, and there was no superficial bruising to suggest a struggle had taken place. Don't you find that odd?'

'Not when she was bound to the chair with duct tape, as her movements would have been heavily restricted.'

'So how did she get into that position in the first place?' Carlisle pointed towards the straight back wooden chair. 'Surely she must have put up some sort of resistance?'

Mason folded his arms, a defensive stance.

'Maybe he threatened her, and she froze.'

'Possible, but highly unlikely don't you think?'

Mason hummed with nervous energy. 'He could have knocked her unconscious, of course.'

Carlisle said nothing.

On reaching the upstairs landing, Mason turned to face him. 'There's a lot of arterial spray and cast off everywhere. Walls, ceilings, and floors.' Mason pointed to it. 'Henderson had obviously fought his way this far before collapsing to the floor. Now in a confused state of shock, the killer remorselessly set about his business. This was unquestionably a prolonged knife attack, and every single thrust was driven deep into the victim's body.'

'And the angle of the wounds?'

'Good question. The killer straddled his victim at this point, which obviously makes him right handed.'

'Yes, of course.'

Turning his attention towards the graffiti adorned walls, Carlisle bent down to take a closer look. This wasn't a vendetta killing, this crime had all the hallmarks of a psychopath at work. Child-like smiley images drawn using the victim's blood wasn't normal. He closed his eyes and searched for a moment of inspiration that would bring them ever closer. Who was this man who could show such utter contempt towards humanity? No, he thought. The act was too final. Too well organised, as if it had been planned. All the warning signs were there, the little idiosyncrasies that psychopaths had. Normally these people developed with each passing murder – growing in confidence as they tried out more bizarre techniques. Curious, Carlisle checked the blood spatter again. Then it struck him. This wasn't his first; these killings were far too advanced.

Carlisle fell silent, deep in thought.

Motive was the problem: why such a frenzied knife attack? And another thing he noted, moving round, there was an awful lot of victim blood transfer between the two murder scenes. In other words, the killer was moving freely between them. Full of misguided thoughts, was this the point at which the killer had turned his attentions back to Jennifer Oakwell? No, he reasoned, even though the evidence was pointing to her being the killer's intended target, there were too many unanswered questions.

Mason stared at him subdued.

'As you can see, there's an awful lot of arterial blood spatter radiating out from where Henderson's body lay.' Mason pointed to it. 'Plunging a four-inch steel blade repeatedly through flesh and muscle thirty-two times would have been extremely tiring work.'

'So, Henderson wasn't dismembered here?'

'No, not here.'

Alarm bells started to ring in Carlisle's inquisitive mind. If the killer had used the same roll of heavy duty duct tape to restrain his victims, it meant he'd come prepared. There again, he argued, according to the PM report there was no duct tape residue found on the dead woman's face or hair. In which case she wasn't gagged.

Then it hit him – *what if she knew her killer?*

'He's organised,' Carlisle said, thinking out aloud.

'What do you mean. . . organised?'

'These murders have all the hallmarks of a serial killer at work.'

'Bollocks,' Mason said in his usual assertive manner. 'This is an open and shut case of witness elimination.'

'In which case, why didn't he remove Jennifer Oakwell's body from the premises?'

Mason stared at him confused. 'Simple. He was sending out a warning signal.'

'No, Jack. Jennifer Oakwell wasn't his intended target.'

'*What!* You think Henderson was?'

'I'm convinced of it.'

'That's ridiculous; even the forensic evidence doesn't point to that.'

'Something's not right,' said Carlisle, turning to face Mason. 'Too many pieces of the jigsaw puzzle don't fit.'

'Let's not get carried away here.'

Carlisle wasn't being fobbed off that easily. 'Just because the evidence points to the woman being silenced first, doesn't mean she was the intended target.'

Mason rolled his eyes, and Carlisle knew he'd overstepped the mark.

'This isn't a straightforward case, I realise that, and that's why we brought you in to assist.' Mason gave him a friendly pat on the back. 'Don't over complicate things. Let's stick with the programme for the time being, and less of this profiler mumbo-jumbo.'

'Fine by me, but why did the killer keep moving between the two crime scenes?'

'That's obvious. After he dragged Henderson's body to a position at the top of the landing stairs, that's when he removed him from the premises. We know that much from the blood trail he left behind.'

'So why not remove Jennifer Oakwell's body whilst he was at it?'

'Like I've said, he was warning someone.'

'Okay, so what's his motive for killing Henderson?'

Mason shrugged. 'Wrong place, right time. He simply got in the way.'

At least Mason was forthright in his answers and didn't pull any punches. No, he thought. It was time to put the record straight and settle their professional differences once and for all.

'No, Jack, he probably killed Colin Henderson for the same reason he killed his latest victim.'

'And that is?'

'I've yet to decide.'

'So, you don't have a motive then?'

'Not yet, but he's extremely irritated about something.'

'Christ! Even I can see that.'

'Think about it. He's targeting young males. . . cutting their bodies up because he's angry about someone, or something. It was Jennifer Oakwell who got in his way, not Colin Henderson, and that's why he never cut her up.'

Mason looked at him gobsmacked.

Chapter Fifteen

Having set up an incident room to deal with university students returning for the start of Summer Term, the police were kept busy. It was painstaking work, and not all students were willing to cooperate. Information was the police's lifeblood. No matter what form it came in. Even so, it was a fellow student who had brought Jack Mason his first real breakthrough. Colin Henderson had experimented in narcotics. Not in a big way, but he'd dabbled in them nevertheless. It wasn't much to go on, but it was enough to send Mason into overdrive.

After thousands of DNA records had been checked by a team of genealogy specialists at a local forensics laboratory, they'd finally discovered a match. Their latest victim, found at the Blaydon Waste and Recycling Centre, had been positively identified as Thomas Wilkinson. Things were moving at a pace, prompting dozens of new lines of enquiry to open.

Mason ran the word serial killer ritualistically around the tip of his tongue. He toyed with it, twisting its meaning until mentally conjuring up a picture of what it entailed. Physically exhausted after viciously stabbing his victim to death, the killer then tried to dispose of his body. Running back over the coroner's report, there was insufficient evidence to pacify all his anxieties. Henderson had died at the hands of a professional – stabbed no fewer than thirty-two times. To say he was blissfully unaware of the terrible fate that awaited him would have been a foolhardy judgement. Henderson had seen his death coming.

After driving north, DS Savage pulled up opposite a large red-brick building. Set back from the rest of the urban sprawl of Westgate Road, *Fat Sam's* nightclub was the in-place to be seen. Soon every police officer on the force would familiarise themselves with the area, trawling through thousands of witness statements and carrying out door-to-door enquiries. Westgate Road would never be the same again. The area reminded Mason of the West End streets of London he'd patrolled as a young undercover detective, a place where outsiders were regarded with deep suspicion. There was a subtle difference, of course. This was modern day Tyneside.

Mason gave DS Savage a withering look. 'Are you sure this is the place?'

'I'm positive, boss.'

'Christ, what a dump. To think I spent the best part of my youth visiting shitholes like this it's a wonder I'm still alive.'

Mason banged on the heavy steel door, and a familiar face appeared around the corner. Not the sharpest tool in the box, Rolex Roy was a former member of the Newcastle Gremlins – a notorious football hooligan gang. Having switched his allegiance to enhance his criminal career as a nightclub bouncer, he'd rapidly gained a reputation for peddling counterfeit watches.

'Inspector, Mason,' Rolex said. 'What brings you to this neck of the woods?'

Mason looked straight past him and pointed towards the nightclub main entrance. 'Is your gaffer in?'

Rolex nodded. 'Follow me.'

Seconds later they were inside and ascending a steep narrow staircase. It was ten o'clock, and perhaps a little early. From what Mason could see, Fat Sam's was a rabbit warren of sleazy alcoves. It had low ceilings, flashing strobe lights, and a multi-million-pound sound system nicked from a well-known Manchester strip club. He'd visited some dodgy establishments in his career, but this one cut the cake.

The Area Commander had wanted him to go in heavy-handed, but Mason had urged against it. The fact the two of them had entered the premises without the slightest resistance, had backed his theory up. Still smarting from the grilling he'd had from Acting Superintendent Sutherland that morning, it was becoming rather messy, Mason thought.

Next to a steel door, through which ran another short flight of stairs, stood a gorilla-faced henchman. Clearly off limits to patrons, they were entering the inner sanctum. This wasn't a place to get lost in – reinforced windows, security key locks on every door, and CCTV cameras covering all exits.

It was Fox who spoke first. 'What's your problem today, Jack? Got out of the wrong side of the bed, have we?'

'I'm looking for information.'

'What kind of information?'

Mason pulled a crumpled photograph from an inside pocket and placed it on the desk in front of him. 'I'm looking for the person who killed these two young men.'

'What about them?' said Fox guardedly.

'Recognise their faces?'

'No. Never seen them before. Why?'

'It might pay you to take a closer look,' Mason insisted. 'The guy on the right is called Colin Henderson. He was a friend of Jennifer Oakwell. . . Frank Wiseman's ex-wife. Nice lad, university student who was doing really well for himself apparently.'

'You know me, Jack. I like to run a tight ship.' Fox stared down at the photograph and shuffled awkwardly. 'I swear on my mother's life I've never seen these people before.'

'What about this one?' Mason said, pointing a finger at the second image.

'Nope, never seen him before. Who is he?'

'His name's Thomas Wilkinson. Rumour has it he dabbled in cannabis from time to time and liked to inject himself full of crap. In and out of trouble and of no fixed abode, he was a regular here I'm told.'

'Nope, I can't say as I've ever seen him before.'

'Think carefully, Tony. Your licence may depend on—'

'What the fuck do you think I'm doing?'

Mason hunched his shoulders in a show of contempt. 'With so many cameras around the place, I guess you run a pretty tight ship.'

Fox swallowed hard. 'What does that mean?'

'It means we may have to search your premises.'

'You'll find nothing here,' Fox replied bluntly.

'What makes you think that?'

'Anyone caught handling illegal substances on my premises is automatically banned for life – even people like you.'

'And which life is this?' Mason smiled.

'Ask around,' Fox insisted. 'Check it out for yourself.'

'No need to, we already have.'

Fox smiled in defeat, and quickly changed the subject. 'I hear you've been talking to Frank Wiseman lately.'

'I could have, but that's none of your business.'

The gangster swallowed hard. 'My oh my, we are tetchy today.'

Mason's eyes toured the room. Apart from a strong smell of cheap aftershave, the room reeked of cigar smoke. It hung in the air like a forgotten memory. Men's clubs, after dinner speeches, and the odd Rotary Club dinners he'd attended.

Unimpressed with Fox's credentials and attitude, DS Savage frowned, then said, 'The man responsible for killing these two young men is a dangerous predator who needs to be taken off the streets.'

'And who the fuck is he?' Fox said turning sharply to face Mason.

'Never mind that,' Mason replied. 'This is the type of shithole that Wilkinson would have felt at home in.'

'What are you trying to say?'

'We're close to making an arrest,' Mason brazenly lied. 'If you do happen to know who's responsible for these killings, now's the time to make a name for yourself.'

Fox laughed. 'There's a million people out there who fit the description of *the Suitcase Man*. If I could help, I would. It's as simple as that.'

'Is that so?' said Mason, annoyingly shaking his head.

Fox looked at each of them in turn. 'Why don't you throw a name at me?'

'You know we can't do that.'

'Then how do you expect me to help you, for fuck's sake?'

Silence.

'It's not that simple, and you know it,' Mason replied.

Fox stared at them and said nothing. Like most gangsters that Mason had come across, they thrived on attention. His friend at the press office was right. If anyone in the West End was tied up in these murders, it was Tony Fox.

Savage leaned in closer. 'We have it on good authority your club's been shifting bucket loads of shit lately, and its top-quality stuff.'

'Who told you that crap?'

'You'd be surprised.' DS Savage smiled. 'Thing is, we're thinking of closing you down.'

'*What the—*'

'We've never been more serious.'

Mason watched as the muscles round Fox's neck tightened. Head and shoulders above the detective sergeant, he wasn't a guy to be messed with. The problem was, whatever Fox put his hand to, it invariably involved narcotics. So perhaps he was involved, and maybe he did know who the killer was. But that was the nature of the beast – you never knew which side of the fence Fox sat on.

Fox muttered something inaudible to himself, having thought through the implications of closing his club down. 'What is it you people are after?'

'Names, Tony.'

'Names—'

Mason grinned. 'What do you know about these Eastern European gangs who are moving into the area, do you think they could be involved?'

'No!' Fox insisted. 'I've already spoken with them.'

'And what did they say?'

'They're just as keen as you are to catch this monster.'

Full of contradictions, Fox was clutching at straws and it wasn't looking good suddenly. He needed to produce suspects, and fast.

★★★

Twenty minutes later, Mason thumbed through the pages of his little black notebook and rolled his eyes. It was 11:30 am, and the day ahead looked another long one. Sitting alongside him in the silver Ford Focus undercover vehicle, Rob Savage was weighing up the facts. Fox couldn't be trusted, everyone knew that. But was he telling the truth?

Savage turned to face him. 'If these aren't gangland killings, then where do we go from here?'

'Whatever his motives are, our killer's a loner who is able to wear the mask of sanity.'

'He could be anyone in other words.'

Mason stiffened. 'Yeah, which makes him a difficult person to pin down.'

'I'm beginning to think as you do, boss. There's far too many people are tied up in this.'

These past few weeks hadn't gone at all well for Jack Mason. Instead of looking at the bigger picture, he was too absorbed in the criminal world to be effective in hunting down a serial killer. Not only that, he was spending far too much time in pubs lately. He was drinking heavily, as if he had a point to prove to himself. Trying to preserve an image that he could drink anyone under the table who fancied the challenge, was slowly beginning to destroy him. He wasn't getting any younger and his hard-fought reputation was slowly slipping away from him.

'I've been giving it some thought lately,' Mason began. 'There are a lot of aspects about this case that remind me of the Dennis Nilsen murders.'

'Like what?'

'Nearly all of Nilsen's victims were students or homeless dropouts whom he'd picked up in bars. After he killed them and cut them up using butchery skills he'd learned in the army, he had very little recollection of what he'd done,' Mason explained in a little more detail. 'Up until 1981 Nilsen had access to a large garden, so he was able to burn the bodies of his victims. Then, after moving to an upstairs flat in London, he found it more difficult to dispose of them.'

Savage held his gaze. 'Yeah, I remember the case. Didn't they catch up with him after he'd blocked the sewerage drains with body parts?'

'That's my point. These individuals are such egotistical sods they couldn't care less how many people's lives they destroy along the way.'

'Remind me,' Savage said. 'How did they eventually catch up with him?'

'When the police raided Nilsen's new flat in London, they discovered a suitcase full of human remains stuffed in a wardrobe. After tearing the rest of the house apart, they found several plastic bags full of body parts hidden under the floorboards.'

'Blimey!'

'I know, and that's what we are up against here.'

'Do you think we could have a copy-cat killer on our hands?'

Typical Rob Savage, thought Mason. Jump in both feet first without the slightest hesitation. 'I'm not sure about that, but we do know our killer stores his body parts in a deep freezer. What if he was running out of freezer space?'

'*Christ!*' Savage gasped. 'Is that why he's trying to get rid of the body parts?'

'Just a hunch.'

Savage's whole demeanour seemed to have changed. 'Where the hell do you dream your ideas up, boss?'

'That's why I'm a DCI with loads of money.'

Savage smiled, then fell silent for a moment.

'He could be cutting them up at home, of course.'

'He probably is, especially if that's where he's luring them.'

'Shit,' Savage said, 'and we're still missing body parts.'

'I wouldn't get too hung up about that, as he's probably disposed of them by now.'

'This is pretty gruesome stuff, and I'd never given it much thought. You're right about one thing, though. What if he lives in a house without a garden?'

'It's another way of looking at it.'

Savage drummed his fingers on the steering wheel and laughed.'Don't go and spoil it, boss, not when I'm beginning to warm to the idea.'

'Something's not right.'

'I know, and I'm getting bad vibes about this one's evil intent.'

Mason saw what Savage was getting at, but the fact that a sexual assault had never taken place, heartened him. 'Whilst it doesn't rule out these killings are opportunistically motivated, it does lessen the odds.'

'Yeah, but what triggers him, boss?'

'Opportunist killers are normally sexually motivated by a desire to torture their victims, and he's certainly not that. This killer has a point to prove, I'm convinced of it.'

The sergeant's eyes were full of unnerving coldness. 'You could be right. The fact that he drew smiley faces on Jennifer Oakwell's walls demonstrates he's angry about something. God forbid we're dealing with another Wharf Butcher here.'

'Don't even go there,' Mason replied.

They both fell silent, thinking.

Chapter Sixteen

The years had worked on Peter Carter's features like a caricaturist's pen. Not an assertive man, Carter had always shied away from the limelight, believing he was just ordinary. Now eighty-one, he was resigned to the fact that most of his life was now behind him. Having worked for the Port Dock Authorities as a ship's pilot for thirty-seven years, a colourful career had been tragically cut short because of major heart surgery. Forced into early retirement, he'd rented a stone-built cottage overlooking the magnificent views of Cullercoats Harbour. Living out a frugal existence, Carter's sole passion in life was painting seascapes of his beloved North-East coastline.

Cleaning the last of his paintbrushes, Carter dropped them into a large earthenware jar and turned back to their previous conversation. In many ways, he reminded Carlisle of an old recluse he'd once met. A hermit who'd lived out his days on Holy Island collecting seashells and selling them back to holidaymakers as lucky charm bracelets. He'd made a small fortune from it, but always claimed he was penniless. He wasn't, of course. After he passed away, his entire estate had been willed to a local children's hospital in Newcastle. Two million pounds, and not a penny less. It was a huge sum of money, and the charity was eternally grateful for his act of kindness.

'So,' Carter began, 'you'd like to take your father out on a sea fishing adventure?'

'That's if you're still up for it.'

Carter's frown lines corrugated. 'Why the sudden change of mind?'

'Dad's always fancied his hand at sea fishing and has gone on about it for years. He's not getting any younger and is a little unsteady on his feet nowadays.'

'That answers a lot,' said Carter thoughtfully. 'Sea fishing's totally different from river angling, of course, and a lot more challenging.'

'I realise that, but I thought the North Sea air might do him the world of good.'

'If it doesn't finish him off,' Carter chuckled.

'Try stopping him.'

Peter Carter had been a family friend for as long as Carlisle could remember, and his pride and joy was a forty-foot motor yacht called *Thunder*. When Carlisle was an impressionable young schoolboy, he'd sailed out to sea in her many times. Moored up in South Shields, as he remembered it, she had twin Mercury Marine engines that could cut through water like a knife through butter. Those were the days. Packed lunches wrapped in greaseproof paper, bottles of fizzy pop, and a box full of rag worm for bait. It was a life-changing experience, the stuff of childhood dreams.

'Tell me,' said Carter. 'Did your father ever catch that sea trout he was after?'

'You mean, Herman?'

'Ah, yes, that's the one,' Carter said, stroking his chin. 'The last time we met, your father never stopped talking about it. I've often wondered how true the story was, or whether it was a figment of his imagination. It's funny how some things stick in your mind.'

Carlisle smiled resignedly to himself. 'As far as I know, Herman's still swimming around in the River Coquet. Mind, he's snapped a good few fishing lines trying to catch him over the years and it's landed him in deep waters on more than one occasion.'

Carter chuckled to himself.

'He still hasn't managed to catch it then?'

'No. Not yet, he hasn't.'

'How old did you say your father was?'

'He's coming up to seventy-nine.'

'Gosh! None of us are getting any younger, Davy boy. Where have all those years gone? It seems only yesterday I was playing cricket for the local parish team, and there's not many of us left these days. Most of them have passed on to greener playing fields —' His voice trailed off in thought.

'That must be twenty years ago.'

'You don't have to remind me.' Carter stroked a pointed chin in thought. 'You were just starting off in the Met as I remember. A young whippersnapper, keen as mustard having just passed your police entry exams. Your father was so proud of you; he couldn't stop talking about it.'

'You're right,' Carlisle remarked, 'none of us are getting any younger. It was around that time that we went—'

Carlisle's mobile phone suddenly rang. He checked the display.

'Hello?' he asked. 'Who am I talking to?'

'*Angelica*—'

The voice on the other end fell to a whisper on the last syllable of her name. At least she'd told him that much.

'How can I help you, Angelica?'

'It's about the body the police recently found—' Her voice trailed off again.

She had a foreign accent, Eastern European. Carlisle was on the edge of his seat but had no idea why. Perhaps it was the name. He took a deep breath and tried to focus his mind. 'Which body might this be? There's been quite a few lately.'

There followed an awkward silence between them, a gathering of wits. She was breathing heavily. Hyperventilating, as if starting a panic attack. What's more, there was shouting in the background and he made a mental note of it.

'The one they found in Forth Street,' she finally replied.

Carlisle felt an adrenaline rush. 'Is that near the Central Station?'

'That's the one.'

He could hardly believe his ears. Feeling on edge, he began to question what other dark secrets this young woman might have in store. Just out of habit, he opened his notebook and flipped through the pages until reaching an empty sheet. Why hadn't she gone to the police? Strange, he thought. Foremost in his mind was how to build up a relationship of trust between them. Force the issue and you could easily lose contact.

The phone line crackled.

'Are you still there?'

'Uh-huh.'

Carlisle sensed hesitation.

'I need to share some information with you,' she said bluntly.

'And what might that be?'

The line went silent. This type of call was a regular occurrence these days. The city was full of rumour-mongers. False sightings of potential serial killers walking the streets were common place. But this caller appeared genuine, as if desperate to share her information with someone. Pencil in hand, Carlisle scribbled down the details and tried to build up a rapport. She was young, he imagined. How young he had yet to decide. His head full of dangerous thoughts, it was like playing a game of Russian roulette.

'Have you spoken to anyone else about this before now?' he asked.

'No.'

'Not even to the police?'

'No police, you're the only person I will speak to.'

He remained silent for a second, thinking.

'Okay,' he said. 'No police. That's a promise.'

'Do I have your word on that?'

'Yes, of course.'

'Thank you.'

Carlisle lowered the tone in his voice, using a more sympathetic approach. 'One question if I may, Angelica. How did you come by my name?'

She hesitated, and then said, 'I saw your advert in one of the local newspapers and ran a check on you. You're a private investigator, are you not?'

'Yes, I am.'

The background noises had kicked off again, as if the argument had turned ugly.

'Perhaps we could meet up somewhere?' he suggested.

'Not today.'

'When, then?'

There was another long pause. 'I'll call you back.'

The man in the background screamed at her in a foreign tongue. More Eastern bloc than Germanic, he thought. Carlisle pondered his next move.

'Tell me—'

The connection suddenly went dead.

He checked the display. Number withheld. Whoever Angelica was, she seemed desperate. But why hadn't she gone to the police before now? Why had she chosen him of all people? There again, he thought. No matter how small or seemly insignificant her information was, it could be of major interest to the police.

He pocketed his phone.

'I'm sorry, Peter.'

'Trouble at mill?' Carter acknowledged, his face showing concern.

Carlisle looked at him, feeling uncomfortable suddenly. 'There's never a dull moment, I'm afraid.'

'No, I suppose not.'

He watched as the old man gathered a few empty plates and returned to the kitchen with them. Still thinking about his conversation with Angelica, he decided to give Jack Mason a call.

The ring tone had nearly played out when the Detective Chief Inspector answered it. His voice was uncharacteristically restrained.

'I'm in a meeting – can I call you back?'

Carlisle could barely breathe, let alone talk.

'There's been a new development, Jack.'

'Give me a few minutes,' Mason acknowledged. 'I'll ring you back.'

The connection went dead.

Chapter Seventeen

David Carlisle had taken the Metro train that afternoon, which seemed a pleasant change from driving in heavy traffic. Besides, parking in Newcastle was expensive these days, but finding a space an even bigger headache. Thinking about his forthcoming meeting with Angelica, he made his way down Grey Street before turning right into High Bridge. Now a listed building, the Old George Inn was reputed to be one of the city's oldest surviving pubs. Not the best of meeting places – he would have preferred somewhere quieter, more low-key.

Despite her secretive stance, he had no idea what Angelica looked like. Was she an attractive young woman, or just plain and ordinary-looking? He knew he would recognise her voice if he heard it again, especially over the telephone. Sometimes it was best to keep an open mind about these things, not get carried away. Foremost on his mind – *would she bother to turn up?*

Entering the cobbled courtyard, he saw the Old George Inn was busy. All the bench seats were taken, and people were standing round chatting. Close to the main entrance door, a busker was playing an old accordion rather badly, Carlisle thought. He hadn't collected much money either, as no one paid a blind bit of attention to him. His dog, a flea ridden mongrel, lay stretched out on a blanket beside him looking bored out of its mind.

The clock above the bar was perpetually stuck at eleven-thirty-two. It had been that way for years. Looking around, he ordered a pint of Theakston's Old Peculier and found himself a corner seat overlooking the lounge. Now back in the swing of things, Carlisle hadn't felt this way in a long time. Not since his days in the Metropolitan's Murder Investigation Team, come to think of it. Fresh out of training back then, he was eager to learn. Those were the happiest years of his life: a trained criminal profiler tracking down psychopaths, and the occasional hostage-taker who threatened national security. Above all else, though, there was nothing like getting inside a serial killer's head and trying to unravel the mystery of what made these people tick. It was like a drug to him, and he couldn't get enough of it.

Well, he thought, he only had himself to blame. Half past three and still no sign of Angelica showing. He'd been warned to stay clear of her, but still hadn't bothered to listen to Jack Mason's advice. Typical, he cursed.

Then the barman's voice cut through the rest.

'David Carlisle?'

'That's me.'

'It's for you,' he said, handing him the pub telephone.

Carlisle instantly recognised the broken English on the other end of the phone. 'Is that you, Angelica?'

'We agreed no police!'

'I came alone, so what's your problem?'

'You were followed.'

It wasn't looking good suddenly. 'That's ridiculous,' he protested.

'There's a man at the end of the bar wearing a blue baseball cap and dark horn-rimmed glasses. . . can you see him?'

'Yes, I can.'

'He's an undercover police officer.'

'That's impossible. How could you possibly know that?'

'If not, then why has he been following you the last fifteen minutes?'

Carlisle stared at a thickset man entrenched at the end of the bar and saw a flicker of recognition in his eyes. He wasn't a gambling man, but guessed it was one of Jack Mason's old cronies sent to trail in his wake.

'Where are you now?'

'Never mind that,' she replied. 'Do you still wish to meet up with me?'

'Yes, of course I do.'

'Listen carefully then.' Her voice was brusque. Agitated. 'There's a little Costa coffee shop inside the Central railway station . . . meet me there in twenty minutes.'

With that she hung up.

The barman rolled his eyes. 'Frustrated girlfriend?'

Carlisle feigned a smile and handed him the pub telephone. It was time to leave.

The Cloth Market wasn't overly busy this time of day. Mainly office workers and businessmen moving between appointments. Sliding his hands into his pockets, he made towards the Haymarket before doubling back on himself. If there were undercover police officers following him, this was the perfect place to lose them. On reaching the bottom of Westgate Road, he stepped up his pace and slipped into one of the many narrow back-lanes.

Why me, he kept asking himself? He knew his movements were under scrutiny, but his head was so mixed up with half-cocked rumours that he was beginning to doubt his own judgement. This was ridiculous. Which side of the fence were the police sitting on?

Then it struck him: Mason was using him as bait.

★★★

Two miles north, Jack Mason looked at his watch and smiled. What Henry Bannister didn't know about the criminal fraternity, wasn't worth knowing. A born loser, Bannister's main source of income nowadays was off-loading cheap cigarettes into the local community. Brought over from Amsterdam in huge quantities, thousands of pounds were exchanging hands – none of it was traceable, and all of it contraband as far as the Customs and Excise were concerned. According to police intelligence, Mason's informant dealt mainly in the popular brands – the easy stuff to shift. It was a lucrative business, and everyone wanted in on it.

It didn't take long for the word to get around. The mere presence of a police undercover vehicle was enough. Tower hamlets weren't the friendliest environments to hang around in, not at any time of day. Full of prying eyes, once people got wind you were working with the police, reprisals could be severe. The trouble was, he wasn't quite sure how he would handle his visit here today. Cultivating moles was tricky, as it usually took years to build up a degree of reciprocal trust. Once your credibility was lost, it was all downhill from then on.

Walls full of graffiti, doors in need of a lick of paint. Mason rang the doorbell. Seconds later a man answered the door in a black polo neck sweater and jeans.

'How are you, Henry?' Mason asked.

'All the better for seeing you, Jack.'

'Someone giving you grief, are they?'

'You could say that, yes.'

Ignoring him, Mason was under no illusions that his informant was a dangerous man to deal with. Moles had a knack of trading information with you, occasionally to the press, but mainly to the police. It was all about trust, and that was another thing that had niggled away at him lately. Bannister had overstepped the mark, double crossed the police and was about to be taken off the streets. Soon he would be left with a massive intelligence void to fill and would need to find a replacement.

Ten floors up with views overlooking Byker and the surrounding districts, was the rendezvous on this beautiful sunny day. Checking the coast was clear, Mason stuck his foot over the door threshold to stop the door from closing.

'Do I know who this person is?'

'Ah-huh. He's one of your local bizzies, and he's a right pain in the arse.'

'How can I help?'

'That depends...'

Seconds later he was inside.

The living room was cramped, piled high with suspicious looking packages. Quite often he knew when he was onto a good thing, as the evidence was always plain to see. He made a mental note of it but refrained from confronting Bannister over his latest scam as he had more important things to talk about.

'Tell me who this PCSO is, and I'll have a quiet word.'

'I'd appreciate that.'

'Before I do that, there's something I need you to do for me first.'

'That depends.'

Mason turned sharply. 'Depends!'

'Yeah. What kind of information is it you're looking for?'

'That's a new one,' Mason growled. 'What are you trying to say?'

'Everything has a price, Jack. Even you know that.'

Bannister looked fit and energetic, despite being in his sixties. Not the best of starts, Mason thought; he would need to take back control.

'If that's how you wish to play it, that's fine by me.'

'What do you mean?'

'Asking a PCSO to turn a blind eye on your little cigarette scam could cost you twenty grand.'

'That's bollocks!'

'But is it?' Mason eyes toured the room. 'Doing you a favour means I'm putting my police pension at risk.'

'Life's tough, Jack.'

'I couldn't agree more.'

Bannister stared at him with deep rooted suspicion. 'What is it you're after?'

'The thing is, offloading dodgy cigarettes carries a hefty penalty. It's almost as bad as piracy, even worse than lying to a judge. Handling contraband is Crown prosecution stuff, and I doubt her Majesty would take too kindly to you fiddling her out of thousands of pounds of taxpayers' money.' Mason supressed a grin. 'People have been hanged for less.'

'Who said this stuff was contraband?' Bannister quizzed.

'Why don't we open it up and see?' Mason was enjoying himself. 'Mind, if it isn't kosher then we'll probably confiscate the lot and burn it in an incinerator.'

Banister's eyes narrowed a fraction. 'What is it you're wanting to know?'

'What do you know about the *Suitcase Man?*'

Bannister was silent for a moment and had every right to be. Paying informants was a cost-effective method of securing information, but the risks were enormous. The thing was, there was a lot of money to be had from it and that's what drove these people into doing it.

'You mean this geek who's going around chopping people's bodies up?'

'That's the one.' Mason nodded.

'Not a lot, why?'

'I need a name, Henry.' Mason looked at him hard. 'I need this bastard taken off the streets before he commits further atrocities.'

'Easier said than done. This so-called Suitcase Man doesn't hang about.'

Mason's mood was irritable, having been up all night with toothache. He paused, watching Bannister's eyes closely and guessed what his informant was thinking. 'Name your price, and I'll see to it my mates don't close your little operation down.'

'What operation is this?' Bannister replied nervously.

'Don't piss me about, you've been under our radar for months now. We know what you're up to, we've been tracking you for weeks. From the shops you offload to, the people you supply. . . everything about you.'

Bannister swallowed hard. Suddenly the general conversation was over, and Mason could feel the change of intensity in Bannister's voice. 'It's only rumours, Jack.'

'Maybe, but I'm not liking what I'm hearing.'

'It's purely rumours.'

'If you say so, Henry. But I'm only looking after your interests here.' Mason gave him a neighbourly tap on the shoulder. 'Just give me a name, there's a good lad.'

Judging by Bannister's response, he wasn't a happy customer suddenly. Caught red-handed with a living room crammed full of illegal cigarettes, there wasn't a lot he could do about it. Mason had him by the balls, and he was slowly tightening the screws.

'I'll ask around, see what I can find out.'

'Don't take too long over it,' Mason replied. 'The clock is already ticking.'

'You know me, Jack. If I can help you, I will.'

Mason eyed him with suspicion. 'It's been a pleasure talking to you, Henry. I'll see myself out.'

'Gan canny. . . Inspector.'

'I will, Henry.' Mason swivelled on his heels. 'If you can think of anything else that's stopping you from sleeping at night, you know where to find me.'

He'd barely crossed the threshold, when he heard the dead bolts snap shut behind him. It was that kind of neighbourhood.

Chapter Eighteen

Inside the little Costa coffee shop on Newcastle's Central Station, Carlisle had found a corner seat. There were dozens of young women passing the time of day and drinking coffee, but which one was his contact?

His mobile phone pinged.

'Raise your hand above your head,' the young woman's voice instructed.

'And—'

'Now I see you.'

'Where are you?' Carlisle insisted.

'When you step outside the Costa cafe, turn left towards the main entrance and wait for me under the train arrivals board.'

His phone went dead.

He suddenly felt like the actor in the film Phone Booth, where the main protagonist was being controlled by telephone calls. Whoever Angelica was, she certainly knew how to send his adrenaline racing. But there lay his problem. This was his best lead in town, and just because Jack Mason's team were shadowing his every movement he wasn't giving up that easily.

His mobile phone pinged again.

'Mr Carlisle—'

He turned sharply.

'Where are you now? How will I recognise you?'

'I'm twenty metres away,' she replied. 'Walk back towards the station's main entrance.'

Still holding the iPhone up to his ear, Carlisle did as he was instructed. Then, through a gap in the crowd, he spotted her. Not a tall woman, petite, with ice blue eyes. Her hair was the colour of ripe corn, and her makeup minimal. She had an intelligent face, slim legs, and she carried a large bag slung loosely over her shoulder. Dressed in a plain red coat, black jeans and wearing red baseball boots with long white laces, she conveyed a mystical presence.

Being a private investigator was all about trust – putting your client at ease. This meeting was different, though, full of dark secrets and suspicion. Then it struck him. There were no CCTV cameras in this section of the station – just electronic notice boards.

He walked towards her. Warily.

'You must be, Angelica?'

She was quiet for a moment. 'I won't keep you long, Mr Carlisle. As you will have gathered, I'm not from your country. Where I live, you learn not to make contact over the telephone. It's far too dangerous. You are a private investigator and will know all about electronic surveillance devices,' she said with a nod; 'you never can be too careful these days.'

As far he could tell, Angelica was alone. But that didn't mean to say they weren't being watched. He tried to steady himself, but the way she looked at him was unnerving.

'So,' Carlisle began, 'what is it you wish to talk to me about?'

'You're moving too fast. How do I know I can trust you?'

Carlisle considered the question but wasn't about to answer. Whoever she was, she had certainly done her homework. One false move and she'd be off like a shot.

'You don't,' he replied calmly.

'What do you know about Eastern European drugs gangs operating within the UK?'

'Not a lot. Why?'

She told him more. About Britain's proximity to the Netherlands, which was now regarded as the epicentre of Europe's narcotics industry. What's more, gang leaders were using the smuggling routes to traffic their illegal human cargoes to England. Despite her age, Angelica – *if that was her real name* – was remarkably informed. Too well, if the truth be known. As more of her story began to unfold, Carlisle had to pinch himself to take it all in. There was venom in her voice, but her delivery was guarded and full of underlying riddles. This was a dangerous game she was playing, but she spoke with confidence as though she understood the situation perfectly.

'Tell me what you saw in Forth Street,' he asked.

She looked at him with frank surprise. 'Can I trust you?'

'Yes, of course you can.'

Her posture had suddenly changed, and he sensed uncertainty. 'It had just turned seven o'clock when he drew up into one of the side lanes in Forth Street. The car's headlights were switched off, but I could still hear the engine running.' She checked over her shoulder again. 'Most men are usually friendly when you approach them, but some like to feel in control. It's a defensive thing, as most customers have secrets to hide. This time felt different, though, as if something nasty was about to happen to me. It was then I decided to question him.'

'Question who?'

Her shoulders slumped, and she glanced coyly away. 'Men often pull up in cars to talk to us girls. It's a quiet area, Mr Carlisle. That's how we operate.'

He thought about it, but not for long. Forth Street wasn't a known red-light district, and yet she was a working prostitute. There again, he thought. Tucked back from the hustle and bustle of city life it was the perfect environment for a woman of the night to operate in.

He didn't press the matter further.

'What happened next?'

'The moment I approached the driver's door, his electric door window wound down. I knew then he wasn't looking for sex.' She smiled. 'You can always tell by the tone of their voice.'

'What did he say to you?'

'He was foul mouthed, and nasty with it. He told me to clear off or he would fetch the police to me.'

'And did he?'

'I was too scared. Some men can be extremely violent towards you, and I try to steer well clear of those types of customers.'

Whilst she spoke English fluently, Carlisle was convinced she was Eastern European. Her face was angelic as her name suggested, but that's where the similarities ended.

'What did he look like, this man?'

There was panic in her voice, and fear in her eyes. 'Not like the rest.'

'What do you mean by that?'

'I didn't get a good look at him,' she replied. 'I was trying to get away from him. It was dark, and I was working alone in the area that night.'

'Sorry,' Carlisle replied almost apologetically. 'So, what happened next?'

'I moved to a quieter spot. . . but still kept a watchful eye on him.' She turned her head towards him but spoke as if he wasn't there. 'Something wasn't right, I could tell from the tone of his voice. At first, I thought he was waiting for one of the other girls to appear. That's what some men do, they like to stick with the same girl every time. It's much safer that way, and they know what they're letting themselves in for.' She steadied herself. 'When no one else showed up, and he didn't drive off, that's when I began to panic.'

Carlisle thought a minute.

'Was he a regular client, this man you talk of?'

'No. I'd never seen him before.' Her eyes widened as she turned towards him. 'If any of the girls feel uncomfortable about a client they're meeting, they text the car registration details to each other. Things can go wrong and do. But at least it puts our minds at rest.'

Clever move, he thought.

'And did *you* text anyone that night?'

'Why would I do that? I certainly wasn't getting into his car.'

'No, I suppose not.' He thought of something. 'What makes you think he had anything to do with this recent murder?'

The look she gave him, told him he'd overstepped the mark. He apologised.

'There was something about him. Something I couldn't quite put my finger on. Then, just when I was about to walk away, that's when he got out of his car and moved to the rear of it.' She smiled. 'He wasn't a tall man, five-nine, and he struggled to lift a large blue suitcase out from the boot.'

Carlisle felt a sudden adrenaline rush.

'A *blue* suitcase. How did you know it was blue if it was dark?'

'The car boot lights were on.' She frowned. 'It looked extremely heavy from what I could see. It had two thick luggage straps to stop it from bursting open, but it still bulged at the sides.' There was a sudden eagerness in her voice. 'Moments later he dragged it into the Storage Company.'

'Why haven't you gone to the police with this information before now?'

'No police!' She panicked.

Carlisle shook his head, annoyed at himself for having pressed the matter. He needed more thinking time, but things were moving too fast for him.

He looked at her. Her eyes were heavy, and her mouth drawn tight. 'Are you in some sort of trouble with the police, Angelica?'

She didn't answer.

'If you are, I may be able to help you.'

She arched her back, a stretching motion. 'I would need to think about that, Mr Carlisle.'

'Yes, of course. Take your time.'

She smiled. 'I know I can trust you, but I don't have the confidence.'

'Are you here illegally, Angelica?' he asked outright.

'What makes you say that?'

'Just asking the question.'

He felt in his pocket for his mobile. Either she didn't realise it, or just didn't care, but if she didn't replace her SIM card at some stage soon he might be able to trace her call.

'No more questions,' she insisted.

Carlisle felt sorry for her, as if she was stuck in a negative downward spiral. Much as he hated to admit, there were some elements of her story he didn't believe. Not all, but some. Normally good at weighing up other people, this time he was struggling. There was a darker side to all of this – far removed and difficult to comprehend.

'This man you saw that night. How would you best describe him?'

She turned sharply to confront him. 'Now you're making me nervous.'

'But I'm—'

She waved her hand and cut him off mid-sentence. 'Please don't follow me, Mr Carlisle. That would be a very foolish thing to do.'

'But surely we can—'

She turned sharply and began to walk away from him.

'Angelica, wait—'

She didn't answer.

He tried running after her, but she'd already melted back into the crowd.

It was a funny old world, Carlisle thought. You could spend weeks trying to force an opening, then everything would fall on your lap. If nothing else, he now had a reasonable explanation as to how the victim's body may have turned up at the Storage Company that night.

En route back to the car park and his car, Carlisle decided to give Jack Mason a call. He pressed the call button on his iPhone and waited for a dialling tone.

Seconds later the automatic voice recorder kicked in.

'You have reached the phone of DCI Mason. I'm sorry, but—'

Chapter Nineteen

Jack Mason spread his hands on the table, palms face down. It had taken him all of twelve minutes to reach the little Costa café on Newcastle's Central Station. Now onto his second cup of black coffee, Carlisle eased back in his seat. Knowing his former workmate as he did, this was far from an easy conversation. Even though he still had the upper hand, it still didn't mean a thing. Mason was hot-headed, temperamental, and could fly off the handle at the slightest provocation. The problem was, hot leads had a nasty habit of going cold and you had to react quickly to them.

'First things first,' Mason announced, 'care to tell me why you haven't contacted me before now?'

'What do you mean?'

'You were meeting a key witness who is probably withholding vital information.'

Carlisle glanced at his watch – a diversionary tactic.

'Well?' Mason insisted.

Carlisle braced himself for the worst and tried to stay calm. Still no mention of the undercover surveillance operation that Mason had put in place that day; he was beginning to feel isolated. Sometimes he got the impression he was talking to a brick wall, and the DCI wasn't listening. Mason was thick-skinned, inflexible, and unwilling to give ground.

'It wasn't my call, Jack. What else was I to do?'

Mason paused just as the coffee cup reached his lips. 'I'm still listening.'

'Look,' Carlisle replied, sucking the air. 'Whatever problem this young woman is facing, she's determined to call all the shots.'

'So, it seems,' Mason scoffed.

Carlisle lowered his voice, realising that people were looking at them. 'Well she categorically refuses to talk to you people and will only speak to me on her terms. What else could I do?'

Mason scooted his seat, and his expression showed concern. 'Here's my problem. I've got a shit load of angry senior officers on my back, and every one of them demands answers. What do you suggest I do – tell them I've got an eighteen-year-old prostitute who knows who the killer is?'

Carlisle remained silent.

'You should have rung me earlier,' Mason insisted. 'At least to run it past me.'

'If you think I'm going to call you every time this young woman decides to spring a surprise meeting on me? It's not going to happen, Jack.'

There, it was said.

Mason's eyebrow lifted a fraction. 'You're forgetting who's in charge here, my friend. Three people are dead, and I'm determined to get to the bottom of it.'

'I realise that, but I've told you everything I know.'

Mason stroked his stubble as he pondered over his next line of attack. 'Rest assured, prostitutes aren't the world's most reliable witnesses. Most are natural born liars; it goes with the profession. And another thing, who's to say she's not here illegally?'

'Wait a minute—'

'How do you know we can trust her?'

'We don't.'

'That's my point.' Mason stabbed a finger in his direction. 'This young woman seems to be clear about a lot of things, but is she telling you the truth?'

'I believe she is.'

'It's all bollocks!'

Carlisle remained silent.

'Besides, prostitutes normally tout for business by poking their heads in through the driver's open window. It's a little trick they use. Once a client gets a whiff of their perfume, it's normally a done deal.'

'Speaking from experience, are we?'

'Don't push it!' Mason snorted.

Late afternoon Newcastle seemed darker than ever, reflecting the Detective Chief Inspector's mood. It was pointless arguing; there was nothing to be gained from it. Mason was goading him, and all he could do was take it on the chin.

'There has to be some truth in what she's saying.'

'Okay, then how come she knew he wasn't a regular client and yet she can't even describe his features to you? Then there's the question of the suitcase, which she could have read about in the papers.'

'Well that's what she told me she saw.'

'She's a liar,' Mason insisted. 'Can't you get that into your head?'

'You're making a grave mistake, Jack.'

'Do you think so?'

'I know so. Her account is too detailed, even down to the colour of the suitcase and the two luggage straps that were wrapped around it.'

'This city is full of rumour-mongers. If this *was* the killer's car she claims to have seen, then why wasn't it picked up during our CCTV sweep of the area?'

'He could have driven there on false number plates.'

'True, but highly unlikely, don't you think?'

'Well that's how I would have done it.'

Mason eyed him with suspicion. 'She's a liar. . . goddammit. I wouldn't trust her as far as I could throw her.'

The atmosphere was strained, and Carlisle knew he wasn't getting anywhere. Best not rush into it. Mason was a creature of habit, notorious for back-of-a-fag-packet plans. Confused at first, then angry with himself, Carlisle tried to focus his mind. And yes, in his experience serial killers were egotistical predators who would stop at nothing to accomplish their goals. Whoever had killed these young men could be driven by sexual lust. And yet, he argued, sex wasn't his primary motivation. This killer was organised, and methodically cunning, and most of his crimes were committed out of his area of residence. No, he thought, his behaviour patterns were far too consistent – *he was winning over these people's confidence before killing them.*

Mason gave him a look that said it all. 'You should know the procedure by now: you'll need to come in and make out a written statement. In the meantime, I'll get Forth Banks Police Station to run a few checks on the area. If she is a working prostitute as she claims, she'll not be too difficult to pick out.'

Carlisle took another sip of his coffee and began to ponder his options. Trying to read into Jack Mason's mind was like staring into a black hole. He would need to work on it, find a better way of relaying his information back to him in future. As it was, he still had a shit load of explaining to do and wasn't looking forward to that.

Chapter Twenty

Naked, stretched out on the cold bathroom floor, he inhaled the sickly-sweet smell of death. Physically exhausted and emotionally drained from his recent overindulgent exertions, an overwhelming sense of calm washed over him. Beautiful strains of music filled the air – *The Tempest* – coming from another part of the building. Wasp loved the sound that a full symphony orchestra made as it played out its dark brooding passages, and this part of the performance was magnificent. Particularly the string articulation, tranquil, unlike the overpowering climax to follow. That would be different, of course. Nature breathing its fury as the sea moved from calm breezy moods to the thundering gust of a tempest – Sibelius at his best.

Alone in his thoughts, Wasp stared at the young man's lifeless body now sprawled out on the floor next to him. Two weeks of watching him. Fantasising. Following his every move until it all came down to this.

"Death was a door through which everyone must pass," he whispered. *"Death was inevitable."*

Wasp, not a tall man, wiry with short cropped hair, playfully fingered the knife. Building rapport and trust between you and the client was all part of the fun. It was all about timing, choosing the right moment to execute your plans. Sometimes he felt an uplifting affiliation towards his victims as if they didn't deserve to die. Regrets seemed futile now, as events had overtaken them.

Exhausted, he would sleep later – when his work was done here.

Then he remembered his Facebook account – he'd almost forgotten about that. Time to open a new account and seek out another potential candidate. The timing was right, and he couldn't have chosen a better place. It was quiet round here at nights and people had lost the art of conversation. He stared at the bathroom tiles and smiled. Blood everywhere, ceilings, walls, and all of it his own doing. It was the thrill of the chase that excited him above all else – trying to separate the vulnerable from the rest of the pack. That was the easy part; it was the next bit that was tricky.

Not long now!

His heart racing, he reached over and wrapped his long slender fingers around the cold plastic handle of the saw. It felt good. Exhilarating. Just as it had done on every other occasion. He tilted his head back slightly, rolled his eyes in their sockets till only the whites were showing. The moment he pressed the start button, his mind flew into hyperdrive. The noise it made was better than drugs, he felt, far more exhilarating than anything else he had ever experienced in the past.

Wasp toyed with the start button and sensed the tiny vibrations running through his fingertips. There was nothing like the sound of a powered surgical saw slicing through human flesh at sixteen inches per minute. It felt good, invigorating. He always wore a visor, of course, as pieces of flying bone could easily blind a person.

Wasp wasn't that daft!

With heels trailing the tiles, head lolloping to one side, he dragged the limp corpse the short distance towards the edge of the bath. Overcome with emotion, he felt another surge of adrenaline rushing through his veins. Not for the first time, he needed to take a rest.

Slowly at first – hands gripped firmly under the young man's arms – he hauled his latest victim onto the lip of the bath. Once the legs had cleared the floor tiles, only then did he let go. He shuddered as the body slid effortlessly over the side of the bath and down towards the drain plug. This time it was perfect – he couldn't have positioned it any better had he tried.

Nearly done.

Quiet for a moment, he mentally walked through the various scenarios he'd meticulously planned in his head. This bit wasn't simple, far from it. Experience had taught him always to hold the surgical saw in your right hand, as it was much easier that way – more accurate. Then, gripping the victim's arm with his left hand, he made his first incision. Not hurried, precise. Just as the surgeon's book had taught him – straight along the suture line.

Looking good, he smiled.

Chapter Twenty-One

Carlisle's taste buds were alerted the minute he stepped into the Northumberland Arms in Newcastle city centre. It was lunchtime, and the place reeked of chicken curry and other tempting aromas. A regular haunt for off-duty police officers, today it was jam-packed with pensioners. Two meals for the price of one, not bad considering. He ordered a beer and found an empty seat. Running your own private investigation business could be a dreary existence at times. Endless hours spent snooping around some seedy partner's nocturnal activities could drive a man mad. Not today, it wasn't. Today he was having a good day.

Despite everything Angelica had told him, according to Jack Mason there wasn't a single prostitute working in Forth Street. They'd all been moved on years ago. Thinking this through, Eastern European gangs were notorious masters at ensnaring innocent young women into illicit sex crimes, so maybe they'd got wind of it.

Having carried out a cognitive interview with Tom Hedley's forensics team earlier that morning, Carlisle was relieved it was now over. Not an exact science, they'd managed to cobble together an e-fit image of Angelica, which he thought bore a remarkable likeness. All that remained now was to circulate it to every police force in the land in the hope that someone would recognise her.

Carlisle had almost forgotten it was Monday. The weekend had flown by. Pint in hand, he paid for his drink and managed to squeeze into a side booth overlooking the bar. He sat for a while, trying to put things into perspective. In a way, he felt sorry for Angelica. Yes, she could exaggerate, but that didn't make her a hoaxer. The problem was, Jack Mason liked to rub people up the wrong way and could be a bit of a sexist-bastard at times. Not everything was rosy in the garden, though. Thinking back, organised gang threats were much broader and more complex than they ever were ten years ago. In the wake of the Soviet Union collapse, Russian mobsters had moved into Europe's major cities and were causing all kinds of havoc amongst decent folk. Drugs, human trafficking and financial scams were now the scourge of modern day society. People were becoming tired of it, and frontline policing wasn't the same anymore. Not only that, Eastern European gangs were extremely good at what they did and that's what made him think as he did.

He couldn't be sure, but the man stood next to the gaming machine carried a familiar look. He wasn't a tall man, lean, with long blond hair tied at the back. Dressed in a blue open neck shirt, jeans and black leather bomber jacket, it was his demeanour that was the giveaway. Then it twigged – he was one of Jack Mason's new recruits brought in to bolster the numbers.

Carlisle decided against having another pint, as he still had a ton of things to do. He exited the pub into bright sunshine, heading south towards the Quayside. On entering Grey Street, he caught sight of the figure out of the corner of his eye. He turned and looked towards where the man was standing and knew then he was being followed. On reaching Dean Street he dropped into the multi-storey car park and boarded the elevator. As the doors swished open to level four, he began to formulate a plan. It didn't take much, but it was enough to put him on edge. Whoever the tail was, he was determined to keep him in his sights.

Twenty feet below he heard people talking, then saw the elevator floor level lights flicker. It was on its way back up. Minutes later he heard the doors open and the sound of footsteps approaching. No longer alone, it was time to make his move.

'This is as far as it goes,' Carlisle said, stepping out from behind a parked van.

The stranger stopped dead in his tracks.

'And who the hell are you?'

'Never mind who I am. You've been following me ever since I left the Northumberland Arms.'

'What makes you think that?'

'You were propped up against the gaming machine as I remember.'

Reaching into an inside pocket, the stranger held up his warrant card. 'Detective Constable Carver, Northumbria Police. I have reason to believe you—'

'Never mind the bullshit,' Carlisle said angrily pushing the detectives hand aside, 'your cover's been blown, son.'

'Cover, what the hell are you on about?'

'You know what I'm on about. Tell Jack Mason to pick someone with a little more experience next time.'

Annoyed, Carlisle pushed past him taking the steps to the ground floor. On reaching the car park entrance ramp he scoured the street in search of the backup officer. These jerks usually worked in pairs. It was one of the tricks he'd learned whilst working undercover with the Met. Signal your partner, exchange shadowing duties, and your suspect is none the wiser. It worked every time and was one of Mason's favourite tricks.

Not this time, it didn't.

'Why are you two jerks shadowing me?'

'Who the hell are you?' the backup officer announced angrily.

'Never mind who I am, whose orders are you working on?'

The young detective adjusted his Ray-Ban sunglasses as if it was a natural thing to do. 'What's it got to do with you?'

Carlisle had already taken an instant disliking to him. The man had attitude and was cocky with it. 'Best talk with your friend on level four, the one with his arse hanging out of his jeans.'

'Carry on like that, and I'll arrest you for obstructing a police officer.'

'Try pulling the other leg, son.'

'I must warn you that it's—'

Carlisle brushed his warrant card aside. 'It's time to sling your hook and head back to Gateshead police station.'

Chuffed with himself, Carlisle pushed on towards the Monument leaving the two disgruntled police officers deep in discussion. Descending into the bowels of the Metro station, his felt his mobile vibrate in his pocket. He checked the display, and sure enough Jack Mason's name popped up on the screen.

'Where are you now?'

'I thought you'd know that already.'

'Yeah, well.'

'Why have—

'Enough of this Get Carter stuff,' Mason interrupted, 'there's been another development.'

Carlisle suddenly felt the hairs on his neck prickle. 'If it's got anything to do with the two undercover officers you've had tailing me, forget it.'

'It hasn't. Just get your arse over to the little café opposite Wetherspoons in Gateshead, I'll meet you there in twenty minutes.'

His phone went dead.

Now it made sense. If there was any trouble to be had, the two undercover officers were merely there for his protection. God! He cursed. He'd cocked up big style and hadn't even bothered to think it through. It was true what they say about mistrust. The truth hurts, lies poison, but suspicion is torture.

Chapter Twenty-Two

The little café on Gateshead High Street was far from full. A sprinkling of pensioners, a young mother with kids, and an obese lowlife who gave him a look that said: *who the hell are you staring at?* Carlisle wasn't overly keen on the place anyway. The service was crap, and the food always served cold. Besides, he liked his coffee black, the stronger the better.

He found Jack Mason sat at a corner seat overlooking the busy High Street. Engrossed in a handy-man's magazine, Mason barely lifted his head as he took up a seat opposite. Sometimes Carlisle felt the DCI enjoyed making people feel uncomfortable in his presence. Mason was old school and cared little for police protocols nor the requisites of case law.

'Another body has turned up,' Mason announced bluntly.

'Blimey. . . he doesn't hang about, Jack.'

'No, it would appear not.'

'When was this?'

Eyes glazed over after another heavy night drinking session, Mason stared up at him from behind his magazine. 'Five-fifty this morning. . . a man out walking his dog.'

'Not the best of starts to someone's day,' Carlisle said. 'Where was this?'

'Close to a council estate in Byker.'

'Thank God it wasn't schoolkids who found him.' Carlisle paused in thought. 'Another vicious knife attack, no doubt?'

'How did you guess?' Mason sounded crestfallen. 'Tom Hedley's currently sifting through the crime scene, so I'm hoping for a quick response.'

'Has he said anything to you yet?'

'Not to me he hasn't.' Mason put his magazine down and folded his arms across his chest. A defensive stance. 'One thing for sure, this bastard gains an awful lot of pleasure from delivering his victims' to us in suitcases.'

'It's the way their minds work; after a while they become predictable.'

'I had a feeling you'd say that,' Mason said, adjusting his shirt collar. 'I dread to think what the media will make of it once they get their hands on it – the city will go into hibernation no doubt.'

'What's the Acting Superintendent's reaction?'

'It's hard to say. The last I heard she was waiting for the Home Office pathologist's report to filter through.'

Wise move, thought Carlisle. Things were getting out of hand, and the police hadn't a clue where *the Suitcase Man* would strike next. He decided to dig deeper whilst Mason was still in an amicable mood.

'What state was the body in?'

'Multiple stab wounds to the upper body and neck. He'd been hacked to pieces, only this time none of the body parts were missing.'

Carlisle turned sharply to face him. 'That's new! He likes to keep us guessing by retaining some of their body parts.'

'God knows what he's thinking.'

'Do we know who the victim is?'

'His name's John Lawrence and he was picked up on our DNA database.'

'That makes it a lot easier.'

Mason steadied himself. 'Where is it all going to end? That's my question.'

'He's not going to stop now, Jack.'

'No. It would appear not.'

'He's changing the rules, gaining in confidence and stepping up his game plan. Psychopaths are grandiose by their very nature, thinking they're smarter than anyone else. They're charming, manipulative, and can hide behind a well-cultivated mask of normality and yet commit the most heinous crimes. Let's not—'

Mason held his hand up. 'The last thing I need right now is a lecture on psychology. There's dozens of police officers out questioning anyone seen dragging a suitcase around town, and yet he still he slips through the net.'

He understood Mason's frustrations but refused to be intimidated by him. A serial killer was at large, and they didn't have the luxury of time. It was then he recalled the heinous crimes of Jeffrey Dahmer, an American serial killer who lured his victims back to his small urban apartment with promises of sex and drugs. In late 1987, he took his second victim back to a hotel room and drank. When he eventually awoke to find him dead, Dahmer had no recollection of the previous night's activities. As Carlisle remembered it, Dahmer transported the body in a large suitcase back to his grandmother's basement, where he dismembered the corpse before disposing of the remains. This case had a similar ring to it, and he was slowly beginning to piece together a mental picture of what the killer was about.

Mason swivelled to face him.

'The Acting Superintendent is holding an emergency meeting in MR-1, eight o'clock in the morning. Everyone's to attend.' Mason's brow corrugated as he stared into the bottom of his cup. 'She wants you to write a summary report on the killer's behavioural patterns. Don't over-elaborate, try keeping it simple.'

'I'll do my best.'

Mason's face remained expressionless. 'Before we both attend the meeting tomorrow, let's spend a few minutes in my office together. We need to think about the killer's movements – kill zone, drop zone, that sort of thing.' Mason tapped his finger on the table in front of him as if to emphasise a point. 'Why does he select mainly young males? Why does he hack their bodies up? Those are the type of questions the Area Commander is bound to ask.'

'What time?'

Mason screwed his face up as if to jog a memory. 'The press office has set up a media briefing for ten o'clock, so we'd better make it seven.'

'Busy times, eh?' Carlisle sighed.

'There's not enough time in the day, my friend.' Mason stared down at the handy-man's magazine, with thoughts elsewhere. 'It's out of my hands, but Sutherland is considering making a media appeal on this one.'

'What... *Crimewatch!*'

'No, at tomorrow's local media briefing.' Mason rounded on him. 'She's particularly looking for information regarding this Eastern European woman you've been in contact with.'

'So, she's finally come around to my way of thinking at last.'

'No, quite the opposite,' Mason said stoically. 'She's scaling that side of the operation down—'

'What!'

'Well, not in as many words.'

'So why bother to go public?'

'Police tactics. Let the local community believe we're on to something.'

'I don't disagree with her logic, but what if Angelica *is* telling the truth?'

'That's the Acting Superintendent's problem, not mine.'

Carlisle thought a moment. 'Anything I can do to help?'

'Not now.'

'So, where does that leave me?'

Mason looked at him then stared out of the café window again. 'Make sure your report's ready in time for tomorrow's briefing and keep it brief. . . no waffle.'

'I will.'

There was something unnerving in Mason's calmness that sent shivers down Carlisle's spine. He felt trapped, isolated, left out in the cold again. He knew the Detective Chief Inspector was defending his own corner against signs of incompetence, as most senior police officers usually did in times of trouble. This time it felt different.

'This woman's story doesn't stack up. She's like a million other wannabes out there. . . anxious to have her two minutes of glory. You need to tread carefully, my friend. Whatever Angelica's up to, don't get sucked into her web of deceit.'

Like hell, Carlisle thought. There had to be some truth in what she was telling him. After all, he was the profiler, the man brought in to assist the police in their investigations. He'd often wondered what went on behind closed doors, and now he knew. Far too many senior police officers were keen to build a team of fall guys around them. People like Jack Mason, people they could readily lay blame on. To get to the top required guile. It was a game of kidology where only the strongest survived.

Carlisle needed a plan, and right now he couldn't think of one.

'So, what is your programme for the rest of the day?'

'I'm still waiting for Tom Hedley's forensic report to filter through, but there's a few things we need to tie up on John Lawrence's background.'

'Do we know much about him?'

'Not a lot at this stage, but we're working on it.'

Carlisle stood to leave. 'Seven o'clock tomorrow morning then. . .'

'I'll keep you informed of any new developments.'

It had been one of those days, Carlisle felt.

Chapter Twenty-Three

Carlisle could see the mountain of paperwork on Acting Superintendent Sutherland's desk had grown considerably these past few weeks. The longer this case went on the more reports the team would generate. It was a vicious circle, and somewhere beneath the pile of case files lay his report. He'd tried keeping it simple. Basic stuff. The trouble was, behavioural psychology wasn't the easiest subject matter to write about, particularly one involving a serial killer. Despite his simplistic approach, he was now having grave doubts as to whether the team would grasp the gist of it.

Except for Dr Colin Brown, all the usual suspects were present that morning. It was a large turnout – *full of hot-air and contradiction*. This was the nineteenth team briefing of Operation Walrus, and they still had an awful lot of ground to cover. The team had got their wires crossed and needed to look at the bigger picture.

Amidst small talk, the Acting Superintendent took up a central position in front of the crime board. Wearing a spotless, freshly pressed uniform, she stared at her notebook before jotting something down. The problem was, Jack Mason wasn't the right man to handle the press anymore and everyone knew it.

'In what can only be described as a frenzied knife attack, Jennifer Oakwell is found dead at a house in Bensham, and a second victim's body is missing. Ten days later, on Monday 10th March a headless torso turns up in a blue suitcase at the Storage Company in Forth Street. The head and hands are missing, but the victim was later identified as Colin Henderson. Now let's turn our attention to the following sequence of events. Timeline, Friday 11th April,' Sutherland said, pointing to a monochrome photograph pinned to the events board. 'Thomas Wilkinson, a well-known local petty-criminal is last seen drinking in the Eagle bar on Scotswood Road. Shortly before closing time, around 11:15

pm, he finishes his drink and leaves via the pub's back door. Where did he go? Who was he meeting?' Sutherland looked down at the table in front of her and moved her head in the affirmative as she spoke. 'Three days later, 14th April, young Colin Henderson's missing body parts turn up at a Waste and Recycling Centre in Blaydon along with Wilkinson's torso. Found hidden inside a large black suitcase by one of the lorry drivers. A thorough search of the site reveals nothing.' Sutherland raised her eyebrows a fraction. 'We know the killer used the same powered surgical saw to cut his victim's bodies up. . . but where did he purchase it?'

Despite her composed appearance, Carlisle detected an underlying nervousness in her voice. He wanted to say something, anything, but the words got stuck in his throat.

'At 10:15 pm on 21st May, John Lawrence is seen leaving the Blue Bell public house in Gateshead. Twenty minutes later, at 10:35 pm, he is picked up on High Street CCTV cameras again. Worse for wear after a heavy night drinking session, he appears to be heading towards the Gateshead Metro Station. . . but we still cannot be certain at this point.' She spun to face them. 'So, if he wasn't intending to catch a Metro train that night, what other arrangements had he made?'

The noise levels heightened.

'What about the other CCTV cameras in the area, ma'am?' asked DS Holt.

'No, nothing. We've drawn a complete blank. What we do know, is that two days after John Lawrence went missing in Gateshead, his body turns up on open waste ground in Byker.' She opened her hands up expansively, as she moved to address the team. 'Three young males, all aged between nineteen and twenty-five, and all killed using the same murder weapon. What links them?'

It was Jack Mason who spoke next.

'Every bar within a two-mile radius of the River Tyne is now under scrutiny. If he is local, and we believe he is, our aim is to flush him out.'

'Apart from this grainy image,' said Sutherland thoughtfully, 'what else do we know about the killer?'

Rob Savage put his hand up to speak, and Sutherland nodded. 'According to the PM report, John Lawrence suffered multiple stab wounds separated into three distinct clusters – neck, back, and chest. Two of the three stab wounds to the left side of the neck, severed the Carotid Artery. Suffering from heavy blood loss, the victim now attempts to stem the blood flow and that's when he was stabbed in the back.'

Tom Hedley pointed to the crime board. 'Looking at the SOC photographs, these are classic downward arc stab wounds and of some considerable force. His attacker is right handed, and approximately five-ten in height. At this stage in the proceedings we know the victim fell backwards to the ground, and wounds to the upper chest suggest the attacker straddled his victim before repeatedly driving the knife home with both hands.' The senior forensic scientist paused in reflection for a moment. 'Stab wounds to the back and chest are elliptic in shape, and indicate the knife was double edged. What's far more interesting are small contusions found above and below each of the puncture marks, which point to some sort of finger guard attached to it.'

'Could this be the same double-edged combat knife?' Mason asked.

'Yes, that would fit. The wounds are consistent with those found on the previous victim's bodies.'

'Good work, gentlemen,' Sutherland acknowledged. 'Has anyone got anything to add?'

'There is one other point, ma'am,' Hedley acknowledged. 'Fibre strands found on the victim's body are consistent with those discovered at two of the crime scenes.'

'What about fingerprints?'

'No, ma'am. We believe he wore rubber gloves.'

DC Manley who had sat quietly throughout the briefing that morning suddenly chipped in. 'He must be a pretty strong bastard.'

'How do you make that out, Harry?' Mason asked.

'What is the average human body weight – one-hundred and seventy pounds?'

The room held its breath

'If you say so,' Mason nodded.

'Dragging a suitcase over uneven waste-ground for more than half a mile would take an awful lot of effort.'

Hedley looked at Manley, bemused. 'More awkward than anything, don't you think?'

'True,' Sutherland nodded, a smile of gratification showing.

Manley looked at Hedley. 'He could be a fitness fanatic, of course.'

'It's possible.'

Sutherland referred to her notes. 'What else do we know about the suitcase, Tom?'

'Common type, purchased from the same charity shop in Low Fell.'

Mason spread his hands like a Baptist priest offering an Amen. 'Just for the record, we've now interviewed everyone at the charity shop and they all seem to remember a young woman purchasing them. She paid by cash unfortunately, so we don't have a bank trace to a card.'

The mere mention of a young woman hit Carlisle hard. Something didn't stack up and it was bothering him.

Sutherland wrote something down, then turned to face Carlisle. 'Are we on to something here?'

'The weapon used is a very important factor in this case, as the use of a combat knife demonstrates a great deal of pent-up anger. There is a significant difference, from a psychological standpoint, to that of shooting someone, of course.'

Sutherland stared at him. 'Yes, but there was nothing in your report to suggest it was part of his behavioural pattern?'

'It's not an exact science, ma'am. The killer could be suffering from an inferiority complex or may have failed miserably at some time in his life. There are far too many variations to take into consideration to make an honest prognosis at this stage.'

'Is he hedonistic?'

'I doubt it. I get the distinct impression he's not at all popular with the rest of society. He's probably an outsider, someone shunned by his counterparts. We know he's egotistic hence the smiley faces he's drawn on Jennifer Oakwell's walls.'

Tom Hedley raised a hand to speak, and Sutherland gave a nod. 'Yes, Tom?'

'What drives him?' Hedley asked.

'That's a strange one,' Carlisle admitted. 'He seems to be egged on by someone, or something. Again, I'm finding it difficult to come up with a motive at this stage.'

'Could a partner be involved?'

Carlisle drew breath; the questions were coming thick and fast.

'That possibility has crossed my mind, but I'm still not convinced.'

Eager to move on, Sutherland moved to the crime board again. 'Three young males, all killed by the same murder weapon, and all dismembered using the same surgical saw. Apart from Jennifer Oakwell, there seems to be a distinct pattern taking place here.'

Mason cocked his head to one side. 'Young men, all picked up from bars and nightclubs. What does that tell us?'

'According to the toxicology report, the concentration of alcohol in blood in Thomas Wilkinson and John Lawrence's bodies was uncharacteristically high,' Hedley confirmed.

Carlisle eased forward in his seat. 'Which suggests he's priming his victims with alcohol before moving in for the kill. If he *is* using alcohol as a stimulus, it certainly demonstrates his ability to manipulate vulnerable men in a drink-fuelled environment.'

'That's a very salient point,' Hedley conceded; 'perhaps we should take a closer look.'

Carlisle shook his head as the coffee slipped down his throat like bitter mud. At least someone agreed with him, which was more than he could have hoped for half an hour ago. 'I couldn't agree more, Tom. He does seem to be gaining the victims' trust, only to abuse it in a most appalling manner.'

'Ah!' Mason said with a grin. 'We're coming back to this Dennis Nilsen theory of mine.'

'*Dennis Nilsen!*' Sutherland looked at Mason sternly. 'What the hell's he got to do with the case?'

The room sat silent as Mason explained.

Chapter
Twenty-Four

Spring was going out with a bang, Jack Mason felt, as he stared out through the unmarked police car's windscreen. The tulips had taken a terrible battering from the recent high winds, and his garden fence was badly in need of repair. Deep down he couldn't give a damn about the changing seasons anymore. Perhaps it was a man's thing, his way of dealing with it. When he was younger he would spend hours in the garden with his mother, and there was always lots to do. His mother, God bless her, always ensured they had plenty of cold drinks to keep them going on a hot summer's day. Ginger beer was his favourite. It had always sounded such a manly drink when he was a schoolboy, as if part of growing up. It was strange how your mind worked when you were a thirteen-year-old boy. Innocent thoughts, nothing unpleasant.

Sunday was always his preferred day of the week, as he used to go train spotting with friends. Taking down the engine numbers and marking them off in a book that his mother had bought for him from one of the local stationery stores. Things had moved on since then, and teenagers today spent most of their time in front of their computer screens. Life was one big adventure when he was a kid. Not like being stuck in a bedroom playing on digital gadgets all day.

Mason's dark expression said it all. 'The place looks closed.'

'It's hard to tell from the outside, boss,' DS Savage replied.

'It's closed, believe me. These bastards are playing for time. We need to get a search warrant and take them by storm.'

Both turned their heads as another car sped past them. A Ford Mondeo this time, with yellow spoilers and flash silver trims. Seconds later it disappeared, and the street fell quiet again. The longer this went on, the more pissed off the Detective Chief Inspector was becoming. This was the second day they'd spent parked up outside Fat Sam's nightclub, and it was sorely testing his patience. Then, as the nightclub doors cracked open a fraction, an unfamiliar figure stepped onto the pavement. A short man, with huge biceps and a face resembling a bulldog.

Mason was onto him like a flash. 'Is your gaffer in?' he announced.

'And what if he is?' the man replied.

Mason slid from the driver's seat and pushed his warrant card under the man's nose. If there was any trouble to be had, Fat Sam's was the place to find it.

'This is police business.'

'Really?'

'We're not here to check the fucking gas meters out. . . there's a good lad!'

There was doubt in the man's eyes. Hesitation.

'Best follow me,' the man finally said.

Two floors down and they were treading familiar territory again. The air reeked of cigar smoke, and something a little stronger this time – *cannabis.*

Fox looked at them hard for a moment. 'Why, if it isn't Jack Mason and his sidekick DS Savage. You people are never away from the place nowadays. What's on your mind this time?'

'We're here to close you down,' Mason announced authoritatively.

The Newcastle gangster glared up at them from behind a large oak desk and signalled to one of his minders. No one was going anywhere, that much was obvious.

'What do you mean, close me down?' said Fox. 'What are the charges?'

'Walls have ears, Tony, and people like to talk. The word on the street is that one of the young men who frequented your nightclub is one of my murder victims. It's not looking good and my boss keeps asking me a shit load of questions.'

Fox laughed. 'We've been over this ground before, you and me, and you're beginning to sound like a stuck record.'

'Just cut the crap.' Mason grinned. 'We have it on camera this time.'

'Touchy today, are we?'

'I'm in no mood for small talk, so stop giving me grief.'

Fox fidgeted uneasily and stared across at them. 'What's on your mind, Jack?'

Mason pulled an e-fit image out of an inside pocket and slid it across the desk towards him. The room felt cold, as if the air-conditioning had been switched on full blast.

'Recognise this young woman?' Mason asked.

'More photographs.' Fox sniggered. 'You should have a been a photographer, Jack.'

'Just answer my question.'

Fox shook his head. 'Nope, who is she?'

'Her name's Angelica, and she's Eastern European.'

'What's she been up to?'

'We're keen to talk to her about a recent murder that took place in Newcastle.'

'Sounds about right,' said Fox, all white teeth and insincerity. 'I wouldn't trust these foreigners as far as I could throw them. What is it with these people?'

'Never mind the bullshit,' Mason interrupted, 'where can she be found?'

Fox went quiet for a moment, thinking.

'She probably arrived here through the back door.'

'Meaning?'

'Human trafficking in Europe is rife with these people, and there's an awful lot of money changing hands. Young women are a bonus as they're much easier commodities to shift.'

'Sounds a bit like the second-hand car market,' Mason smugly replied.

'Funny.'

Mason pointed a finger at Fox. 'Someone in your organisation must know who she is?'

'Maybe they do, but it ain't me.'

'Who then?'

Mason eyed up the two bouncers who had suddenly appeared in the doorway. One was small and chubby, the other taller and fair. Maybe they carried weapons in their pockets, or perhaps they didn't. Either way, neither of them looked the friendly type.

'You need to open up your mind,' said Fox, suddenly brimming with confidence. 'Smugglers are paid good money to get these illegals across our borders; it's a lucrative business. Once here, that's where the financial transaction ends.' Fox went quiet for a moment. 'If it's trafficking this young woman is involved in, that's a different ball game, of course.'

'What's trafficking got to do with this?'

Fox explained. 'Trafficking means bringing these illegals into an on-going situation, and that's when a lot of women get forced into prostitution.'

'You're well informed.' Mason smiled.

Fox fell silent for a moment. 'Not really. It's just what I've read in the papers.'

'That's a new one, Tony. I didn't know you could read.'

'I was always good at school, Jack. That's what made me what I am today.'

It was Mason's turn to laugh. 'What, a second-rate nightclub owner who is about to be shut down?'

'There's no smoke without fire,' Fox replied sharply.

Mason's dark expression said it all. 'So, you think this woman is here illegally?'

'I didn't say that.' Fox made a grinding noise with his teeth, as if bored by it all. 'I was merely making a point. Anyway, how do you know her real name is Angelica?'

'We don't, but that's what she calls herself.'

Fox glowered back. 'These Eastern Europeans are difficult people to deal with, and I try to steer well clear of them. They slip across our borders like the March winds, and nobody can put a stop to it. Not even the politicians.'

'Let's not even go there.' Mason shrugged. 'Just give me a name.'

'You know me, Jack. If I could, I would. But I swear on my mother's life I've never seen this woman before.'

'This is beginning to sound like the last favour I asked you to do for me.'

Fox's head dropped. 'Nobody's heard hide nor hair of the person who killed those two young men you were asking after. Even Wiseman's crew are none the wiser.'

'What about your friends on the east side?'

Fox shot him a nasty look. 'It's difficult these days, as nobody's willing to talk.'

'What about Frank Wiseman, could he be involved?'

'How the hell would I know. The last I heard, he was still serving time in Durham prison.'

Their eyes met.

'One thing's for sure,' Mason said with a grin, 'Wiseman isn't happy about this recent takeover bid you and your cronies are plotting.'

'Who told you that shit?'

Mason tapped the desk with an index finger. 'There could be a way out of this for you.'

'Oh, and what might that be?'

'What if you were to talk to your Eastern European counterparts, find out what they know about this Angelica woman. You never know, I might even turn a blind eye to closing you down.'

Fox stood to his feet before he spoke. He was a towering man – head and shoulders above Jack Mason. 'You're talking shit again?'

'Don't piss me about, Tony. We know one of the victims regularly visited your club, as we have it on camera.'

Fox took in a long intake of air and tried to recover his composure. 'These Eastern Europeans won't take too kindly to me asking them questions about this Angelica woman. . . especially if she's one of their own.'

'Yeah, but my neck's not on the line here.'

'Hold on!' said Fox. 'Who said I would talk to these people?'

'Your face tells me otherwise.'

'It's like that, is it?'

'Afraid so.' Mason smiled. 'You look nervous, Tony. Do these foreigners frighten you?'

Fox laughed. 'Give me a fucking break; it's time you went to Specsavers, Jack.'

'There's nothing wrong with *my* eyesight, or my sense of smell,' Mason replied.

'What the hell's smell got to do with it?'

Mason wrinkled his nose. 'Do you know what, I could have sworn I smelt cannabis the minute I stepped into the building.'

Fox moved to protest, but quickly thought the better of it.

'We need to come to some sort of arrangement, Jack?'

Mason glowered at him. 'Who mentioned anything about arrangements?'

'Nobody did, but I just thought I'd mention it, that's all.' Fox looked at him anxiously and swore through gritted teeth. 'What's going on?'

'Murder, and one of the victims was caught on camera frequenting your club. All we need is a contact name, and we'll go easy on the accelerator pedal.'

'And in return?'

'I'll see to it you stay open.'

'I need assurances. Even you should know that.'

Mason's stupid grin broadened. 'You have my word, Tony.'

Fox picked up the e-fit image and studied it again. The gangster's confidence had gone, and he was struggling to form his words. 'Like I say, these people are nasty bastards to deal with.'

'I'm sure you will cope.'

The minders now standing in the doorway looked across at them perturbed. One wrong word and things could turn ugly.

Mason swung sharply to face Fox. 'You have three days to get me the information I'm looking for.'

'You're joking!'

'After that, I'll be round with a dozen of my best men and they know how to switch your lights off.'

Fox glared at them, annoyed. 'Let's hope Angelica is her real name. If it's not, then we're all in the shit.'

As they made their way back across the dance floor, Mason felt a deepening sense of unease. Heavily outnumbered, they still had a long flight of stairs to climb and it was an awful long way to the top from where he was standing. Even though a deal had been struck, Fox couldn't be trusted, and this place was no longer safe anymore.

Chapter
Twenty-Five

It had rained non-stop throughout the night, and the sky over Newcastle hung as a solid grey curtain. Now it was bouncing off the roof of his Rover P4 100 as Carlisle slid from the driver's seat and made a dash towards the stone-brick building opposite. Earlier, Tom Hedley had won him over with his encyclopaedic knowledge of forensic methodology. Latent fingerprints found at two of the crime scenes were considered a perfect match. It was a huge development, enough to send a ripple of excitement amongst the senior backroom staff. For the moment, at least.

The task force had assembled at five-thirty that morning, and everywhere was crawling with police. Close to the waste ground where John Lawrence's body had been found, CCTV footage had revealed a slightly built man passing a local corner shop in the early hours of the morning. Wearing black tracksuit bottoms, a hoody, and white Nike trainers on his feet, the suspect was seen dragging a large suitcase behind him. It was the breakthrough they'd been looking for, opening a whole raft of new leads.

He checked his watch. Nine-thirty, and there was still ample time to persuade local magistrates to sign a few more search warrants. It was Friday, so there could be possible delays. Beyond the yellow barrier tape marked: CRIME SCENE DO NOT CROSS, Carlisle spotted the slightly built figure of Peter Davenport. Soaked to the skin, the rain bouncing off the brim of his cap, the SOC photographer seemed oblivious to the appalling weather conditions surrounding him. Further afield, he caught a glimpse of a team of forensic officers. Fully suited up, they were crawling on hands and knees in an extended line and desperately searching for clues. It was painstaking work, but all too often a fingertip search would throw up all kinds of new leads. Not today it wouldn't. What little evidence there was to be had was lost in a river of mud.

'If it's DCI Mason you're looking for,' the PCSO announced, 'he's over by the old lorry park.'

'And where might that be?' Carlisle asked.

'It's at the rear of the building, sir.'

Parked close to the outer perimeter fence, the mobile Incident Command Unit was soon spotted by Carlisle. All the interior lights were on, and a set of mud spattered steps had been propped up against the side door. Bracing himself against the elements, the private investigator tried to get a fix on his bearings. Close to a series of loading bays, several police vehicles were parked. Beyond that, a tall metal girder structure contoured the skyline. It reminded him of a piece of modern artwork he'd once seen in a local art exhibition. Not that he was an art lover. He wasn't. Looking round, he saw that many of the surrounding buildings had fallen into disrepair. Some of them health and safety hazards, others not. Now a ghost of its past, this once thriving chemical plant was little more than a bomb site.

'Nothing yet,' Mason announced, staring down at him from inside the command vehicle.

'Why here?'

'This is where the killer may have parked his vehicle that night. The date and time display on the security CCTV footage confirms he passed Bean Street at precisely 2.32 am.'

'At that time of the morning, anyone seen dragging a suitcase around the streets would surely have raised suspicion.'

'Not really.' Mason shrugged.

'And why not?'

'People tend to take off for airports that time of day. What with a three-hour security check-in, it's not uncommon nowadays.'

'No. I suppose not.'

Mason said nothing.

'How do we know it was the killer's vehicle?' Carlisle asked.

Mason stared at him, perplexed. 'We don't, but there's no public transport running that time of night and a taxi would have been out of the question – far too risky.'

'He could be local.'

'Possible, but why dump a body on your own doorstep?'

Carlisle thought a moment. 'He's not that selective.'

This case had obviously got under Mason's skin, as he seemed to have an answer for everything. He was exhaling heavily and a lot of it from sheer frustration. With four murders to contemplate, there was little wonder he was struggling to come to terms with it all. People wanted facts, but until you'd obtained them you played around with theories. The press wasn't helping either. *The Suitcase Man,* as he was now better known as, had sure drummed up a lot of public interest.

Carlisle peered at the large map pinned to the command vehicle wall. Why this estate, and why here? He questioned. Was this a random selection, or was this all part of the killer's plans? He tried to look at the bigger picture – think things through logically. If the killer was using a Transit van to transport his victims' bodies around in, it meant the kill zone could be miles from the drop zone. It wasn't easy, and they would need to think outside of the box on this one. The problem was the killer had undeniably gained the upper hand, which made matters more difficult.

As the door swung open, they were joined by DS Holt.

'Just the man,' said Mason.

'You talking to me, boss?'

'Who else?' Mason smiled. 'I need you to establish whether the killer lives in the area. Take a few men with you and do nothing else. While you're at it, get hold of as many eye witness accounts as you can. Find out who was drinking in any of the local bars that night, and who hung around after closing time.'

'What are we looking for?'

'You need to start here and work your way back towards this area.' Mason pointed to a small section of the map where John Lawrence's body had been found. 'Ask around, find out who was still up at home that time of night. Had they heard or seen anything suspicious? We know the killer was last seen around here at 2.30 am, so where did he go after the pubs had closed?'

Holt touched his forehead in an imaginary salute and disappeared out of the door. It had barely closed behind him when DC Manley appeared on the scene. Notebook in hand, rain dripping off the detective's long parka coat, Manley looked a forlorn figure.

'Any luck?' Mason asked.

The detective constable stood in silence for a moment. 'I think he may have left us a clue, boss.'

Mason eyed him with suspicion. 'Like what?'

'A set of number plates were nicked from a local resident's Transit van.'

'When was this?'

'Late Thursday night. Shortly after ten o'clock.'

'Both plates?'

'Yeah, front and rear apparently.'

'Good work.' Mason grinned.

Carlisle shuddered inwardly, sensing the vulgarity. If this was the killer's doing, he was obviously covering his tracks. He thought about it, but not for long. If the number plates had been stolen from the north side of the estate, it meant he'd taken a different route back to his vehicle that night.

Inside the tiny command unit, the air felt oppressive. He didn't know why, but Carlisle suddenly felt a close affinity with the killer. How situations can quickly change, he thought. One minute you were wallowing around in a sea of mud, the next all hell was let loose.

Manley allowed himself a brief, wry smile and wiped the rain droplets from his face. 'Should we broaden our search, boss?'

'No, Harry. Let's stick with the plan.' Mason made a little sweeping hand gesture. 'You need to release the stolen plate details to the media. . . first thing tomorrow morning. In the meantime, I'll get Road Traffic to set up a few discreet road checks using ANPR. If it is him, and there's no reason to believe otherwise, he can't be far away.'

Manley peered up at the wall map, his wet finger circling a large area of ground. 'How much of the estate should we cover?'

'Let me see.'

Mason reached over and pulled out a couple of well-thumbed images from one of the case files and placed them on the table in front of him. Next, he consulted the wall map. 'CCTV footage confirms a forty-minute gap from the time the suspect passed the corner shop to the time this person came into view.' He pointed to an image on the table. 'Find out who this man is, and you should find the answers you are looking for.'

'There's one other thing, boss. The streets would have been relatively quiet that time of the morning, don't you think?'

'What if were dealing with a shift worker here?'

Manley smacked his forehead with the flat of his hand. 'Do you know what, I'd never given it much thought.'

'Someone out there must know something, surely. Ask around – talk to local shop keepers, find out if they saw or heard anything.'

'Local gossip should throw up a few interesting stories, boss.'

Mason stuck his hands deep into his trouser pockets and glanced up at the timeline. Not a good sign, Carlisle thought. For days now, he'd wrestled with the notion the DCI had finally lost the plot, and too much attention had been paid to Fat Sam's nightclub and Tony Fox. It was this and the trivial things that worried him most, like the lack of attention to the killer's geographical movements. They were looking in all the wrong places, and needlessly covering old ground.

Carlisle stood for a moment, thinking. A part of him hoped that Jack Mason would finally come to his senses, but there was little chance of that ever happening. Compromise would be the last thing on the Detective Chief Inspector's mind. Short tempered and unpredictable, Mason was more likely to fly off the handle than anything. No, he thought. They needed a plan, but right now he couldn't think of one.

The rain had eased considerably when Carlisle finally stepped out from the mobile Incident Command Unit. Squinting left, he noticed one of the forensic team was carrying a transparent plastic evidence bag in his hand. It may not be much, but it didn't take much. If there was a breakthrough to be had, it would come from the most unlikely of sources. Then he remembered. The suitcases the killer had used had been bought from a local charity shop in Low Fell by a young woman who paid for them with cash. Who was she, and what did she look like?

It was time to find out.

Chapter Twenty-Six

The Acting Superintendent had thought better of seeking the general public's assistance over the stolen Transit van's number plates. She'd been well advised. If this was the killer's doing, the more control the police had over the proceedings the greater chance they had of catching him. There was no easy solution to this, and with dozens of roadside checks now in place, Gateshead Police Station had never been as busy in a long time.

Five miles south, it wasn't the best of driving conditions at ten o'clock that morning. After pulling over another unsuspecting van driver, little did Constable Clarke realise what he was letting himself in for. Following the temporary line of cones, he watched as a fellow officer re-directed the van driver towards a designated holding area. In what had been a well-run operation, two lanes of the A1(M) motorway had been closed off to all north-bound traffic. With long tailbacks building up, tempers were fraying as hundreds of commercial vehicles were held up in the queue.

Clipboard in hand, Constable Clarke felt an air of authority as he approached the latest arrival. A cursory check of the tyres, and he tapped on the driver's side window with the end of his pen. The solution to solving some crimes often lay in a person's demeanour. If they reacted positively towards you, it usually meant they were genuine. If not, it meant they had something to hide. It was all about attitude, and Constable Clarke could tell within the first five seconds of questioning someone what type of person he was dealing with.

He waited for the driver's electric window to wind down before firing off that all important first question. 'Is this your vehicle, sir?'

'No, it belongs to a friend,' the van driver said in broken English.

'Mind telling me his name?'

'Alex.'

Pen poised, the constable gave him a withering look. 'Alex who?'

'I don't know his other name. He's a friend of a friend.'

'I see—'

Suspicions aroused, the constable moved round to the front of the vehicle and took down the registration details. He was in no hurry. On first impressions, the driver seemed a genuine sort of guy. Hard working like him. As the offside cab door swung open and the occupant jumped onto the hard tarmac in front of him, Clarke smiled. He wasn't a tall man, five-ten, with a round rubbery face, sticky out ears and an unruly mop of black hair. His T-shirt was torn, and his trousers in need of a wash. Officially, this was a murder enquiry and nothing to do with vehicle checks. This time felt different, though, as the Transit van had come up on the Automatic Number Plate Recognition system as stolen.

'Mind telling me the registration number of your vehicle?' the constable enquired.

'I can't remember it.'

'I take it that's a *no, sir.*'

The van driver remained tight lipped.

Clarke stepped back a pace and signalled for assistance. Seconds later, blue spinner-lights flashing, a marked patrol car pulled up in front of them. Wearing a Hi-Vis jacket and a no-nonsense expression on his face, the sergeant in charge squeezed his portly frame out from the front passenger seat of the vehicle and ambled towards them.

'Morning,' the sergeant said by way of introduction. 'Mind handing me the keys to your vehicle, sir?'

Taken aback, the van driver reached into his trouser pocket and dutifully obliged. His English wasn't good, but he understood the sergeant's demands perfectly.

'What's going on?' the van driver asked. 'Why are you people questioning everyone?'

'This will only take a few minutes, sir.'

The arrival of a second marked police vehicle only added to the confusion. Poking his head out of the passenger window, the officer inside gestured towards the stationary Transit van. 'You guys in need of any assistance?'

'No thanks,' the sergeant replied. 'Everything's under control.'

Bracing himself, Constable Clarke scratched the side of his head with his pen. 'We best check the VIN, Sarge.'

As the bonnet catch sprung open, the sergeant dutifully thrust his head inside the engine block. Sometimes it was better to say nothing, keep an open mind about these things. But there was something odd about the van driver's demeanour, and Clarke couldn't put his finger on it.

'Guess what?' the sergeant suddenly announced.

'What is it, Sarge?'

'The VIN doesn't match.'

Bracing himself, the constable instinctively grabbed hold of the van driver's arm. He'd been down this avenue before, many times. Just when you least expected it, the suspect would do a runner. Not today he wouldn't; Clarke had everything under control.

'Do you carry any form of identification with you?'

'Not with me, I don't.'

'A log book, vehicle insurance details... a passport perhaps?'

'No.'

Clearly the focus of attention, there was a new buzz of excitement in the air. There were two trains of thought here. One, the suspect spoke broken English. The other, he was driving on false number plates. Either way they were about to slap a fixed penalty fine on him, or better still, arrest him on suspicion of murder.

The arrival of a Mercedes-Benz Sprinter van only added more commotion to the proceedings. Clarke recognised the driver, along with another Road Policing Officer sitting alongside him. He blew a sigh of relief and glanced at his watch.

'Mind telling me what's in the back of your vehicle?' the sergeant asked.

The moment the van's rear doors flew open, a crowd of police officers gathered around.

'What is it with you people... what are you looking for?' the bemused van driver asked.

'This won't take a minute, sir. I can assure you of that.'

'So why search my van? I have nothing to hide.'

'Let me be the judge of that.'

The words had barely left the sergeant's lips, before he'd clambered into the back of the van and started rummaging around. Piled high with builders' equipment, everything seemed in order.

Then the sound of surprise could be heard.

'Well I'll be damned,' the sergeant muttered aloud. 'Look what we have here.'

'What is it, Sarge?'

'It's a chain saw.'

Constable Clarke reached for his handcuffs, as a second officer grabbed hold of the suspect's other arm. What had started as a routine road check, was now a full-blown murder inquiry.

The sergeant's smile broadened. 'Mind telling me who the chain saw belongs to?'

'I didn't even know it was there.'

'If it's not yours, then whose is it?'

The driver looked at him confused. 'Like I've already explained to you people, I'm delivering the van to a friend.'

'Not now, you're not,' Constable Clarke announced. 'This van was reportedly stolen two weeks ago.'

Clarke watched as the sergeant jumped out from the back of the Transit van and dusted himself down. Now in official mode, he cautioned the suspect on suspicion of murder then led him towards the waiting Mercedes-Benz Sprinter van. As another young officer appeared on the scene carrying a fresh roll of police tape, they began cordoning the area off. Soon the Scientific Support Unit would arrive, and Constable Clarke's part of the operation would be over.

'Excellent work,' the sergeant announced.

'Thanks, Sarge.'

'No doubt you'll have plenty to report.'

'Yes, Sarge.'

The sergeant nodded. 'Good, I'll catch up with you back at the station.'

Clipboard in hand, Clarke tipped his peaked cap in salute and returned to guarding the Transit van. The next twenty-four hours would be crucial if they were going to make the charges stick. Some talked, but most hardened criminals refused to cooperate on the grounds they might implicate themselves. Once their solicitors were involved that would be an entirely different matter, of course. It was all about timing and breaking down the prisoner's will to put up a fight.

Clarke watched as the prisoner cage doors slammed shut and the sergeant banged on the Mercedes-Benz Sprinter's roof. Seconds later, it edged forward a few yards, before heading off in the direction of Gateshead Police Station.

Well I'll be damned, Constable Clarke chuckled to himself. Incidents such as this seldom happened on Road Traffic, and never on his shift. Just when he thought it was all a waste of time, everything had clicked into place.

Chapter Twenty-Seven

After another mad hour spent haring around the living room, Benjamin was fast asleep on top of the kitchen units. The young kitten had certainly led him a merry dance these past few hours, and Carlisle had all but given up on him. Nothing was sacred anymore. Everything he owned was fair game. They'd been getting along fine together until now, but things had changed for the worse. Having clawed his way into the back of his favourite sofa bed, the kitten's antics meant Carlisle was at his wits end. Loath to admit it, he should never have listened to Jane Collins in the first place. He'd been conned – or at least he thought he had – by a business partner who simply adored cats. Why hadn't he gone with his instincts and done things differently? Too late now, he thought, they should have taken Benjamin to the local cat rescue centre and ended it there and then. He hadn't, and now he was left to pick up the pieces – and what was left of his sofa bed.

By the time he'd finished his breakfast cereals, it was starting to get light. Still unable to think of a clear-cut motive as to why the killer was dismembering only his male victims, he was having to second guess. What made the killer tick? And why was he so angry over this group of young men? It was time to regroup and return to basics.

Thinking out loud, Carlisle slotted the memory stick into the USB port of his laptop and waited for the autopsy images to appear on the screen. At a glance, the torso looked bloated, the flesh mottled brown and green. Zooming in, he studied the puncture marks – mainly around the left sternal. Patterns. He was looking for patterns. Something to bring them ever closer. The next set of images he came to, revealed an open black suitcase and close-up images of the lid and interior lining. It wasn't an expensive suitcase, and the locks were nothing flash either. He knew from his own investigations that a young woman had purchased them from a local charity shop in Low Fell, but that was all. Described as late teens, with long brown hair tied back – it wasn't an awful lot to go on. Remember the golden rule, he thought to himself: never jump to conclusions.

Carlisle cupped his hands to his face and tried to think as the killer did. Once he'd cut the body up into manageable chunks, he would need a freezer to store them in. It had to be big, large enough to hold at least two of his victims' bodies at any one given time. Anything smaller wouldn't work. Disposal would come later, when things had quietened down a tad. It was all about timing, and the killer had a good understanding of that.

No, he thought. These weren't spontaneous killings; these crimes were too well organised. Mixing the body parts up was all part of the killer's plan – a means of keeping the police guessing whilst maintaining control over everything else. And, if he was perfectly honest, the suspect needn't operate within the city of Newcastle.

Now back in the real world, Carlisle closed the lid of his laptop computer and rubbed his tired eyes. There was a great satisfaction to be had from solving some crimes, but this one was doing his head in. Had they overlooked something? A small piece of vital evidence perhaps. He looked at his notes and questioned why the killer had made such a hash of getting rid of John Lawrence's body. Had he been disturbed at some point?

Carlisle parked that idea to one side for a moment and thought about the latest drop zone. He'd missed out on an awful lot of information lately, and there were a million things to catch up on. Annoyed at the fact that Angelica still hadn't contacted him over the weekend, had now left him with a lot of explaining to do. He wasn't alone, of course. Jack Mason's arrangements with Tony Fox had also fallen on deaf ears. It had now been four days since their last visit to Fat Sam's nightclub, and still Fox hadn't got back to them. Whoever Angelica was, she sure was a hard nut to crack. Deep down Carlisle felt sorry for her, especially if she'd been forced into slave prostitution. All the signs were there. Her reluctance to go to the police, and her knowledge of how the human trafficking system worked.

Frustrated, Carlisle gazed at the street map again not wanting to lose heart. The question often asked of him was how do serial killers select their victims? Most were territorial predators who liked to work within their comfort zones. This case was chillingly different, though, as the killer was using large chunks of the local landscape to scope out his potential targets. He was picking his victims up in bars before taking them to a place of execution. Not only were his selection criteria consistent, he was gaining these people's trust with ease. He knew from experience that visionary serial killers generally suffered some form of psychosis where their delusions and hallucinations commanded them to kill, but wasn't this the case?

His problem was, he'd changed his mind so many times these past few weeks that he was beginning to doubt his own judgement. And yet there was a distinct pattern to the killer's modus operandi, and his choice of victims. The more he thought about it, the more confused he became. Yes, there was an awful lot of pent up anger inside the killer, but what was he trying to achieve?

His phone rang, and Jack Mason's number popped up on the screen. It was time to jump into action, it seemed.

★★★

The minute Carlisle stepped into Jack Mason's office, the smell of black coffee hit him. Sat at his desk, chair tilted back and both feet propped up on a pile of box files, the Detective Chief Inspector was deep in conversation over the telephone. As Carlisle waited for him to finish, Mason suddenly sat bolt upright.

'That was the Acting Superintendent I was speaking to, and she's not a happy camper.'

'What's her problem now?'

'She wants an update on the latest developments, and why we're no further forward in catching this monster.' Mason stared at him. 'What do you make of that?'

Carlisle was having to think on his feet. Ever since his divorce settlement, Mason had turned into a bit of an arsehole lately. Drinking heavily, rumours were rife he'd hooked up with another married woman. How much was true he had no idea, but the last time that had happened Mason had ended up in all kinds of trouble.

'What about this Polish guy picked out during yesterday's roadside checks? Are you any further on in making an arrest?' Carlisle asked.

'He's not the killer, if that's what you're thinking, but we've charged him with theft of a vehicle and driving without insurance.'

'That's disappointing; I thought he may have been connected.'

'You're beginning to sound like the Acting Superintendent. . . full of wind and piss!'

'Hang on a minute—'

Mason glanced at the pile of paperwork cluttering his desk and sighed. Still seething with anger from his run-in with the Acting Superintendent, he folded his arms and slouched back in his seat. 'There must be a way of getting to the killer, surely?'

'It's not that simple, Jack.'

'This geographic profiling research you recently carried out – how reliable is it?'

'We've used it before.'

'I know, but what does it tell us this time?'

'Quite a lot actually,' Carlisle insisted.

'Like what?'

'I've spent days going back over witness statements and mapping out possible sightings of the suspect's movements.' Carlisle blew into his coffee and tried to avoid confrontation. 'After adding in the kill zones, I applied some basic statistical concepts to the formula. Mean, standard deviation, that sort of thing.'

'This all sounds very complicated,' Mason huffed.

'Not really.'

'So, what's the bottom line?'

Carlisle put his mug down. 'As you well know, mapping isn't an exact science. That said, it's becoming increasingly more sophisticated with things such as global positioning systems, digital photography, and the likes of videography. What my latest analysis has shown is there are two areas he's most likely to strike again in. One comes out at forty per cent. The other at ninety-two.'

'Yes, yes,' Mason said impatiently. 'Just give me a location.'

The room fell silent for a moment.

'In all probability, his next strike will be within a five-mile radius of Newcastle's city centre.'

'So, he *is* local!'

'I'm not sure about that.'

Mason's disappoint showed. 'What, you think he's slipping under the radar from another location?'

'It's possible, and we know he doesn't have a local accent.'

'I'm surprised we haven't caught up with him during these recent roadside checks.'

'He's obviously avoiding them, Jack.'

Mason thought a moment, then sighed. 'This Angelica woman is taking up far too much of your valuable time. If you want my—'

Carlisle's mobile phone suddenly buzzed, and he checked the display. Number withheld.

'Hello, is that you, Angelica?'

Mason stared up at him from behind his desk and mouthed the words – '*Speak of the devil.*'

'Okay,' Carlisle whispered. 'I'll meet you there.'

Mason's glare hardened. Although he was still the man in charge of a murder investigation, Carlisle wasn't giving in that easily. No doubt the backroom boys would be trying to get a trace on her call, and he tried to keep her engaged.

His phone suddenly went dead.

'I take it she wants to meet up with you?'

Carlisle pocketed his phone. 'She claims to have seen the killer again.'

'You know my views on this woman.'

'What about Tony Fox – have you heard anything more from him lately?' he said, quickly changing the subject.

'No, and I'm not expecting to either.' Mason put a pencil against his lips and thought for a moment. 'What are your real interests in this Eastern European woman?'

A fresh pot of coffee arrived, brought in on a tray by one of the canteen ladies. A short woman, dressed in a summery frock and loafers on her feet. She smiled and pushed a small plate of cream biscuits under Mason's nose.

'Will that be all?' she asked.

'Yes, Marg. That'll do fine, thank you.'

The moment the door closed behind her, Carlisle picked up on their conversation again.

'I've been thinking about these Eastern European gangs. If Angelica is caught up in a human trafficking ring, she could be in an awful lot of trouble.'

'That's strictly a police matter and has sod-all to do with criminal profiling.'

Carlisle remained tight lipped.

'I know when I'm right.' Mason shot him a warning glance. 'Stay clear of her and let the police deal with those matters.'

'But she claims to have seen the killer again – dragging a suitcase through the streets of Byker this time.'

Mason huffed. 'We've been over this ground before.'

'Well that's who she claims she saw.' Carlisle took a sip of his coffee, thinking. 'Hold on a minute, I thought we'd withheld that kind of information from the press.'

'Stop talking in riddles, what kind of information is this?'

'The suitcase the killer delivered John Lawrence's body in.'

Mason shifted his weight. 'We did. Why?'

'Then how could she have known it was *GREEN*?'

Mason's jaw dropped.

Chapter
Twenty-Eight

A compromise had been reached, and Jack Mason's undercover surveillance team had been called off. Carlisle's only remit, if he could call it that, was to unlock this woman's dark secrets and get the hell out of there. If police backup was required during his meeting with Angelica, then a small group of specially trained officers were on hand. Eastern European gangs were notoriously dangerous people to deal with; it's what drove the crime figures up, according to Jack Mason. Sudden deaths and people going missing were all too common place nowadays.

Despite Jack Mason's last-minute interventions, the rush hour traffic had gone when Carlisle drove into Bensham that evening. Turning right at the bottom of a steep bank, he pulled up in front of an old nineteenth century stone building and switched off the car's engine. Hands gripping the steering wheel, the tension inside him mounting, he tried to steady himself. This area was no longer considered safe and was full of troublemakers according to DS Holt.

At the back of the building he found a door. He placed his shoulder against it and gave it a gentle shove. It opened.

'Is anyone there?' he called out.

Silence.

Reaching the end of a long narrow corridor his wind-up torch went dead. Eyes straining through darkness, he frantically wound it up again. It was pitch black inside, humid, and all the windows had been boarded up. Why anyone would want to meet him here beggared belief. Still no sign of Angelica showing, his mouth felt dry and the lump at the back of his throat threatened to choke him.

Given the choice, he would have preferred backup. Spent needles everywhere, a strong smell of urine, this wasn't a safe environment to hang around in. As his mind began to drift, he searched for signs of life.

The room was large and spacious, with cathedral ceilings and graffiti filled walls. Existence in the gutter could be tough, it seemed, and full of unpleasant things.

As the last rays of daylight played through a gap in one of the window panels, he made his way into the next room. Not the best place to be caught up in, he figured, the denizens who hung around here were full of hopelessness and despair. No room had been left untouched, each the same as the last. Floorboards ripped up, copper piping torn away, and doors used as makeshift drug mixing tables. He often wondered how owners could allow such terrible things to happen to their properties, and why they didn't get involved. If this building was anything to go by, then no wonder drugs had a bad reputation.

Then he heard footsteps from another part of the building.

'Who's there?' he shouted.

Uncertainty gripped him.

'It's me, Mr Carlisle,' a familiar voice called out.

'Are you alone?'

'I should be asking you that question.'

At last, he sighed.

Now picked out in his torch light, Angelica looked the epitome of innocence. But there was a darker side, unexplained, that he craved to get to the bottom of.

'What is it you wish to talk to me about?'

'I bumped into that man again.'

'Which man was this?'

'The same one I saw in Forth Street.'

'What about him?'

Angelica clung to the shadows. 'He was in Byker this time and getting out of the back of a Transit van. He had another suitcase with him. This one was green.'

'What's unusual about that?' Carlisle said, acting dumbly.

'The last time I saw him he was dragging a suitcase out of his car, remember?'

'Yes, and the police found a body inside that one.'

'Well then. . .'

'You seem to know an awful lot for someone who professes to know so little.'

Angelica stared at him, her eyes full of suspicion. 'What are you inferring?'

'Millions of people drag suitcases round towns and cities every day, so how can you be sure this was the same person?'

'It was him all right. Same height, same top, and the same Nike trainers on his feet.'

'What colour trainers?'

She frowned. 'They were white.'

Carlisle's heart sank, and he sensed uncertainty. 'What makes you think there was a body inside the suitcase this time?'

'I never mentioned anything about a body.'

'But you inferred there was a body inside. If not, then why did you mention it?'

She managed a smile, but it did not reach her eyes.

'What makes you think I can trust you?' Carlisle asked.

'If you don't, then why did you come here this evening?'

Clever answer, he thought.

'The last time we met, you told me you were working as a prostitute in Forth Street. You saw this man that night, and he was sitting alone in his car. You approached him, and he told you to go away. If not, he would fetch the police to you. You were scared, so you hid in the shadows to see what he was up to. Minutes later he opened the boot of his car and struggled to lift a large blue suitcase from it. He wasn't a tall man, you said, but he somehow managed to drag it into the storage company.'

'Why are you telling me all of this?'

Carlisle moved closer. 'The problem is, there are no prostitutes working in Forth Street anymore. They were moved on years ago. What's more, there is no CCTV evidence to support your story of a car being parked anywhere near where you said it was that night.'

'But I am a prostitute,' she argued. 'And I *was* working in Forth Street.'

Wait a minute, Carlisle thought. Hadn't she told him it was dark that night and she never saw the suspect's face?

'What is it you're hiding from me, Angelica?'

'I did see this man in Byker again, and he was dragging a large suitcase behind him. It was GREEN!' she insisted.

Carlisle, clearly confused, fell silent for a moment. Hadn't Tom Hedley confirmed that the same matching fibres had been found at all three crime scenes?

'Tell me,' he said. 'Is Angelica your real name, or is that made up too?'

'Why would I lie to you?'

'I'm a private investigator, remember.'

'Well then!'

Carlisle detected a slight movement in the corner of her eye and knew then she was lying. 'Are you in some sort of trouble with the police?'

'What makes you say that?'

'If not, why are you refusing to talk to them?'

'That's none of your business, Mr Carlisle.'

'And it's not a clever answer, Angelica.'

'In my country, we do things very differently.'

'But you're not in your country now, you're in England.'

She'd lied to him about so many things that he'd lost all track of the truth. And yet her description of the clothes the suspect wore was unnervingly accurate. Same hoodie, same colour shoes, and the same method of transporting his victims' bodies around. Then there was the question of the green suitcase – how could she have possibly known that?

Carlisle watched as she placed her hand on the door stanchion. He could not be sure, but she may have applied enough contact pressure to obtain a latent palm print from it.

He made a mental note of it.

'I'm sorry for asking so many awkward questions,' Carlisle said almost apologetically, 'but I'm confused.'

'Confused. . . confused about what?'

'This man you recently saw in Byker, what did he look like?'

'He wasn't a tall man, about your height. He—'

Plunged into sudden darkness, Carlisle frantically cranked the windup torch handle again. It didn't take long, but in those precious few seconds she'd vanished without trace.

He checked the building. Inside and out.

Nothing!

Then it dawned on him.

★★★

The watchers were less than one hundred metres away. Their orders, crude as they were, to assist the criminal profiler if trouble broke out. Stuck in the back of an undercover police van on Jack Mason's instructions wasn't a clever idea. It was cramped inside, uncomfortable, and there were far too many people moving about. As the officer lifted the binoculars to his face, he took in a long intake of air. Parked up outside the old retirement home was a stationary Rover P4 100. It belonged to the profiler. He knew that much – they'd been following it for days. Then out of the corner of his eye he caught a flurry of activity at the rear of the premises and adjusted the binocular focusing ring. Three kids kicking a football against the outer perimeter security fence.

Officer two smiled. 'Jumpy tonight are we, George?'

'No, just bored out of my mind.'

'Relax. It's just a bit of harmless fun.'

'Yeah, a bunch of fucking toe-rag kids more like.'

This neck of the woods was a dangerous place to carry out undercover surveillance, that went without question. House burglaries were commonplace, drug crime prolific, and if you needed a car you stole one.

He checked his watch. 'Time check 9.20 pm,' he announced.

'Roger that,' officer two confirmed, as he wrote it down in the log.

Fifty metres away, he watched as a young woman appeared pushing a buggy with a small child inside. She was young, far too young to be a mother, he thought. Had that been his daughter out walking the streets at night, he would have probably given her a good talking to.

Seconds later he contacted control and the operator re-routed his call to a cell-phone in Forest Hall. Ten miles north he could hear Jack Mason's phone ringing out, and impatiently waited for a connection.

The line suddenly clicked.

'Jack Mason—'

Officer one could clearly hear laughter in the background and guessed then his contact was in a pub drinking. Lucky bastard, he thought, what he wouldn't give for a pint. Reporting his findings as ongoing, he gave a brief overview of the events so far.

Message gratefully received, the officer's phone went dead.

Head stooped slightly forward, he lifted the binoculars up to his eyes and zoomed in. Thirty metres away, he could just make out the criminal profiler as he appeared from the side of the building. Alone, and still no sign of the Eastern European woman showing, the officer yawned. Then, as he swung his binoculars back towards the young woman pushing the buggy, the penny suddenly dropped.

'That's her,' he screamed.

'Shit,' officer two cursed.

Seconds later, she'd disappeared into the night.

Chapter Twenty-Nine

Including David Carlisle, there were over forty police officers present when Jack Mason entered MR-1 that Wednesday morning. Glancing up, he instructed them to be seated before taking up a central position in front of a large cork board. Covered with post-its, maps, photographs, newspaper cuttings, and all linked together with pieces of red string, it was difficult to grasp the full picture.

Mason sounded subdued. 'Late yesterday evening a successful sting operation was carried out at a disused retirement home in Byker, where contact was made with this young woman.' Mason pointed to an e-fit image pinned to the top left-hand corner of the cork board. 'Eastern European, approximately eighteen years old, she goes under the pseudonym Angelica. After extensive checks with Immigration Control, we have reason to believe she may have connections to human trafficking gangs operating out of Holland.'

No one spoke.

Mason turned to Tom Hedley. 'What's the latest on fingerprints, Tom?'

The senior forensic scientist ran his fingers through unkempt hair and pushed back in his seat. He had an owl shaped face, strong jawline, thick bushy eyebrows, and brown eyes. Quiet by nature, Hedley was the easiest of persons to get along with.

'Latent fingerprints lifted from yesterday's crime scene have so far drawn a blank. If Angelica *is* an illegal entry, she'll not be picked up on our database.'

'What about Interpol?' Mason asked.

'The same applies. Unless she's committed a criminal offence in another European country, it's unlikely she'll be on record.'

'Mason turned to DS Holt. 'Where are we with phone tracking?'

'No, nothing. She's obviously using some sort of pay and go system and throwing the sim card away immediately after contact.'

Mason thought a minute then turned to David Carlisle. 'So, what's this new theory of yours?'

There were mixed feelings at the morning briefing, and things hadn't quite gone to plan. A relatively new field with few set boundaries or definitions, criminal profiling could be very insular at times. Not all agreed with the methodology or the terminology, and the term *"profiling"* often rested uneasily with some police officers on the force. Clearly at odds with the rest of the team, there were those present who perceived Angelica to be a hoaxer. They were right, of course, but not entirely for the right reasons.

Carlisle spent the next five minutes explaining his latest theory, concluding that Angelica was in some way involved in these murders. Convincing the team would be difficult, as it was a massive step change in direction.

Mason's voice betrayed his astonishment. 'You're not suggesting Angelica's in cahoots with the killer, are you – surely not?'

All eyes were now on him.

'Yes I am.'

Holt raised his hand. 'When did you first realise that something was wrong?'

'Sometimes it's the trivial things that can change a person's views,' Carlisle began, 'but Angelica's graphic descriptions of events are not only remarkably accurate, they're unnerving.'

DC Manley shuffled awkwardly. 'If she couldn't identify the suspect in Forth Street, then how come she recognised him in Byker?'

'That's a bloody good point,' Mason added.

Carlisle turned to Mason. 'I've been struggling to come to terms with that myself,' he admitted, 'but it's my view that Angelica is toying with us and drip feeding us vital information about the killer's activities and movements. That's how she's getting her kicks.'

Mason looked at him inquisitively.

'And what do you base your facts on?'

'I'm no expert in linguistics, but I can tell from a person's body language when it comes to uncovering blatant deception. And that's what changed my views about her.'

More mumblings could be heard as DS Holt pointed to the cork board. 'I must admit, she does have an uncanny knack of being in the drop zone at all the right moments.'

Mason remained unruffled. He did not do conventional; it wasn't his style. Where most senior police officers hung certificates of achievements on their office walls, Mason did not. The only thing he was ever known to have proudly displayed, was a twenty-five-yard swimming certificate for breaststroke. And that, according to his cleaning lady, was screwed to the back of his toilet door.

The senior forensic scientist turned to Mason. 'If I'm completely honest with you, I've had my doubts about this woman for several weeks now. Her knowledge of the facts is remarkably accurate, and there's no way she could have picked this up from the media.' Hedley cleared his throat. 'I presume that's where David is coming from.'

'Yes, it is, Tom. There's an awful lot of information the media don't even know about, including last night's meeting with her. So, unless we have a mole in the camp, or someone is drip-feeding information to her, there's no other explanation for it.'

'I doubt anyone on the force is leaking information,' DS Savage added.

Mason shook his head. 'So, what made you change your mind?'

'When I questioned her about the Transit van, she told me it was near a run-down factory close to a Byker council estate.'

'That sounds remarkably like the old chemical plant.' DC Manley nodded.

Hedley concurred. 'The fact she told you the suspect wore the same clothes on two separate sightings, matches perfectly with forensics findings.'

'Something's not right,' Savage agreed.

'Yes, Rob, but after much deliberation I've finally reached the conclusion that she may be suffering from a form of hybristophilia.'

'Ah! Folie á deux,' Hedley said, excitedly rubbing his hands together.

Mason looked on puzzled. 'Are we talking at cross purposes here, or am I missing something? What the hell is *hybristophilia*?'

'It's sometimes referred to as Bonnie and Clyde syndrome,' Carlisle replied, 'and occurs more often in women than men. It's described as a paraphilia that takes on two forms, either passive or aggressive. The aggressive form is what Bonnie Parker displayed when she helped Clyde Barrow in their infamous 1930's bank robberies. It can also take the form of sexual arousal, fascination, or is reached through having a strong affinity with someone who commits atrocious crimes.'

Mason raised an eyebrow. 'You're not asking me to believe she's the killer's accomplice? Surely not!'

Carlisle nodded, reluctant to be drawn in.

Mason switched his mobile on, and frantically searched the internet. 'The woman's a liar and I've said so all along.'

'I too have had my doubts, but not after last night's meeting with her.'

'You're cutting a fine line here. It's a big ask.'

Carlisle guessed what Mason was thinking, that much was blatantly obvious. Not one for compromise, the DCI preferred to act on impulse. It was like flipping a coin in a game of pitch and toss when you never knew which side the coin would land on.

Hedley broke the tension between them.

'I do find it strange that she was able to describe the exact colour of each suitcase.'

'And the clothes he wore,' DS Holt added.

'She's a hoaxer,' Mason groaned.

Carlisle shrugged. 'I can only base my opinions on facts.'

'*Really?*'

The room fell silent as Mason held eye contact with him. Lateral thinking was one way of looking at it, but complex psychological theories all too often went over a lot of people's heads. There were some present, only a handful, who were beginning to question the DCI's hard stance. Mason was hot-headed and renowned for being inflexible, and that was the problem he now faced.

'Do you know what?' Holt suddenly announced. 'The more I think about it the more this case smacks of Maxine Carr and the Soham murderer, Ian Huntley.'

Holt rolled his eyes in a show of contempt as Mason read out aloud from his iPhone. 'It says here that some believe hybristophiliacs are submissive subjects, while others believe they are narcissistic enablers who are pulled in to power. If there is a hint of truth in what you're saying, then what's this woman's role in all of this?'

A chance to explain, thought Carlisle.

'Without going into detail, there are two parts to hybristophilia,' Carlisle began. 'There's the taboo danger part to it, and there's this hyper-masculine aggressive part that can be very appealing to some women. Without knowing Angelica's full background, if our killer is much older than she is, she may regard him as a father figure. Someone to look up to.'

'And if he's not?' Mason replied.

'Then her role could form part of a "Bonnie and Clyde syndrome".'

DC Manley's mouth slowly twisted into a thin smile. 'Guessing by the number of stab wounds we found on the victims' bodies, he's more likely to be a younger man, don't you think?'

'True,' Hedley acknowledged. 'And there's plenty of forensic evidence to support such a claim.'

Ever the optimist, Mason paced the floor. Short on ideas, and time, he was struggling to come to terms with it all. 'I'm still not convinced,' he said, shaking his head. 'It's a massive shift in direction, and it still doesn't answer her connection to the killer.'

'I'll admit it's a bit of a long shot,' said Hedley, 'but this new theory does answer a lot of questions.'

'Okay.' Mason looked at his watch. 'We need to put an end to the matter, once and for all. It's only a theory at this stage, another way of looking at it. So, let's not get carried away here.'

'What are you proposing we do?' Hedley asked.

'Let's put a warrant out for her arrest.'

'On what charges?'

'Being an illegal immigrant should do the trick.' Mason glanced at his watch again, as if he had another appointment to keep. 'Before we go running around like headless chickens, let's see what forensics throws up after last night's operations. If Interpol does draw a blank, then we know this woman hasn't got previous.'

'What if she decides to skip the country?' asked Holt.

'We'll cross that bridge when we come to it.' Mason looked Carlisle directly in the eye. 'Let's hope this isn't another red herring, or you'll have an awful lot of explaining to do.'

Carlisle nodded. 'With any luck, she may even lead us to the killer.'

'I'm not convinced of that either.'

'And why not?' Holt queried.

'A copper's instinct, George.' Mason tapped the end of his nose. 'And twenty years of service at the sharp end of things.'

Tom Hedley came to Carlisle's rescue. 'I quite like David's new theory, and the evidence certainly stacks up.'

Mason stared at the crime board as if looking for divine intervention. The table in front of him was strewn with case files, and there wasn't a scrap of evidence to suggest why the killer had committed such heinous crimes, let alone work with an accomplice.

'Okay,' Mason announced. 'Let me spell it out to you. If this Eastern European woman *is* an accessory in these crimes, what's her involvement? We need to dig deeper, go back over old case files and unpick people's statements. If there is a connection in there, we need to uncover it, and fast.' Mason jotted some notes down on a pad. 'Let's talk to the victims' close-knit families and friends, see if a young woman was ever involved. If Angelica is in cahoots with the killer, is she the one who is grooming them?'

Carlisle was about to speak, but Hedley beat him to it.

'Perhaps we should take another look at the victims' social media accounts, chat room sites, Facebook, Twitter accounts, that sort of thing. If Angelica is involved, the killer could be using her as bait to lure these young men in.'

Mason tilted his head back. 'Best leave that to the tech boys, otherwise we'll be wasting more valuable resources.'

'What about revisiting old CCTV coverage, boss?' Manley asked.

'No, Harry. We need to treat this as just another theory at this stage. Take another look at old case files, see if we haven't missed something.'

'Leave that with me.' Manley grinned.

There was a new buzz of excitement in the air, and Mason was unwittingly being sucked into it. As the meeting came to an end, everyone broke into small groups.

Mason turned to Hedley. 'What do you think, Tom?'

'I quite like the idea, Jack. The evidence stacks up, and it's given us a new sense of direction.'

Could Mason be warming to his new theory? Carlisle wondered. Probably not!

Chapter Thirty

Leeds Ripper territory

Jack Mason had driven down to Leeds that morning. A white Transit van stolen from Byker, had been picked up near the Seacroft area using automatic number plate recognition technology – ANPR. Now with the West Yorkshire Police Crime Investigation team, the van had been taken away for further forensic examination. Things were moving at a pace, and a lot of satisfactory progress was being made. Ever the optimist, Jack Mason was hoping to fill in a few more gaps in his quest to catch the killer. Still keeping an open mind about the profiler's latest theory, he remained sceptical.

'*Turn left at the next junction,*' the Satnav's voice instructed.

'Got it,' Mason grunted.

Located on the eastern side of Leeds, behind the façade of this modern office-block building, Killingbeck Police Station covered a large sector of the city, including the infamous Halton Moor Estate, the seat of several hardy criminal gangs. Met at reception by a fastidious desk Sergeant who insisted on taking down his full details, he was ushered into a back room and offered coffee.

He did not wait long.

'Ah! Detective Chief Inspector Mason.'

As soon as he heard the high-pitched voice behind him, he almost choked on his coffee. Inspector William Greystone was a tall man, late-forties, with slicked back black hair and touches of grey at the sides. Their paths had crossed on several occasions over the years. Mainly police training stuff, and the odd seminar he'd attended back in his early policing days. Not an easy person to get on with, Greystone was a knobhead as far as Mason was concerned. A born-again Christian who loved nothing more than to spout off religious verse at the most inconvenient times, he was still a hard-working copper nevertheless.

'How was your journey south?' Greystone asked.

'The A1(M)'s not good,' Mason confessed. 'Other than that, it was fine.'

'These motorway improvements are never ending,' Greystone sighed. 'Fifty miles an hour and dozens of average speed cameras constantly monitoring your progress – who'd want to be a long-distance driver?'

'No, I suppose not.'

The Inspector took up a seat opposite and flicked open one of the case files he'd brought with him. 'I've just had a lengthy discussion with Tom Hedley, your Senior Forensic Scientist up in Gateshead. It seems that latent fingerprints we found on a stolen white Ford Transit van, match those recovered from a retirement home in Byker.' Greystone cleared his throat. 'If these belong to this Eastern European woman you're looking for, she doesn't appear on the Police National Fingerprint Database.'

'Yes, we're already aware of that.' Mason nodded. 'She's obviously here illegally.'

'Pity,' sighed Greystone, 'as I was rather hoping for a quick breakthrough.'

'What about the van driver?'

'Nothing much in the way of fingerprints, and the van had been wiped clean apparently. That said, forensics did manage to collect soil samples from the vehicle's cab foot-well, and traces of blood were found in the back of the vehicle.' Greystone conferred with his notes. 'They've been sent for further analysis.'

'Do we know who the van belonged to?'

'Yes, a local lease hire company. According to our records, it was reported stolen from the Seacroft area three weeks ago.'

Mason did a quick mental calculation. 'You mentioned it was abandoned?'

'Yes. When we first came upon it, it wouldn't start up. Whoever had stolen it, must have realised that something was seriously wrong with the engine.'

'It's a wonder it wasn't torched.'

Greystone laughed. 'Another day and the local hooligans would have seen to that, no doubt. Fortunately, one of our keen-eyed RT officers had picked up on it.'

Mason jotted down some notes. 'So where exactly was it stolen from?'

'Here in Seacroft, close to the A64.' Greystone smiled. 'Two builders had leased it to carry out some house renovations they were working on. Parked up outside the property with the keys left sticking out of the ignition, there's little wonder it was stolen.'

Mason stared at Greystone. 'He's an opportunist!'

'Yes. It would appear so.' The Inspector recovered his composure. 'We also found a set of stolen registration plates hidden under the passenger seat. So, he'd obviously intended to avoid detection at some later stage.'

Mason scratched the side of his head. 'If it was stolen in Leeds and driven up to Newcastle and back, there's every chance he's local.'

'We've already considered that angle,' Greystone replied. 'If your suspect does work in Leeds, then the van may have been stolen to order. It would be much safer that way, especially if the number plates were changed.'

Mason ignored his comment.

'What else did you recover from the vehicle?'

'Not a lot,' Greystone admitted. 'A couple of petrol receipts, and a spent roll of heavy duty duct-tape wedged down the back of the driver's seat. Your man must have overlooked them during his clean-up operation.'

Mason felt a sudden adrenaline rush. 'Is it possible to have a full analysis done on the duct-tape?'

'It's already under investigation. I'll be sending you a full written report as soon as we get the test results.'

'Copied in triplicate?'

'Yes, of course.' Greystone nodded.

Unlike Gateshead police station, this building had a contemporary look. Plush furnishings, state of the art technology, and plenty of parking space at the rear. Even so, Mason wasn't overly impressed. He preferred a more lived in environment, plain and simple. This building was too clinical to be a police station, he thought, and way over the top.

'Just out of interest,' Greystone began, 'have you managed to uncover a motive yet?'

'We're still working on it.' Mason ran his hand over the top of his head. 'We've drafted in a criminal profiler to help us in that side of our investigations.'

'A criminal profiler—'

'Yes, but I'd rather not elaborate at this stage.'

'Of course, that's understandable.'

'He's worked with us before, so we know what to expect.' Mason smiled.

Greystone nodded. 'How does that tie in with the psychological aspects. Do you—'

'These petrol receipts,' Mason said quickly changing the subject.

'Yes. What about them?'

'They were all dated, I presume?'

Greystone was taken aback. A rank below him he dutifully fell into line. 'They were mainly centred around Leeds, but there is one from a Gateshead filling station that may be of interest to you. Low Fell, wherever that is.'

Got him. Mason grinned.

For Greystone, everything was a matter of fact and Mason's opinion of him hadn't changed one iota. The inspector was still a knobhead as far as he was concerned, and there was no getting away from it. Mason fumbled around in an inside jacket pocket and pulled out an e-fit image of Angelica.

'Ah. The Eastern European woman,' Greystone said immediately. 'We've recently circulated that to every officer on the Yorkshire force. If she is local, there's every chance we'll find her for you.'

'She goes under the alias, Angelica.'

Greystone made a note of it and pushed back in his seat.

'What's her involvement in all of this?'

Mason explained.

A fresh pot of coffee arrived, brought in by the fastidious desk Sergeant who insisted on pouring it out. Close to retirement; if not, he'd suffered one hell of a paper round, Mason thought. Sometimes he envied other police officers' roles – far less hassle, no responsibility, and a shit load of free time on your hands. There again, he argued. Sitting behind a computer desk all day somehow didn't appeal. He preferred old school policing, down to earth encounters with the real hardened criminals.

Surprisingly, Greystone had fallen over backwards to assist him, which was more than Mason had anticipated. Police work was all about contacts, and the more contacts you had the better chance you had of solving a case.

'What more can you tell me about his victims?' Greystone asked, breaking his thoughts.

Mason explained but refused to elaborate.

As the morning wore on, the DCI's mind began to drift to other things. What if the killer lived in Leeds – what then? Would the case fall outside their regional jurisdiction? There again, he reasoned. These murders were all committed up north, ninety-five miles away to be exact.

He'd checked it before driving south that morning.

Greystone stood to leave.

'This is a nasty business, and I certainly don't envy your task.'

Mason closed his notebook and reached out a hand. 'Thanks for all your assistance, William. You've been most helpful.'

'No problem,' Greystone said, lapping up the adulation like a ten-year old schoolboy receiving his first school certificate. 'If there is anything else we can help you with, you know where to find us.'

More than pleased with his findings, at least Mason now had a better understanding of the killer's movements. Despite all that was going on, the profiler was right: Angelica was involved. If not, then how come her fingerprints were all over the stolen Transit van?

A sprinkling of black clouds had formed over the horizon as he drove north towards Wetherby and the A1(M). Feeling peckish, it was then he remembered the New Inn in Scarcroft. It was only a twenty-minute drive away, and the beer was usually good. His mind already made up, he contacted the office and relayed some further instructions to DS Holt. He wasn't going to make it home for hours yet, and he needed some thinking time. At least he could draft his report and prepare for tomorrow's briefing.

Yes, Mason thought. *Brilliant idea!*

Chapter Thirty-One

Throughout the morning, the area around Byker had been a hot-bed of activity. With every available police officer drafted into the area, by mid-afternoon the arrival of the mobile Incident Command Unit brought with it a temporary respite from the inclement weather. More importantly, it meant that Jack Mason now had coffee-making facilities.

On first impressions, the DCI seemed more than pleased with the way his operations were developing. They'd plugged a few gaps, opened a few fresh leads, and generally made their presence felt. Having split the area into six zones, Mason was examining every possibility. As more and more police officers poured into the outlying districts, the hunt for the killer was relentless. There was no easy solution to the problem, but Mason was working on a three-week window – from the time the white Transit van was stolen in Leeds to when it had been recovered. Keen to fill in the gaps, no stones were being left unturned. Garages, pubs, restaurant and supermarket car parks were all under scrutiny.

Officially this was now a Northumbria police murder investigation, even though the killer had links to Leeds. If nothing else, Mason's recent dealings with the West Yorkshire Police had certainly clarified matters. Any notion that the enquiry would be switched to another division had finally been crushed. Mason was still the man in charge.

Looking around, nine detectives crammed into a tiny incident unit no bigger than a broom cupboard was always going to be a tight squeeze. If nothing else, it demonstrated Mason's inability to plan things.

'You okay, Carrington?' the DCI said, glancing up. 'It appears you've drawn the short straw this morning.'

Now wedged between two big strapping police officers, the young female detective smiled without humour. 'Is this some sort of joke, boss?' she groaned.

'I know it's a tight squeeze.'

'*Tight squeeze!*' DC Carrington gasped. 'There's not enough room to swing a cat.'

'Try spreading some feminine charm about the place and see if that works.'

Laughter broke out.

'There's little chance of that happening with this bunch of morons.'

Mason gathered a few loose papers together and looked at her quizzically. 'You ever played rugby?'

'My father did. Why?' Carrington replied.

'Was he good?'

'I don't know, I only ever saw him play the once.'

'There's a part in the game called the scrum.' Mason smirked. 'It's a bit like a big man's cuddle. After a lot of pushing and shoving everyone breaks free and a big space opens up in front of you.'

'Not in here it doesn't.'

More laughter broke out.

'Okay,' Mason said, the serious side surfacing. 'I know we're going back over old ground here, but from what we now know from the West Yorkshire police, of particular interest is a white Ford Transit short wheel base. If blood samples found in the back of it matches John Lawrence, it proves our killer used it to transport his body around. Where was it parked? Who saw it? Did anyone see the driver?'

'What else do we know about the vehicle?' asked DS Holt.

'Stolen from Leeds, it had PROPERTY RENOVATIONS splashed all over it,' Mason paused to let his words sink in. 'Someone out there must have seen it, surely?'

'Anything more on the Low Fell petrol station receipt?' DS Savage asked.

'The diesel was paid for in cash, so we don't have a bank card trace.'

'What about CCTV coverage?'

'There was none.'

'Typical,' Savage muttered.

Carrington raised a hand to speak. 'So, what are my instructions, boss?'

Mason handed everyone a brown envelope and flicked back over a few pages in his notebook. 'You'll be working in pairs on this one. . . so try keeping it simple. We know the suspect was last seen in the area during the early hours of Friday the twenty-third, and we know a set of registration plates were nicked from one of the residents' Transit vans. If Angelica is involved, did anyone see or hear anything?'

Carlisle stared down at the brown envelope and saw Carrington's name scribbled across the top of it in bold black capital letters. At least Jack Mason had got something right for once.

'What more do we know about the Eastern European woman?' DC Manley asked.

'I'm coming to that,' Mason replied.

Outlining his plans, Mason asked for a summary of what the team had found so far. It didn't amount to much. As is often the case surrounding illegal immigrants, there were more questions than answers. Without a surname, Angelica was becoming a bit of an enigma.

Manley turned to Mason. 'This woman could be acting as the lookout.'

'So, you haven't read my report.'

'It's the bairns, boss. They've been keeping me and the missus up all night—'

Mason cut Manley short by holding his hand up. 'Angelica claims she saw the suspect dragging a green suitcase out of the back of a white Transit van that night, and we know he was later caught on CCTV passing Bean Street at 2.32 am. What did she get up to in the meantime? Who was she with?'

'That's easy.' Manley grinned. 'She was out nicking number plates.'

'Hmm. It's a thought. We need to fill in the gaps, jog people's memories.'

It was the coordinator who took them by surprise.

'You okay?' Mason asked.

Sweating profusely, it was like an oven inside the tiny command unit and the coordinator's face had turned ashen. Mason signalled for the back door to be opened. In what had been another demonstration of Mason's inability to plan things, everyone breathed a sigh of relief as they pushed out through the door.

★★★

Checking his street map, David Carlisle estimated there were at least a dozen pubs within easy walking distance of the mobile Incident Command Unit, which meant a busy afternoon. It was a large catchment area, but Carlisle remained optimistic.

Carrington sidled up to him. 'You've not been in contact in a while.'

'I've been extremely busy, Sue.'

She gave him a disapproving glance. 'Are you avoiding me, or is there someone else in your life?'

'No. Why?'

'If there is someone, that's fine by me.'

Carlisle stiffened. 'It's funny you should mention it but there is someone actually.'

She looked at him dejectedly. 'Anyone I know?'

'I doubt it.'

Her face clouded over as her eyes rested upon his. 'I always thought the right person would come along one day. Pity, cos I thought I was in with a chance.'

Carlisle smiled inwardly. 'His name's Benjamin, and we're living together.'

'Benjamin!' she huffed.

Carlisle burst out laughing. 'It's not what you think. Benjamin's a stray kitten I've recently adopted.'

Carrington blushed, having blown her feelings towards him.

It had been months since they'd last worked together. Now an established member of Jack Mason's team, Carrington wasn't pushy like the rest. Apart from getting on well together, he really liked her. He would need to tread warily though. Rushing into any sort of meaningful relationship with another woman might not end up the fairy tale they were looking for. Carrington had an enthusiastic little-girl quality that was infectious. There again, he reasoned, younger women were far less likely to carry baggage with them and may be far less hassle.

He pushed those thoughts to one side.

It was mid-afternoon when they eventually entered the Cumberland Arms in Ouseburn. The place was busy, standing room only. Checking his surroundings, Carlisle spotted a space at the end of the bar and made a beeline towards it.

'Police,' Carrington said, holding up her warrant card in front of the barman's face. 'We're looking for information regarding a recent murder which took place close to St Anthony's Park. Are you the regular barman here?'

'That's me.' He smiled. 'What can I get you people?'

'Nothing,' Carrington replied bluntly, 'but I'd appreciate some answers.'

'I gave you people a statement a few weeks back.'

'Yes, I'm aware of that too.'

'Listen,' the barman replied, 'it's not convenient right now – mind popping back later?'

Undeterred, the detective reached into her handbag and dug out an e-fit image of Angelica. 'Ever seen this young woman in here before?'

The barman's eyes narrowed a fraction. 'Can't say as I have. Mind, there's thousands of pretty young girls get in here every week.'

Annoyed, Carlisle had heard enough. Without thinking he reached over and grabbed hold of the barman's arm. 'Don't try to be clever, son. If you continue to mess us around, we'll sharp shut you down.'

The barman stood gobsmacked.

'So, what's it to be?'

'I'm sorry.'

Carlisle picked up the e-fit image and held it under the barman's nose again. 'This young woman we asked you about, she may have come here with a fella – average height, white trainers, and always wears a black hoodie.'

'Yeah, but. . . no,' the barman stammered, 'he sounds like dozens of customers who drink here.'

'This guy's shifty looking,' Carlisle exaggerated. 'Drives a white Transit van and likes to keep his distance.'

The barman hesitated. 'I'm not sure I should be telling you this, but there's a guy gets in here who I think you should talk to.'

'Talk to about what?' Carrington asked.

'It might be nothing, but I overheard this conversation one night. He was telling his mate he'd arranged to meet this foreign woman here who was offering him promises of sex. When he went outside with her, her fella was waiting for him. He sounded a real nasty piece of work by all accounts.'

'What happened exactly?'

'He managed to get away from them.'

'And what's this customer's name?'

'Reg—'

'Reg who?' Carrington demanded.

'How the hell would I know? He's not been back since.'

Carlisle checked the sign above the bar and pointed to it. 'I see you do bed and breakfast here.'

'That's right, thirty quid a night.'

Carrington stared at Carlisle.

'I need to see your guest book,' she demanded.

Reaching below the counter, the barman reluctantly handed her a large red diary. Curious, Carrington flipped through the pages before tucking it under her arm. 'We need this as evidence,' she said sternly. 'I'll drop it back when we've finished with it.'

The barman rested his knuckles on the edge of the bar, and there was urgency in his voice. 'I'll need to speak with the landlady about that.'

'Why, is there a problem?'

'It's not for me to say.'

'Perhaps I should have a word?' said Carlisle.

'No, that won't be necessary.'

Carrington handed the barman one of her business cards. 'The next time you see Reg, you're to ring this number.'

The barman looked at her bemused.

It was Carlisle's turn. 'Does this place operate security cameras?'

'No. We got rid of them years ago.'

'What other security arrangements do you have?'

'The pub is burglar alarmed if that's what you mean.'

Carlisle didn't suppose the barman was really interested, but he still felt the necessity to emphasise the point. 'You're to ring that number if Reg turns up.'

'Leave it with me,' the barman sighed.

Carrington flashed her big blue eyes at him. 'Good man!'

The moment they stepped outside, Carlisle felt a cool breeze on his face. Not more than a ten-minute walk from Manors Metro Station and fifteen from Newcastle's Quayside, the Cumberland Arms was ideally situated. Halfway down a steep bank, with views overlooking the Ouseburn Valley – he couldn't think of a better place for a serial killer to lie low. But there lay another problem: three of his victims had been kept in a deep freezer. No, he thought. They could rule this place out.

Back at the mobile Incident Command Unit, Carlisle's mind was all over the place. Why on earth would the killer travel all the way from Leeds to carry out his murders? There again, he thought. If his work took him to Leeds, he could be stealing his Transit vans to order. The only issue with that, if he was stealing them to transport his victim's bodies about, where was he cutting them up? Unless the killer was lining the van's interior with heavy duty plastic sheeting and cutting them up in the back of it, then it had to be somewhere else.

There again, serial killers were territorial and liked to stick within their comfort zones. The closer to home the better!

'Penny for your thoughts?' Carrington smiled.

'Angelica,' he replied. 'If she's grooming these young men with promises of sex, where are they being slaughtered?'

'Somewhere out of the way, I'd wager.'

'It makes sense,' Carlisle agreed, 'but their van was found in Leeds, don't forget.'

'What if they live there?'

'If they do, then why does Angelica always use the Metro trains?'

Carrington wrinkled her nose. 'I've no idea; you're the so-called expert.'

'No, Sue. The killer works in Leeds, but his home is here in Newcastle.'

The young detective looked at him confused.

'This profiling malarkey is doing my head in.'

Sometimes it was best to say nothing -- keep your thoughts to yourself.

Chapter
Thirty-Two

The mood in MR-1 was subdued. Still without a motive, yesterday's investigations had thrown up very little in the way of fresh leads. Now standing in front of the operations team, DCI Mason had brought in two new additions. Both were senior Road Traffic officers, and both extremely experienced in their jobs. Mason's plan was to keep a close eye on the two main arterial roads covering the North East of England – namely the A1(M) and A19. If the killer was commuting regularly between Newcastle and Leeds, then he would need to come under their radar.

The moment Tom Hedley appeared in the doorway, Mason's face dropped. Looking like a man possessed, the senior forensic scientist was frantically waving a sheet of paper in the air.

'I've just received an email from the West Yorkshire Police.'

'What's up now, Tom?' Mason asked.

'Good news, gentlemen. The blood sample found in the back of the stolen Transit van is a ninety-nine percent match to John Lawrence's DNA. In other words, the van was used to transport the victim's body around.'

'Anything else?'

Tom Hedley glanced at the report. 'The forensic evidence is unequivocal. The roll of duct tape found wedged down the back of the driver's seat is the same composition and identical to that used in the Jennifer Oakwell murder.'

Mason pushed forward keen to learn more. 'Does it say where it was purchased?'

'No, but the manufacturer's batch code tells us it was distributed throughout North East hardware stores in June 2013.'

Mason stroked his chin in thought. 'Do we know where exactly?'

'It doesn't say.'

'So, we've no idea of when or where it was purchased?'

'No,' Carlisle cut in, 'but it does tell us our suspect was here when he bought it.'

Mason shot him a glance. 'So, he could be living in the area?'

Carlisle nodded. 'I believe so. His knowledge of it and his ability to move around in it certainly suggests he's territorial. This one sticks rigidly to set routines... even down to the clothes he wears.'

'What are the chances he travels down to Leeds to work?' Hedley asked.

'If he does,' said DS Holt, 'it's odds on he's a tradesman of some sort.'

'Hold on a minute,' Mason said raising a hand. 'Let's stick with the duct tape for a second. What else does the report tell us?'

Hedley raised his eyebrows a fraction. 'We know he did a clean-up job on the Transit van, but after further examination forensics found traces of a distinct mix of brick dust in the foot-well of the vehicle.'

'And?' said Mason, disquiet clearly showing on his face.

'It's identical in chemical composition to a footpath close to where John Lawrence's body was found. What's more, traces of pollen and thirty-six types of plant were also discovered in the vehicle... one of them rare.'

'Got him,' Mason said.

Hedley allowed himself a brief, self-assured smile. 'If that hasn't convinced you, fibres discovered on the driver's seat match those found at all three murder scenes.'

Chatter broke out amongst the team.

'Okay,' Mason said, turning to face them. 'We know where John Lawrence's body was found, when it was found, and how it got there. The one vital piece of information still missing is, who killed him?'

'What does the report say about this Angelica woman?' asked Holt.

Hedley elaborated. 'In addition to fingerprints recovered from the van's dashboard, a strand of hair was found. The annoying thing is, there's nothing in any database systems to say who she is.'

'She's obviously here illegally,' Mason sighed, 'which begs the question: what nationality our killer is?'

Carlisle thought about it, but not for long. 'He's definitely territorial, someone who commits his crime within a twenty-mile striking radius of Newcastle. If his partner does suffer from hybristophilia, then her infatuation towards him could lead us to his whereabouts.'

Mason was first to react.

'In other words, find the woman and we find the killer.'

'Precisely.' Carlisle nodded.

Tom Hedley shuffled awkwardly. 'Easier said than done. Where do you suggest we start looking for her?'

Inspector Dick Harris peered hard at his notes, his fifteen years with Road Traffic invaluable. 'For what it's worth, gentlemen, these people seem to be avoiding detection by stealing legitimate number plates and putting them on stolen vehicles. The problem with that is, stolen plates are seldom reported to the police so they're difficult to pick up on the ANPR system.'

'We need to find a way round it, Dick.'

Harris nodded. 'We could set up more roadside checks, of course.'

'Let's do it,' Mason insisted.

DS Holt raised a hand to speak. 'What are the chances of her contacting us again—'

'Slim,' Mason replied stoically. 'But if she does contact David's mobile phone again, we've fitted a call tracker device on it.'

'So, it's a waiting game?'

'Unless you can up with a better plan.'

Carlisle checked the key location markers again. Everything that could go wrong, had gone wrong. It was time to think outside the box and look at a different approach. 'Have we heard any more from Tony Fox lately?' he asked.

'No, nothing,' Mason shrugged. 'Which reminds me, it's time we paid him another visit.'

'I wouldn't hang my hat on it,' said Holt.

Mason offered a thin smile. 'No, I suppose not.'

'Perhaps we should go public on this one?'

'No. Not at this stage, Tom.'

'Why not? It's worked for us in the past.'

Mason angled his head in thought. 'Yes, but we know this woman's a control freak. If we do go public, it will force her to go to ground.'

'There is that aspect to it,' Hedley acknowledged, 'but what other alternatives do we have?'

Carlisle studied the map and shook his head in frustration. If these people were operating locally, their best plan of action would be to flush them out into the open. It was a large catchment area, densely populated, and no easy task. There were probably a few better ways of doing it, but right now he couldn't think of one.

He thought a moment. 'If her real name isn't Angelica, then why has she chosen to call herself that?'

'That's a bloody good point,' Mason agreed.

Holt wasn't convinced. 'Nah, it definitely sounds East European to me.'

'Hang on a minute,' said Hedley. 'When I spoke with my counterpart in Leeds, he told me his wife's favourite restaurant is called Angelica's.'

'That's stretching it a bit.' Holt chuckled.

'Not really,' Mason argued, 'I rather like the idea.'

'Perhaps we should all go down to Leeds and have a meal in the place,' Manley jested. 'Find out who the owners are.'

Mason was about to speak, when the Acting Superintendent suddenly appeared in the doorway. Dressed in full uniform and carrying a bundle of case files under her arm, her expression was subdued. 'Ah, Detective Chief Inspector,' she said, staring directly across at him. 'Has there been any more developments on this Transit van?'

'Yes, ma'am. We've just received a full written report from West Yorkshire Police.'

The senior forensic scientist reached forward and handed her the report and pointed to the relevant information.

She stared at it for a few seconds, then smiled. 'Excellent news, I'm on my way over to the Area Commander's office. He's bound to ask.'

Mason nodded but said nothing.

'What about yesterday's operation – anything to report on that?'

'Not yet, ma'am. We're still working through the detail.'

Sutherland thought a minute. 'And this joint operation with Leeds – where are we with that?'

'Operation *Sparrow Hawk* takes effect from midnight tonight. All arterial roads in and out of the North East will come under the scrutiny of the Durham Constabulary. If the killer and his accomplice do travel to Leeds, they're bound to come under our radar.'

'Good.' Sutherland nodded. 'I'll inform the Area Commander that we're making satisfactory progress.'

As the door closed firmly shut behind her, Mason let out a long sigh of relief.

Chapter
Thirty-Three

Foot hard to the floor, the speedometer on 112 mph, Mason took the next slip road towards Corbridge. If his gamble had paid off, and it was Angelica sitting in the front passenger seat of the stolen BMW, he might just make a name for himself. Now the most wanted woman on the National Crime Agency's rogue's gallery, every police officer in the country was on the lookout for her.

"Angelica's Curse," he softly whispered to himself.

As the road up ahead suddenly narrowed, Mason caught his first glimpse of flashing blue lights. Fast closing in, his car radio suddenly crackled into life. Seconds later, after taking a sharp left-hand bend, he was flagged down by an irate road traffic officer. Dressed in a Hi-Vis yellow jacket, and carrying a traffic cone under his arm, Mason braked to a halt.

'DCI Mason, Northumbria Police,' he said, holding out his warrant card.

'There's been a single vehicle accident some fifty metres up ahead,' the officer confirmed. 'We're closing this section of the road to traffic.'

'Was this a silver BMW 1 series?'

'Yes, it was, sir.'

'What do we know about the occupants?'

'As far as I'm aware, we still have a young woman trapped inside the vehicle but the driver's done a runner.'

'Is she alive?'

'The last I heard she was unconscious and breathing,' a second officer announced, as he approached from behind his marked BMW X5 Traffic vehicle.

'Who's in charge?' Mason asked next.

'Sergeant Fallon. He's over by the crash scene.'

On a good day, the target response time for the emergency services was nineteen minutes. Now hot on the trail of a serial killer, Mason was only yards away from the seat of the accident. With no idea of what to expect next, he approached the T-junction with trepidation. He saw the stationary green and yellow chequered paramedic's vehicle and decided to head towards it. Blue spinners flashing, doors thrown open in haste, the occupants were nowhere to be seen. It was then he noticed the skid marks.

From what he could deduce, the driver of the stolen BMW had failed to make a sharp right turn at the T-junction with Jacks Lane. Travelling at speed, it had glanced off a tree, flipped onto its roof, and was lying upside down in the bottom of a dry ditch. Glass everywhere, it reminded him of a scene out of a Clint Eastwood film he'd seen.

'DCI Jack Mason, Northumbria police,' he announced.

Barely visible through the tree line, the Sergeant stared back up at him.

'Sergeant Fallon,' the police officer called out. 'There's a bit of a footpath just to the left of your position, sir.'

'I see it,' Mason acknowledged.

At the bottom of a steep ditch, Mason stood in silence for a moment. Apart from a slight whiff of woodland flora, the air reeked of petrol fumes. Curious, the detective chief inspector dropped down on his hunkers and peered in through the driver's shattered door frame. Entering an upside-down world of uncertainty, he felt an eerie presence. As his eyes adjusted to the gloom, every now and then he heard the metallic clicking sound of cooling metal.

Now stretched out over a crumpled roof, a middle-aged paramedic was attending to a female passenger still strapped in by her seatbelt. It didn't look good suddenly. Her hair was matted in blood, and her face carried that all too familiar haunted look of death.

She was barely alive.

'How did you managed to beat the rescue teams?' the sergeant asked.

Mason swung to face him. 'Pure luck. I was on my way to Riding Mill when the response call came in over my radio.'

The sergeant removed his peaked cap and scratched the top of his balding head. Late forties, squat, with a square jawline, he had inquisitive mouse-like eyes that were constantly on the lookout for clues.

'Not the best of endings, I'm afraid.'

Mason nodded. 'No, I suppose not. What happened exactly?'

'It all started with a minor road traffic violation and quickly escalated out of control. After I'd pulled them over along the Western Bypass, I instantly recognised the female passenger. When I checked the ANPR system, their vehicle was down as a 3 series.' The sergeant turned and pointed to the overturned BMW. 'This one is a 1 series, and it was then I realised that something was wrong.'

'A copper's nose.' Mason shrugged.

'You could say that.' The sergeant blew through his teeth. 'When I asked the driver to accompany me back to my vehicle, that's when he took off like a bat out of hell. Before we'd even reached the A69, he was doing over a hundred and twenty.'

Mason stared at the wreckage. 'So how did it eventually end up down here?'

'Approaching the T-junction, he clipped the nearside verge, and the vehicle rolled over several times before ending up down here. Not the prettiest of manoeuvres, I guess.'

'Where's the driver now?'

'There's a team out looking for him.'

Mason stepped back and looked out across the countryside before speaking. 'In which direction did he go?'

'East,' the sergeant replied, pointing a finger in the general direction of the treeline. 'He'll not get far, though, there's a helicopter on its way.'

'Good man.' Mason nodded.

'Did you manage to get a good look at him?'

'Not really, he was wearing a baseball cap and dark tinted glasses.' The sergeant shook his head. 'It all happened so quickly to tell you the truth, but I'd certainly recognise his voice if I heard it again.'

'What accent?'

'Hard to say. He had a funny sort of Yorkshire twang.'

'Middlesbrough, you think?'

'No, more Leeds.'

Mason heard the helicopter but could not see it.

Moments later they were joined by the Fire and Rescue teams. Then, through a gap in the treeline, Mason caught sight of the scene of crime manager. Early fifties, tall, with an unruly mop of hair, Stan Johnson was a welcome addition on the scene. A stickler for detail, the SOC manager was standing at the top of a worn footpath and barking instructions to anyone and everyone in sight.

Mason stared up at him, and then shouted. 'I'm down here, Stan.'

'Jack! I'm surprised to see you here so quickly.'

'I heard the response call over my radio, and decided to join in.'

Reaching the bottom of the ditch, Johnson turned to face him. 'So, what have we got?'

'One female still trapped in the passenger seat of the stolen BMW. . . and suffering from extensive head injuries. The driver's male, around five-ten, and was last seen heading off in an easterly direction.'

'He'll not get far,' Johnson confirmed. 'There's a search team already out looking for him.'

'Be careful, Stan. He may be the *Suitcase Man*.'

'Well I'll be damned,' said Johnson. 'So, who's the female passenger?'

'She calls herself Angelica, and we suspect she's the killer's accomplice.' Mason's eyes toured the crash scene. 'There's a paramedic already in attendance, and an ambulance is on its way.'

'What a mess!'

'It was obviously taken without the owner's consent,' Mason said.

Their eyes met. 'I heard it was stolen from a Tesco's car park in Jesmond. . . just after ten-fifteen this morning.'

'You people don't hang about, Stan.'

'No,' the scene of crime manager replied. 'This operation *Sparrow Hawk* has certainly kept everyone on their toes.'

'Something had to give.'

'If he *is* out there, we'll find him.'

'What about the dog teams?'

'They're on their way and should be with us shortly.'

Every few minutes Mason's mobile phone kept ringing. This wasn't the right time or place he decided, and he switched it off. The moment the ambulance arrived on the scene, he heard the paramedic relay his findings back to the hospital's crash team. His words sounded hollow, matter of fact: *"Large scalp lacerations to the skull, subdural haematoma. . ."*

What other injuries this young woman was suffering from, Mason dreaded to think. These things could go either way, and usually did. From what he could see they would soon have her out of there and he prayed to God she would survive. Even so, he wasn't pinning any hopes on questioning her, not with severe head trauma injuries he wasn't.

Stan Johnson was right – this was one hell of a mess.

Chapter Thirty-Four

David Carlisle had chosen to steer well clear of Jack Mason's celebrations that evening; he thought them premature. Now fighting for her life in an intensive care unit, there were grave doubts as to whether Angelica would pull through. It had taken emergency crews all of forty-five minutes to free her from the wreckage of the stolen BMW. Apart from a great blood loss and lacerated flesh, paramedics had difficulty in inserting a breathing tube during the twenty-minute ambulance ride to a Newcastle hospital. After a CT scan had shown swelling to the right side of her brain, Angelica had been rushed into surgery where neurosurgeons had removed the right side of her skull and part of the left to stop multiple brain haemorrhages. Though she was still in a coma, security was tight. Even so, there seemed very little chance of Angelica regaining consciousness and achieving a meaningful recovery. It didn't look good, and most neurosurgeons acknowledged that an early prognosis was extremely difficult as many patients defied all sense of reasoning. Not so in this young woman's case – her life was barely hanging by a thread.

News travelled fast, and Angelica's capture had certainly stirred up a lot of public interest. Strange as it was, neither the media nor the police had the foggiest idea who she was. At this crucial stage in their investigations, Carlisle was more concerned about what was going on inside the killer's head than anything else. Still out there, the man was a dangerous predator who would stop at nothing to accomplish his goals. Having ran away from the scene of the crash, the police believed he'd flagged an unsuspecting motorist down to make good his escape. Anything was possible but having gone to ground so quickly there was no other explanation for it. The motives to kill were complex, but the outcomes more difficult to comprehend. Now that Angelica had been placed on electronic monitoring, God knows how the killer would react to it.

It had just turned four o'clock when DC Carrington finally pulled up outside the snooker centre in Gateshead. Barely a five-minute drive from the High West Street police station, this was their final call of the day.

Carrington turned to Carlisle. 'This latest CCTV footage Harry Manley picked up...'

'What about it?'

'The guy caught on camera has a remarkable likeness to the man last seen passing the corner shop close to where John Lawrence's body was dumped.'

Carlisle unbuckled his seat belt and stared out of the undercover car's windscreen in thought. 'What was the quality like?'

'Not good, I'm afraid.'

'Anyone with him?'

'Just the Eastern European woman.'

'That's interesting,' Carlisle acknowledged. 'What time was this?'

'Thursday evening, just after six.'

'Rush hour, which means they could live local.'

'Those were my thoughts,' Carrington smiled, 'but it's pure speculation at this stage, and what we need are facts.'

Stopped at the check-in desk, Carrington showed her warrant card to a doorman in his late sixties and signed the visitors book. Seconds later, they were ushered into a small back room and away from the table action. As luck would have it, their suspect was already sat waiting for them. A fellow student of Colin Henderson, Terence Walker looked much older than nineteen. Not a tall man, he wasn't sporty looking either. His huge pot belly hung over baggy jeans, and his T-shirt was covered in curry slops.

Over the years Carlisle had learned that some thoughts were best kept to yourself. His job was to get inside the killer's head and not get bogged down in everyday police affairs. Even so, the small team of detectives who'd travelled to Leeds that morning was wasting its time as far as he was concerned. The killer was hiding in Newcastle but where, he had yet to decide.

After brief introductions, they sat in a corner seat away from further distractions.

'So,' Carrington began, 'you were out drinking with Colin Henderson the night before he was murdered. Mind telling us why you haven't gone to the police before now?'

Walker blushed. 'I was—'

'You were what?' Carrington said, pen poised.

Walker cleared his throat. 'I gave you people a statement a couple of weeks ago. . . .what more do you want from me?'

'Answers,' Carrington groaned. 'And, may I add, you're still under oath.'

Walker said nothing.

'The night Colin Henderson went missing,' Carrington went on, 'you were seen drinking with him in the Whickham House on Bensham Road. According to a previous statement you alleged Colin was accompanied by a young female that night?'

'Did I?'

'Don't try to be clever with me, Mr Walker. We've got you on CCTV.'

The suspect's face drained. 'What is it you people want this time?'

Carrington handed Walker an e-fit image of Angelica, and then said, 'Is this the young woman you and Colin were out with that night?'

'I'm not sure.'

'It's important,' Carrington insisted. 'Take a closer look.'

Walker gave the slightest shake of the head and muttered something inaudible.

'When I rang you earlier this morning, you told me Colin's new partner didn't sit right with you. What did you mean by that exactly?'

'I had difficulty in connecting with her.'

The detective raised an eyebrow. 'But you obviously spoke with her.'

'Yes, but she wasn't interested in anything I had to say.'

'She froze you out of her conversation, in other words.'

'You could say that.'

Walker seemed reluctant to cooperate, and Carrington had picked up on it. She hardened in her approach. 'I'm confused, Mr Walker. This was your friend's first big date, and yet you still went ahead, and gate-crashed the party.'

'That's not true.'

'So why join them?'

'Colin didn't fancy the idea of going it alone and asked me to accompany him.'

Carlisle listened as Walker huffed and puffed his way into another tight corner. The more he opened his mouth, the deeper the hole he dug. It was that kind of interview.

'What confuses me,' Carrington said, 'is why you went to the pub in the first place. It seems only natural they'd want to be alone on their first date, don't you think?'

Walker hesitated. 'Yeah, I suppose so.'

'*I know so,*' Carrington insisted.

Walker looked at her, annoyed. 'It may have been the first time they'd met in the flesh, but they'd chatted to one another over the Internet for weeks beforehand.'

Carrington shot Carlisle a puzzled look.

'You never mentioned anything about this in your statement to us.'

'I was never asked,' Walker replied.

Carrington leaned forward in her seat. 'Was this a chat room site that Colin was involved in by any chance?'

'Yeah. Why?'

'Do you happen to know which one?'

'No, Colin was involved in several as I remember.'

'And this young woman was offering your friend an enjoyable time no doubt?'

Walker reddened. 'I'm not sure where this is heading.'

'Oh, come on,' said Carrington. 'I wasn't born yesterday. That's why he invited you along with him, wasn't it? You thought you were onto a good thing. . . didn't you?'

Walker remained silent.

Carrington checked her briefing notes. Something didn't sit right, and whatever it was she seemed determined to get to the bottom of it.

'What else didn't sit right with you that night, Mr Walker?'

Walker paused, as a puzzled expression swept across his face. 'It was weird,' he sighed.

'Weird?' Carrington replied. 'What was weird?'

'There was this van parked up in the pub carpark that night; it was facing the entrance door.' Walker leaned back in his seat, his fingers gripping the armrest. 'I'll be straight with you, I still like the odd spliff now and then. . . but I'm not addicted in any way.' He smiled philosophically as if glad to have broached the fact. 'Anyway, every time I went outside for a ciggy, this guy in the van kept staring at me.'

'Perhaps he was waiting for someone?'

'I wouldn't say that.' Walker shrugged.

'What did he look like this guy?'

Walker sighed. 'It's difficult to say, as he was wearing a hoodie and dark sunglasses.'

Carlisle felt a sudden adrenaline rush.

'How old was he?'

'Thirtyish.'

Carrington remained silent for a moment, thinking. 'I'm struggling to find a connection here, Mr Walker. What does a thirtyish van driver have in common with this eighteen-year-old woman your friend was dating? Is there something you're not telling me here?'

Walker swallowed hard. 'Look,' he said. 'I don't like playing these guessing games, but if you must know I was scared.'

'So, you were spooked by his appearance. Is that what you're trying to tell me?'

'Yeah.'

'What happened next?'

'We were all drinking lager that night. Nothing out of the ordinary, if you know what I mean. Anyway, we'd finished our drinks and I decided to get another round in.' Walker sighed and shifted position. 'It was then they announced they were leaving—'

'Leaving to go where?' Carrington interrupted.

'They didn't say.'

'Okay, so what did you do then?'

'I ordered myself another pint and went outside to say my goodbyes.'

'And?'

Walker drew back. 'They'd gone.'

'Gone where?'

'How the hell would I know? They were nowhere to be seen!'

'What time was this?' Carrington asked flatly.

'Around ten o'clock.'

'And that was the last time you saw Colin?'

Walker lowered his head. 'Yes, I believe it was.'

'This van driver you spoke of. Where was he in all of this?'

'When I went outside to look for them, he'd completely disappeared.'

Carlisle felt his pulse race but said nothing. Carrington was doing just fine.

'Perhaps they'd booked a taxi?'

'Not that I'm aware of, they hadn't.'

A ghost of a smile swept across Carrington's face. 'Okay. Maybe this young woman had a car, and maybe they left in it together.'

'If they did, she was well over the legal limit.'

Pen poised at the ready, the young detective let the silence hang for a moment. 'Do you know what, Mr Walker? I find it hard to believe that you've not gone to the police with your story before now.'

Walker protested bitterly. 'I gave you people a statement a few weeks ago and have heard nothing since.'

'Yes, but none of this information was in your statement.'

Walker's jaw dropped. 'You people never asked.'

It was easy in hindsight, thought Carlisle. At the time of Walker's interview, nobody knew that Angelica was the killer's accomplice. Had they done so, things may have turned out differently.

Carlisle consulted his notes. 'After your friend left the pub that night, did you ever contact him again?'

'I tried ringing his mobile several times, but it went straight to voicemail.'

Carrington cast him a look of disapproval. 'Mr Walker, you were the last person to be seen with Colin Henderson.'

'What do you mean by that?'

Carlisle folded his arms across his chest and continued his silent observation. *Why hadn't Walker gone to the police before now?* The man was in deep trouble and didn't understand the severity of the situation he was in.

Carrington closed her notebook, the official side surfacing. 'Mr Walker,' she began. 'I need you to accompany me back to Gateshead police station. And before you say anything that may be used against you in court, I would advise you find yourself a good solicitor.'

'What the hell for?' Walker protested. 'I've done nowt.'

'The night Colin Henderson was murdered, you were the last known person to be seen with him.'

'That's a ridiculous statement. How can you possibly say that?'

'That's my point,' Carrington said, her eyebrows drawing together. 'This is all new to us, and none of it was ever mentioned in your previous statement.'

Walker's face darkened. 'What's going on here, I've done nowt.'

'That's for us to decide,' the young detective said, pursing her lips. 'Had you been forthright in the first place, I doubt we'd be sat here talking to you.'

Walker lowered his head as though about to be sentenced to death. His hands were shaking, and he was perspiring profusely. This case had suddenly taken on a whole new twist, and things were falling into place. Now up to his neck in trouble, it still didn't mean that Walker was the killer. From what Carlisle had gleaned, it seemed that Angelica was luring her victims into a web of deceit by using the internet chatrooms. It was a dangerous game she was playing, and one with deadly consequences. There again, he reasoned, what if her relationship with the killer had suddenly turned sour and he became jealous of her dark past? It wasn't looking good suddenly.

Chapter Thirty-Five

Nobody socialised much with Jack Mason nowadays, not since his bust up with the fancy woman. She wasn't attractive either. Mid-forties, with peroxide blonde dyed hair and lacking in feminine attributes. On the few occasions they had met, Carlisle couldn't think of anything nice to say about her. Taciturn and undemonstrative, she was a woman of few words. He'd often wondered whether Mason was genuinely looking for a new love in his life, or in it just for the sex. The latter sprang to mind!

'Take a seat,' Mason whispered, as he entered the DCI's office.

It was mid-afternoon, and Carlisle imagined, as he often did, that he was sitting in front of the headmaster's desk waiting to be reprimanded. Finding Mason in an irritable mood had the same effect on his stomach as a dodgy landing at Newcastle airport. No one claimed he was a bad copper, just that he bent the rules to suit himself.

Dressed in a black open neck shirt, jeans and brown leather shoes, Mason was wearing the office carpet out. Not the best of starts, Carlisle thought, as he waited for Mason to finish his call.

'What's up with Sutherland these days?' he asked a little nervously.

'The stuck-up bitch wants me to hold another press conference.'

'Oh!'

Mason threw his mobile phone on his desk in a show of contempt. 'She's got some bloody nerve.'

'What's up now, are they beginning to get twitchy upstairs?'

'If you're willing to stick your head above the parapet, someone's bound to take a pop at it. It's par for the course, and this is what policing has come down to.'

Carlisle nodded. 'I can't help you there, I'm afraid.'

'No. I guess not. Things have moved on considerably since your days in the force.' Mason blew out his cheeks. 'Everyone's answerable, and it's all about political correctness nowadays.'

'Sounds like I got out at just the right time.'

'You probably did.'

Carlisle was accustomed to seeing people's pride being crushed, but this was ridiculous. Things had got off to a bad start that morning, even the team briefing had ended up a bad-tempered affair. Not a lot of progress had been made, and everyone was scratching around for answers. The trouble was, the police were looking in all the wrong places but that didn't stop them from searching all the same.

Mason's face contorted into something almost unrecognisable.

'There's forms for just about everything nowadays, and everyone's bogged down with paperwork.'

'Life in the fast lane, eh?'

Mason shook his head in resignation. 'All we need now is another victim on our hands and this place will implode on itself.'

'We need to put a stop to it, Jack.'

'Yeah, but how is the question. I've got dozens of police officers out searching for him, and still he slips through the net.'

'It's the way their minds work, they have a knack of avoiding us. They're predictable to the point of being monotonous, and that's what we're up against.'

'Where the hell is he?'

There was silence. Only the sound of the window blinds flapping in the breeze.

'Something to bear in mind is, a lioness always protects her cubs no matter what the circumstances are.'

Mason craned his neck forward. 'Yet another one of your infamous riddles to think about!'

'He's bound to come to her rescue at some point.'

'To do what exactly?'

'It's difficult to say, but you'll need to keep a watchful eye on this Angelica woman.'

Mason looked at him puzzled, as though his words were stuck in his throat. 'There's no way he can snatch her out of her hospital bed, not with armed police officers patrolling the ward.'

'The moment he feels ready, he's bound to make his move.'

'That's insane.' Mason groaned.

Carlisle shuffled in his seat. Whoever Angelica was, it sure was making him nervous. Short on clues, and ideas, Mason was pinning his hopes on

Interpol getting back to him. Without a name or country of origin, any form of identification was proving difficult.

'Just out of interest,' Carlisle asked, 'how was the BMW stolen?'

'Some stupid bitch returning her empty supermarket trolley back to the trolley collection point.' The DCI laughed. 'She left her car keys sticking out of the ignition.'

'They're making it far too easy for him.'

'Tell me about it, and he doesn't hang about.'

'What about fingerprints?'

'We believe he wore gloves.' Mason shook his head annoyed. 'And, might I add, after an extensive fingertip search of the crash scene we found nothing by the way of a blood sample.'

'Lucky escape by the sounds of it.'

'Remarkable, I'd say.' Mason twisted his face again. 'If this bastard doesn't have a police record on file, he'll be difficult to track down.'

'How come he managed to escape the accident unscathed?'

'The impact was all on the passenger side of the vehicle.' Mason stood and glanced out of the window and down onto the traffic below. 'If she did have a handbag or cell phone with her at the time, he obviously grabbed them before he ran off.'

'He's organised, Jack. And intelligent with it.'

'Tell me about it.'

'How can we be certain it's our man?' Carlisle asked.

Mason shook his head like he couldn't believe what he was hearing. 'Footprints found at the accident scene match those lifted from previous murder scenes — it's as simple as that.'

'So, it was him.'

Mason nodded. 'I was never in doubt. Let's see what forensics throw up before we go making assumptions.'

Carlisle didn't speak, just fought his usual interior battle about exactly when to give up a lost cause. Angelica was obviously the key in all of this, but Mason wasn't letting on about it. Still in intensive care, there was little chance of her being questioned. Patience. They would need bags of it, but Mason didn't have any to give.

'What's the latest hospital bulletin?' Carlisle asked casually.

'It's not looking good.' The detective chief inspector's fingers hovered over his key-pad, having quietened down a tad. 'The neurologist reckons it could be weeks before she comes out of her coma, and there's no way of knowing whether there's any permanent brain damage.'

'What about the suspect we picked up from the Gateshead snooker club?'

'You mean, Walker?'

'Yes.' Carlisle nodded.

'He's not the killer, if that's what you're thinking.'

'No, I didn't think he was.' Carlisle veered from the cutting edge. 'He's definitely holding back on something, though.'

Mason checked his watch. 'This chatroom site that Colin Henderson was involved in. His wall has been taken down and all of his posts removed from the site.'

'So, they were grooming him?'

'It would appear so.'

'When did you discover this?'

'When Walker was brought in for questioning, the tech boys seized his mobile phone. Angelica was offering them promises of sex, it seems.'

'I had a feeling that's how she was operating.'

Mason shook his head slowly. 'The question is, how will the killer react now he knows his accomplice is being held in police custody?'

'He'll not stop now. Not whilst he has a taste for it.'

Mason's face dropped. 'What does that mean?'

'Nothing will get in the way of a serial killer, even you should know that. Apart from missing her adulation, it means he'll need to work harder from now on.'

'Pity.' Mason groaned. 'I was hoping you'd say otherwise.'

Carlisle straightened. 'Any more developments from West Yorkshire Police?'

'Nothing regarding the killer's whereabouts; they've drawn another blank.' Mason looked at him hard for a moment. 'You were right about one thing, though. Inspector Greystone believes the killer resides in the North East, and suspects he's travelling down to Leeds to work.'

Carlisle watched the skin around Mason's mouth tighten.

'That narrows it down.'

'With any luck Road Traffic will catch him,' Mason forced a wry smile. 'We're still covering the A1(M) in both directions, and further restricting his movements.'

Carlisle stared at the map on Mason's office wall and pointed a finger at it. 'If he's stealing his vans to order, he'll need a place to store them. Not just the vehicles, but somewhere to carry out his dirty work.'

'A lock-up, perhaps?'

'That's how I'd be going about it, and it ties in nicely with him having a large freezer at his disposal.' Carlisle circled the map with the tip of his pen. 'You may wish to broaden your searches to cover this area.'

'Easier said than done. We don't have the resources.'

'What other options do we have?'

Mason gave him a studious look. 'This geographical profiling stuff you've been working on, is there any chance of narrowing down the field?'

There followed a sharp rap on Mason's office door, and DC Manley entered.

'Yes, Harry?' Mason nodded.

The detectives grin broadened. 'Is this a private confab, or can anyone join in?'

There were smiles, but no laughter.

'What can we do for you, Harry?'

'This Reg Duncan bloke. The one from the Cumberland Arms—'

'What about him?' Mason asked.

'He's just been released after questioning.' Manley looked at them warily. 'I've been reading through his statement notes, and he reckons he met this woman through a dating website called *Cherubini's*.'

'Never heard of it.' Mason shrugged.

Manley puckered his lips. 'You don't know what you've been missing, boss.'

'Sod off, Harry. Get to the point.'

'I've been trawling the Internet and may have found something of interest.'

Mason cocked his head to one side, as if his interest buds had been pricked. 'Oh. And what might that be?'

'This dating site Duncan was involved in, it specialises in Eastern European women offering promises of sex.'

Mason laughed. 'I wouldn't expect them to be selling anything else.'

'I know, but this Reg bloke had arranged to meet this woman in the Cumberland Arms.'

'I thought Rob Savage was dealing with that?'

'He is.'

'So why are you getting involved?'

Manley let out a long sigh. 'I know it's not much, but when I overheard that Eastern European women were involved, I thought I'd drop by and mention it.'

'Good man.' Mason nodded. 'I'll catch up with you later.'

'There is one other thing,' Manley said, as he turned back at the door, 'there's no mention of this Angelica on the *Cherubini's* site.'

Mason stared at Carlisle. 'I doubt that's her real name anyway.'

'No, probably not.'

Carlisle had thought about a lot of things lately, and chatroom sites were high on his priority list. If these people were grooming their victims through the Internet sites, then where were they taking them to be slaughtered? He'd tried to think as they did, unravel the killer's inner thoughts and try to make the connection. If there was a clear motive to be had, then jealously sprang to mind. At least it made sense, and he was only targeting young males.

He jotted it down in his notebook, and circled it with his pen: *Jealousy? Must consider.*

Chapter Thirty-Six

Wasp had seen enough for one day. Obnoxious TV presenters, so-called media experts dragging up buckets full of bullshit about everything and nothing. Who did they think they were? Truth be known, most hospital security officers were ward based and spent most of their time walking around corridors and challenging people. Druggies and drunks mainly, and mostly at weekends. High security was a different matter. Armed police officers dressed in bulletproof Kevlar jackets, press button keypad entry on every door, and heaps of cameras to manoeuvre around. Hospital security was tight. It had to be, as that's what security was, all layers. Even so, he knew the main entrance was packed full of closed circuit cameras and several layers of secondary security further back in the building. More importantly, to Wasp that is, was the Fat Controller's room. Get a life, he groaned. If he did have a purpose in life, it was to stare at millions of images all day.

He smiled as another ambulance drew up alongside A&E and prepared to drop off its sick patient. This was the third in as many minutes. He'd counted them in, every single one of them. One o'clock was always the busiest time of day – much quieter during the night, of course. Not surprisingly, these people worked round the clock. It's what they did every day of their lives. However long that was, he chuckled.

Wasp wasn't daft, that's why he carried a sting in his tail. He'd kind of grown fond of his name lately, as it did have an aggressive quality. His psychiatrist told him he had 'a screw loose', but what the hell did he know about these things? Most psychiatrists were nuts anyway and had a long history of destroying sane people's intelligence. He'd read somewhere that psychiatrists had put millions of people on toxic drugs programmes and ruined their quality of life. It was devastating stuff, heart-wrenching, and these parasites were making big bucks out of it. What he wouldn't give to get even with them — put the record straight.

So far, his disguise had worked perfectly. Dressed in green scrubs, a stethoscope casually slung around his neck, he knew how to blend into the background. And according to the site utility map he was carrying in his pocket, he wasn't far from Neurology. No doubt it would be heavily fortified — twenty-four-seven security. Auxiliary was the way to go, and he did have a spare uniform.

As he made his way down another long corridor, the only thing on his mind was how to snatch her out of there. She was trapped — sedated up to her eyeballs to stop her from escaping from her hospital bed. He'd read somewhere how to reverse the process. It was all clever stuff and he needed to dig deeper, find out how to unravel its secrets.

Still following the direction signs, he pushed on through the big double doors with SURGERY SUITE written all over them. It was quiet back here, but he was entering a part of the building he despised most. Plain glossed walls, polished floors, and a strong smell of disinfectant everywhere. When he was a kid he'd suffered from all kinds of allergic reactions to chemical cleaning fluids. Not anymore; he'd stopped using them.

Gripped by uncertainty, Wasp stopped dead in his tracks.

No more cameras beyond this point.

The fire door clanked as he pushed the panic bar — it wasn't alarmed. Isolated from the rest of the building, he poked his head through the tiny opening and checked his surroundings. He could see the staff car park wasn't far away and he could just make out the student quarters. What he didn't know, or maybe he did, was just how far it was to the main entrance door. Yes, there was excellent ground cover to wheel a bed-trolley around in, and plenty of room for manoeuvre. *But what else lay beyond the building?*

Still thinking about the fat controller's room, Wasp pushed on regardless. Less than twenty metres away, another short corridor opened in front of him. Confused at first, he opened the hospital site plans and tried to get a fix on his bearings. When that didn't work, and he still couldn't fathom out where he was, he pocketed the plans. Deep down he hated map reading anyway, as the people who had taught him never had a nice word to say about him.

Then, beyond the double swing doors, he came across the X-ray department. Set back from the rest of the building, he guessed this is where the MRI scans were carried out. It wasn't as he'd expected to find, and he quickly doubled back on himself. Then, just when he had almost given up on it, he spotted the neurology ward. He missed her. Missed her more than he'd ever missed any human.

Twenty minutes later, after leaving by one of the side doors, he paid for his parking and strolled back to the stolen black Peugeot 408. There were still a few things he needed to fix, but Wasp was more than pleased with his findings.

'*Not long now*,' he whispered.

Chapter
Thirty-Seven

Working on a tip-off, Jack Mason had summoned a select group of officers to his office. Things were moving at a pace, but not fast enough according to the Acting Superintendent. With thoughts of Angelica foremost on everyone's mind, Gateshead Police Station was unusually busy when David Carlisle checked in at the reception desk. Tough decisions were being made, and according to the desk Sergeant, everyone was monitoring the hospital situation closely. It hadn't been possible to question her, not since the accident. But they were ready and waiting.

Hand hovering over the telephone receiver, Mason stared up at him from behind his desk the moment Carlisle entered the office. 'Coffee?' he whispered.

'I'd love a cup,' Carlisle replied.

Mason garbled some inaudible instructions down the other end of the phone and dropped the receiver back on its cradle. Ignoring a few sarcastic quips about the age and speed of his Rover P4 100, Carlisle took up a seat along with the rest of the team. Everyone seemed to be in jovial spirits that morning, as if they'd had a tickle on the lottery. He knew they ran an office syndicate of some sort, but surely, they hadn't come up trumps. The only other feasible explanation he could think of was that Tony Fox had been badly beaten up by a gang of ruffians. Not that Fox didn't deserve it – the question was, who was responsible?

'Good news from the Home Office,' Mason announced, as he held up one of the many files cluttering his desk. 'The Eastern European woman turns out to be Estonian. Her name is Angelica Glebova, and according to the Dutch police she's wanted about a series of credit card fraud scams in Amsterdam.'

'So, she *is* here illegally,' Holt remarked.

Mason nodded. 'I'm reliably informed by UK Border Security that she may have arrived here on fake passport documents. It seems the Dutch authorities lost track of her six months ago, so that would account for her going missing in Holland.'

Carlisle thought a moment. 'What do we know about her background?'

Mason looked at his briefing notes. 'Glebova was born in St Petersburg, Russia . . . and into a working-class family. Brought up as a Russian Orthodox, when she was two the family moved to Tallinn in Estonia where she attended a basic comprehensive school not far from the old city walls. When she was seven her father died from a heart attack and the family were forced to move to Kopli, a district of Tallinn with a lot of early twentieth century houses, some of which would have been impressive in their heyday. Young families live there now, mainly mixed race, with a hard-core smattering of drunks and drug addicts. Reading between the lines, after she left school at the age of sixteen, that's when she sought a better life and decided to move west.'

'Sounds like she had a rough start to life,' said Holt, shaking his head.

'It's usually the case,' Carlisle agreed, 'and that's how vulnerable young women normally get caught up with human trafficking gangs. Forced into slave prostitution, there's little wonder she fell into the wrong hands, as she did.'

'That's all very well and good,' Mason huffed, 'but let's not forget she's an evil bitch and none of us should underestimate her cunning.'

Mason's sudden outburst had taken everyone by surprise.

'Do the Dutch authorities have an Amsterdam address?' Hedley asked.

'Yes, but she vacated the premises six months ago.'

'I presume that's when she slipped into the UK?'

Mason took a sip of his coffee and stared down at his notebook again. 'As far as human traffickers being involved, the Dutch police have no evidence to support such a claim.'

'If she's wanted about a credit card fraud, she's bound to be part of a gang.'

'You would think so,' Mason agreed.

'Credit card fraud is rife in Eastern Europe,' added Holt.

Mason rasped his two-day stubble. 'Let's not jump to conclusions here. Now we have a name to work with, I've circulated her details to every police force in the land.'

Carlisle was pleased with Mason's comments but refrained from saying so. Sex trafficking was one thing, but murder was a whole different ball game.

Then Tom Hedley's voice cut through the rest. 'Do we have any more news on this young woman's progress?'

'She's out of the coma but not fully responding to sights and sounds,' Mason replied. 'They're doing more CT scans tomorrow morning, so hopefully we may get some better news.'

'Do we know if any permanent brain damage has been done?' Hedley asked.

'Not at this stage we don't.' Mason's eyes lit up. 'Any changes in her condition, and the hospital staff will keep us informed.'

'Shit,' Manley swore, 'that means we still can't question her.'

Mason allowed himself a brief smile. 'Not yet we can't.'

'It could go either way by the sound of things,' DC Carrington added.

'Very true.' Mason turned to Carlisle. 'Any thoughts as to what the killer's next move might be?'

At that, Carlisle snapped open his briefcase and pulled out a file. 'I've been looking at the landscape lately and trying to get a fix on possible locations where the killer might be hiding. My biggest concerns are, when the incredible surge of power wears off he'll need to replenish his desires.'

Hedley cocked his head to one side. 'But if Angelica was responsible for luring his victims through the social media sites, then how will he operate without her?'

'He'll work on it, Tom,' Carlisle replied. 'Like I've said before, it's in his nature to continue. Once these people get a thirst for it, it's difficult for them to stop.'

'So, he's likely to strike again?'

'Yes, I'm convinced of that.'

Mason thought for a minute as their conversation splintered into smaller groups.

'What if this young woman makes a remarkable recovery?' Holt suddenly announced.

Carlisle shook his head. 'She'll not talk to any of us, if that's what you're thinking.'

'Not even to you?'

'I doubt it.'

'Is this something to do with this hybristophilia thing?'

'She's obviously infatuated by him, and probably worships the very ground he walks on.'

Mason gave Carlisle a withering look. 'Yeah, but a sheep can be meat and it can also be wool.'

Carlisle smiled but said nothing.

More coffee arrived, and Mason gave out a few hurried instructions as the meeting began to wind down. It wasn't a great plan, Carlisle felt, more on the spur of the moment. Even so, they were slowly building up a mental picture of how Angelica had arrived in the country, and what she'd got up to in the meantime. As the office began to empty, DC Carrington, who had said very little throughout, was asked to stay behind. Something was afoot, and whatever it was, Carlisle was curious to find out.

Mason stood unusually quiet for a moment, thinking.

'This theory of yours about the killer having some sort of lock-up, I've been giving it a lot of thought lately. I know you've done a lot of work on geographical profiling and may have a few places in mind. In which case, I need you and Detective Carrington here to do some digging around for me.'

'Is this on a full-time basis, boss?' Carrington asked.

'Until I tell you otherwise.' Mason spun back from the window to face her. 'Is there a problem with that?'

'No, boss. I just like to be clear about my instructions, that's all.'

'Good!'

It was Carlisle's turn.

'What about access to properties... search warrants, that kind of thing?'

Mason helped himself to a fresh mug of coffee and sat down at his desk again. Carlisle knew the DCI liked to rub people up the wrong way – accomplished young women like Sue Carrington. This time felt different, though, and Carlisle could sense a distinct change in Mason's demeanour.

'That's where Detective Carrington comes in handy, as she'll be representing the police.' Mason made a friendly little hand gesture. 'Besides, you two seem to work well together and you're both level headed.'

Carrington blushed.

'Does that mean we have a free hand in everything?' Carlisle smiled.

'Until I say otherwise.'

Carlisle considered his options, happy in the knowledge he was no longer bogged down by police protocols.

And he already had a plan in mind.

Chapter
Thirty-Eight

DC Carrington swung the unmarked Ford Focus estate onto the garage forecourt in Wallsend and switched the car's engine off. It wasn't exactly a tourist attraction, more a run-down shantytown than anything. Row upon row of terraced houses, and bored kids hanging around on street corners. Leave your vehicle unattended round here overnight, and it would be stripped for spare parts or torched. This was the rough end of town, a place where strangers were no longer made welcome.

Carrington stared across at Carlisle, and then said, 'So, where to now?'

'There's an industrial estate just north of here I think we should look at.'

'Why do we always have to go snooping around shit-holes like this? Why can't we go up market for a change?'

'Because that's where the toe-rags hang out.'

'Get a life,' the young detective sighed. 'I thought we were looking at factory units?'

'We are, trust me.'

A group of young thugs had caught Carlisle's attention. Fifteen or twenty of them, closing in and chanting abuse. As Carrington turned the ignition key and coolly eased off the garage forecourt, he kept a watchful eye on them. Half-expecting a brick to land through the rear window at any moment, Carlisle feared the worst. Seconds later, Carrington's foot hit the accelerator pedal hard, and his neck pressed against the seat rest. It was a close-run thing, but they both fell about laughing afterwards.

Twenty minutes later, the young detective got out of the undercover car and looked around. Most of the factory units in the area were run-down, and none of them appeared to be occupied. They'd visited some shady establishments in their travels that morning, but these were among the worst.

'Typical,' Carrington huffed. 'There's nobody about.'

'I was waiting for you to say that.'

'But it's true,' she groaned.

'We need to take a closer look.'

'What ever happened to that sixth sense of yours?'

'If you must know, I have a bad feeling about this one.'

The detective gave him a withering look. 'We'd best get going then.'

No sooner had they stepped onto the tarmac when a Group 4 security van drew up alongside them. Not the friendliest of introductions either.

'What are you people looking for?' the pug-faced security guard announced.

'Police,' Carrington said, flashing her warrant card. 'Who owns these properties?'

'A company down south, but they've gone into liquidation.'

'So, none of these units are occupied?'

'Only the end one, why?'

Carlisle checked the company name above the unit door and made a mental note of it. 'What do you know about the people who run Auto Parts Distribution?' he asked, pointing to the crudely hand-painted sign attached to the door.

'Not a lot, why?'

'Regular guys are they – here every day?'

The security guard stared at him as though it were a statement and not a question. 'I can't say that I've ever noticed before. What's your problem?'

'Who would know for certain?' Carrington asked forcibly.

'You'd need to check with head office about that. What these people get up to has nothing to do with me. . . my only concern around here is security.'

Carlisle smiled. 'Do you run CCTV monitoring?'

'Yes, we do. That's how I caught you two sniffing around.'

'So, you must operate from a control room somewhere?'

'That's me.'

'And what about master keys, are you in charge of those too?' Carrington asked.

'I am, but they can only be used in an emergency.'

'What about murder?' Carrington said, pointing up at one of the cameras. 'Is that classed as an emergency?'

The stupid grin on the security guard's face had suddenly disappeared. 'Murder! Around here?'

'Uh-huh, that's why we need you to open up for us.'

★★★

The key had barely turned in the lock before an overwhelming stench of diesel fumes hit them. It wasn't a particularly large unit, half brick and half double-stud walls. The floors were solid concrete and heavily impregnated with oil, and a roof fitted with skylights. Running along one wall stood a series of steel storage racks, and in front of them a couple of small work benches. Cluttered with old vehicle parts, nothing had moved in months by the amount of dust that had gathered on them. Carlisle picked up an empty packing box and searched for contact details.

There weren't any.

Looking around, there wasn't much in the way of machinery or plant which felt kind of odd, Carlisle thought. Perhaps it was the presence of a white Transit van that had unsettled him, and yes, its number plates were missing. He knew from experience that this estate had a bad reputation, but it wasn't that kind of feeling he was experiencing. Get a grip, he shuddered. You're a criminal profiler; this isn't supposed to happen to you.

Close to the rear of the building they found a door. Curious, he was half expecting it to be locked. It wasn't. Fumbling around in the dark, the moment his finger flicked the light switch on it gave off a strange ominous orange glow.

Spooky.

The room was 'L' shaped, airless, and ice cold at the touch. Following in Carrington's footsteps, the place had a weird feel, unnerving. The walls, red-brick, were windowless, with no other exits other than the one they'd just stepped through. At the back of the room hung a pair of heavy duty plastic curtains. Crudely nailed to the ceiling by a thick batten of wood, they looked at odds with the rest of their surroundings. As his eyes began to drift, the hairs on his neck suddenly stood on end. What lay beyond the plastic curtains he had no idea, but his instincts kept pulling him towards them.

Gripped by uncertainty, he tried to focus his mind.

'Over there,' Carrington whispered.

'What is it?'

'I thought I heard something.'

'Rats,' he cursed. 'The damn things get everywhere.'

As his eyes adjusted to the light, Carlisle moved deeper into the building and closer towards the plastic curtains. At first it didn't register. Then it did.

A large deep chest freezer unit!

Carrington had spotted it too, but her detective instincts kicked in.

'Touch nothing, we may need to use it as evidence.'

He could see the padlock on the freezer lid was hanging loose and open and decided to take a closer look. Smothering the lock with his handkerchief, he gently tugged on the hasp and stepped back a pace in silence. Not knowing what to find next, he slowly lifted the lid. It was heavy at first, awkward, and on reaching mid-point he felt a sudden rush of chilled air waft his face. His mind implanted with evil thoughts, the moment the freezer's interior lights came on, he bent down to take a closer look.

He froze!

Eyes glazed over and staring back at him. He took a step back. He thought he saw them move, but that was impossible as the head had been severed from the upper torso. Carlisle felt his stomach lurch. Now lying at the opposite end of the freezer, it was then he caught the real horror. Severed mid-thigh, the legs had been painstakingly arranged down either side of the torso. Then he spotted the hands. They too had been meticulously arranged and paired together using heavy duty duct tape. If he did need proof that these were indeed a serial killer's trophies, he need look no further.

As his grip on the freezer lid slackened, it slipped through his fingers with a thud.

Carrington shrieked.

'Sorry, Sue,' he whispered

Terrified, the young detective's face had drained of all colour and she was uncontrollably shaking with fright. 'You scared the living shit out of me,' she croaked. 'What's inside?'

'You don't even want to go there.'

'And why not?'

'Best ring Jack Mason,' he instructed.

His entire world now pressing down on him, Carlisle was finding it difficult to breathe let alone think straight. No matter how many corpses he'd dealt with over his career, it never got any easier. He'd seen mutilation before, but nothing compared to this. This was insanity gone mad, and there were no other words to describe it.

'I need to look for myself,' Carrington said, grabbing hold of the freezer lid handle.

Carlisle stared at her.

'I wouldn't advise it.'

He watched as the young detective struggled to lift the heavy lid and waited for her reaction.

He didn't wait long!

Chapter Thirty-Nine

Sometimes Jack Mason wondered where the time went. Huddled around a computer screen, they'd spent the best part of the morning going back over hundreds of hours of CCTV footage. In what had been a long drawn out session, tempers were frayed, with very little progress being made. The security company's footage wasn't the best quality he'd ever come across. The images were jerky and constantly kept going out of focus.

Holt at the controls, the detective sergeant annoyingly twiddled with the brightness controls – which seemed to take an eternity to get right. Still no better, they'd all but given up on it when a woman appeared at the bottom of the screen, quickly followed by a white Transit van. Mason noted the digital time display and watched as the driver slid from his cab and unlocked the roller-shutter doors. Not a tall man, he was wearing a black hoodie and white trainers on his feet.

DS Holt spoke first. 'Isn't that the Estonian woman operating the roller-shutter doors?'

All eyes now moved to the top left-hand corner of the screen.

'Can we sharpen up the image?' Mason asked.

'I doubt it, boss. The quality is crap.'

The moment Holt clicked the pause button, Mason shuffled awkwardly. 'Hold it right there,' he said, pointing his pen at the screen. 'That's her.'

The room fell silent as minds began to focus.

'It certainly looks like her,' Holt agreed.

'Let's grab a screenshot and make a few facial comparisons.'

'I'm on it, boss.'

Mason exhaled loudly, as he latched on to something else of interest. 'There,' he announced, 'isn't that one of the stolen Transit vans?'

Holt zoomed in.

His mind all over the place, Mason leaned over to take a closer look.

Sure enough, there was no mistaking the big green advertising slogan splashed along its side.

'Well I'll be damned,' a voice from the back of the room declared. 'That's the vehicle the West Yorkshire Police have been whinging on about.'

Holt shook his head in dismay. 'This bastard doesn't know when to stop, he's—'

'Never mind his sodding plans,' Mason interrupted, 'where's he cutting the bodies up?'

'Not at the factory unit,' the senior forensic scientist replied stoically. 'He's been using that purely as a storage base.'

Mason exchanged glances with Hedley. 'What are the chances he lives within easy walking distance of the industrial estate?'

'It's possible.'

'Probable more like.'

Hedley stared at the monitor screen. 'What do we know about this latest victim?'

'Not a lot. Young man, early twenties, Caucasian, with a shock-white head of hair. I'm still waiting for the DNA and pathologist's reports to filter through.' Mason scratched his forehead in thought. 'There's been a few reports of people going missing lately, so we'll need to check them out.'

'He could have lived on his own,' Manley pointed out.

'He may well have done, Harry.'

Carlisle, who had said very little so far, pointed to the screen. 'To catch a psychopath throws up all kinds of challenges. This one lacks empathy, so the loss of an accomplice is merely an inconvenience. To him it's a battle of wits, and the only way to stop him is to catch him at his own game.'

Mason twisted his face in a show of frustration. 'And how do you propose we do that? We don't have the resources to keep an eye on every pub in the city, let alone the thousands of young men who frequent them every night.'

Carlisle drew back in seat. 'There must be a way.'

'Like what?'

'Here we go,' Holt suddenly announced. 'They're leaving the factory unit.'

Sure enough, no sooner had the roller shutter doors come down, when their suspect reappeared at the entrance door. His back to the camera – making any form of facial recognition impossible – they moved left of screen.

'They're heading towards Wallsend by the look of things.'

'And on foot,' Carlisle added.

Mason wrinkled his nose. 'That should make your geographical profiling much easier.'

'There,' Manley pointed out. 'That's a better mug shot.'

Holt rewound the tape and grabbed a screenshot of the suspect's face.

'You were right, George.' Mason remarked. 'The quality is crap.'

Manley annoyingly popped another humbug into his mouth and sat back smiling. 'Just out of interest, the owners went into liquidation six months ago.'

'That must make these people squatters.'

'It would appear so, boss.'

'So much for site security. What more do we know about Auto Parts Distribution?'

'Established in 2006, they had a wide customer base covering the whole of the North-East of England.'

'That's interesting,' DS Holt interrupted. 'Van hire companies, auto distributors, and now factory units. There seems to be a general pattern running here.'

'Duct tape. . .' Mason remarked.

Everyone froze.

'Of course—'

'I want a list of every employer who ever worked for the company. What they did, how long they worked for them, and the names of every distribution outlet they were involved in.'

'Anything else, boss?' Manley sniggered.

'We'll be asking everyone to give a DNA sample – completely voluntary at this stage.'

'What about the owners?'

'The killer's an opportunist, and may have known the financial difficulties the company was in. We still need to check on them nevertheless.'

Hedley checked his notes. 'Do you still think the motive could be jealousy?'

'It's difficult to say.' Mason shrugged. 'What are your thoughts, David?'

Carlisle stared at the CCTV image. 'He's certainly angry about something, and jealousy could well be his motive. If the killer didn't know that Angelica was a prostitute before he met her, he sure would be angry the moment he found out. Jealousy is a strange thing, it can destroy a person's way of thinking.'

'You're right,' Manley added. 'Perhaps that's what caused him to snap?'

'It's possible,' Carlisle agreed. 'Mission-Orientated serial killers murder because they're motivated to seek revenge or eliminate a specific group of people; they seldom move away from their selection criteria. That said, there's plenty of convincing evidence to suggest that Angelica was grooming her victims through Internet chatroom sites. Working together as they did, would have made them a lethal cocktail.'

'Hang on a minute,' Mason interrupted. 'If jealousy is the motive here, that may account for his anger towards these young men. Let's wind the clock back a couple of months. If his initial target was young Colin Henderson, it proves Jennifer Oakwell wasn't part of his plans. The only question remaining, is why he killed her.'

'What if she egged him into doing it?' Manley suggested.

Mason looked on perplexed. 'I doubt it, Harry.'

'What about this Bonnie and Clyde thing?'

Plenty of officers got along fine with each other, but not so in Mason's case. The Detective Chief Inspector was a grumpy old sod, and the recent bust up with his fancy woman wasn't helping either. No one was willing to challenge him nowadays, not even Harry Manley, which was surprisingly unusual as the detective constable was renowned for making snide quips.

'Do you know what?' Mason suddenly announced. 'That's the best thing I've heard all day.'

Holt turned to Carlisle and winked. 'Had you not found the factory unit in the first place I doubt we'd be sitting here talking like this.'

'Let's not get carried away,' Mason groaned. 'There's still an awful lot to think about.'

Taking a momentary break, Mason caught up with Carlisle along the corridor. It was Monday, and the growing bottleneck of weekend crime had finally caught up with them. Every police cell in the building was full, and the duty solicitors were having to work flat out to clear the backlog. By the end of the day it would have quietened down a tad, and things would be back to normal – whatever normal meant.

'Here's my problem,' Mason suddenly announced. 'According to her doctors, Angelica is now conscious but can't remember a damn thing about her past.'

'What are her solicitors saying?' Carlisle shrugged.

'Not a lot.' Mason lowered the tone of his voice. 'We've yet to charge her with murder, and I'm in no hurry to do that.'

'And why not?'

Mason tapped the side of his forehead and smiled philosophically. 'On the surface, she appears to be suffering from temporary memory loss. What she doesn't know, not even her doctors, is that a team of trained undercover officers are constantly monitoring her progress. It's a painstakingly slow process, but I don't want to rush it. Not whilst she's talking to one of my undercover officers, I don't.'

'You've lost me – I thought she was suffering from temporary memory loss.'

Mason gave him a hapless look. 'That's how it appears on the surface, but she appears to have gained the trust of one of my female officers, believing she's a sympathetic staff nurse. She's not, of course. She's a trained psychologist, with a shit load of qualifications to her name.'

'Clever—'

Mason glanced back at the empty corridor, as if to check his surroundings. 'Shortly after Angelica arrived in this country, she told my undercover psychologist she'd been forced into prostitution.'

'That's exactly what I thought had happened to her.'

'You were wrong,' Mason said flatly. 'She's a liar, and I wouldn't trust her as far as I could throw her.'

'Did she say who this person was?' asked Carlisle.

'No. She claims to have been in a steady relationship with an older man but has yet to mention his name. What she has told us is that when the relationship finally soured he'd committed numerous sexual offences against her.'

'What! He forced her to have intercourse against her will?'

'Not in as many words.'

'It's time I talked to her, Jack. She may open up to me?'

Mason gave him a withering look. 'Her solicitors would never allow it.'

'No, maybe not.'

Mason smiled wryly. 'We could always ask Sutherland, of course.'

Chapter Forty

Soil samples found at the factory unit had drawn Jack Mason's investigations back to Byker that afternoon, a district north of the River Tyne. As the hunt for the killer intensified, no stones were being left unturned. Forensics had been kept busy, and the young man's body found in the deep freezer had formally been identified as Kevin Price, a 26-year-old local engineer who had recently returned to Newcastle after working in France. Reported missing by a relative, after he failed to turn up for work, Price was last seen hanging around in bars on Wallsend High Street. Single and living on his own, detectives involved in the investigation had carried out extensive CCTV and house-to-house-enquires and believed that Price may have been seeing a young woman at the time. Sadly, from the evidence gained so far, Price was murdered before he was reported missing. There wasn't much to go on, and without a murder scene the team were severely hampered. Finding out where Price had been murdered and who the young woman was, was now paramount to solving the case.

Sitting in his undercover Ford Focus, Mason took another swig from his bottle of water and stared at the building opposite. It was 2.15 pm, and his police radio had gone into hibernation again. Earlier that morning, reports of a stolen Transit van seen in the vicinity had scrambled the team into action. He'd heard nothing since. Now parked just a few blocks from where John Lawrence's broken body was found, Mason was taking no chances. If this was the killer's hunting ground, they would need to be on their guard.

Kevin Price's violent ending had hung heavily on the Detective Chief Inspector's mind that morning. It was a shocking discovery, and one he'd wished he'd never witnessed. Not all of Price's body parts had been recovered from the freezer; some parts were still missing. After hours spent labelling and trying to match dismembered limbs, some of Thomas Wilkinson's missing body parts had finally turned up. It was a harrowing experience, and one that most police officers present were keen to forget.

Now facing the biggest murder inquiry in his entire career, Mason knew exactly what was going on inside Chief Constable Ronald Gregory's mind when the Yorkshire Ripper was at the height of his killing spree. When they finally caught up with Peter Sutcliffe – a Bradford lorry driver and former grave digger – 13 murders had been committed. God forbid the *Suitcase Man* should reach such staggering figures; it didn't bear thinking about.

The moment his radio spewed out some inaudible instructions, he managed to catch the gist of it. A mile east, a stolen Transit van was heading his way and moving in heavy traffic. Just as a precaution he banned all marked cars from the area but wasn't pinning his hopes on it. If this was the killer's vehicle approaching, and he believed it could be, they would need to stay vigilant.

Then he heard a sharp rap on his nearside window and flicked the door release button. Moments later the criminal profiler slid into the passenger seat.

'Heard anything yet?' Carlisle asked.

'We're getting reports of a stolen Transit van heading in this direction.'

'Sounds encouraging.'

'Don't get carried away, this is the third today.'

'Really?'

Mason craned his neck as he peered out of the rear window – nothing yet. He steadied himself. 'More importantly Sutherland wants me to charge the Estonian woman with murder.'

'It's a bit premature, don't you think?'

Mason twisted his face. 'I've expressed my concerns to her in no uncertain terms. Not that she'll take a blind bit of notice of me the stupid bitch is determined to go ahead with it. Media interviews, reconstructions, you name it she wants it.'

'It's not a clever idea... not under the current circumstances. It could spark him into committing all kinds of atrocities.'

Mason shook his head. 'Once Sutherland gets the bit between her teeth there's no stopping her.'

'But this killer will stop at nothing, Jack.'

'Tell me about it.'

'I can't say I blame you for putting up a fight.'

It was time to settle their differences, find out the profiler's inner thoughts.

'If you could change one thing right now, what would it be?' he asked.

'That's a hypothetical question.'

'Maybe, but you're not tied down like the rest of us.'

'What are you getting at?'

Mason sighed. 'What with Sutherland's crazy new demands, I'm finding it impossible to duck under the radar nowadays.'

Carlisle burst out laughing. 'Get a life, Jack. The minute I did that you'd be all over me like a rash.'

'I'm trying to be serious here.'

'So am I.'

Mason exchanged glances, determined to get his point across. 'Let's park that to one side for a moment. We know the killer's a cunning bastard, and I don't have to tell you that. The team's overstretched but knowing where to concentrate my resources is my biggest concern.'

Carlisle looked at him surprised. 'The one thing I've learned about serial killers is they stick rigidly to set plans. This one's no different, and his methodology hasn't changed one iota since his partner's arrest.' He made a little sweeping gesture with his hand. 'If I were in your shoes, I'd be concentrating my efforts on the people who previously occupied the factory lock-up.'

'So, you think the killer could be an ex-employee?'

'Think about it. If you didn't know why the factory unit had remained empty these past few months, you wouldn't dare store body parts in it?'

'That's a good point but checking out hundreds of distribution outlets will be a massive drain on resources.'

'He's local, Jack, and he knows his way around this city like the back of his hand.'

'Mmm.'

Carlisle grinned. 'I'm not a gambling man, but it wouldn't surprise me to find he's still working in the auto parts trade.'

'It makes sense.'

'I agree it's a massive undertaking, but you need to be patient.'

'You and I should talk more often, my friend.'

Carlisle smiled. 'I doubt you'd listen?'

Mason lifted his eyes to the rear-view mirror, just as a white Transit van came into view. He checked the NPRS, and sure enough it was stolen. But that didn't mean a thing, as the killer had a nasty habit of switching number plates.

He pressed the clutch in and turned the key.

'Hold onto your hat.' Mason grinned.

The moment the Transit van's red tail lights grew brighter, he swung behind it. Eyes glued to the rear-view mirror, DS Holt's undercover pool car was up close and intimate. Too close, he thought, and he switched his hazard warning lights on to signal his intentions. Seconds later, Holt's unmarked vehicle pulled out of the pursuit.

'Looking at the Google GPS,' Carlisle said, staring down at his mobile phone app, 'if he doesn't join the Coast Road at the next junction, he could be heading for Freeman Hospital.'

Mason felt an adrenaline rush. 'How far is that away?'

'Barely half a mile from here.'

Sticking rigidly to the speed limit, at the next mini roundabout the Transit van swung left. At least the driver hadn't spotted them, which was always a good sign.

'He's turning onto Freeman Road,' Carlisle announced.

'What the hell is he playing at?'

'He's obviously checking the lie of the land.'

Mason slowed as he approached the hospital turn in, then stopped at the car park entrance barrier. Thirty feet ahead, he watched as the Transit van turned into the first available parking space and came to a halt. He drove up behind it, and boxed in.

'Police,' Mason shouted, hammering on the driver's window and holding up his warrant card. 'Mind telling me the registration number of your vehicle?'

The driver wound down his window and looked at him confused. 'Beta, Gamma, Victor, Ninety-Six.'

'It's not what it says on the tin.'

Jumping out of his cab, the van driver moved to the front of his vehicle. Seconds later he turned to face them. 'Some bastard has switched the number plates.'

'Is this your vehicle, sir?' Mason asked.

'No, it belongs to the company. I'm a delivery driver for FastTrack.'

His mind all over the place, Mason felt his stomach churn. 'Tell me,' he said, 'where do you leave your vehicle at night?'

'Outside my house. Why?'

Realising the plates had been switched, Mason pulled out his notebook. 'Mind telling me where that is?'

'Yeah, Barry Street in Walker.'

Mason turned to Carlisle. 'Sounds likes he's active again.'

'If it is him.'

Mason managed a thin smile. 'If not, I'll show my arse in Fenwick's window.'

The van driver stared at them gobsmacked.

Chapter Forty-One

Within weeks of Thomas Wilkinson's dismembered body being discovered at a local waste recycling centre in Blaydon, a local miscreant named Andrew Martin had come under Mason's radar. The evidence was thin, but the police knew that Martin had hung around with Wilkinson's associates, and that he didn't technically have a job. Apart from social benefits, Martin had carried out a dodgy door to door leaflet distribution service to pay for his iPhone and drug habits. Although Martin seemed an unlikely target for a resource-intensive surveillance operation, when Jack Mason received a call from a local newspaper reporter informing him that Martin was involved in high end car theft, it all made sense. Fox now had a lot to answer for, it seemed.

As the cell door swung open, Andrew Martin moved awkwardly towards Interview Room Two. There were no smiles, no friendly banter, only serious expressions. Brought in for questioning the previous evening and held on suspicion of murder, Martin looked exhausted. After a thorough search of the suspect's property, a knife found hidden inside a bag of sand was currently being examined by forensics. Anticipating a quick result, Mason remained upbeat.

Holt activated the recording tape and announced the time, date, and those present. Sitting directly opposite him, Mason could tell when a suspect was out of their comfort zone, as they always wore that nervous look on their face. It reminded him of a frightened rabbit trapped in the headlights of a car – not knowing which way to turn.

Mason stared down at his interview notes as he spoke. 'Let's talk about your friend, Thomas Wilkinson.'

Martin nodded but said nothing.

'After a thorough search of your bedsit, we recovered a vital piece of evidence that puts you close to the crime scene the night Thomas was murdered. Care to explain where you were on Friday, April 11, around 7:30 pm?'

Mason stared Martin in the eye and watched for signs of weakness.

'I've told you all I know, I was in Newcastle.'

'According to your previous statement, you were drinking with friends that evening.'

'So what?'

Mason shuffled awkwardly anticipating *No Comment* to every question he posed. So far so good, he thought. He waited patiently and felt his heart beat faster. His next question, when it came, was far more reaching. 'Your account of what happened that evening doesn't seem to stack up. At 7:20 pm you were caught on CCTV cameras outside the Globe bar in Railway Street. What's more, you were seen talking to Thomas Wilkinson and wearing a black hoodie, jogging bottoms and white trainers.'

'Was I?'

As IR-2 fell silent, the atmosphere was strained.

'For purposes of the tape,' Mason said, 'I'm showing Mr Martin exhibit AD54.'

Mason slid a monochrome photograph in front of Martin and took up an unfriendly posture. 'At 9:30 pm, you were caught on CCTV camera outside the Yard Bar in Newcastle. That's you there, isn't it, Mr Martin?' Mason pointed to the photograph.

'It looks like me, but it's not.'

'Care to tell me why you murdered Thomas Wilkinson?'

'Fuck you, Inspector,' Martin replied angrily. 'You can't pin that one on me.'

'Tell me,' said Mason calmly, 'what did you do with the knife after you killed Thomas? Did you try to hide it somewhere safe?'

Martin glared at him. 'I don't own a bladed weapon, and there's no way I would stab my best friend with one. That's a crazy statement.'

'Who mentioned anything about stabbing anyone?'

'Everyone knows Thomas was stabbed to death. It was in all the newspapers.'

'You're going to have to stop lying to us,' DS Holt said assertively, 'you're not making a very good job of it. The fact is, early this morning we recovered a six-inch bladed weapon from your property identical to the one that killed Thomas Wilkinson.'

Martin shrugged but remained silent.

It wasn't looking good suddenly, and Mason was unhappy at the way the interview was progressing. Martin was digging a hole for himself, and his solicitor was allowing it to happen. Strange, he thought. Getting the suspect to cooperate was proving more difficult than he'd imagined. He knew he could only hold Martin in custody for twenty-four-hours; after that they would need to apply for an extension. He was floundering, and he still didn't have sufficient evidence to charge him.

Mason turned to his files and slid another photograph towards Martin. 'For purposes of the tape, I'm showing Mr Martin exhibit AD43.'

The suspect glared at him but said nothing.

'Just for the record, what were you doing in the Yard Bar at 9:42 pm that night?'

'I went there for a drink, why?'

'Isn't that on Scotswood Road?'

'Yeah, you know it is.'

'Did you go there with the intention to meet up with someone?'

'I may have done?'

'Just answer the question.'

Martin drew back in his seat, his demeanour defensive. 'Like I said, I was out drinking in all my usual haunts. The same as I do every Friday night.'

'We're not stupid,' said DS Holt shaking his head. 'Whilst you've been detained in custody we've been busy going over your property. It's what we do best. It's what we're trained to do. The problem is, we've recovered items of interest about you, including your computer.'

Martin stared at them but refused to be drawn in.

Holt smiled. 'Do you know what, it's amazing what computer files can throw up. Facebook accounts, twitter contacts, that sort of thing. There's even a chatroom forum that tells us where you were on Friday, April 11, at 5:30 pm. It's all there, Mr Martin. You'd arranged to meet up with a Joseph Trotter that evening, hadn't you?'

'I may have done—'

'Don't lie to me. You did meet up with him, didn't you?'

Martin said nothing.

'Now here's my problem,' said DS Holt shaking his head. 'We know you messaged a Joseph Trotter that afternoon at 3:22 pm. What you don't know, or perhaps you do, is that Joseph Trotter is an undercover police officer.'

Martin's face dropped. 'It was just a bit of fun, I—'

'Fun, Mr Martin? This isn't some sort of chat show, and I'm not a TV host sitting here. That's how you always arrange to meet your men, isn't it? You message them on Internet chatroom sites and build up a rapport with them.' Holt held eye contact. 'I'd say you were grooming them. . . trying to win these people over.'

'There's nothing wrong with that. I just like chatting to people, that's all.'

'No, I suppose not,' Holt agreed, 'but what worries me is what goes on after you've taken them back home with you.'

'What are you inferring?'

'Well,' Mason began. 'What did you intend to do with Joseph Trotter after you'd met up with him that night?'

'He was an interesting guy to talk to. Why?'

'I bet he was. Just like the other young men you supposedly chatted up.'

Martin sneered back at them. 'That's how some guys like to operate, Inspector.'

'What worries me,' said Holt, 'is the night Thomas Wilkinson was murdered *you* were one of the last people to be seen with him. We're not stupid, Mr Martin. After you'd teamed up with him outside the Globe bar in Railway Street, you'd arranged to meet up with him later that evening.'

'That's not true. I'm not that sort of person.'

'Oh, but I think you are.'

'I'm not—'

'You took advantage of him, didn't you?' Mason shuffled awkwardly as he slid another vital piece of evidence across the table towards Martin. 'For the purposes of the tape, I'm showing Mr Martin exhibit AD69. It's a picture of the so-called *Suitcase Man,* taken outside a corner shop in Bean Street, Byker.' Mason glared across at Martin and tapped the photograph with his pen. 'That is, you is it not?'

Martin said nothing.

'The night you met Thomas Wilkinson, you were dressed in a black hoodie, jogging bottoms, and wearing white Nike trainers.' Mason's eyes narrowed a fraction. 'Do you know what, they are identical to the ones this person is seen wearing.' Mason drummed the photograph with the end of his pen and watched for a reaction.

'Whoever this person is, it's not me.'

'How can you possibly say that? I haven't even told you what time this picture was taken, or anything else about it for that matter. You're lying, Mr Martin, and you're making a really bad job of it.'

'Perhaps we can take a break, gentlemen,' Martin's solicitor suddenly announced. 'I need to talk to my client.'

DS Holt leaned over and switched off the interview tape.

'Yes, of course,' Mason replied. 'Take your time. Your client will soon have plenty of that on his hands.'

'Let's not get facetious, Detective Chief Inspector. My client is completely innocent, and you people know it.'

Mason smiled. 'Surely that's up to a jury to decide, not me?'

'True,' Martin's solicitor contemptuously replied, 'but before you even think about going down that avenue, perhaps you should ask my client where he was on the night that Colin Henderson was murdered. Had you done so, then you'd have approached this interview very differently.'

Mason glared across at him realising he must have reasonable grounds to prove his client's whereabouts. Surely not, he groaned.

Chapter
Forty-Two

Wasp braked hard the moment he spotted the marked patrol car – *just in case*. He needn't have bothered. The officer inside seemed placid enough, but you could never be too careful at this time of night. Much to his relief, except for a few security lights guarding the back of the hospital grounds, this part of the complex was in darkness. No cameras to worry about here – they were all at the front of the building and covering the main entrance. There was always the fat controller's room to consider, but that would come later.

The moment Wasp slid into the designated parking lot, he gave a sigh of relief. There was an air of quiet, orderly calm, as he opened the rear doors to the Transit van. His first task was to secure his escape route; without that he was nothing. Seconds later, he dragged the folding ROAD CLOSED sign out from the back of the vehicle and erected it close to the approach road. Next, he slid the ramp into position and rolled out the wheelchair. One final check before he was ready to rock and roll.

Perfect.

Deep in the night Wasp heard a siren wailing. This place never stopped. There was always plenty to keep the hospital staff occupied, no matter what was going on around him. Breathing heavily, he trundled the empty wheelchair towards the rear of the staff accommodation wing, double-checking the curtains and smiling. All that remained now was to prise open the fire door – the one he'd wedged earlier that day. Once inside it would all run like clockwork. Nothing to worry about, he laughed, everyone was asleep.

Wearing a clean white shirt, navy slacks and a comfortable pair of black shoes, Wasp felt a million dollars in his new porter's uniform. His wig was a tad uncomfortable, and perhaps a little too tight. If anything, he was more than pleased with the Swiss medical watch he'd borrowed from the local charity shop. God, it looked awesome.

Gripped by uncertainty, he hung in the shadows and waited. Wasp wasn't sure, but he could have sworn he'd heard a high-pitched beeping noise the moment he entered the hospital building. Physically shaken, it was only natural he should feel on edge. Security was tight, it had to be, and every door in the building was locked and alarmed against night predators. Not to worry, though, the route he was taking was barely fifty metres away from his intended target.

He hesitated and stared once more at the operating theatre doors. There was an interesting myth doing the rounds that some limbs could be reattached to another person's body as many as four days after amputation. He'd read about it in one of the many medical journals he'd bought – and he was training himself to be a surgeon. Cross-transfer of human body parts was his biggest fascination, and he was obsessed by what these people could do. Some surgeons had amazing skills and could do a lot more than just reattach body parts to people. Not much use if you were dead, though.

He'd heard somewhere that surgeons had transplanted a healthy hand from a dead patient to a living one, which was kind of awesome when you thought about it. How it would work with fingertip recognition he had no idea, but he would need to investigate it.

Suddenly two men came scurrying along a long corridor, their footsteps echoing their arrival. One was carrying a human organ box, the other wearing green scrubs. He put his head down and kept on walking and wasn't sure if they'd noticed him. If they had, it hadn't shown. His body clock wasn't functioning as well as it ought to be this time of night, and things had looked totally different in broad daylight. Anxious, and breathing heavily, Wasp pushed on.

Then, he spotted the neurological ward.

He tried the door – it was locked.

The moment he peered in through one of the side glass panels a middle-aged woman joined him. Wearing a blue staff nurse uniform, he tried to hide his surprise from her. There had to be a better plan than this, surely.

Hold your nerve!

Then much to his surprise, she punched a series of numbers into the push button keypad and he made a mental note of the code. As the door swished quietly shut behind him, she turned, and said. 'How can I help you?'

'I'm here to pick up a patient. She's due down at the Imaging Department in twenty minutes' time.'

Wasp smiled as he assuredly patted the empty wheelchair seat.

'Do you have a name?'

He hesitated. Big mistake.

She looked him up and down, causing him to drop the clipboard he'd brought with him. He recovered it and pointed up to the list of names on the roster board that hung on the wall.

'It's the foreign lady, and I always have difficulty in pronouncing it.'

'Ah, you mean Angelica Glebova?'

'Yes. That's the one.'

She looked him up and down, then glanced down at the computer screen again. Something was wrong, and whatever it was she was making him nervous. Wasp drew himself into the scene and tried not to think negative thoughts. He'd covered a lot of ground that evening and wasn't giving in that easily. He should have done things differently – thought of a better plan. Even though he couldn't see her, he still sensed Angelica's presence. Excitement gripped him, and he was holding back the tears.

Then, glancing up, he spotted an armed police officer. Not a tall man, docile looking, and dressed in a familiar black combat uniform.

'Who sent you?' the duty staff nurse asked authoritatively.

'Why, is there a problem?'

'There seems to be some sort of mix-up. Miss Glebova has had another *subdural haematoma* and is back in intensive care.'

'Intensive care. . .' whispered Wasp.

'Yes. The doctors are in with her now.'

'Dearie, dearie me. I hope she's not in a whole lot of trouble.'

Niceties dispensed with, the duty staff nurse turned to face him again. 'I can run a check for you,' she said, her hand hovering over the telephone receiver. 'It's always best to err on the safe side.'

He forced a smile, as he slowly turned to leave.

'Best not waste any more of your precious time,' Wasp said, using his best sympathetic voice. 'I know you're very busy.'

'We are.' The duty staff nurse smiled.

Concealing his anger, Wasp punched the red door release button and watched as the ward doors swung open. At least he now had the security code and knew exactly where to find her.

It's always best to err on the safe side, he mused.

He rather liked that.

Chapter Forty-Three

Having been dragged out of bed at an unearthly hour, Jack Mason wasn't in the best of moods. Someone had breached hospital security, and an attempt had been made to snatch the Estonian woman from her sick bed.

'Where the fuck's the hospital security manager?' Mason screamed.

Blue spinner lights flashing, his iPhone buzzing in his pocket, Detective Sergeant Holt stood before him dripping with sweat. 'We've covered every inch of the grounds, boss. Except for the staff car park. There isn't a lot more we can do until the dog teams have completed their sweep.'

'What about the rest of the buildings – how do we know he's not posing as a patient?'

'We don't.' Holt shrugged. 'That's down to each individual ward to check out.'

The time was now 6:00 am, and another shift change was imminent. With more new arrivals to worry about, Jack Mason was livid at the lack of hospital security. To make matters worse, he wasn't in immediate radio contact with anyone on the team and was having to muddle his way through. The arrival of Stan Johnson brought an immediate calming effect. If there were flaws in his plans, the SOC manager would fix them. Stan was a reliable officer, and never missed a trick when it came to be managing a crime scene.

'If he wasn't a genuine hospital porter,' the SOC manager said thoughtfully, 'then how come he knew the security keycode to access the neurological ward?'

Johnson had asked a question that no one else had that morning, and it had taken them by surprise. Holt was the first to react. 'The duty staff nurse should know the answer to that.'

'If he's not a member of staff, he'll not hang around longer than necessary.'

'Damn!' Mason cursed.

Johnson shot Mason a quizzical glance. 'If it was the Estonia woman he was after, what was he intending to do to her?'

'God knows,' Mason shrugged, 'but it's not looking good.'

'She's obviously in no fit state to be moved, let alone be pushed around in a bloody wheelchair,' Holt added.

Mason groaned. 'There's far too many *ifs* for my liking.'

'Whoever's in charge of hospital security is obviously facing an internal enquiry.' Johnson thought a minute. 'If the hospital security has been breached, it's down to us to ensure the public is kept safe.'

'You're right,' Mason replied, grateful of some sound advice at last. 'It's time to throw a security cordon around the complex.'

Johnson stared into the distance, thinking. 'If he's posing as a hospital porter to penetrate security, it shouldn't be difficult to fix.

'You wouldn't have thought so,' Holt agreed.

There followed an awkward exchange of glances between them.

'It's not the best of situations,' Mason said guardedly. 'Surely it's down to these people to vet their own staff?'

Johnson nodded. 'This was obviously planned, as he escaped via a broken fire door at the back of the building. There's a dog team out looking for him, so let's hope they soon catch up with him.'

By nine o'clock the sun had appeared, and it promised to be another beautiful day. The warm weather had come suddenly, in what had been a damp and dismal June. The cruel irony was, it was Hexham Races on Saturday and Mason had been looking forward to that. Just when he thought he'd got to grips with the case, everything was turned on its head. Even Tom Hedley's team had thrown up very little in the way of fresh leads. These things took time, he realised that, but nothing seemed straightforward anymore. Loath to admit, it was time to involve the criminal profiler – bring some lateral thinking to the team.

'Ah, if it isn't Inspector Jack Mason,' a familiar voice called out.

The moment he clocked Christopher Sykes, Mason's stomach lurched. Where Sykes got his information from, was beyond him. Sleazebag journalists were the last people he needed right now.

Mason took a deep breath. 'What can I do for you?'

Pen poised at the ready, Sykes habitually brushed the flecks of dandruff from his jacket and turned to face him. 'Excuse the pun, Inspector, but there does seem to be a rather large gathering of police officers around the place. I hope it has nothing to do with this. . . *Suitcase Man!* There again, I've heard rumours there's been a breach in the hospital's security.'

Mason nodded but said nothing.

'Mind telling me what's going on?'

Mason pretended to act dumb. The last time he'd spoken with Sykes, he'd ended up complaining to the Independent Press Standards Organisation about running what he claimed were inaccurate stories on a major crime case he was working on. He'd got nowhere.

'Why not check with hospital security?' Mason replied. 'Find out what they know.'

'I already have. I just thought I'd run it past you as well.'

Sykes was weird, and not to be trusted. Rumour had it that he'd been caught messing around with young teenage girls in one of the local park toilets. Nobody could pin a thing on him, and that was the problem. The most likely scenario, as far as Mason could make out, was that people were trying to get their own back on Sykes.

'What do we know about this intruder?' the journalist asked.

'Not a lot. Why?'

'That's odd. I'd heard he'd tried to snatch one of the patients out of her hospital bed. Came through the back door, apparently.'

'What else have you heard?' Mason quizzed.

'Some say it was this Angelica woman he was after,' Sykes dribbled. 'You know me, Jack. I always try to keep my readers informed.'

Like hell, Mason thought. Sykes only interest lay in selling headline stories, no matter how many people's toes he trod on. It's what sold newspapers, what made scumbags like Sykes such an enemy of the police.

It was time to put the record books straight.

'Okay,' Mason began, 'don't quote me on this, but a few of my trusted lieutenants are currently out searching for him.'

'And?'

Mason lowered his voice a fraction and pretended to check over his shoulder. 'We've just received reports he's heading towards the Quayside.'

Sykes stared at him and laughed. 'Why is it I don't believe you, Inspector?'

'It's Detective Chief Inspector, actually,' Mason condescendingly replied.

'Yeah, well. What do you think my readers will say when they read a lunatic is running amok on the streets of Newcastle?'

Mason glared at him, annoyed. 'No doubt you'll think of something to say.'

Sykes bottom lip quivered. 'Don't tempt me.'

'You asked, and I delivered.'

'Like you, I'm just doing my job, Inspector.' Sykes swivelled on his heels. 'Which reminds me. This Andrew Martin chap you recently brought in for questioning on suspicion of murder.'

'What about him?'

'A little bird tells me the charges against him have been dropped. Mind, his solicitors are not very happy chappies. They've written to the Police Complaints Commission about their client's abusive treatment and having to spend two nights locked up in a Gateshead police cell. Have you heard anything from them yet?'

'You should have been a detective,' Mason smiled wryly.

'No thanks. I'll stick to what I do best.'

DC Manley joined them from the hospital's main car park carrying a plastic forensic bag in his hand, and Sykes made a note of it. 'One last question if I may,' the newspaper reporter sneered. 'Is anywhere out of bounds?'

'If you're thinking about having a kidney transplant,' Manley scoffed, 'the surgical suite's still open.'

The newspaper reporter's face darkened.

'Don't push me, Detective Constable. I'm in no mood for small-talk.'

Mason burst out laughing. 'You've gone and done it again, Harry.'

'Done what?' Manley asked.

'I'm having steak and kidney pie for tea.'

There was a bit of a stand-off between them before Sykes finally stormed off towards the hospital main admissions. Just what the evening tabloids would make of it, Mason shuddered to think. One thing for sure, Manley's quip had certainly brought a smile to everyone's face.

Chapter Forty-Four

Tommy Nolan was a slightly built man, mid-forties, with a high forehead and long hooked nose. Dressed in a blue open necked shirt, grey suit, and black brogue shoes, he certainly looked the part. Mason had a notion about slick car salesmen, believing they could sell snow to the Eskimos. It was this aspect, among other things, that had brought him here today. Close to the A1, and two miles north of Newcastle city centre, the car dealership showroom reminded him of an oversized greenhouse. Even so, it had a fine range of high-end luxury cars on display, and there were plenty of cars to choose from. Mason sat for a moment quietly weighing up the prices. There were none to suit his wallet, though he did fancy a test drive in one he'd spotted.

'Okay,' Mason said, as he sat back in a plush leather upholstered seat that stank of saddle polish and squeaked when he moved around in it. 'After Auto Parts Distribution went into liquidation, you tried your hand as a supermarket manager. When that didn't work out, you ended up here as the Senior Sales Manager.'

'That's right, Inspector.'

Nolan was irritatingly chatty and didn't know when to keep his mouth shut. The advantages from Mason's viewpoint was there wasn't a damn thing he didn't know about Auto Parts Distribution. He'd read about them in Companies House and was trying to catch Nolan off guard. If one of its ex-employees was a potential serial killer, he was determined to weed him out. He peered at the exquisite Audi R8 coup again and began to let his mind drift. It had beautiful contour lines, luxurious interior, and a full range of fancy new gadgets to admire. He could well imagine himself parading up and down the High Street in one, and watching the young women turn their heads in awe.

Then he fell to earth again.

'How long did you say you worked for Auto Parts Distribution?'

'Three years.'

'And how many people did the company employ?'

'There were fourteen of us in total.'

'And you worked in the warehouse, you say?'

'That's right. Me and a guy called, Bob Stanton.'

Mason cocked his head to one side. 'Friendly atmosphere would you say?'

'Yeah, you could say that.'

'What about staff turnover?'

'There was only one as I remember, and that was due to ill health.'

Mason sat for a moment. 'Apart from the owner's wife, I take it the rest of the staff were male?'

'Yes, they were.' The senior sales manager looked at him quizzically. 'Mind telling me what this is all about, Inspector?'

Mason pushed back in his seat, pleased in the knowledge he was finally getting somewhere. He wasn't usually sentimental about victims, but the image of young Kevin Price's dismembered body was still indelibly etched on his mind. It could have been *his* daughter lying in the freezer, or any one of his best friend's kids come to think of it. Still fired up by it all, he was determined to put a stop to this monster's killings.

'Sounds like it was a good company to work for. Were you in it from the start?'

'Yes, I was. I joined the company as the distribution manager. Well, that's how they initially described the position in their advert.' Nolan's eyes dropped. 'The owners were in the process of setting up a distribution hub in Yorkshire and were looking for a new manager to run it. It never materialised, unfortunately.'

'I see. And what exactly did your job entail?'

'Most days were spent making up shipment orders for the distribution drivers. Apart from re-ordering and replenishing stock, the job was mainly warehouse-based.'

'No doubt you complained to the owners about it?'

'Yes, bitterly. And on more than one occasion might I add.'

'And how did they react?'

'They were very apologetic about it at first.'

'Any reason why they never went ahead with their expansions?'

'It's a cut-throat business, Inspector. Besides, the company had big cash flow problems as I remember. It was something to do with ninety-day payments.'

Mason nodded, already knowing the answer to that. 'And that would be an accounts problem, I guess?'

'Yes, it was.' Nolan nodded.

'Tell me,' Mason said, thoughtfully. 'Apart from you, what did the other members of staff do in the organisation?'

Nolan went on in great lengths to explain the Auto Parts Distribution set-up, its customer base, its methods of supply, everything about the company. By the time he'd finished, Mason's head was in bits.

'These distribution outlets,' Mason quizzed, 'where were they located?'

'All over the North East and as far south as Sheffield. At one point, there was even talk of expanding into Nottingham.'

Mason ears pricked up. 'What about Leeds?'

'Yes, we had an excellent customer base there,' Nolan explained.

'Were all of your delivery drivers involved with the Leeds distributions?'

'No, only three of them were.'

Mason made a note of it. 'Anything out of the ordinary occur in Leeds?'

'Like what!'

'You know what I mean, men always like to brag about their conquests after a few drinks.'

'No. There was none of that shenanigans going on to my knowledge.'

Mason took another sip of his coffee and tried to gather his thoughts. Nolan was a family man and didn't have a bad word to say about anyone – let alone kill someone. This wasn't as easy as he had first thought, and a lot of water had passed under the bridge since the company had gone into liquidation. If the killer was an ex-employee, it certainly wasn't evident from what Nolan was telling him.

Then Mason remembered. 'Tell me,' he said, pen poised. 'Did the company ever deal in heavy duty duct tape?'

'We did, and it was one of our most popular product lines. It's funny you should mention Leeds, as that's where most of it was sold.'

'Who to exactly?'

'A paint company in Seacroft.'

Alarm bells ringing, Mason jotted down some notes.

'The three Leeds delivery van drivers you talked about,' Mason said. 'Have you met up with any of them since?'

'Yes, I occasionally bump into one of them. Why do you ask?'

'Most are married, I suspect?'

'Yes, they are.'

Mason suddenly remembered what Carlisle had told him about the killer sticking rigidly to set routines and decided to probe deeper. 'That's interesting. After the company went into liquidation, did any of them ever go back into the distribution business?'

'A few did as I remember, and—'

'Would you know who, exactly?'

Nolan reeled off a couple of names, but Mason was reluctant to divulge why he needed the information in the first place. If the press ever got a whiff of it, his investigations would be blown out of the water. He glanced at the blue Audi R8 coup again.

'Nice car,' he said, pointing to it. 'What does something like that set you back?'

'Interested in buying one, Inspector?'

Nolan had automatically switched back into sales mode, and Mason had picked up on it.

'No, just curious, that's all.'

'Around one-hundred and twenty-grand, but they're a beautiful looking car. Three hundred and ninety-seven horsepower, nought to 62 mph in 3.2 seconds, and a whole lot of extras thrown in. It certainly looks your type of motor, Inspector. Would you like to test drive one?'

Mason gave him a look that said, *you must be joking bonny lad.*

'Just for the record,' Mason said, as he stood to leave. 'Did anyone at Auto Spares Distribution ever team up with a Russian woman?'

'A Russian woman. . .' Nolan repeated, as he stared back at him bemused. 'Not that I'm aware of. Why?'

'Internet chat-rooms, that sort of thing?'

'Hell no. Besides, it's not the sort of thing that anyone would discuss at work.'

'No, I suppose not,' Mason grinned, 'but it *is* the kind of thing that someone might brag about!'

Nolan shook his head, as if puzzled by it all. 'Can't say as they ever did.'

'Thanks for your time.' Mason extended out a hand. 'You've been most helpful.'

He left the dealership showroom into bright sunshine, pausing to take one last lingering look at the beautiful blue Audi R8 coup. *One-hundred and twenty thousand pounds,* he whispered, cheap at half the price. There again, Mason thought, he would need to reach Chief of Police to own something new of that value.

Chapter Forty-Five

It had rained briefly that morning, and damp puddles still clung to the pavement. The estate had changed very little over the years. Not exactly the Ritz, it still carried an element of hopelessness about it, as if stuck in a time warp. There was quite a mix of houses in the street, and those unoccupied had overgrown gardens full of junk. Across the street, a rusty old Ford Escort was jacked up on bricks. Its wheels were missing, and the exhaust pipe had fallen to the ground like some jouster's broken lance in battle. Mason folded his arms across his chest as he climbed out from the silver Ford Focus. The people who lived here didn't give a toss about the material things in life, only drugs.

He stood for a moment and glanced at his watch. Strangely enough, he was having another quiet day. All his clear thinking had paid dividends that morning. They'd made a few calls, eliminated several people from his enquiries, and generally made their presence felt. Approaching thirty-six, Patrick Stanley was the last of the three Auto Spares Distribution drivers on his list to interview. And that, he told himself, was the purpose of his visit here today.

From the outside, the house looked deserted. All the upstairs curtains were drawn, and there was junk mail sticking out of the letterbox. Peering in through the broken kitchen window blinds, Mason felt the hairs on the back of his neck prickle. He could not be sure, but there was something about the place that told him to stay focused.

'He's not answering the door,' Carlisle announced, as he approached from the side of the building.

'He's probably in bed and smacked out of his mind on drugs.'

'It's not the safest of areas to hang around in, that's for sure.'

Mason hesitated for a second, then authoritatively rapped on the kitchen door. He'd been over this ground too many times these past few days and was beginning to tire of it. People who had secrets to hide always refused to answer their doors. Curious, he peered in through the window blinds but could not see movement.

'Who are you looking for?' an unfriendly voice called out from a neighbouring fence.

'Police,' Mason replied. 'And you are?'

'I live here. What is it you're after?'

Mason stared at him full of suspicion. To call him a stout man would have been an understatement. His centre of gravity was located around his mid-riff and reminded Mason of an overgrown Teletubby. Then, out of the corner of his eye he caught movement. It wasn't much, but enough to draw his attention towards the hostile dog now sat observing him. It was baring its teeth, and if he wasn't mistaken it was a Pit Bull Terrier and one of the four dog breeds banned from the UK.

Mason flashed his warrant card under the man's nose and watched the frown lines ripple. He wouldn't pull him over his dog now — that would come later.

'Does Patrick Stanley live here?' Mason asked.

'He's out, why?'

'Out where?'

'How the hell would I know?'

Mason checked the door. It wasn't locked.

'If Stanley does return,' Mason said, stepping inside the building. 'Tell him he's got visitors.'

They entered a long narrow passage, their shoes squelching on wet carpets. Then, after flicking the hall lights on, Mason slipped into detective mode. Whilst Carlisle checked the downstairs rooms, he dashed up a short flight of stairs to gain the element of surprise. He'd barely reached the top of the landing when he stopped dead in his tracks.

'Good God!' he gasped.

'You okay?'

Panic gripped him, and he could feel himself hyperventilating. 'Touch nothing,' he shouted, 'this place is now a murder scene.'

Eyes full of curiosity, Carlisle stared up at him from the bottom of the stairs. 'What is it you've found, Jack?'

Mason took another deep breath and steadied himself against the bannister rail. The bathroom door was ajar, and he could barely believe his eyes. 'It's like a slaughter house up here,' he said pushing the door open with the toe of his shoe. 'There's blood everywhere, and what appears to be chunks of human flesh lying in the bottom of the bath.'

'Any footprints?'

'There's plenty of those around.'

Carlisle stood transfixed. 'Blimey—'

'We need to suit up and secure the building before the rest of the cavalry arrive.'

★★★

Twenty minutes later, the estate resembled an impregnable fortress. Feeling like a kid in a sweetshop, Mason watched as a team of forensic officers crawled on hands and knees over the suspect's back garden searching for clues. Amongst other things, they were looking for body parts or buried victims clothing. These things took time, but time was fast catching up on them. There were jobs to be done, fresh plans to set in motion, and new lines of enquiries to explore. Once they'd carried out a thorough examination of the suspect's property, it was a simple matter of legwork. Nowhere was safe for Patrick Stanley anymore, wherever he ran. But that wasn't all, and the Detective Chief Inspector was staring at a much bigger problem – the arrival of the Area Commander's entourage.

Mason's instincts as a working detective told him they were gradually closing in. Whoever the killer was, there weren't a lot of options left open to him. He smiled inwardly as the profiler reappeared in the doorway.

'Well there was a turn up for the books.'

'I had a hunch we were close, the minute we entered the estate.'

'If I hadn't have known you better, I'd have sworn you'd been tipped off.'

'It's not over yet,' Carlisle said shaking his head. 'The killings may have stopped, but Stanley will be a difficult person to track down.'

'I'd already guessed as much.' Mason blew out his cheeks, his eyes fixed firmly ahead. 'No doubt the Acting Superintendent is itching to go public on this one.'

'Let's hope not, as it could cause all sorts of problems.'

'I know,' Mason sighed, 'but I doubt she'll listen to me. She's more concerned about what Mad Frankie might get up to once he finds out who killed his ex-wife.'

Carlisle stared at him. 'I'd almost forgotten about Wiseman.'

'We need to get to Stanley first, before the criminal fraternity beats us to it.'

'He'll probably lie low for a while; it's in his best interest.'

'Yeah, but *where* is the question?'

'The answer to that may be hidden in the detail.'

Mason put a pencil against his lips and thought for a moment. 'Stanley's bound to make life difficult for everyone – there's no other options left open to him.'

'Not with Frank Wiseman breathing down his neck, there isn't.'

'You're right. The fewer people who know about this, the better.' Mason thought a minute. 'Do you think he'll head for Leeds?'

'It's difficult to say. Although he may still have a few contacts there.'

'One thing's for sure, he'll get far less hassle down there than here. Perhaps that's what lies behind the Acting Superintendent's thinking.'

'I would think so.'

'Bugger.' Mason groaned. 'I was hoping for a quick result, but it's not going to happen.'

'These people are always one step ahead of the game. Just when you think you have them in the palm of your hand they slip through your fingers like grains of sand.'

Mason gave a little shake of the head. 'No doubt the Area Commander's cronies will want to get involved, which leaves me little room for manoeuvre.'

'Our biggest threat right now is the media. Once they get hold of the story we'll all be catapulted into the stratosphere.'

'You can say that again.'

'Stanley's a popular guy – in more ways than one.'

Mason adjusted his stance. 'It'll be interesting to see what forensic throws up.'

'I doubt they'll find anything we don't know already.'

'No, I suppose not.'

There was nothing either of them could do, not until the SOC manager had given clearance. Entering the hall, it was the serious look on Tom Hedley's face that suddenly caught their attention. Carrying a large brown paper bag in his hand, the senior forensic scientist's posture was guarded.

'What's up now?' Mason asked.

'You guys should look at this,' Hedley insisted.

They both stared at one another.

Mason blew through his teeth. 'Don't tell me you've found more body parts. I couldn't handle much more of this bastard's handy work.'

'Not this time, but you'd be surprised what's hidden under the floorboards.'

'Like what?'

Hedley opened the brown paper bag and Carlisle stuck his head inside. 'Well I'll be dammed.'

'What the hell is it?' Mason demanded.

Carlisle smiled as he turned to face Mason. 'It's a powered surgical saw—'

'That's strange,' Mason shrugged. 'Why leave the house doors unlocked with chunks of human flesh in the bath, and hide a surgical saw under the floorboards?'

Carlisle winked at him. 'That's why you employ a criminal profiler, Jack.'

Chapter Forty-Six

The damp getting to his bones, DS Savage shuddered inwardly. He'd encountered Tony Fox's nefarious organisation on more than one occasion in the past and could think of far better places to meet on a windswept night. The dimly lit back lanes of Low Fell weren't exactly the safest of places to hang around in, not at any time. The problem was, if ever they were going to make inroads into catching the man responsible for such heinous crimes, they would need to take risks. DCI Mason's meeting with Tony Fox had initially set the wheels in motion, but Fox had gained the upper hand, and was giving the police a run for their money. With claims that Patrick Stanley had once worked as a barman at Fat Sam's nightclub, could the gangster be bluffing?

The detective sergeant stood perfectly still for a moment, fists clenched, legs slightly apart and ready to spring into action. He'd been in this situation before, but it never got any easier. Deep down there was a much darker side to all of this, and one involving a serial killer. His boss was right, he should have agreed to backup instead of going it alone. He hadn't, and now he was faced with an even bigger challenge.

Then, just when he was about to make his move, a figure emerged. He wasn't a tall man, squat, with rounded shoulders and wearing a baseball cap pulled down over his face.

'I assume Jack Mason sent you?'

'Yes, and you are?'

'That's not important.'

The stranger had turned aggressive suddenly, as though trying to force the issue. It wasn't the best of situations to be in either, as dark alleys had a nasty habit of kicking off just when you least expected them to.

'You came alone?'

'Yep! Just as arranged,' the sergeant replied.

'I which case I'll not keep you longer than necessary.'

The terms of engagement having been agreed, Savage was under no illusions as to where this was heading. There was a hint of hostility in the stranger's voice, enough to throw him off balance. He'd been involved in numerous clandestine meetings over the years, and the rules of engagement never changed. No weapons, no concealed recording devises, and no hidden agenda up your sleeve. Break the rules, and the consequences could be disastrous.

'How do I know we can trust you?'

'You don't,' the stranger replied. There followed an awkward stand-off between them, a coming together of minds. 'A friend of mine tells me you're seeking Wasp's whereabouts?'

'Yes, we are.'

Another uncomfortable silence.

'He's still in the city as far as we know, but that's as much as I can tell you.'

'Where exactly?'

The stranger held his hand up in front of the sergeant's face. 'Not so fast, my friend. There's a few things we need to iron out first.'

'At least tell me which part of the city Stanley's in.'

'That's not possible either. Not until you people have agreed to our terms.'

'*Terms?* What terms are those?'

'Not so fast—'

The moment the stranger reached into his coat pocket, the detective's heart sank. Things were moving at speed, and he was having to think on his feet.

'What is it you people are looking for?' DS Savage asked.

'Assurances,' the stranger replied.

'Regarding what?'

The stranger handed him a crumpled brown envelope. 'If you want to know Stanley's whereabouts, you're to turn a blind eye to *Fat Sam's*.'

'Why haven't you gone to Jack Mason direct?'

'It's not my call.'

'Whose call is it then?'

'Like you, I'm merely the messenger here.'

Still curious as to who was pulling the strings, the sergeant wracked his brains. If Tony Fox did know Patrick Stanley's whereabouts, who else did? There were always the Eastern Europeans, of course, but that was highly unlikely.

'So, what's the deal?' DS Savage insisted.

The stranger pointed to the envelope and dropped back into the shadows again. 'If Mason agrees to our terms, he's to call that number.'

'And what if he doesn't?'

The stranger seemed taken aback, as if no wasn't the answer he was looking for. 'What do you mean. . . doesn't?'

'I'm merely the messenger here, so I can't speak for Jack Mason.'

'Let's just say he'd be wise not to refuse.'

There was urgency in the stranger's voice. Threatening. There again, plea bargaining with gangsters always carried an element of risk. Get it wrong, and your world could be turned upside down. It was a fine balancing act, and everything was at stake here.

'When are your people expecting an answer?' the sergeant said, playing on his words.

'Sooner rather than later.'

'And what sort of assurances do *we* have?'

'There are no guarantees, as the whole damn city is out looking for Wasp.'

'I take it he no longer works at Fat Sam's?'

The stranger shrugged as if not knowing, but the eyes were the giveaway. Patrick Stanley, alias Wasp, had obviously worked at Tony Fox's nightclub at some stage, which was the perfect environment to win over his victim's.

The narrative coming together, DS Savage tucked the envelope into his pocket and tried not to dwell on it. He'd spent seventeen years in the force, and his instinct was to believe nothing at all. His boss was right: far too many people were involved in the case, and everyone wanted a piece of it. At least the killings had stopped, and that's all that really mattered as far as the public was concerned.

No sooner had the stranger disappeared into the night, the sergeant pressed the call button on his iPhone.

'*Jack Mason.*'

'It's me, boss. DS Savage.'

The line went quiet for a second.

'*How did your meeting go?*'

The detective sergeant sucked the air in through clenched teeth. 'You're not going to believe this. . .'

Chapter Forty-Seven

Wasp lit up another cigarette and took a deep drag, then blew out a long smoke trail. He'd packed up smoking years ago, but his nerves had finally got the better of him. After another sleepless night spent cooped up in the old mineral bottling plant, he was suffering from bouts of claustrophobia. Not that he was complaining any; he wasn't. Hell, he'd not felt this safe in a long time.

The room was small and stifling. Even with the windows left open it didn't make much difference. Bats in the loft, mice everywhere, and a million dust mites to contend with. Strange he should call this place home. When he was a youngster he used to hang around here after school. His foster mother worked here. Lifting heavy bottle crates and stacking them onto long wooden pallets so tall they'd almost touch the ceiling. She'd worked on one of the bottling lines, sticking on labels and checking for quality issues. A happy go lucky woman who always had wonderful things to say about him. He was friends with most of the men too. Kind souls, who took pity on him and gave him biscuits and treats to see him through his day. Such fond memories. What he wouldn't give to have them back again.

As another smoke trail drifted aimlessly towards the ceiling, Wasp eased back in his seat. Maybe they'd transferred Angelica to another hospital ward, one he hadn't visited yet. He would need to get her out of there, whisk her back to Estonia, where she had contacts. Reliable people who could smuggle them across borders. The thought of it excited him, and he was gaining in confidence with each passing day. Those miserable bastards who had abused her would surely pay for their sins. Damn cockroaches every single one of them.

It didn't take a rocket scientist to figure out the police were still out looking for him. This place was crawling with armed officers every night.

He'd often wondered how they'd cope without people like him to chase around all day. Maybe the system would collapse, maybe it wouldn't; who gave a toss anyway? There was always the ultimate game to play, and that's why he trawled the Internet every night. Hoovering up scumbags like Thomas Wilkinson, people who preyed on vulnerable young women like Angelica. The police were never going to deal with it, and that's why he'd chosen to get involved.

Wasp crushed the cigarette butt out in a saucer and sat back and thought about it. There was nothing of any value here, just security. He had a makeshift bed and an old camping stove that he could boil a pan of water on — what more could he wish for? Sometimes he questioned what all the fuss was about, and why people bothered to complain. If you'd never had a television to watch at night you were none the wiser of what was going on in the world. He still missed the hourly news bulletins, though, listening to the anchor man talking about his exploits and how good he was at his job.

Somewhere in the distance he heard a helicopter hovering. It was out searching for someone. This area was full of scumbags, and there were always plenty of distractions to keep the police occupied. There were times when he wondered what all the fuss was about, and why they even bothered to look for him. They'd never find him — not in a million years.

Wasp stood in front of the mirror for a second and felt a new wave of excitement wash over him. Wiping the skin around his hairline with a cotton pad dipped into an alcohol solution, he removed the oils from his forehead. Then, holding the back of the wig with both hands, he slid it over his head in a front to back motion. Finally, he aligned the ear tabs and ensured the front hairline was in place

God, it was amazing.

The moment he felt the urge of a nicotine fix, he lit another cigarette and took a deep drag. Money talked, it got you into places where other people couldn't go — and that was incredibly important to him. Once he'd finished his workload here, they would catch the overnight ferry to Amsterdam. First-class, executive suite, the best that money could buy. It wasn't the greatest plan he'd ever come up with, but he certainly knew it would work. And, if he wasn't mistaken, once they'd crossed the English Channel Angelica's friends would be waiting for them.

He knew he could trust her, and she never went back on her promises. That's why he had to snatch her out of there, so he could keep his promise with her.

Wasp thumped the table with the flat of his hand. *Don't give up on me, young lady, we'll have you out of here before you can say Jack Robinson!*

Chapter Forty-Eight

The focus of attention that morning was damage limitation. As usual, the moment Jack Mason read out his summary to the assembled operations team, you could have heard a pin drop. The story had made big headlines, prompting dozens of people to come forward. Ten people had been arrested, three had been released, and two of those released were now out on bail. Working on a tip off, there had been dozens of raids on properties in Newcastle and Gateshead, and numerous items of interest had been seized. All that remained now was to sift through the detail, including a large quantity of data found on the killer's computer.

It was a mixed bag of officers who had turned up for the briefing, but Carlisle knew most of them. There was almost a sense of expectation in the room, as if something big was about to happen. Now that DC Carrington had returned after a specialist firearms training course, Carlisle was looking forward to working alongside her again. At least something had gone in his favour, even though very little else had lately.

Much to everyone's surprise, Jack Mason's arrangements with Tony Fox had fallen on deaf ears. Everything that could go wrong had gone wrong. They'd been conned, big style, and the Detective Chief Inspector was now left with egg on his face. If Fox did know the killer's whereabouts, he wasn't letting on about it.

'Okay,' Mason announced. 'Everything's in place for tonight's raid on Fat Sam's nightclub, and we now have search warrants to that effect. If Fox hasn't responded with information about Stanley's whereabouts, his nightclub licence will be revoked.'

A loud cheer broke out.

As Mason sped through the summaries, Carlisle began to ponder over the last message found on the killer's computer: MEET YA SOON. It wasn't much, but it was still of significant interest from a criminal profiling standpoint. Could someone be harbouring Stanley, or worse still, had he found another unsuspecting victim? Anything was possible.

'What if the killer has fled to Leeds?' Manley suddenly suggested. 'We know he has contacts there.'

Stoney-faced, Mason's voice deepened. 'It's highly unlikely, don't you think, as his main interests lie in Newcastle.'

'Well, that's what I'd be doing if I were in his shoes.'

Mason thought a moment. 'What are your views, David?'

Carlisle looked up at the large street map now covered in post-its. There were thousands of places the killer could hide, but which one of them would he choose? The game plan was changing, and everyone was getting tetchy.

'He'll not budge from the city, not whilst his accomplice remains in the area. Stanley is territorial, so he'll stick to his comfort zones.'

Mason's look was relief. 'Yeah, but will he attempt to snatch her out of her hospital bed again?'

'Looking at past killer partnerships, the Moors Murders are a classic example of how these things work. Serial killers have a real affinity with power, even when caught and they know the game is up. Stanley's predictable; he's a narcissist who likes to exert his control over people. In his mind, he probably sees Angelica as the real mastermind in all of this. . . even to the point of blaming her for all of his own sadistic wrongdoings.'

'Sounds like the gang of flying monkeys,' Manley chuckled.

'What the hell are you on about now?' Mason glowered.

'It's a scene from the Wizard of Oz, boss. When the Wicked Witch of the West sent her flying monkeys to do all the dirty work for her, she couldn't stop laughing about it.'

'Mason shook his head. 'Sometimes you frighten the shit out of me, Harry.'

Rob Savage suddenly chipped in. 'What about our undercover team at the hospital – have we heard anything more back from them lately?'

'Nothing much in the way of covert information,' Mason acknowledged. 'Angelica's solicitors are playing devil's advocate claiming she's in no fit state to be interviewed.'

'Compos mentis, and all that,' Tom Hedley remarked.

'Bollock's more like.'

'What about Stanley's neighbours?' asked Holt.

'If they do know anything, they're not letting on about it.'

Savage cleared his throat. 'It's time we applied some pressure, boss.'

'And how do you propose we do that?'

Carpe Diem, thought Carlisle. 'What if we informed Christopher Sykes that we're about to make a significant arrest. Sykes is as much in the dark as we are as to the killer's whereabouts, so he's bound to make a big headline splash over it.'

'That's not a bad idea,' Mason agreed, pointing at finger at the cork board, 'and it may force him out into the open.'

Hedley leaned forward thoughtfully. 'But will Sykes swallow it?'

There was a knock on the door – soft knuckles by the sound. Seconds later, Acting Superintendent Sutherland appeared in the doorway dressed in full uniform. 'When you have a spare minute, Detective Chief Inspector,' she announced, 'the Area Commander wishes to speak to the two of us about tonight's raid.'

'We're almost done here, ma'am.'

'Good.' Sutherland smiled. 'I'll be up in my office.'

As the meeting ended abruptly, no one was any the wiser as to the killer's whereabouts. It was a roller coaster-ride, and Stanley was proving an elusive figure to track down. But that was the nature of the beast, and it was causing havoc amongst the senior backroom staff.

★★★

Stepping from the shadows, fifty officers drawn from the police tactical unit stormed in through the front door of Fat Sam's nightclub. It was the early hours of the morning, and the ground underfoot felt damp. Dressed in their familiar black armoured vests, and wearing black balaclavas over their heads, the building was secured within minutes. The speed and execution of the operation was breath-taking, and even took Jack Mason by surprise. Codenamed Operation Peppercorn, undercover officers had begun covert surveillance operations as early as three days beforehand. Popular with celebrities and wannabe playboys, Fat Sam's had become something of a rite of passage these past few weeks. Not all patrons were here for the music, of course, that much was obvious.

Scurrying across the dance floor, Mason bumped into one of the nightclub's bouncers. A tall guy, with a mouth full of gold teeth and a face like a Pitbull terrier. He was standing next to the DJ's booth with a big fat cheesy grin on his face. The music was at full blast, and Mason could feel the floor vibrating beneath his feet. Undeterred, he pushed on through the steel security door leading to the basement and ran down a steep flight of stairs – he wasn't alone.

'If you're looking for the gaffer, he's not here,' Rolex Roy loudly announced.

'Where is he?' Mason demanded.

'What is it with you people?'

Amid the noise and confusion, Mason felt as though his ears were about to pop. Even in the fortified basement of Tony Fox's sanctuary, the noise level was unbearable.

'Do yourself a favour, Rolex. Tell your gorilla upstairs to turn the fucking music down, it's doing my head in.'

The doorman glared at him as if about to throw a punch. Then, quite unexpectedly, Fox's office door flew open. Standing there in his boxer shorts and black socks, the Newcastle gangster looked at him as if he couldn't believe his eyes.

'What's all the fucking noise about, Roy? What's going on upstairs?'

'We've got visitors, chief, hundreds of them.'

Fox looked at the doorman, then back to Mason, before glancing back into his office. 'Get dressed, Polly. Make yourself look respectable. . . there's a good girl.'

Mason grinned but said nothing. He'd seen enough for one night.

Chapter
Forty-Nine

'So,' Acting Superintendent Sutherland began, 'I hear last night's operation was a complete success. Has Tony Fox said anything to you about Stanley's whereabouts?'

'Not yet, he hasn't,' Mason replied.

'What about the others who were brought in for questioning?'

'We've made ten arrests for possession of class A drugs, but nobody has seen hide nor hair of Stanley. Although he did work as a barman at Fat Sam's nightclub, he packed in shortly after the killings had started.'

'That's strange, surely someone must know Stanley's whereabouts?'

'Apparently not.' Mason shuffled awkwardly. 'Although we do have several eye witness accounts testifying that Angelica frequented the nightclub regularly, the details are somewhat sketchy.'

'Have we checked on the nightclub's CCTV?'

'Indeed, ma'am.'

'What about Fox, does he know anything about this?'

'Fox's lawyers are a right pain in the arse, and most of his cronies are refusing to cooperate.'

Sutherland ran a finger over the charge sheet, and then remarked, 'They're obviously plea-bargaining and looking for ways to lessen the charges against their client. Perhaps we should contact the prison governor at Durham jail, find out what Mr Wiseman is up to nowadays. No doubt the bush telegraph will be mad hot after last night's police raid.'

'Yes, that could be useful, ma'am.'

Sutherland looked puzzled. 'We may have closed Fox's nightclub down, but we're still a million miles from finding Stanley's whereabouts. Do we have any thoughts?'

'The profiler believes he's still in the area.'

'What about Leeds?'

Mason was quick to answer. 'No, ma'am. Carlisle's adamant he's holed up in Newcastle somewhere, and I tend to agree with him on that. Just on the off chance he does decide to travel south, I've contacted West Yorkshire Police to keep an eye out for him.'

'The sooner Stanley's brought to justice, the better,' Sutherland sighed. She rested her hands on the edge of the desk and pushed back in her seat. 'What are your thoughts on getting the media involved?'

'We've already started the ball rolling to some degree. I've arranged to meet with a group of resident journalists to drum up some local interest.'

'This wouldn't involve Christopher Sykes, would it?'

'Yes, ma'am. Do you have a problem with that?'

'No, but after your last run in with the Independent Press Standards people, I would have thought you'd have learnt your lesson by now. Besides, I was thinking more on a national scale.'

'I don't think that would be a wise move at this stage, ma'am.'

'Oh, and why not?'

'The last thing we need to do is to spook Stanley into going to ground.'

Sutherland checked her briefing notes. 'Talking of local interests, this council property that Patrick Stanley was renting in Gateshead, have forensics found anything that might suggest his whereabouts?'

'Not yet, they haven't.'

'There must be plenty of hard evidence available, though?'

'There is. . .'

The room fell silent; only the noise of car horn could be heard.

'What about this message found on Stanley's computer?'

Mason blew through his teeth in frustration. 'You mean – MEET YA SOON!'

'Yes. Do we have any idea who it was intended for?'

'No, and we haven't found any links to Stanley's close associates either.'

'What about this alias he goes under. . . Wasp?'

'No. Nothing of any interest has shown up on that one either.'

'Pity, I was hoping there might be a connection of some sort.' Sutherland shook her head dismissively. 'We're missing a trick here, and we may need to tighten up on our investigatory procedures by the sound of things.'

The tension was building, and Mason was beginning to get agitated. Okay, he wouldn't tolerate incompetent policing, not at any level. If mistakes had been made, he would admit to them. They hadn't, and this type of comment was totally unnecessary. Besides, he disliked the tone in

Sutherland's voice. He knew she was desperate for answers, but he didn't have any to give. Pity, he thought. Just when they were beginning to see eye to eye with one another again, this had to turn up. There again, he thought, one of the senior backroom staff could be pulling her strings – forcing her to react.

Mason sighed. 'It's turning into a bit of a minefield, and—'

'It's time we stopped pussy-footing around and got to the bottom of it.'

Mason smiled wryly and raised an eyebrow as if in agreement. 'I know it's not much, but the profiler believes he could be using some of his old thespian skills to slip in and out of society. If he is using disguise as a weapon, he'll be difficult to spot.'

There was a knock on her door, and DS Savage walked in.

'Yes, Sergeant,'

'She's gone—'

'*Gone!* Who's gone?' Sutherland demanded.

'Angelica Glebova, ma'am.'

Sutherland stared at Mason, and then back at DS Savage. 'Gone where exactly?'

'God knows, but she's completely disappeared from the hospital.'

'She can't just disappear, Sergeant. She must be there somewhere. . .'

'With all due respect,' Mason cut in, 'we're not mind readers here. These NHS people have some queer ideas as to how a high security operation should be run, especially one involving high-risk prisoners.'

'This just won't do.' Sutherland slapped the palm of her hand on top of a pile of case files and stared at them annoyed. 'Both suspects are now missing, and neither of you have the faintest idea where either of them is.'

'There's obviously a weakness in the hospital's security system,' Mason replied firmly.

'What do you mean, *weakness?* I thought you had this covered.'

'We do, ma'am. But the hospital's security keeps throwing the Human Rights Act at us.'

'Yes, but I was under the impression we had 24/7-armed security protecting the public, particularly after Stanley's last failed attempt to snatch her out of there.'

'We still do,' DS Holt insisted.

'It's all very well saying she's gone missing, Sergeant, but it's me who's answerable to the Area Commander.'

Shit, Mason cursed. If this bastard was to kill again, they'd all be assigned to desk jobs for the rest of their days. The only person most likely to know the answer to Stanley's whereabouts, was the profiler. He stared down at his phone and thought about making a connection, but it was Savage who broke his thoughts.

'According to the security manager, Angelica was on her way for a CT scan when she went AWOL.'

Mason stared at his watch. 'What time was this?'

'The alarm was raised barely fifteen minutes ago, boss.'

'And what have we done in the meantime?'

'Four members of the team are on their way over.'

'And uniforms?'

'They're out covering the hospital grounds,' the Sergeant replied.

'Good man.' Mason was having to think on his feet, but that's what he did best in these situations. 'What's Road Traffic up to?'

'The last I heard they were running road checks on all the surrounding access roads.'

Mason suddenly remembered the last time Stanley had tried to snatch Angelica out of the Neurology ward, and fifteen minutes didn't seem a long time. Maybe they were lying low somewhere. Choosing their moment.

His mind running amok, Mason leaned in closer. 'Let's get hospital security involved – close down all the hospital car parks and all exit roads in and out of the complex.'

'Sounds like a plan of action at last,' Sutherland acknowledged. 'Do we know what sort of physical shape Angelica is in?'

'Not a very good one, I'd wager.'

Sutherland drummed her fingers on the edge of her desk. 'Who's behind it, Jack?'

'Patrick Stanley no doubt.'

'I agree, as there's no way she could walk out of there on her own accord.'

'The question is, what is he intending to do with her?' Mason replied.

'Looking at the case files, Stanley didn't have a very good upbringing by all accounts, and that could be part of his problem. We know his mother was an alcoholic and died of cirrhosis of the liver when he was five.' Sutherland gave a thoughtful shake of the head. 'In and out of prison, his father was well-known to us, and that's why Social Services got involved. The sad thing is, young Stanley was brought up in foster care on a rough council estate in Byker, so he knows the area well.'

Mason nodded. 'A loner, with an attitude problem doesn't bode well, ma'am.'

'What did he do after leaving school?'

'We know he failed miserably at stage school, and that's why he went to work for Auto Parts Distribution.'

Sutherland's jaw dropped. 'There must be a connection somewhere.'

'The profiler believes there is.'

'It has to be Stanley—'

Mason leaned closer to express his frustration. 'Apart from Frank Wiseman and a couple of Tony Fox's cronies, I can't think of anyone else who fits the frame.'

'Which brings us nicely onto Tony Fox.'

'Indeed, ma'am.'

Sutherland checked her files again. 'If Fox is giving Wiseman a run for his money over this takeover bid, could he be using this woman's kidnap as a smokescreen?'

'I wouldn't go as far as that, but the longer this goes on the less chance we have of catching him,' Mason said, staring at his watch.

'What are Carlisle's views?'

'He's been right on more than one occasion lately and has an incredible knack of getting inside the killer's mind. Carlisle believes that Stanley has a split personality and is living out a double life.'

'*What!* A Jekyll and Hyde?'

'It's something to do with this stage acting malarkey. Having failed miserably at drama school, Carlisle believes he's trying to prove a point. Hence his possible use of disguises.'

'Perhaps we should give Mr Carlisle a wider role. . . a free hand in trying to track Stanley down.'

'We already have to some extent.'

'Sounds like we've done something right,' Sutherland said sarcastically.

Mason stared at Acting Superintendent and then across at DS Savage. 'The main reason we assigned DC Carrington to work with the criminal profiler, is due to her proficiency in reporting back to us.'

'In which case, we should probably leave well alone,' Sutherland confirmed.

Furious, Mason stood to leave. 'No disrespect, ma'am, but we can't just sit here waffling about it. . . there's plenty to be getting on with.'

'Yes, of course.'

Mason picked up his files and smiled. 'In the meantime, I'll contact West Yorkshire Police and see if they can offer us some technical assistance.'

'Never a dull a moment,' Sutherland replied dismissively.
Mason gave her a look that said it all.

Chapter Fifty

Tucked away in one of the many backrooms in Gateshead's Metrocentre, was the Retail Crime Unit. Not a large building, its small team of plain-clothes security officers covered every inch of the shopping mall. One of the largest shopping centres in Europe, with over 340 shops, this was a shoplifter's paradise. Not today it wasn't. Security was tight, and nothing was getting under their radar.

Now taking centre stage, the man's image that suddenly exploded across a dozen monitor screens seemed to cut a familiar figure with David Carlisle. Dressed in familiar black tracksuit bottoms, hoodie, and sporting dark Ray-Ban Aviator sunglasses, the suspect was heading towards the Red (shoppers') multi-storey car park.

Carlisle's stomach churned the moment the suspect picked up pace and ran towards the automatic swing doors. 'How long have you people been monitoring him?' he asked.

'Ever since we first made contacted with you.' The controller proffered a smile. 'Is he your man?'

'I'm not sure. What do you think, Sue?'

'He looks familiar. . . can we zoom in?' Carrington said anxiously.

Harassed, the operator clicked on the man's image and watched as it flashed across a dozen monitor screens.

'It certainly looks like him, but I'm not a hundred percent.'

'Can we put a marker on him?' Carrington asked.

The moment the suspect entered Level Three car park, he glanced over his shoulder. There was purpose in his stride, as if in a hurry. Trying to predict his movements would be difficult, but Carlisle knew what he was after – a black Peugeot 308. Seconds later he was inside one and heading down the steep spiral exit ramp.

'He's alone,' Carrington announced.

'Unless she's hidden on the back seat.'

The detective stared at Carlisle. 'Let's not get carried away here.'

'He's descending into Level Two,' the controller announced.

'Is there anyway of stopping him?' Carrington asked.

'We've circulated the car's registration number, make and model to your people. The best we can hope for is that he's held up at the next set of traffic lights.'

Carrington smiled faintly, as she relayed her findings back to Gateshead Police Station. Still no signs of the Peugeot 308 showing, the tension was building.

'It's Road Traffic,' she whispered, turning to Carlisle. 'The vehicle was stolen from Byker early yesterday morning.'

Carlisle felt his stomach tighten.

'It has to be him.'

'They've already put a marker on it, and they're setting up road checks.'

'If he heads towards the Angel of the North, there's fixed camera units all the way.'

'Finger's crossed—'

Then, from the ground floor a black Peugeot 308 emerged. Slowly at first, it inched its way towards the mainstream traffic before pulling to a halt at the traffic lights.

'What other cameras do you have covering the Red Zone?' Carrington asked excitedly.

'Just what you see,' the controller replied. 'Once he joins the circular, he'll be out of camera range.'

His mind all over the place, Carlisle tried to piece together the possibilities. Geographical profiling could be a useful tool, especially in predicting a serial killer's movements. Knowing Stanley as he did, he would operate within his comfort zone – and Byker immediately sprang to mind. And, if he remembered correctly, that's where he grew up in foster care. Suddenly the pieces were falling into place, and things were beginning to make sense.

'The Red Zone is now closed to all traffic,' the controller confirmed.

Carrington pointed to the central bank of monitor screens. 'What about the other zones?'

'Your people are dealing with it.'

'So, it's down to us.' She smiled.

Things were happening too quickly, and it was difficult to keep track.

'He's moving again.'

'*Jesus!*' Carlisle shouted aloud. 'He's heading in the opposite direction.'
All eyes were on him, and he suddenly felt a right prat.

***

Carlisle sat thinking as DC Carrington pulled up outside his house in
Whitburn. It was 7.00 pm, and he was utterly exhausted. Having spent
the best part of the afternoon looking for a stolen black Peugeot 308,
the search had finally been called off. So much for his theory of the killer
returning to Byker – Stanley was nowhere to be seen.

Carrington turned to face him. 'Aren't you going to invite me in?'

'Sorry—'

'I thought you might at least introduce me to this new partner of
yours.'

Not believing what he was hearing, Carlisle proffered a smile. 'You
mean Benjamin?'

'Why, is there someone else in your life?'

'No. Why do you ask?'

'Well, then.'

The moment Carlisle stepped into the kitchen, the young kitten ran
towards him. It had been a long day, and Benjamin seemed more than
pleased to see him back at the house again. Without thinking, Carlisle
took two glasses from the kitchen cupboard and grabbed a bottle of
Chardonnay from the fridge.

'Wine,' he asked, 'or would you prefer coffee?'

'Wine's fine.' She smiled.

Carlisle filled two good measures, screwed the bottle top back on,
and moved into the living room. Surprised at Carrington's forthright
approach, he made himself comfortable in his favourite armchair.
As conversation moved, as it invariably did, to Patrick Stanley and his
accomplice Angelica, Carrington appeared reluctant to engage.

'Make yourself at home, that's if Benjamin will allow you.'

'He's fine,' she said. 'It seems I've made a new friend.'

'He can be a very demanding little bugger at times.'

'Cats don't normally take to me like this,' Carrington admitted, 'they're
usually very choosy as to who they make friends with.'

'Benjamin's not normal, I can assure you of that. I'm positive he thinks
he's a dog.'

'Really!'

'Try throwing something for him to fetch, and he'll bring it back to you.'

'That's hilarious.' She laughed.

Moving towards the sound system, Carlisle felt a fleeting moment of calm as he put on one of his favourite tracks from JJ Cale's *Really* album. 'I've been thinking what Patrick Stanley's next move might be, and where he may have gone to ground.'

Carrington sighed, and gave him a withering look. 'Does that brain of yours ever shut down, or is that a criminal profiler thing?'

'Sometimes, but very rarely,' Carlisle admitted. 'It's weird how the brain works. Most people assume that our memories are accurate records of what has happened to us. The trouble is, our brains tweak and alter our memories all the time. Recreating partial recollections, imagining different outcomes, and modifying an existing memory until it's quite different to what actually happened.'

'Try giving it a rest,' Carrington groaned. 'We've done enough running around for one day, and *my* brain is in bits.'

Carlisle walked over to the window, and Benjamin followed him. 'Can I ask you a personal question?'

'You may, but whether I answer it is another matter.'

'Do you like curry?'

'Yes, of course I do. Why do you ask?'

'Good, would you mind if I order us a take-away?'

An hour later, their food arrived. Delivered by a middle-aged oriental man who arrived on a red scooter carrying a large white box strapped on the back of it. Neither of them had eaten since breakfast that morning, and apart from grabbing a quick coffee between enquiries, they were both famished. Sitting with a tray resting on her lap, Carrington tucked into her starters. The food was delicious; even Carlisle was surprised by it. By the time they'd finished the main course, he felt his stomach was about to explode.

Easy to get on with, Carrington reminded him of his late wife in many ways. He knew he could be withdrawn at times, and self-centred come to think of it, but the young detective had a way with words that made him sit up and listen to her. Now half-way through their second bottle of wine, the conversation was varied, and he was finally beginning to relax. They talked about many things that evening, and Carlisle was surprised just how much in common they had. Beneath the angelic charm there was a definite mean streak – one of the requisites of close protection selection, he guessed. Intelligent, incredibly quick witted, not to mention a slightly wry sense of humour, Carrington was easy company. Not that it ever showed in her work, but her parents were well-to-do people, which could account for her confident outlook on life.

'Jesus!' Carrington suddenly announced. 'Look at the time. It's almost eleven-thirty and I'm well over the legal limit. I'd better phone a taxi and pick up the pool car tomorrow morning.'

There was panic in her voice.

Carlisle thought about it, but not for long. 'There's a spare bed in the back room you can hunker down in. It's not exactly the Ritz, but you're more than welcome to stop the night.'

'The perfect gentleman.' She smiled coyly.

'I wouldn't say that,' he confessed. 'But you may have company during the night.'

Carrington looked at him wearily. 'What do you mean. . . company?'

'Your little friend.' Carlisle smiled, pointing to Benjamin who was now comfortably curled up on her lap.

Carrington flashed her big brown eyes at him. 'Let's drink to that.'

Chapter Fifty-One

Mary Leech lived in a terraced house just off Shields Road in Byker, within easy walking distance of the local Metro Station. Not a tall woman, she reminded Carlisle of his late mother in many ways. A sweet old lady with dyed auburn hair, deep blue eyes, and a sharp retentive mind. Over the years, Mary had been a foster parent to no less than seventeen children, all of them through Social Services. No stranger to troublesome children, Mary had a way of ironing things out with them. Known for her kind-hearted approach, no matter what a child's background, she always cared for them as though they were her own. Through Mary's generosity, many a child had been given the hope and aspirations they desperately needed in life. Not so in Patrick Stanley's case; that was a very different story.

Emotionally detached and unable to connect with people, Stanley had shown little or no empathy towards another person's suffering. Aged ten, young Patrick had set fire to the next-door neighbour's garden shed having previously slaughtered all their pet rabbits. If that wasn't bad enough, he'd stolen the poor box from the local parish church and spent all the money on cigarettes.

Carlisle sat quietly as Mary's incredible story began to unfold. A troublesome child, long before the age of ten, Stanley had unnerved people by his odd behaviour. Unquestionably violent and to make matters worse, Stanley didn't give a damn how many people's lives he destroyed – just that he got his own way!

'Excuse me for asking,' said Carrington softly, 'but when you first took charge of Patrick from Social Services, how would you best describe him?'

The old lady looked a little nervous, as well she might be. 'He was such a pleasant little boy when he first arrived at the house. Well-mannered, polite, as if butter wouldn't melt in his mouth.'

'Was he a lovable child, do you think?'

'At first, he was, but that soon changed.'

'When did you first realise that something was wrong?' Carlisle asked.

Mary leaned back and regarded him quizzically through narrowed eyes. She wore a plain white top, black trousers, and a pair of comfortable flat shoes. Not an overly confident woman, mid-seventies, she still possessed a sharp mind.

'Patrick was a very disruptive child and difficult to keep in check,' Mary finally replied. 'None of his school teachers knew how to handle him, and that was a major problem.'

'In what way?'

'Whenever the teachers tried to bring him in line with the other children in class, he would throw tantrums in front of them.'

Carlisle couldn't help feeling sorry for the old woman. There were so many factors to consider, and every one of them complex. Having told them so much about Stanley's disruptive past, it was obviously taking its toll.

'Would I be right in saying that Patrick had serious anger issues?'

'Yes, he did. Unlike the other children we took into care, you could never reach out to Patrick. Nobody could. Not even Social Services.'

'Did he ever threaten you at all?'

'He frightened me, especially if he couldn't get his own way.'

Carrington checked her notes. 'And what did Social Services have to say about that?'

'Not a lot. They referred him to a specialist doctor.' Mary gave Carrington a long-suffering look. 'For anxiety management.'

After spending the previous evening going back over the case files, Carlisle was more than aware of the details. Stanley had shown little or no emotional attachment towards his foster parents, having isolated himself from them. Unable to tolerate criticism – even constructive criticism – Stanley was terrified of being embarrassed. And, if anyone did feel the need to challenge him, he didn't have the social skills to cope. Perhaps that's why he reacted as he did. It was his way of dealing with it. All the little idiosyncrasies were there – interpersonal dominance, aggression, excessive self-esteem – it didn't take much.

Carlisle thought for a moment as he tried to get his head around it all. Some experts believed that anxieties could manifest themselves in a variety of ways, based on a psychological response to a threat in the environment. It was this response that maximised the body's ability to either face danger or escape it. Patrick Stanley's reactive behaviour to an uncomfortable situation had obviously been misread as anger or opposition. The problem with this was, none of it had been picked up in his adult life and no one had addressed the uncontrollable anxiety attacks. Just as a ticking timebomb lay dormant until someone pressed the trigger, Stanley had gone into meltdown.

Grave mistake!

'And how did Patrick respond to his treatment,' Carlisle asked thoughtfully, 'did the disruptive behaviour finally go away?'

'Yes, at first it did. . . but it soon returned.'

'It sounds as if you were left on your own to deal with it.'

Mary stared back at them. 'There were times when I felt totally incapable of handling the situation.'

'The only real failure is the failure to try, Mrs Leech.' Carlisle shook his head sympathetically. 'You did your best, and under very difficult circumstances you coped admirably well.'

She blushed. 'I tried my best.'

Carrington said nothing. Whether she understood where this was heading, Carlisle was unable to tell. His main aim was to establish Stanley's childhood comfort zones – which environments he felt most safe in. Most serial killers turned inwards on themselves when confronted by authority. It was their way of dealing with it. If Stanley had gone to ground, had he returned to his childhood roots? He knew it was a long shot, but anything was worth a try.

'What about Patrick's friends?' Carlisle asked.

'He had no friends,' Mary replied unreservedly. 'Patrick didn't mix with other children; he isolated himself from them. If he couldn't get his own way, he became aggressive towards them.' She stared pitifully across at Carlisle. 'The other kids called him *Wasp*, and who would want to play with someone like that?'

The early signs of power and control were all there, and Stanley had obviously developed into what he now was – a narcissistic control freak who was prone to violate the rules of society, at any cost.

'Tell me,' said Carlisle, 'what did Patrick do with himself apart from school? Did he hang around in his bedroom all day?'

'Most of his spare time was spent down at the bottling plant.'

Carlisle suddenly sat bolt upright. 'Bottling plant—'

'Yes, I worked there for several years. Patrick had a lot of friends there too.'

'Excuse me for asking, but I thought you said he had no friends.'

'Not at school he didn't. These were people I worked with at the plant. Patrick used to run errands for them.' The old woman shuffled awkwardly in her seat. 'As a reward, they gave him their loose change and unwanted sandwiches they couldn't eat.'

'Ah, that explains it,' Carlisle smiled. 'And this bottling plant is down by the River Tyne I presume?'

'Yes, but it closed down many years ago.' Mary thought a moment. 'To tell you the truth, it's been ages since I was last down there and I'm not sure if it's there anymore.'

'I'm forgetting,' said Carlisle, shaking his head and smiling, 'this all happened fifteen years ago.'

'Time waits for no one, Mr Carlisle.'

He sat quietly for a moment, thinking. 'When did you last see Patrick?'

'Not since he left my care.'

'And neither of you have made contact since?'

'No, we haven't.'

Mary told them more, then flopped back into her chair looking utterly exhausted. It was time to call it a day, thought Carlisle. There was nothing to be gained from talking to her anymore, and she'd told them more than they needed to know.

He thanked her and stood to leave.

'If Patrick does happen to contact you,' Carrington said, handing her a business card, 'could you please ring this number?'

The old woman's face reddened. 'Is Patrick in some sort of trouble?'

Carlisle smiled thinly. 'We don't wish to cause you alarm, Mrs Leech. But if you do have any concerns, you're to ring that number.'

'Yes, I will.'

Perhaps they'd been a little harsh on the old lady. Overstayed their welcome. After all, this wasn't a police interview, more a fact-finding mission. Even so, they'd uncovered a multitude of new leads and were both itching to get going again.

Chapter Fifty-Two

Newcastle was bathed in bright morning sunshine with clear blue skies. As the city's rejuvenation programmes slowly began to shine through, the Quayside flourished. Middle class England, it seemed, was willing to open its wallets to the North East and long weekend breaks were now the in thing. As the affluent south poured into the metropolis nightlife, Geordie hospitality was alive and kicking. But there was a darker side, a side where tourists never ventured.

Carlisle's instincts told him to turn left at the next T-junction, but they had to make a short detour first. After dropping down a steep bank, they passed a series of derelict buildings before finally reaching their destination. There were no gates at the front of the building, just a narrow back lane leading to another part of the complex. Some of the surrounding units had been demolished, but a few of the old worker's terraced houses remained.

Pulling up behind a mud-spattered dumper truck, Carrington switched off the undercover car's engine. Not twenty metres away, two men dressed in Hi-Vis jackets were digging a hole in the middle of the road. One guy was tall and lean, the other was stocky with a weather-beaten face. Neither paid much attention to them.

'Are you sure this is the right place?' Carrington asked, sliding out of the driver's seat.

Carlisle frowned. 'According to the Satnav it is.'

She stared at him quizzically. 'I think we should get uniforms involved.'

He knew what Carrington was thinking but chose to ignore her.

No lights came from the old bottling plant, and there were no vehicles parked outside. If Stanley was lying low here, he was obviously covering his tracks. Moving down a narrow lane, Carlisle tried the first door he came to. It was locked. Swearing quietly to himself, he took a step back and reconsidered his options. There was nothing to suggest that anyone was hiding here, and most of the ground floor windows had been bricked up. All kinds of emotions tugged, and it wasn't curiosity.

'What's up now?' Carrington shrugged.

'I'm not sure.'

'Why don't you try another door?'

'I have done, and they're locked.'

'So what?' She smiled. 'This is a murder inquiry and there isn't time to apply for a search warrant. It's not going to happen.'

After several attempts at gaining entry, Carlisle placed the flat of his hand on one of the central door panels and gave it a gentle shove. He could see it wasn't bolted and was only held by a central mounted lock. Taking a step back, he employed a forceful well-placed kick to the side panel and watched as the door flew inwards. Seconds later they were inside and staring into a vast open abyss.

'This must be it,' said Carlisle, gazing up at the skylights. 'There's a small courtyard at the back of the building, and what appears to be a row of offices.'

Carrington smiled. 'We'd better check them out.'

Built on two levels, the upper floor was slightly set back from the rest. Obviously used by management at some stage, as the lower level offices were decked out with cheap floor tiles and had low-level strip lights attached to their ceilings. He tried the switches, but none of them worked. It was then he spotted the large brown suitcase, its price tag still attached.

He pointed to it.

'It can't be—' Carrington gasped.

As his grip on the handle tightened, Carlisle felt his pulse race.

Oh shit! Oh no! Please don't let there be a body inside.

That wasn't all, there was something in Carrington's voice that sent shockwaves down his spine. From the darkness of the interior, she pointed to the other office walls. All had been daubed with big red smiley faces, but none of them in blood. Crude as it was, alarm bells were ringing in Carlisle's head. Nothing was black and white anymore, everything was surreal.

As his eyes toured the rest of the building, Carlisle tried to get his mind around it all. He didn't know why, but it suddenly felt as if his entire world was spiralling inwards on him.

'Best check the upper floor level,' Carrington said a little nervously.

They moved up a narrow flight of stairs together. If they were expecting to spring the element of surprise, their cover had already been blown. All they could do now, was hope the killer wasn't lying in wait for them.

'There,' Carlisle whispered.

At the top of the narrow stairs was a small annex, beyond that a sliding partition door. And, if those were Stanley's footprints leading from it, it meant they had to be close. As Carrington knelt to take a closer look, he noted her hands were shaking.

'You okay?' he whispered.

'I think so.'

Carlisle took another deep breath and tried to steady himself. Looking for Stanley was like searching for a needle in a haystack. The man was an elusive predator and wouldn't think twice about plunging a knife into them.

They inched their way closer.

Carlisle noticed, after he'd slid back the partition door, a strong pungent smell. It wasn't a spacious room, oblong, with two narrow slit windows and a bank of office cabinets running the entire length of one wall. He stood for a moment, his eyes adjusting to the light.

'Over there,' Carrington gasped, pointing her Taser Gun to the corner of the room.

They crept forward together. Cautiously.

Then he heard a whimpering sound. Pitiful, like the cry of some wounded animal. The next thing he noticed, after he bent down, was the terrified look on a young woman's face.

Carlisle felt his stomach lurch.

From what he could see her wrists had been bound to the wheelchair rests with heavy duty duct tape, and her ankles strapped to the side frames with rope. Still conscious, she was barely alive. Adjusting to the light, he noticed the IV bag hanging over the backrest of the wheelchair had run dry. It wasn't looking good suddenly, and whatever lifesaving fluids had been flowing into her veins had finally come to an end.

'Angelica,' he whispered.

Her lips moved to speak, but her voice was pitifully weak.

'Where's Patrick Stanley?' Carrington asked authoritatively.

Angelica craned her neck towards them, then back to the partition door.

'It's okay. Help's coming. There's an ambulance on its way.'

Drifting in and out of consciousness, her arms were so badly swollen from the lack of circulation that Carlisle could barely look at them, let alone touch them. As Carrington pulled her iPhone out of her pocket, she made a few frantic calls. Now in police mode, her voice sounded authoritarian as she barked out a set of instructions.

'I want full forensic deployment, and the area in lockdown.'

Carlisle checked out the rest of the rooms and heard a siren in the distance. Faint at first, but rapidly getting louder. Then he heard another, quickly followed by a third. As he moved towards the window to take a better look, a splinter of blue light flashed past his eyes. Suddenly the whole courtyard was alive and buzzing with police officers.

★★★

Carlisle watched the ambulance arrive, followed by a Mercedes Sprinter full of police officers kitted out in body armour. As a stern-faced Sergeant slid from the passenger seat, he moved towards the front of the building.

'I want your men to cover every inch of the ground,' a familiar voice called out.

Moments later Jack Mason appeared in the doorway.

Carrington spoke first. 'This young woman is badly in need of medical assistance, boss.'

Angelica rolled her head to one side, as if trying to tell them something. Not that Jack Mason was interested – his mind was now on other things. Then, just when he was about to apply his handcuffs to her wrists, he thought better of it.

'It looks like her circulation is restricted.'

Carrington nodded. 'Shall I cut her free, boss?'

'No, best leave that to the medical experts.'

Mason stood for a few moments, his eyes taking in the detail.

'Has anyone searched the rest of the building?'

'No, boss.'

'Any signs of Stanley?'

'No, this is the only part of the building we've been in.'

'So, you've not been here long, I take it?'

'Fifteen minutes at the most, I phoned as soon as we found her.'

'Well done.' Mason nodded.

A man's voice suddenly boomed out from the lower level of the building.

'Are you there, Jack?'

'I'm up here,' Mason shouted back.

Carlisle stepped aside as a SOC photographer entered the room. A tall man, garbed in a white sterile paper suit with a bag full of camera equipment slung over his shoulder. He nodded, exchanged information with Mason, then jotted something down in a red notebook.

Mason swung to face them. 'This building has been cleared, so Stanley can't be too far away.'

'Do you think he'll return?' asked Carrington.

'I doubt he's left her here to rot.'

'No, I suppose not.'

'Try not to touch or disturb anything, I'll be back in a jiffy.'

Carlisle said nothing; Mason's expression said it all. Over the years he'd grown accustomed to this kind of rhetoric – which usually meant the suspect was long gone. Mason lacked patience and was straining at the bit to get going again. Not so in their case. Not until the Crime Scene Manager had given them clearance at least.

As his eyes toured the room, Carlisle suddenly felt cold inside. He sensed an evil presence, a feeling of disquiet. He was closer now, closer than ever before. As his head began to clear of vile thoughts, he closed his eyes and let his mind drift to other places.

Where are you, Patrick?

Chapter Fifty-Three

Wasp looked on in confusion. Blue spinner lights everywhere, marked patrol cars on every street corner, and a shit load of armed police officers to contend with. Not looking good, he cursed. This place was no longer safe.

Abandoning the stolen Peugeot 308, he made his way towards the old bottling plant. The master of disguise, Wasp knew his outfit would keep him out of trouble, at least for now it would. Even he was amazed at some of the incredible costumes he'd dreamt up lately. He should have been a make-up artist, as that's where his future lay. It was good to dress up, and he did have a favourite costume like the black hoodie he always wore on night manoeuvres. Instantly recognisable, it had become his personal trademark.

The Suitcase Man, he chuckled.

Whoever dreamt that one up was pure genius.

The road up ahead was long and exposed, with only a handful of red-brick buildings on either side for protection. Even so, there wasn't much he didn't know about the local community, including resident gossip. On reaching the blue and white police cordon tape, Wasp suddenly felt vulnerable. This area was no stranger to police officers, it's where the bad guys hung out. But he'd been brought up in foster care here, and this district was second nature to him. The shipyards had long gone, but he didn't remember them anyway.

It was the gravelly voice that shattered Wasp's concentration. A stout man, with long sideburns, and inquisitive brown eyes that looked down on him as though he was carrying a box of dynamite. Next to him, dressed in a grey suit, white shirt and purple tie, stood an alert man-mountain detective. He made a mental note of it and began a search for a better spot. It was a large turnout – network satellite vans tipping the skyline, newspaper reporters everywhere, and anchor men making their presence felt.

Then he spotted the ambulance. Stationary, its back doors had been flung open, and the driver was nowhere to be seen. He knew from experience that government targets required that crews reach Category-A emergencies within eight minutes of receiving a 999 call. Not bad when you thought about it.

Excitement gripped him, and he could barely breathe let alone contain his emotions. God, this was awesome. By the time he'd found a new place to lay claim to, a large crowd of onlookers had gathered. Not all had gone to plan of course, but nothing was ever straightforward where the police were concerned. He checked his pocket and pulled out his iPhone, then switched it to camera. Lifting his arm high above the crowd, he fired off a couple of shots. He liked to keep a record of everything, just for posterity's sake. Not that he was narcissistic or anything – he wasn't. His plans were coming along nicely, though, and he was beginning to enjoy the celebrity status he was attracting.

Then two paramedics appeared. Dressed in their familiar green uniforms they were pushing an EMS stretcher towards the back of the stationary ambulance. He knew she was alive, as he could see the fresh IV dripline they'd attached to her arm. He would follow them, find out which hospital they were taking her to. Newcastle General seemed the most logical place, but there was always the Freeman, of course. Which ward he had no idea, but he knew the layout well.

He glanced at his watch.

Time to get going.

Chapter
Fifty-Four

Mason had just finished his call with the Acting Superintendent when there was a sharp rap on his office door, and Rob Savage walked in. A former boxing champion, the Detective Sergeant wasn't a specialist at anything, more a jack of all trades.

'What can I do for you, Rob?' Mason asked.

'We've just received reports of a stolen Transit van travelling on Dutch number plates.'

'Where exactly?'

'North Shields.'

'And where is it now?'

'About to board the DFDS Ferry for Amsterdam.'

'If you haven't already done so, you'd better inform the port authorities. No doubt they'll want to get involved.'

'There's something else you should know,' said Savage excitedly.

'Like what?'

'The van driver is wearing the uniform of the Royal Dutch Touring Club ANWB. It's the equivalent of the UK's Automobile Association.'

'What is this, a fashion show?'

'No, but one of the security officers at the ferry terminal reckons the guy's an imposter.'

Mason put his pen down, his interest levels heightened. 'Where's the driver now?'

'He boarded the ferry, boss.'

Mason moved from behind his desk and put on his jacket. 'Grab half a dozen men and meet me down in the car park in five minutes.'

The Sergeant's grin broadened. 'We think it could be Patrick Stanley.'

'Chance would be a fine thing.'

Within minutes, two unmarked police cars were speeding east towards the Royal Quays Ferry Terminal in North Shields. His foot hard on the accelerator, the needle the wrong side of 110mph, Savage seemed determined to show off his driving skills.

Not a good move!

'Easy on the cornering, Rob,' Mason demanded. 'We need to get there in one piece.'

'I'm only doing a hundred and ten.' Savage chuckled.

'Seems more like five hundred and ten from where I'm fucking sitting.'

The moment he saw the ship's DFDS funnel markings, Mason heaved a sigh of relief. Thirty minutes more and they'd be staring at an empty quayside. Still loading, the undercover car inched forward in a long queue of waiting lorries before it was redirected towards the ferry terminal.

'Good morning,' a ship's officer announced, as he moved from behind the check-in desk. 'I'm Lars Anson, the ferry's Chief Engineer. How can we help you, Detective Chief Inspector?'

Pleasantries exchanged, Mason handed Anson a photograph of Patrick Stanley. 'We believe this man may have boarded your ferry. He's travelling on stolen Dutch number plates and wearing the uniform of a Royal Dutch Touring Club ANWB.'

'That's a new one.' Anson grinned. 'Illegal immigrants prefer to dress up in crew uniforms.'

Mason gathered his thoughts. 'Stanley's not an illegal immigrant – he's wanted about a number of brutal murders we're investigating.'

'And you think he's on board?'

'It's highly likely he is.'

'In which case, he shouldn't be too difficult to find,' the ship's officer confirmed. 'May I suggest we continue with our loading, then go into ship's lock-down?'

'Sounds good to me.' Mason shrugged.

'I'll get one of the staff officers to check on the van's whereabouts, and we'll take it from there.'

'One other thing,' Mason said, trying to contain his enthusiasm. 'Stanley's a desperate man and may be carrying a bladed weapon. If he is, he won't be frightened to use it.'

'Thank you, Inspector. I'll warn the rest of the crew members.'

Anson radioed the ship's bridge and spoke directly with the captain. It was a tense moment, and Mason was eager to get going. There were things to be done, plans to put in place, besides a whole load of maritime protocols to adhere to.

'Here's the plan,' Anson said turning to face Mason. 'The captain advises that once he's ready to sail, he'll carry out the mandatory lifeboat drill. Whilst the crew clear the lower decks, your men can check on the assembled passengers.'

Mason breathed a sigh of relief. 'Thank you, I'll inform my team.'

'But first we must secure all possible escape routes.'

'Yes, of course.'

Moments later they'd moved onto the lower vehicle loading deck and split into two groups. 'How many men do you have with you, Inspector?' asked Anson.

'There's six of us in total.'

'That's perfect.'

Twenty minutes later, plans in place, the crew made ready to sail. Seven short blasts on the ship's foghorn saw the passengers assemble at their muster stations.

'Let's work in tandem,' Anson instructed. 'Team One will search the forward part of the vessel. Team Two the aft. Once we've cleared the bottom two decks, we'll close the watertight hatches, and only then do we move up to the next level.'

'So, there's only one way he can go,' Mason said, pointing up to the heavens.

'Yes. It's like squeezing a tube of toothpaste.'

Well, that was the theory.

Within minutes of securing the two lower decks, the stolen Transit van had been traced. Whoever had driven it on board the ferry that morning was now the person they were looking for.

'Time to move up a deck,' Anson said, closing the last of the watertight hatch doors.

Now in close contact with the rest of his team, and wearing a bright orange lifejacket, Mason climbed the ladders to the next level. Split into smaller groups, the teams now began to work their way through the accommodation decks. It was a painstakingly slow process, as every cabin had to be checked for signs of life.

Anson swung to address Mason. 'Before the captain gives the all clear on the lifeboat drill, you and I should look at the Columbus deck.'

Mason nodded. 'Okay.'

'I doubt your man will be there, but we need to check it out anyway.'

'There can't be many more decks left,' Mason insisted.

'No, but there's plenty of places to hide.'

The moment they reached the Columbus deck, Mason instinctively poked his head around the double glass doors. Much larger than he'd anticipated, the lounge had a huge dance floor, central stage, and what looked to be a well-stocked bar. Now void of ships passengers, the place had an eerie feel, akin to the Marie Celeste.

Then, out of the corner of his eye, Mason caught a movement. It wasn't much, but enough to draw his attention towards it. Struggling to breathe, he moved slowly and quietly towards the edge of the dance floor. His handset switched to silent, he had all but given up on it when he heard a scraping noise coming from behind the bar.

Not a tall man, stocky, with broad rounded shoulders, Lars Anson had heard it too. Tiptoeing across the dance floor together, the ship's engineer signalled his intentions before peeling off in the opposite direction. Then Stanley appeared – screaming at them like a madman possessed.

Mason spotted the knife.

Fists clenched, feet spread slightly apart, he instinctively shifted his weight to the balls of his feet. Quick as a flash, he lunged out and grabbed tight hold of Stanley's knife arm. Realising his terrible mistake, Mason lashed out at him with both feet. When that didn't work, he automatically twisted his body sideways to throw his assailant off balance. Each time he tried, the killer continued to resist. Wedged between the drinks cabinet and bar, they were now locked in mortal combat. He was trapped, caught on the receiving end of a maniac hell bent on inflicting him terrible harm.

As he clung onto the knife arm for dear life, he tried headbutting Stanley. It was useless, and the killer kept forcing him back. Then, just when Mason thought he'd got the better of him, Stanley caught him a lucky blow to the right upper cheek and he fell to the floor in a heap. Dazed, he tried to scramble to his feet, but it was already too late. As the knife blade flashed towards him, Mason let out a painful scream.

'You bastard!' he yelled.

Staring into the killer's crazed eyes, Mason felt a steady trickle of warm blood running down his sleeve. Pinned down and unable to move, his whole body was on fire. If only he'd carried a gun, he'd have blown the bastard's brains out without the slightest hesitation. He hadn't, and now he was staring certain death in the face. Exhausted, and desperately fighting for his life, he tried to break free from the killer's grip. Stanley was having none of it and kept spinning him around by his ankles to disorientate him. He was toying with him, as a cat plays with a mouse before it moves in for the final kill.

Then he saw the knife arm retract again.

Oh shit. Oh no.

Lars Anson wasn't a tall man, but he was nifty on his feet. Picking up the nearest bar stool, he smashed it over Stanley's head. As the killer's feet buckled from under him, he dropped to the deck like a stone. Blood spurting from a huge gash in the top of the killer's head, Mason thought the ship's officer had slain him.

'You okay?' Anson asked, picking up his communications handset and giving out instructions to the rest of the crew.

'I think the bastard has stabbed me.'

Anson bent down to take a closer look, and immediately radioed for help.

'The ship's doctor is on his way; please try not to move.'

His head spinning 360 degrees, Mason felt physically sick. Then, just when he thought it was over, Stanley rose to his feet again. This time there was hatred in his eyes, as if the wires in his brain had been crossed. Terrified, and taken completely by surprise, Anson desperately tried to defend himself. As the knife blade disappeared deep into the chief engineer's upper left side, he let out a gut-wrenching shriek. Blood spurting everywhere, there was nothing Mason could do to stop him.

Then he saw the knife arm rise again.

Moments later, dozens of crew members appeared at the door. They were yelling abuse at the killer and trying to goad him away from the ship's officer. Outnumbered and hemmed in on all sides, there seemed no way out for Stanley now.

But the killer wasn't finished yet.

Eyes burning with anger, head gushing with blood, Mason could see what Stanley was intending to do. Determined to inflict the maximum harm to those surrounding him, the killer rushed at them like a madman possessed. Panic spread like wildfire, as everyone ran for their lives.

No one had seen it coming, not even one of them.

With one hand gripping the handrail, the other wielding the knife, Stanley flung himself headlong over the side of the ferry. He was gone, but the terrifying scream he let out as he plunged headlong toward certain death, resonated throughout the ship. Seconds later, his head smashed into one of the lifeboat winching cranes and his body was catapulted sideways.

First the splash.

Then silence.

Within minutes of the ship's lifeboat being launched, the river police arrived. Above, a helicopter clattered, its thermal imaging camera pointing at the water's edge. Shivering, and unsteady on his feet, Mason looked for signs of life. Then, one hundred feet below, a ghostlike figure emerged from the river. It was staring up at him like the stone face of a child on a cathedral tomb. At first, he thought he was imagining things, but others had seen it too.

Then, as the Tyne's notorious undercurrents went to work, Stanley slipped silently from view. It was over, and the Suitcase Man's unimaginable reign of terror had finally come to an end. All that remained now was to recover his body and the rest would fall into place.

'You okay, boss?' someone yelled out.

The moment he saw Rob Savage sprinting towards him, Mason knew he was in serious trouble. He tried to stand, but the pain in his side was unbearable and some of his muscle controls were shutting down. Drifting in and out of consciousness, he began to experience the weirdest sensation. He was floating on a silver cloud and peering in on himself as if from another dimension. The next thing he saw, after he'd opened his eyes, he was lying on a hospital bed and surrounded by people dressed in long green gowns. He tried to make the connection, clear his head of crazy thoughts.

Exhausted, and unable to control his innermost feelings, Mason reached out towards the outstretched hand that was drawing him ever closer towards a bright silver light. It was surreal, unimaginably beautiful, and yet more powerful than anything he'd ever witnessed before. As his life flashed before him, his eyelids felt heavy as though they had lead weights attached to them. He wanted to say something, anything, but he couldn't form the words. Then he heard his father's voice telling him there was nothing left for him to fix here anymore. He was free, and it was time to let go.

Then everything sank into inky blackness.

Chapter
Fifty-Five

David Carlisle found a parking spot on Benton Front Street and walked the short distance back to the Ship Inn. Pretty much a man's pub, he'd always felt at home there. Eight weeks had passed since his contract on *Operation Walrus* had been terminated, and he was disappointed not to be involved anymore. Being a private investigator had its benefits, but once the killer had finally been taken off the streets, his part in the operation was over. Not all was despair, though. He now had a big fat pay cheque tucked in his back pocket, and enough money to pay off his creditors.

Despite a huge search operation, which had lasted several weeks, Patrick Stanley's body had never resurfaced again. Missing, presumed drowned, wasn't the result the police had been hoping for, as it always left an element of doubt. Even so, the River Tyne was notorious for its strong tidal undercurrents around the Ferry Terminal, so it may well have been washed out to sea.

'You took your time,' Mason said, checking his watch.

'I got held up, but I could murder a pint.'

Mason turned to face him. 'Talking of murder, we've formally charged Angelica Glebova with two counts of murder.'

'Two counts——'

'I'll be making a statement to that effect at tomorrow morning's press briefing.' Mason did his usual funny little jig like dance. 'Her solicitors are claiming she's suffering from retrograde amnesia and can't remember a damn thing.'

'They're obviously playing the system, Jack.'

'They'll get nowhere.' Mason laughed. 'Not according to the CPS, they won't.'

Against all advice, and barely eight weeks after nearly losing his life, Jack Mason was back at his desk again. He'd had a remarkable escape by all accounts, and had it not been for the type of life jacket he was wearing, he could easily have ended up as Patrick Stanley's last victim. Mason was old school, a no-nonsense copper who was determined to fight his corner at any costs.

The drinks arrived, along with a bag of crisps.

'Stanley certainly had charisma,' Mason chuckled. 'One of his neighbours reckoned he could charm a vulture off a carcass.'

'That's how most serial killers operate, I'm afraid. They know who to make friends with.'

'Let's hope the crabs strip his body clean and the bastard rots in hell.'

'Well at least the killings have stopped.'

Mason laughed again. 'Yes, thankfully.'

'Recovering the murder weapon is one thing, but it's a pity you never found his body.'

'He's dead alright. I saw the bastard go under, along with hundreds of other people on the ferry that day.' Mason took another swig of his beer. 'Once the trial date gets listed at the High Court, no doubt the press will make a meal of it. Those cockroaches never fail.'

Carlisle turned to Mason. 'What really puzzles me about Stanley's last movements, is why he left Angelica behind as he did?'

'It's a strange one.' Mason raised his glass to his lips and paused in thought. 'Mind, if he'd have wanted her dead he would have done it long ago. Theirs was a strange partnership and had all the ingredients of a Greek tragedy.'

'They were definitely an odd couple,' Carlisle agreed, 'and both had the childhood from hell.'

Mason cradled his glass. 'She's bound to talk at some stage or other; most of them usually do once their necks are on the line.'

'You surprise me, Jack.'

'Nah, it's just what I've read in the papers. Even the Moors murderer Myra Hindley severed all contact with Ian Brady in the end . . . professing her innocence in a lifelong campaign to regain her freedom.'

'That's not a bad analogy actually,' Carlisle smiled. 'At least it answers a lot of questions.'

Mason's eyes looked jaded. Heavy. To think he'd almost lost his life barely eight weeks ago, returning to work so soon seemed foolhardy. Mason was tenacious, stubborn, and the day he retired would be the day they broke the mould on old-school detectives.

'There's something you should know.' Mason lowered his voice. 'Tom

Hedley reckons John Lawrence and Kevin Price were dismembered in Stanley's bathroom, and Angelica's fingerprints and DNA were all over the place.'

'What about Stanley's?'

Mason frowned. 'There's plenty of trace evidence and footprints according to the forensic report, and we know Stanley wore rubber gloves to his crimes.'

'So, Angelica did have a hand in it after all. What about dismembering Price's body?'

'Not all is as it appears.' Mason shrugged. 'We know she was the last person to handle John Lawrence's body parts, as her fingerprints were all over the suitcase we found.'

'Why hasn't any of this information come out in the reports before now?'

Mason shrugged. 'The CPS are building a case against her and keeping it back for the trial.'

Carlisle nodded. 'That makes sense.'

'According to the PM, their last two victims were killed over the same weekend. What's more, Angelica's fingerprint sample found on the powered surgical saw shows a probability match of ninety-nine percent.'

'Good God! I would never have expected to hear that. Is that why you're charging her with two counts of murder?'

'Some people never cease to amaze. I don't subscribe to the evil in the world, but I do worry about sending my daughter out into it at times.' Mason's shoulders slumped. 'It's the young men they murdered I feel sorry for, as none of them saw it coming. Once she'd hooked up with them on the Internet chatroom sites, they thought they were onto a good thing.'

Carlisle shook his head. 'There's obviously a lot more to come out of this case by the sounds of things.'

'Undoubtedly, but it proves they were in it together.'

'Who would have thought that six months ago?'

Mason proffered a smile. 'That's why I'm the copper and you're a private investigator, my friend.'

Carlisle thought a moment. 'Let's not forget that Stanley was the dominant partner in all of this, and it was he who had overall control over everything. The issue with Stanley was, he was sexually aroused by a knife entering a human body. The appalling nature of his crimes and the twisted way in which his warped mind worked was plain for all to see.' He paused in reflection. 'That's how he fulfilled his fantasies. . . dismembering his victims' bodies.'

Mason took another sip of his beer and pondered his statement. 'Perhaps we'll never know what really went on behind closed doors.'

'Probably not, but it certainly changes my thoughts as to the killer's motives.'

'Stanley was always an enigma.' Mason frowned. 'Let's leave it at that.'

Outside, the streets were bustling with people. It was another glorious day, clear blue skies and a smattering of cotton wool clouds. Mason was right, serial killers were control freaks by their very nature and perhaps that's why he left Angelica to die as he did. Daft as it may seem, he didn't have the heart to kill her himself.

'What's the latest crack on Frank Wiseman?' Carlisle asked casually.

'In what respect?'

'The last I heard he was out seeking his revenge.'

'Nah. Now he knows his ex-wife's killer is dead, he's quietened down a tad. How he'll react once he learns an Estonian woman was involved in her murder is a different kettle of fish, of course.'

'But Angelica didn't kill Jennifer Oakwell.'

'True, but Tony Fox has more than an interest in the case, and we all know what that slippery bastard can get up to.'

Mason filled him in on the latest developments, and Wiseman's reactions towards Fox's takeover bid. Fox was a cunning sod and knew how to play the system to his advantage, but Mason still had an ace up his sleeve. CCTV coverage grabbed from Fat Sam's nightclub during their early dawn police raid, proved beyond all reasonable doubt that Patrick Stanley had worked there. Not only that, two of his victims had regularly frequented the place, and that's where they'd hooked up with Angelica. It wasn't over yet, not by a long chalk, even though Fox denied all knowledge of it.

'What's the Area Commander's views?' Carlisle asked.

'He's loath to get the CPS involved at this stage. The problem with Fox is, he has influence in high places. Given the opportunity, he'll no doubt make another huge donation to a well-known local charity and that will be the end of the matter.'

'Pity,' Carlisle said, wrinkling his brow. 'Putting Fox behind bars would have been a bonus.'

They chatted a while, about everything and nothing.

Mason glanced at his watch. 'So, my friend. What have you been doing with yourself lately?'

'It's back to the grindstone, I'm afraid.'

'Each to his own, I suppose.' Mason clanked his empty glass on the bar to attract the barman's attention. 'How's your old man keeping nowadays?'

'He's fine, thanks.'

'Do you still manage to go fishing together?'

'Now that you mention it, I've arranged to take him out on a sea fishing trip this weekend.'

'Sounds like fun.'

'It is. As long as the North Sea doesn't finish him off.'

Mason chuckled. 'What does that involve. . . hiring a boat and a skipper for the day?'

'Fortunately, an old family friend owns a sixty-foot converted motor launch and has promised to take us both out in it.'

'That makes life a lot easier.'

'Oddly enough, he keeps it moored up in St Peters Wharf, of all places.'

Mason's jaw suddenly dropped. 'How freaking mad is that?'

'I know, and it's barely a stone's throw from the North Shields Ferry Terminal.'

Mason raised his glass and smiled. 'If you do manage to bump into Wasp on your travels, give him my best regards.'

They both fell about laughing.

Chapter Fifty-Six

Two months later

The Café Frontline in Amsterdam sat on the edge of the red-light district. Like most bars housed in the area, it had a lively atmosphere and played great music. It wasn't one of his favourite bars, but it did serve a good pint and the clientele was friendly enough. Not that he was a regular or anything, but he did enjoy the odd pint of Dutch beer now and then.

Working his way towards the crowded bar, he ordered a bottle of Amstel beer, sipped and watched the world go by. It was Monday, 7:00 pm, and the place was unusually packed. The streets outside were lively too, and a few hours from now the Café Frontline would be heaving. It was that kind of district, dynamic, and always had a great atmosphere.

'*Hoe kan ik helpen*?' the pale-faced barman asked, in a gruff Hollander voice.

'I'm looking for a man called Jack Mason. Do you speak English?'

'A little,' the barman replied. 'What is it you want with him?

'I have some valuable information that I wish to share with him. Does he drink here?'

'And you are?' the barman asked in broken English.

'An old schoolfriend.'

The tall man standing next to him drew on his cigarette and turned to face him. 'If it's Jack Mason you're looking for, then I may be able to help.'

His eyes widened a fraction. 'Do you happen to know his whereabouts?'

'What is it you wish to speak to him about?'

'It's personal. . .'

'I see. And your name is?'

'I'd rather not say.' He smiled. 'But Jack knows who I am.'

'Without a name, how do you expect me to help you?'

Annoyed with himself for having been so disrespectful, he swore under his breath. He should have known better, done things differently instead of flying off at a tangent as he had. These things took time, he realised that. He stood for a minute, thinking. Some things were best left unsaid, and the least people who knew of his presence here the better. Besides, he had a more pressing engagement to keep, and he was desperate to get going.

'The name's Ballantine,' he said, trying to recover the situation. He held out a welcoming hand. 'I'm an old chum of Jack Mason's, we went to the same school.'

'Well, Mr Ballantine, I'm sorry to inform you that Jack Mason is back in England. He's a very busy man these days.'

'Yes, I'm sure he is. Do you happen know when he's due back?'

'Early Friday morning, I believe. He's here visiting a sick friend.'

'Police business?'

'I've absolutely no idea.'

He stood for a moment, thinking. 'Friday morning you say?'

'Yes, he's hoping to be here for the music. . . we're holding a Rolling Stones tribute night.'

'The Rolling Stones?'

'Yes, there's live bands on here every Saturday night . . . it's extremely popular.'

'Sounds fun.'

'It is.' The barman smiled. 'Shall I tell him you called?'

He thought a minute, then handed him a slip of crumpled paper from a pocket. 'Tell Jack Mason I have a proposition to put to him and he's to ring that number the minute he arrives back in the country.'

'Yes, I will—'

Happy in the knowledge he'd finally set the wheels in motion, he slid his empty beer bottle across the bar and walked off into the night.

THE END

You've turned the last page.
But it doesn't have to end there...

If you're looking for more action-packed reading in the Jack Mason crime thriller series, why not subscribe to my monthly newsletter at **www.michaelkfoster.com**

Here you will find behind the scene interviews, discount promotions, signed book giveaways, and more importantly new release dates.

If you enjoyed *The Suitcase Man*, why not drop a review on Amazon and let other readers know what you thought of it. They are dying to hear from you!

Gan canny.

Michael

THE WHARF BUTCHER

(Book 1) in the DCI Mason & Carlisle Crime Thriller series

A serial killer is stalking Tyneside. But there is a pattern to his killing, his choice of victims, and his method of slaughter. David Carlisle, a criminal profiler, is brought in to assist DCI Jack Mason with his task of identifying the killer and stopping him in his tracks.

The Wharf Butcher is a fast-paced thriller that shines a light on the dark forces within the corridors of power, in the boardroom and the police force itself. The clock is ticking to catch the monster that has been unleashed. But first Carlisle must get inside the killer's head...

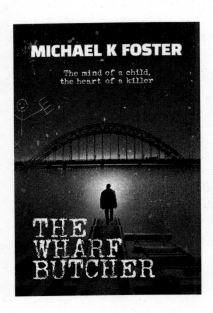

'Start to finish, the author hardly gives you time to catch your breath as horror piles on horror and the killer thumbs his nose at the pursuers.'

The Northern Echo

SATAN'S BECKONING

(Book 2) in the DCI Mason & Carlisle Crime Thriller Series

When a fatal road crash turns out to be murder, JACK MASON is sent to investigate. There are no clues, no motive, and the driver of the car is missing.

Within the seemingly dark vaults of the police missing persons files, lay untold dangers. Young women are easy pickings for a serial killer who is growing increasingly audacious. When criminal profiler DAVID CARLISLE is drafted in to assist, he is not able to protect anyone – least of all himself.

As the investigations intertwine, Jack is forced to face his own demons, but the closer to the truth he gets, the greater the danger he puts them in.

Satan's Beckoning is a fast-paced crime thriller with a cliffhanging conclusion.

'An outstanding writer of considerable talent and with this, his second novel he has proven yet again that he is a new force in British Crime Fiction.'

Booklover Catlady Reviews